The
Naked Ear

by Michael Hoffman

A Blackcover Book

"The Naked Ear," by Michael Hoffman. ISBN 978-1-62137-054-3 (softcover), 978-1-62137-055-0 (eBook).

Manufactured in the United States of America.

Introduction

The Naked Ear is an unpolished, apparently unfinished piece of writing by an author about whom nothing is known, not even his name. The manuscript that chanced to come into my possession in so bizarre a fashion is signed – self-mockingly, one presumes – "John of Silence."

I say "manuscript." John of Silence wrote not on a computer but in longhand, in a cramped, unsightly, difficult to read scrawl that fills to bursting two 200-page, 17 x 24cm notebooks and spills over into a third, which is two-thirds blank. There is in addition a fourth notebook, more tattered and evidently older than the others (though none of them is dated), with a faded and splotched red cover and a coil binding, whereas the other three have blue covers and sewn bindings. This fourth notebook – or rather the first – contains notes and jottings, snippets and fragments, thoughts, proto-ideas, rough drafts, snatches of dialog, apparently scribbled down as they occurred to the author, to be developed later. Many passages in the actual manuscript are traceable to these jottings.

Is *The Naked Ear* a novel? Not in the usual sense, though it does seem to be fiction. Nor, though it is divided into "scenes" instead of chapters, does it aspire to drama. There is no easily discernible plot, no evident beginning, middle, or end; nor is it consistent as to mode, shifting capriciously back and forth between realism and fantasy, sometimes within the same brief "scene" – until at last, towards the end, the fantastic element, or more precisely a dream-like element, seems to overwhelm realism altogether.

I am not a literary scholar – in fact my labors on behalf of *The Naked Ear* proceeded in spite of, I might almost say in defiance of, the express advice of two literary scholars I took the trouble to consult, both of whom, independently of one another, pronounced the manuscript worthless. I am not qualified to disagree with them, and yet I do disagree – so strongly, indeed, that I have devoted years of my spare hours to the task – pleasurable at times, exasperating and frustrating at least as often – whose end result is now before you.

I propose in this preface to explain to the reader my personal involvement with *The Naked Ear* – the weird and bewildering manner in which it fell into my hands, how it gradually and almost against my will became part of my life – at times, I confess, to the point almost of *absorbing* my life. I apologize in advance if I seem to be forcing my personal circumstances on the reader. I will do so only to the extent that it bears on *The Naked Ear* and on my decision, following a long and fruitless search for the author and, as I said, against the advice of two respected and indeed even (in certain circles) revered literary connoisseurs, former teachers of mine, to translate and publish this work in the hope it will enrich other lives as it has (though at a cost!) my own. In a second essay, an "afterward," I will attempt a tentative analysis of the work, addressing myself to those who have read it, laying claim to their attention not on the basis of academic qualifications, in which I am quite lacking, or of literary talent, which I do not claim for myself, but merely on that of having studied and thought about and lived with the text – almost obsessively, as I said – over a period of more years than I like to count!*

A brief self-introduction seems indispensable, and once again I apologize for intruding it upon the reader. I was born in Montreal into an ethnic stew of a family. My father's mother was Jewish, his father Greek; my mother's father was French-Canadian, her mother half Japanese. It was a big, close-knit family, full of uncles, aunts and cousins who all seemed to regard our house as a second home and, in the case of the cousins, my parents almost as their own. They were forever dropping over – for dinner, for afternoon tea or milk and cookies, for after-dinner coffee. There was much laughter and much shouting, especially between my father and one of my uncles, who were constantly at each other's throats across a political fence – my father the "communist" versus my uncle the "fascist." It was very noisy, very convivial, very healthy no doubt, but the fact is that I was a reserved, quiet child, forever craving more privacy and solitude than my own home afforded me.

Of all the languages I was exposed to as a child, it was Japanese I loved best – for its quietness. Later of course I learned that Japanese is no more "quiet" than any other language, but my half-Japanese grandmother happened to be the quietest member of our family, and *her* Japanese certainly was quiet, almost whispery. My earliest memories are of her cradling me in her arms and singing soft Japanese lullabies to me while my older and more spirited cousins played, fought, made up and fought again and our parents carried on their interminable polyglot discussions, arguments and shouting matches, deploying volume as a weapon when logic failed. Japanese, in short, was almost from infancy a kind of *refuge* for me.

I was ten when my grandmother died, by which time I had absorbed a basic command of the language. In university I majored in Japanese Studies, after which I went on to Waseda University in Tokyo for two years of graduate work. This focused less on literature than on economics, for my ambition at that point, since fulfilled, was to become an economic journalist, fluent in the languages of the world's two biggest economies.**

In the summer of 1999 I was in Japan, reporting for the Wall Street Journal on the causes and effects of the prolonged recession. I was at Tokyo Station, waiting to catch a *shinkansen* to Osaka. With an hour to kill before train time, I decided to stash my suitcase in a coin locker and, braving the heat and humidity, go for a stroll around the station.

In the locker whose door I chanced to open I found *The Naked Ear*.

I found the four notebooks, I mean to say. They were simply there – four scruffy-looking notebooks, piled one on top of the other.

My first reaction was peculiar. Instinctive reaction to the unexpected always is, perhaps. I slammed the door shut, as though I'd blundered into a room, thinking it my own, to find a strange couple in the throes of passion. My embarrassment was extreme, but short-lived. A moment later I was laughing at myself. I vividly recall glancing around furtively to see whether I'd been observed, and the relief I felt to see I hadn't been. Then I laughed at that, for that too seemed peculiar. There was one more peculiarity to follow – namely, my agonized indecision as to what on earth I should do. (Later I found a kind of mirror-image of myself, distorted but perhaps the truer for that, in the character Yasushi, whose similar affliction as *The Naked Ear* breaks off seems to threaten, though it is left to the reader's imagination, a descent into madness.)

What to do? Simply pretend I had not seen the notebooks and choose another locker? Take the notebooks to the station office? That seemed reasonable. Their owner would surely return for them. Four notebooks filled to bursting with writing were no trivial thing. Why didn't I do that? To this day, I don't know. I see myself now as I stood there, half-stupefied, as though (again, like Yasushi) the very fate of the universe depended on my decision, a decision I was unable to make, though the only rational course of action was perfectly clear – and all the while darting furtive glances everywhere, like a criminal desperate to escape observation and despairing of doing so!

Then, suddenly, after how much time I don't precisely know – not as much as it seemed, I'm sure – I made my move. Without having reached a conscious decision to do so, with one final furtive look about me, I snatched the notebooks and fled! A safe distance away I tossed them into my bag, all the while thinking to myself, "What am I doing? Why am I doing this?"

Then I boarded the train, sank into my seat and closed my eyes, as though hoping to achieve invisibility thereby – not opening them, though not sleeping, until we pulled into Osaka Station some hours later.

———

I did not open the notebooks in my hotel room that evening, though I didn't leave the room and didn't do anything else. My work kept me in Osaka four days. By day, brisk and professional as usual, I went about my business, but evening seemed to rob me of my competence, my character, my very

v

sanity. I sat in my room, oppressively conscious of the notebooks in my suitcase, not daring to open them. All I knew of them was what I had glimpsed scrawled, in English, on the cover of one of them as I thrust them into the bag: "The Naked Ear. John of Silence." The scrawl was ugly, challenging, threatening – at least it became so in my imagination. It seemed to taunt me, saying, "You were the one whom fate chose to take possession of my notebooks; now the price is yours to pay, and mine the satisfaction of watching you pay it!" To which I would reply in my mind, "I won't read them, I won't so much as glance at them, and as soon as I get back to Tokyo I'll take them to the station office and be rid of them!" "Oh no," came the mocking rejoinder, "you'll read them, you'll read them!"

That is the last thing I remember.

———————

Forgive me, I do no mean to indulge in dramatics. The fact is, I had an attack of some sort, the precise nature of which remains mysterious to this day. I woke up, or came to – whatever the appropriate expression is – not knowing where I was, how I'd got there, how much time I'd been unconscious – nothing. I was in bed, among other people in bed, in a large room, in which ghostly figures draped in white flitted noiselessly about. A hospital, of course, and the ghosts were doctors and nurses. Good. I was reasoning; my mind was working. "Excuse me," I said to a passing nurse – who seemed so startled at my addressing her that I immediately thought, It's not a hospital after all, it's a morgue, I'm supposed to be dead, maybe I am.

But no; the confusion was cleared up; I was alive, it was a hospital, I'd collapsed suddenly, an ambulance had been called, I'd been unconscious three days... About what followed I need not go into detail; I fear I've burdened the reader already with more of me than he needs or wants to know. Suffice it to say that after being kept a few days for recuperation and observation I was released, to all appearances fit both mentally and physically. I felt fine – even, in a sense, better for having had the attack; so it seemed to me, at least. I flew back to New York ready to throw myself back into my old life. Short-term, there was a series of articles to write on Japan; long-term, perhaps the series might be expanded into a book.

I had altogether forgotten *The Naked Ear*. There it was in my suitcase as I unpacked, four notebooks, mocking me and leering at me as before: "You said something, I believe, about getting rid of these at Tokyo Station?"

I read and read, read as I'd never read before, read as *if* I'd never read before. I simply did not know – do not know to this day – how to account for the effect it had on me. All my life I've been a reader, a book-lover. No literary scholar, I can all the same describe myself as well-read in several languages; as a student of Japanese culture I had delved into Japanese literature ancient and modern, and even as a professional in a field quite remote from literature, I retained an amateur's love of the literary arts – fiction, poetry... And here was this "Naked Ear" – ragged, incomplete, unpolished, inconsistent – one needn't be a critic to see its faults! – and yet... and yet what? It seized hold of me, like... the simile that occurs is a bizarre one... like a beggar who latches onto you on the street and simply won't take no for an answer, who attaches himself to you, impervious to your most vigorous efforts to shake him off...

Who was this "John of Silence"? Was he alive? Could he be found? Surely a man doesn't pour out his soul like this into four thick notebooks – and the ragged, jagged quality of the handwriting, by no means easy to decipher, was ample testimony to the feverish intensity of the composition – only to toss them into an unlocked train station locker and resume his everyday life, simply forgetting their existence and indifferent to their fate. No, but as a prologue, so to speak, to suicide it made some sense. Thirty-odd thousand people a year commit suicide in Japan, many of them by jumping in front of moving trains. Had anyone done that in the vicinity of Tokyo Station in the days before my bizarre discovery, or on the very day of it? How could I find out? Macabre though they are, incidents of that sort have become so common – partly as a result of the crippling recession I had gone there to write about – that they rarely even made the newspapers. The police might be helpful, or they might not. Well, I could try. After a few false starts I was put through to a police official who was pleased indeed to be of assistance to a fluent Japanese-speaking Wall Street Journal reporter; he didn't cross paths with many. Yes, he said, there had been two train suicides in the week leading up to my discovery. A woman and a man. Details, of course – he was so sorry – he was not authorized to release. Stupid of me; I should have known. But the effort had one unexpected result – it put an idea into my head that had not occurred to me before: could "John of Silence" be a woman?

Why "John of Silence"? For that matter, why "The Naked Ear"? The phrase does occur in the text, but infrequently, and hardly centrally, unless the author was trying to construct an image that he (or she) failed to fully develop. (There is an abundance of evidence in the text of failed intentions of one sort or another.) Silence – ear; silence – naked ear... How many hours over the years did I spend in my darkened room, lying on my bed, staring up at the ceiling, repeating those syllables – "silence, ear, naked ear, silence" – over and over, like some mantra, striving to tease forth some illuminating, clarifying connection. Googling John of Silence I learned, or more precisely was reminded, that the Danish philosopher Kierkegaard had written *Fear and Trembling* under the name Johannes de silentio. Was that a clue or a mere coincidence? It might even – for I had come to regard my author as a perverse and prickly character – be a willful deception, a false lead, designed to make a fool out of anyone daring to match wits with him – or her.

"Well, we'll see," I thought; "we'll see, *I'll* dare to match wits with you" – for I have a prickly streak myself, dormant most of the time but vigorous enough when roused, and suddenly – or perhaps not suddenly, perhaps it was so from the outset – this unknown, invisible "John of Silence" became an enemy to be hunted down and "dealt with" – that was the expression that came to me; I would find him and "deal with him," whatever that meant. It was while in this frame of mind that I became convinced of something I had only suspected before – that he had *seen* me take the notebooks from the locker, had been lurking in the shadows watching my agonized indecision, my sudden snatching of the notebooks, my furtive glances, my hurried flight from the scene... Yes, he had seen it all, had watched with amusement, with delight, with mockery!

The humiliation I felt as I visualized all this is almost a humiliation in itself, for it was stupid and unreasonable, and yet impervious to, therefore stronger than, intelligence and reason. But of course, so many of our feelings are like that. I digress, perhaps, but it seems important that the reader understand how, at moments, I *hated* this invisible, unknown adversary – to whom I, on the contrary, was visible and known! I will go one step further and confess – for it is in a sense a confession – that never, ever, have I hated anyone as, at moments, I hated "John of Silence"! Meanwhile he, invisible to me, saw my impotent rage as he had seen me furtively snatching his notebooks at the station, and laughed all the harder.

I closed my eyes and tried to visualize that scene at the station. Who had been there? Who could have seen me? Who had those furtive glances of mine taken in? Nobody that made much of an impression, obviously, or I wouldn't have done what I did, and yet the area hadn't been entirely deserted, there had been people around, one of whom could easily have been paying more attention to me than I realized. And at intervals I would seem to recall someone who did seem, in retrospect, to be watching me, a man... yes, yes, I noticed him at the time, fleetingly – he was wearing what looked like an overcoat, and I remembered thinking, "Why would anyone be wearing an overcoat in this heat?" – an overcoat and a hat, an old-fashioned hat, a fedora...

Was I sure? Yes, no... Had I noticed anything else? Was he old, young, straight, stooped, walking, standing still? "He's a figment of my imagination, pure and simple," I'd tell myself indignantly – to which this figment replied, "Why don't you advertise in the Japanese papers requesting that a man in an overcoat and fedora come forward" – at which he would laugh uproariously, and it was laughter, reader, that was as audible to me as if it had been real!

But it gave me an idea, which I hastened to carry out. I did place ads in the Japanese papers, the respectable ones and the tabloids – not for a man in an overcoat but for "John of Silence." I was in possession of *The Naked Ear*, I said and had read it, and could be contacted at such-and-such an email address.

I waited and waited – nothing. Well, it was only to be expected. Either he – or she – is dead, or wants to be thought so, or has no interest in making my acquaintance, or doesn't read the newspapers, or, considering the handwritten manuscript, doesn't know how to send email, like his Professor Horiuchi... What were the chances, after all, of him, or her, simply materializing at my summons: "Here I am, master, yours to command!" Meanwhile, my own life was taking its course. I married, set up a household, fathered a child, wrote my book on the Japanese economy, which made me, if not famous, respected and even to a degree controversial, for my analysis was by no means conventional. Prosperous, busy, happy – for a time I was a popular figure on the lecture circuit – I had no time for *The Naked Ear*, I more or less forgot about it, and about "John of Silence." When, at intervals, I did chance to think of them, I was pleased to return the derisive laughter I used to hear from the phantom-author: "Get lost, brother, I have no time for you."

Abruptly, tragedy struck and changed everything. My wife died. Suddenly. In childbirth. And though the thought was unbidden, and unwanted, it came anyway, and haunted me – oh, how it haunted me! Rogozhin, in *The Naked Ear*, which at that point I had not read in years, had lost his wife in exactly the same way, and his feelings, his destructive, nihilistic grief, were precisely what I myself was going through! The difference was that I had no Tazawa, no willing disciple, to convert my worst thoughts into action, with such hideous results. No, but I had something else, namely a son, then seven years old, and there was a time, a period, an interval, when – my hand trembles as I write this, and yet write it I must! – I could have killed him, I could have murdered him, I felt it, I could have...

In sheer terror of what horrors I might commit, I left the child with my mother, took an extended leave of absence from my job, and vanished. In my knapsack, among the bare necessities of life on the road, was my sole traveling companion – the four notebooks of *The Naked Ear*.

———————

Twelve years have passed since that day in Tokyo Station when those four notebooks invaded my life and altered it irrevocably – for the better or the worse? I naturally ask myself. There is of course no way of answering that, which doesn't nullify the question; quite the contrary. Most of the questions we ask ourselves – all of them, maybe – are unanswerable. Maybe questions are by definition unanswerable. Yes, maybe they are... All I know is, I am not the man I would have been had that long-ago day in Tokyo gone according to plan, had my utterly innocuous action of opening a train station locker door in order to deposit a suitcase had the usual innocuous result.

I remember the room in which I began the translation. It wasn't even a room, properly speaking. Like Maeda at the end (if it is the end) of *The Naked Ear* – though the imitation, if that's what it was, was unconscious – I was traveling on foot, aimlessly, hardly knowing where I was, not caring; I would set out early in the morning and stop for the night wherever I happened to be. Yes, I remember the room – the hallway, rather, or passage – I can see it as clearly as I can the room I'm in now as I write this – and yet the name of the town escapes me; the name of the state too; my aimlessness was that total. The accommodation was a kind of hostel, where people slept six, seven, or eight to a room; I'd been alone for so long I suddenly felt a kind of longing for company, which is why I chose the place in favor of a perfectly adequate-looking hotel not far away, but the longing withered at the first contact. A young fellow staying there asked me, one stranger casually accosting another, "Where're you from?" and my brain froze, it literally froze, I couldn't answer; pretending not to hear or even be aware of his presence, I slipped out into the passage, where there happened to be a little table; I sat down at the table, took the first notebook of The Naked Ear out of the knapsack; there was a pad of memo-paper and a pen on the table; perhaps if there hadn't been, the project would never have got underway... I picked up the pen and, as though doodling, translated the opening line: "Father, can I speak to you?"

———

*The afterward was never written. – Publisher's note.

**China has since, of course, overtaken Japan as the world's second-largest economy.

Part I

Scene One

"Father, can I speak to you?"

"Come in, come in."

"What's that you're reading?" He leans forward across the desk. "Ah." He laughs. "It's Greek to me."

"Me too." A joke we've shared for years.

"Father... I think I'm in love."

"You don't say! Sit down. Tell me about it."

"If I were a poet like you, maybe I'd be able to."

"A poet like me!"

"You have the soul of a poet."

What *is* he babbling about?

"You can speak poetically about love. Not me. All I can do is feel it."

"That in itself is a great deal."

"I was thinking... how about if I brought her home for dinner some night?"

"Home? For dinner?"

"Her name is Tomoko. She's..."

He talks on about his Tomoko. My attention wanders. It's true, he does not speak well. Young people don't. They've lost the power of speech. I notice it in my classes. Language in their hands has become a blunt instrument. It can no longer express nuances. Soon there will be no nuances to express.

1

"By the way. I have a confession to make. I stole 1000 yen from your wallet the other day."

"Oh?"

"And bought a lottery ticket with it. It will win. Tomoko said so."

"What is she, a fortune-teller?"

"No, she just... knows things. She's in tune with the... the... the...

"The forces of the universe? The music of the spheres?"

"She said I had to buy the ticket with money taken from your wallet without your knowledge, or else it wouldn't work. She's never wrong. She's amazing, really. Why don't you let me bring her home? I know you'll like her."

"Who says I won't let you bring her home? It's your home as much as mine."

"It's the way you sort of... flinch when I suggest it."

"I flinch easily these days."

"Oh? Why's that?"

Should I tell him? Why not? "I'm about to lose my job."

"What? Why? What happened?" He finally takes a seat, sitting across from me and leaning his elbows on the desk, as he used to when he was a child.

"They caught me having an affair with one of my students."

"No! You're joking!"

"Why should I be?"

"Well..."

"You're right, I am joking. The fact is, no one's interested in the past anymore."

He waits for me to go on, though really, there's not much more to say.

"My subject is ancient history. Enrollment in my courses is down. People have no time for that sort of thing nowadays, no attention to spare for it.

Who cares that 2500 years ago the Greeks fought the Persians, or that Herodotus, the world's first historian, wrote about it in immortal prose? Who cares about Homer, Sophocles, Plato, or about... Anyway, to make a long story short, I've been asked to take early retirement."

"I see. Well... What are you going to do?"

"I don't know. I could fight it, I suppose. On the other hand..."

"You're too young to retire."

"It's kind of you to say so."

———

I can speak poetically about love, he said. *I*, speak poetically about love! Poetically or prosaically, it's not a subject I have cause to broach very often. Love? What do I know about love? Well, this: that it can turn to hate, and when it does... when it does... I wish the sun would set, or hide behind a cloud... I'll draw the curtain. Look. Not a cloud in the sky. For weeks. No cloud, no rain, nothing but sunshine, relentless sunshine, day in, day out! The earth is parched, the flowers are withered, and still the sun shines... and crows, crows everywhere! What void do they come out of? Hm. The weather forecast in yesterday's evening paper was actually for rain. I should know better than to believe it! Of course I know better. With all the instruments they've got up there, and all the brilliant scientific minds surveying this, measuring that, the weather forecast still seems to be no better than flipping a coin. And yet, knowing that, I still went to bed last night thinking to myself, "Thank the gods, it'll rain tomorrow!" What does that say about human nature? And when I woke up to the same brilliant sunny glare that has tormented me for weeks – how to describe my bitterness? Yes, bitterness, bitterness, bitterness!

3

Against whom? I know, it's absurd, no need to tell me!

Scene Two

The journalist, I forget his name, has a positively astonished look on his face. What did I say? "What's wrong?" I ask.

The sunshine streams in through the windows, flooding the room and obscuring with its glare the young man's face. Perhaps his astonishment is only in my imagination. "Excuse me a moment." I push back my chair and, reaching behind me, draw the curtain. "There, that's better. Really, this sunshine..."

"Don't you like sunshine?"

"Too much of a good thing! The golden mean, as Aristotle said! I'm sorry. I interrupted you. You're from... what newspaper, did you say?"

"The *Maiasa Shimbun*."

I should never have agreed to this interview. What's the point? But he was quite insistent, and it occurred to me that, as the beneficiary of unearned wealth, I have an obligation of sorts to cooperate with people. So the journalist is here, and a photographer, with all his paraphernalia, all those cameras and lenses dangling from his neck. "My face," I said to the photographer, "has absolutely nothing to do with me." I meant it as a joke, because he seemed to be making such a fuss, as though something terribly important were at stake – but he didn't laugh, didn't crack a smile; I may as well not have spoken. Words don't interest him, I suppose.

"You were saying, I think," the journalist resumes, "that your son purchased the ticket – "

"On the advice of his girlfriend, yes, who prophesied – she's a prophetess, you see – that if he bought the ticket with money filched from my wallet – "

"Prophetess?"

"Evidently so, since her prophecy came true."

"And has she any other... prophecies to her credit?"

"I really don't know. Why don't you interview her?"

"And how did you feel when you first heard the news?"

"How did I feel? I don't know... surprised, happy..." What does he want me to say?

They leave at last, the journalist with my feelings, the photographer with my face. Ha ha. Actually, I'm not laughing. Far from it. I am exhausted, drained – emotionally and physically drained. And tomorrow... tomorrow I'll read all about it in the newspaper... Good heavens, what is that? A horrible rattling, clanking... it seems to be rolling this way, getting louder and louder, closer and closer – but when I pull back the curtain and peer out the window into the sunshine I see nothing... It's gone now. Strange. All kinds of things go on out there, all kinds of inexplicable things, things of which I know nothing...

What was I saying? Oh yes, the newspaper. Well, take it in stride. You can't win twenty million yen in a lottery and keep it secret, certainly not in a small town like this. Life doesn't work that way! Why did I have to blurt that out about "the prophetess," though? Stupid, stupid! Anyway – forget it. I won't look at tomorrow's paper, that's all; anyway, it'll be buried somewhere in an inside page, nobody'll notice it, and... hm. Perhaps, just to be on the safe side, I'll vanish for a few days, go away somewhere. By the time I get back – What's

that? The phone? Let it ring, let it ring! I won't
answer it!

Scene Three

"Seriously, Tomoko, do you love me? I mean
– "

"Well? Go on – tell me what you mean. You
can't, because you don't know yourself."

"I *do* know, it's just…"

"Well?"

"I know, but I don't know… it's the *words* I
don't know."

"There's no such thing as love. It's as
nonsensical a notion as God, or the soul, or ether,
or any of a million illusions the human brain has
spun for itself down the millennia. Love! I like your
face, I enjoy your company, I like sleeping with you.
What more can you ask of me?"

"Maybe if you told me you'd feel that way
forever and ever…"

"What a child you are! How can I possibly tell
you such a thing?"

"You could if you wanted to."

"How? How can I possibly know?"

"*I* know that I'll always feel the same about
you."

"You don't. You just think you do."

"Well, tell me you *think* you'll feel – "

"Oh, stop this now! This is beyond
childishness – this is infancy!"

"If the future of your own feelings is so dark to
you, how did you know my father would win the
lottery?"

"I didn't."

"You didn't? But…"

"I told you, it just popped into my head, the way random wisps of thoughts do, out of nowhere. Just a meaningless wisp of thought, that's all it was. I said it out loud, but I could just as easily have kept it to myself. You took me seriously, but could just as easily not have... only you're such a clown, you take *everything* seriously."

"But it came true, didn't it? He really did win the lottery."

"Somebody had to win it. It happened to be him."

"Tomoko – I want you to tell me you love me. Even if it's not true, even if you don't mean it, I want you to tell me."

"I don't understand you! Really I don't! Why should it mean so much to you to have me tell you something that isn't true?"

"Then you don't love me?"

"Why do you insist on making me repeat myself? Love doesn't exist! If it existed, I would love you. There! Won't you be satisfied with that? Come, it's getting late, we better get up. If I'm late for work again they'll fire me."

———

"Her parents are dead. She's working her way through school. Can you believe it? A girl studying astrophysics, whose quest is to discover the nature of the universe – and who surely *will* discover it, with her brains! – working part-time at 7-Eleven! And not minding it, either."

"If you tell me everything about her," I say, smiling, "there'll be nothing for us to talk about at dinner."

He's talked me into it. All right, we'll have us a little dinner party. It's the least I can do, I suppose, since, in a manner of speaking, I owe this sudden fortune of mine – more burden than blessing, I'm inclined to feel (perversely, I admit) – to her.

"I can't help it," he says. "I love talking about her almost as much as I love being with her. What a mind she has, what a mind! What can she possibly see in me, I wonder?"

"Don't sell yourself short! You're a handsome boy, much handsomer than any son of mine has a right to be."

"True – *you're* certainly no beauty!" We both laugh.

"Her parents are dead, you say?"

"Yes, killed in a plane crash in Hawaii in 1989. She was three years old. She has no memory of them at all."

"How terrible! Who raised her?"

"Her grandparents. Kind people, she says, but from another age. Hearts and minds in the past, the present another planet as far as they're concerned."

"Hm."

"I know what you're thinking – that you can sympathize. Right?"

"Right."

"I can read you like a book."

"Wait, my son, wait! One day you'll be old – "

"You're not old!"

"Well, aging. By the way, I'm older than you think I am."

"What do you mean?"

"It was stupid of me, of course, but... I'm not sure what impelled me – What's that?"

"My cell phone. Hang on. Hello? Tomoko!" Jun's momentary excitement immediately turns to dejection. "Oh! I see." It's not difficult to guess what's happening – she's bowing out. "Well, another time then... She can't make it," he says to me as he snaps his phone shut. "There's this paper she has to write. She thought it was due the end of next week, but suddenly remembered it's the end of *this* week. She'll be up all night working on it."

"Oh. Well..." It's relief I feel; I try not show it. It's more shyness than misanthropy, though the latter is probably better suited to my time of life. "What's to stop you and me from going out just the two of us? It's high time I got you drunk! 'In vino veritas,' as Pliny so aptly said."

Scene Four

"What's her paper on?" I ask. "The nature of the universe?"

"She told me but I forget. I have no head for that kind of thing."

"Nor do I. Numbers baffle me. They seem to inhabit a world of their own. A hostile, inhuman world."

"Hostile only to those who don't know them, she says."

"Very likely. More wine?"

"Father?"

"Yes, son."

"Is there such a thing as love?"

"Do you doubt it? Didn't you tell me you were in love?"

"Yes. I'm in love with someone who says there's no such thing as love!"

"There's a famous speech on love by Aristophanes in Plato's *Symposium* – "

"Father?"

"Yes, son."

"You've told me before about Aristophanes' famous speech on love, and also Socrates'. I won't lie and say I remember them, but... you know what I'd like?"

9

"What would you like?"

I'm floating. This really is good wine. I don't know the name of it. I could look at the label on the bottle, of course, but I don't feel like it. Jun ordered it, after a minute scrutiny of the wine list. He's something of a connoisseur, to my surprise.

"I'd like to hear what *you* have to say about love. Not Aristophanes, or Socrates, or Homer, or... what's his name, that Roman. You."

"Me." What I have to say about love. "I loved your mother..."

"Tell me about it."

His mother. "Yes, I loved her..." He's filling my glass; he wants to get me drunk. In vino, veritas. "The only woman I have ever loved. Ever, ever, ever. Ever."

"You love her still," he muses after a moment's silence.

"Your mother..." How strange. I seem to be seeing this for the first time, and yet I am aware enough of my foggy condition to regard this crystal clear perception with skepticism. True, it's clear – but is it true? The perception is that this is the first time Jun has ever asked me about his mother. He was seven when she died. He's nineteen now. What does he remember of her? What feelings does he harbor for her in his heart? How is it he has never spoken of her? Did he sense somehow, as a child, that it was not a fit subject to broach with me, and was this intuition, vague as it must have been, nevertheless powerful enough to make him suppress his natural curiosity?

How I loved her, and then, later, how I hated her! I remember both feelings vividly and yet with surprise. Both are incomprehensible to me now. I don't know what I loved in her, nor what I hated.

"You're not drinking."

I drink.

"We were students together. Like you and Tomoko."

"Tomoko and I aren't really students together. She's in physics and will one day set the world on fire with the power of her mind; me, I'm... I don't know..."

"How did you meet?"

"She picked me up."

"*She* picked *you* up! In my day it was the boy who – "

"I'm telling you, Tomoko's different. She's like nobody on earth. Listen. I'm sitting at a table in the reading room, pretending to study. She sits down beside me. 'What's that you're reading?' Like we're old friends or something. I'm staring into her face, trying to figure out where we could have met. 'Do I know you?' 'My name's Tomoko.' She takes the book out of my hand, turns it over and looks at the cover. 'Natsume Soseki?' 'Mm, it's for my Japanese lit course.' 'Interesting?' 'No.' 'Let's go somewhere where we can talk.' She leaves the room without a backward glance, and I follow. We end up at her apartment, which is just off campus..."

"And what did you talk about?"

"She showed me one of her physics books, mathematical formula after mathematical formula, nothing but numbers and funny little letters and weird symbols, and she said, 'This is the literature of the future.' I said, 'Tomoko, I think I love you.' And she said, 'There's no such thing as love.'"

"She must be very beautiful."

"Was mother beautiful?"

"Seen through a lover's eyes, yes."

"Tomoko's not beautiful even through a lover's eyes. She says to me, 'You have enough beauty for the two of us.'"

"I see what she means."

11

"Would you care for another bottle of wine, sir?"

The waiter has materialized from somewhere; he seems to be speaking Japanese with a French accent; I must be imagining it. Interestingly enough, it's Jun he addresses, not me. Jun nods, looking very wise indeed.

Scene Five

I seem to have fallen in love with the sound of my own voice. It amuses me that Jun thinks I've been a professor all my life – a born professor, so to speak, with all the comic, bookish, unworldly qualities that implies. I amuse him now with tales of my unexpectedly varied life – unexpected to him, that is. As a child I dreamed of being a private detective. That's not uncommon, of course. Kids are full of what they see in the movies, and the movies are full of private detectives. I saw my share of them, but the impetus came from elsewhere – from *tachi-iri kinshi* signs. Seriously. *Tachi-iri kinshi* – No Entry. They seemed everywhere, those signs, and they exercised a mysterious power over me. "Enter," they seemed to say. "Closed to everyone else; open to you." And enter I did. At six or seven or eight years of age I would roam the neighborhood, looking for *tachi-iri kinshi* signs and obeying their whispered command: "Enter." Everything I saw, in weedy vacant lots, abandoned factories, cultivated fields, seemed a secret revelation – secret to everyone else, revealed only to me. I was rich with the consciousness of secret knowledge and confidence in my cleverness. And my secret conviction was that one day I would put it to use, that secret knowledge of mine, in the service of good people in

12

trouble; in short, I would become a private detective.

And I did – or rather, I became an actor. "Oh yes," I say to Jun, whose astonishment looks to me rather like bad acting. "Yes, for a time, I don't mind telling you, I was actually quite famous. This was before you were born, of course..."

"You were in *movies*? *You*?"

"Why not me? In movies and on television. I played, among other characters, two detectives: Eiji Murata and Ken Kon; the former highly intelligent, the latter, as his name suggests, rather a bumbler."

"Tell me the names of the movies; I'll rent them. *You* – an *actor!*"

"Me an actor! Yes, my boy, yes! I was on my way to stardom!"

"What happened?"

"What happened. Well, what happened was... I started reading Sophocles, intending to take the part of the blind prophet Teiresias in *Oedipus the King*. The performance, for one reason or another, never came off – but my encounter with Sophocles changed me forever. This was my first real encounter with what I call 'high life,' life lived on a higher level. It was like the first ever sight of a mountain to someone who'd spent his life on the plain. Or to borrow Plato's metaphor of the cave, like a prisoner in an underground vault seeing the dazzling light of day for the first time. To make a long story short – as I really must, for it's getting late; look, they're getting ready to close, they want us out of here – to make a long story short, I gave up acting, went back to school..."

———

"Come home with me, Tomoko, please. Meet him, talk to him. I'm so confused, I – I feel as if I don't know him anymore."

"How can my meeting him help?"

"Why don't you want to?"

She laughs. "I'm afraid he'll expose me as the fraud I am."

"Fraud?"

"Fake from head to toe. You don't see it, but he will. What is it, exactly, that's confusing you so? That he used to be in movies?"

"Well, yes, that, and... not only that."

"What else? Come, tell your Auntie Tomoko! Tell her everything."

"He said at one point, 'I'm older than you think I am.' What did he mean by that?"

"Why didn't you ask him?"

"I meant to, but the conversation changed, and I forgot."

"What else?"

"He talked about my mother. He's never talked about her before, never. He said, 'The only woman I ever loved. Ever.'"

"Well? What's strange about that?"

"Are you saying that nothing is?"

"Supposing you and I have a child, and I die young. The child grows up. Isn't it possible you will be moved to say to the child, 'Your mother was the only woman I ever loved?'"

"I wish you wouldn't say things like that."

"Like what?"

"About you dying."

"What a child you are! Come to me. Come! Honestly, sometimes when we make love I feel like that woman who's been in the news lately, who was arrested for having an affair with a twelve-year-old. Come. And then, if you like, we'll go to your place, and you can introduce me to your father. How's that? Are you happy?"

14

"Yes, I... I think so."

Scene Six

Haruyuki Maeda came home at the usual time, tossed his cell phone onto the sofa, and said to his wife, "I've quit my job."

"You what?"

"Bring me a beer. No, never mind, I'll have a bath first. This heat! Really, it's unbearable."

"You quit your job?"

"I couldn't take it any more, Yosh. I'm sorry. I became a journalist because I wanted to do serious work, uncover the truth behind the lies, the filth behind the... the civilized veneer. Because that truth, that filth – I *see* it, Yoshi, I *smell* it! But they don't, and they're not interested. All they want is trivia, filler. Day after day after day after day – what do I get sent out to cover? Last week – an old lady's hundredth birthday party. Monday – a ribbon-cutting for the new subway line. Don't they hear themselves? Don't they see themselves? The posturing, the hypocrisy! Today it was some jerk whose claim to national attention is that he won a lottery. No, if that's what journalism is, I'd rather lie on the sofa all day long staring up at the ceiling!"

"And how are we supposed to live, if you don't mind my asking?"

"Are you joking? With what you earn?"

"Are *you* joking?"

"What do you take me for, a fool? Well, if you do you're right. But not an ignorant fool. A fool who knows things. Look at me, I'm all sweaty. A bath, a bath, I need a bath!"

"Have a bath, then."

15

"Listen. There's Kinoshita – news editor, you met him once. How he got into the news business is one of the few mysteries left in this world – or even why a guy like him'd *want* to be in it; he should be shuffling papers in a municipal ward office or something, or tending bar in the sort of place where old men gather to mumble toothlessly over their memories. I go up to him. 'Listen,' I say, 'I've stumbled on a secret cult, a cult that worships evil – '"

"Worships evil?"

"'One of their members,' I tell Kinoshita, 'is a guy I went to school with. He's become disillusioned, and gave me a call. He'll take me today to meet them. Can I go?' 'Today?' says Kinoshita. 'Today.' 'Today? But... ahem!... I was going to send you today to interview that... that professor, that fellow who... ahem!... won the lottery. There's no one else I can send, Hara is on vacation, Sekine is in Hokkaido covering the summit...'"

"But what is this cult?"

"Well, that's what you want to know, isn't it? It's the cult you're asking me about, right? – not the lottery-winner. You couldn't care less about the lottery-winner – right? But it's the lottery-winner I spent the afternoon interviewing, instead of – ah, what's the use. What's the damn use! And then I get back to the office and have to grind out a story about how the guy's daughter-in-law or something is a *prophetess* because she predicted he'd win! 'Prophetess' – that's the word he used, I'm not making it up."

"But to quit over – "

"I know, it's stupid. You're right. Well, we've already agreed I'm a fool. What's the big deal? So what if what's left of my soul gets eroded, destroyed..."

"Oh, you and that soul of yours!"

"Yes, me and that soul of mine!"

"And is being unemployed good for your soul, do you think?"

"I'm not sure."

"Listen to me. Life is a balance between soul and body. A balance. Your soul is unbalanced because – "

"Yoshi! Is this you talking? Is this you? Who have you been speaking to? Who has possessed you? Who is it who's using your tongue as a vehicle? Come! Tell me! Confess! Ah, you're silent, you're blushing, you're confessing without words! Well, I'll have a bath."

"Hot water costs money!"

Scene Seven

"If I don't shoot myself," thought Haruyuki Maeda, "it's for one reason and one reason only – apart, of course, from the fact that I don't have a gun." He laughed. "Yes, one reason only – the pleasure of bathing. Now let's, like the good philosopher we are, pose a philosophical question. You take, on one side, the filth, meanness, stupidity, conniving, degradation and so on that daily life imposes on even the most fortunate among us – to say nothing of the pain and suffering, hunger and disease, war and poverty, etc. etc., endured by those not so fortunate. And then, on the other side: a daily half-hour soak in a hot tub, life's one unadulterated pleasure! So – here's my philosophical question: Is a bath, under these somewhat strained circumstances, an adequate reason for living? Anyone with a grain of philosophy in his soul would obviously say no, and act accordingly. So – why don't I? Because I'm afraid of death? Of course I am – but here's a sure

17

remedy: Just imagine yourself doing what you will surely have to do in order to go on living – namely, crawl before that idiot Kinoshita, apologize for your outburst, beg to be reinstated to a job you despise and that is beneath you... Isn't it better to die? Of course it is! Well?

"What's that noise? Crows. 'Caw caw, caw caw.' They're multiplying like flies, those crows. Hm. What was that strange dream I had last night? A woman, a beautiful, beautiful woman, caught sight of me; she winked and smiled; the sight of me evidently made her radiant with joy; but – she had no teeth. And yet she seemed wholly unconscious of the fact; her smile grew broader and broader; her beautiful face seemed about to burst with happiness – and then I woke up. I think I screamed; I seem to remember hearing myself scream. Who was that woman? Do I know her? Do dreams like that *mean* something?

"Here's another philosophical question: We talk about environmental pollution purely in physical terms, but what if it's affecting our mental processes as well, turning us all into madmen? Is that so implausible? If we inhale dirt with every breath we take, why shouldn't that cause short-circuits in the brain? And if everyone is mad, what is sanity? Hm. Hm! I'll tell you what the trouble with me is. I was born with the worst possible amount of brainpower – too much to be content with the idiotic daily round, not quite enough to rise above it. So? What to do? Get out of the bath and phone Kinoshita? Groveling is easier over the phone than face to face – but is it as effective? No, I'd better go down there. I'll pretend I'm not me. I've done it often enough. I'll send my body in and say to my soul, 'Wait outside, I'll be back in a jiffy.' He's not a bad old guy, Kinoshita, just stupid, stupid, stupid! Short-staffed as they are, he'll be relieved to have me back, and, being

18

stupid, he'll show it. All right then! All right! Let's do it and get it over with."

Hoisting himself out of the bath, Maeda looked down at his dripping body and said, "I am Odysseus landing in the country of the Phaecians, 'streams of brine gushing from my mouth and nostrils.' Soon the lovely Nausicca will appear with her maids, and lead me to her father's royal palace."

He was in fact an extremely well-built young man, lithe and solidly though compactly muscled, and few would blame him for the look of satisfaction that stole across his handsome features as he gazed at himself through the steam clouding the mirror. "Never mind journalism; why don't I take a cue from Yoshi? Join a host club and make some real money?"

He dried himself and, wrapping the towel around his middle, went into the kitchen. "Yosh?" She must have gone out. He took a beer from the fridge, snapped open the can and sank into a chair, his elbows resting on the table, his chin in his hands. The sun streaming in through the window struck him full in the face; would evening never come? Endless, endless summer days – and yet as a child he had loved them; every day had seemed a lifetime, and though he knew that people died, his own personal immortality was beyond question. Was there any link at all between himself as he was now and the child he had been? There was not. Was it the same with other people?

The beer was somehow not cold enough. With a frown more contemptuous than annoyed he slapped the can onto the table, rose to his feet, and went into the living room, not so much with any set purpose as like a zoo tiger marching with grim determination from corner to corner of its cage. On the sofa was his cell phone. Idly he picked it up and, smiling suddenly, pointed to it with his free hand and declaimed, as though facing a TV camera, "With this little device I am in touch with the whole world!"

"Wouldn't it be a nice touch if it rang now, right this instant?" he muttered sardonically. It didn't, but a sudden thought came to him. "Well, so this is where my destiny is leading me." He input a number and was answered almost immediately.

"Tazawa? Maeda. Listen... about that cult of yours... Eh? Yeah, sorry about that, something came up. How about right now?... Good. Splendid. Excellent... Funabashi Station, exit 3, six thirty. Got it."

Scene Eight

Age is no defense against vain hope. Mine – my vain hope – over the past few weeks, has been – I blush to say it – that my students would get up some kind of campaign to protest my dismissal. Ha! How could they, after all? Officially it is not dismissal but early retirement, not under pressure from the administration but freely, of my own accord. What is there to protest? Still, one hopes for *something*, *some* sign of regret at one's passing! – an indication, however faint, that the world will not simply shrug you off and proceed along its accustomed path as though nothing has happened. But nothing *has* happened. Well, never mind. The question now is... what now? What to do with the rest of my life? To the college I've served for twenty-two years I'm superfluous; to the world at large I'm an anachronism. Just the other day Jun said to me, "Seriously, father, why don't you get into computers?" *Get into* computers! No thank you! Probably they'll phase out the history department altogether. In a hundred years, two hundred at most, no one will ever have heard of Plato, Pericles, Sophocles... anyone. The past will dissolve. There'll be nothing but present and future. Every day will see the invention of some new device, magic but of course scientific. Life will grow easier, more pleasant. Troubles will vanish. Death itself will become a distant, fading memory. Historians of the future, in the unlikely event there are any, will divide the human experience into two vast categories: before immortality, and after. They'll do research on what life was like when there was death. How strange it will seem to them; how sad, how awful to live under that grim shadow! Immortal man will have no problems to solve, no death to fear, no goals to strive for... except more and keener pleasures, more and sharper distractions, more and softer comforts. Will he succeed in defeating boredom as he defeated death? Very likely he will. If necessary he'll invent a device to neutralize the part of the brain that generates the sensation of boredom.

Should I write a book? It'll keep me busy and out of trouble, there's that to be said for it; and also, as one of the few remaining (so to speak) custodians of the past, don't I have an obligation to do what little I can, suppressing a sense of utter futility, to preserve it? Well, we'll see, we'll see; we'll give it some thought.

What time is it? Four forty-three. Jun and his friend are coming at six, on the understanding that I'm to cook them a meal, Jun being eager, I suppose, to flaunt my not inconsiderable skills at the cooking stove. Yes, I'm not a bad hand in the kitchen – maybe I can hire myself out to a restaurant! There's an idea. A second career. Professor Masao Horiuchi, chef.

I learned as a boy. My mother was a bit bewildered at my penchant for hanging around the kitchen watching her work. Girls were supposed to do that, not boys; but in that, as in a few other things, my sister and I switched roles, and my mother, far from discouraging me, was pleased to have so eager a pupil. She taught me well, and what I learned was a big help to me as a single father. I wonder if the meals I prepared while Jun was growing up are not part of the reason we're so close today.

I wish I was more eager to meet this friend of his – Tomoko? Tomoko. I wish it because my instinctive aversion for people troubles me. It always has. You'd think my years in the classroom would have cured me of this infantile shyness of mine, but they haven't. I suppose it stems from a feeling of shame. I am ashamed of everything about me, beginning with my face. My thoughts too fill me with horror. Perhaps that's why I trained them to focus on the remote past, as a kind of distraction. But Tomoko isn't likely to be interested in the remote past. What then, in the name of Zeus, will we talk about?

Scene Nine

"The prophetesses of ancient Greece," I hear myself say, "went into trances, they took drugs..."

"Oh, I do nothing of the kind!" says Tomoko gaily. Yes, we are very convivial. We are a perfect threesome. I did the cooking, Jun chose the wine (red; we're on our second bottle); Tomoko supplies the wit. She fairly sparkles. Pity she's so homely. Does Jun actually sleep with her? Ugh – horrible thought! What kind of way is that for a father to... but how to suppress them, these horrible, shameful thoughts? With more wine, perhaps.

22

"Hold out your glass," says Tomoko. Does she read minds too?

"How do you do it then?" I ask.

"Do what?"

"Foretell the future. That is, if it's not a professional secret…"

"Oh no! No, it's terribly simple. All you have to do is empty your mind, empty it utterly."

"And prophecy fills the vacuum?"

"That puts it very well. Yes, prophecy fills the vacuum." She giggles – a ringing, childish laugh; if you closed your eyes you would imagine it coming from a pretty little girl.

"But emptying the mind surely isn't easy?"

"It's like sleeping. You don't fall asleep by trying, sleep simply steals over you. It's the same with this."

"Prophecy simply steals over you."

"You see," she says, turning to Jun and grinning, "I told you he'd see through me!"

"See through you?"

"One doesn't need prophecy to hear the sarcasm in your tone, sir!"

"Sarcasm!" Was I sarcastic? Have I offended her? No, she's laughing.

"Think of a number," she says.

"All right. Between what and what?"

"Between zero and infinity."

"All right."

"Jun tells me you were an actor."

For some reason I feel myself blushing. "I was, once upon a time, yes. A sort of actor…"

"He was saying how surprised he was to learn that your past is not as simple as he had supposed."

"I suppose he supposed – suppose he supposed! – I suppose he supposed my past was simple because I am. But life, you know, has a way of making simple things complex, over time. Live

23

long enough, and you wake up one morning to find yourself complex. Mired in complexity. Hm." I laugh; honestly, I haven't the faintest notion what I'm talking about.

"Go on."

"About...?"

"How does life make simple things complex?"

"Ah, my dear, that's a long and complex story!" I laugh again, then suddenly remember something. "Jun tells me you don't believe in love. Is that true?"

"Oh dear! You've spilt your wine!"

So I have. Some unconscious movement of my hand... a whole glassful, flowing, flowing... from the table onto the floor, onto my pants, flowing interminably... In a sudden rage I seize the glass and hurl it against the far wall; it shatters...

I come to myself in a hot bath, and though I remember everything clearly and vividly, it is as if it happened to someone else, and I feel at ease, at peace – in fact, happy. The window is open, a soft breeze enters, and from where I sit I can see the leaves of the mulberry tree in the garden, awash in moonlight. Is the moon full? Hm. "What a waste of good wine!" I think to myself – "but what the hell! I can afford it!"

The door opens a crack. "Father? Are you all right?"

"Fine, fine. I'll be with you in a minute."

———————

"I told you we should have bought white wine," Tomoko says brightly to Jun. "Those stains won't come out. Still, I did the best I could." She turns to me, her smile revealing her large and slightly protruding, but very white, teeth. "We were talking about love and prophecy. Shall I venture a prophecy about love? And about you? You, professor, will fall in love. There, don't look so surprised!" she says to Jun, who really does look more than a little astonished. "You were right – your papa is more complex than you had imagined!"

Scene Ten

"So! How are you?"

"Good. Good. Gin and tonic," says Maeda to the bartender.

"Gin and tonic?" echoes Tazawa. "Is that what journalists are drinking these days? Beer. Well! It's been a long time."

"So long that... honestly, if you hadn't called out to me, I wouldn't've known you."

"Have I changed so much?"

"Well, it's funny. I'm looking at you now and thinking... no, you haven't, really. You're thinner, of course."

"Of course. From the rigors of my search for truth. Fasting, ascetic practices..."

"And you end up in a cult..."

"Thank you. Cheers!"

"Cheers. You end up in a cult that worships evil!"

"Keep your voice down. Well, one must worship something, you know, and good is pretty elusive these days."

"Why must one worship something?"

"Maybe some people can get along without it. I can't. Can't seem to, anyway. Maybe it's my troubled background. Broken home, abuse. Don't blame me if my character's warped!"

"If you want a shoulder to cry on, mine's free."

"Thank you. I remember your compassion of old, and I'm pleased to see that adulthood has not hardened your heart."

"Oh, no! Adulthood notwithstanding, I'm as softhearted as ever. But seriously, what is this... this business you're involved in?"

"I'll take you to them, wait a bit. Their logic is impeccable. Something like this: God exists, but he's man's enemy. He created the world, but he didn't create man. Man is a kind of freak accident, an unintended by-product of creation, and the proof is... well, it's obvious, isn't it? Everything in creation is iron-bound by the laws of nature; only man is free, only man – if only partially. Listen. If I were a tiger and you were a hare, I would be literally *compelled* by my hunger to devour you. Right? Compelled. But as a man, I can say to my hunger, 'Down, boy! I will endure your pangs, however sharp they are, and even die of them if necessary – but I will not harm that hare – because it's wrong, it's immoral, the hare is innocent, it will suffer...' Etc., etc. You see what I'm saying? Or, alternatively, as a man I can say to myself, 'I am not hungry, this man sitting beside me has nothing I want, he's done me no harm, and yet all the same I will kill him if I feel like it, if the whim strikes me...' A man, you see, is free to that extent! Well?"

"Well what? I follow you so far, though I wish the damn music, if you call it that, wasn't quite so loud, it's giving me a headache... I grant you that man is free relative to hungry tigers. What follows from that?"

"What follows from that? Why – everything follows from that! Everything!"

"For example?"

"That God and man are enemies, irreconcilable enemies. Man's freedom is intolerable to God, and God's power is intolerable to man – though until now he has sublimated his resentment into an attitude he calls worship."

"Tazawa, really..."

"While man cringed, Satan rebelled against God – rebelled against his megalomania, his insistence on being worshipped as omnipotent, omniscient and good. Satan rebelled, and was defeated. Since then he has attempted to win man over as an ally, but man hesitates, vacillates..."

"Maybe he's holding out for better terms."

"You're a perfect example of what I meant when I said before that a man must worship something. Otherwise he becomes cynical, laughs at everything, believes in nothing, grows hollow inside!"

"Are you offering to save me? Is that it?"

"Maybe."

"But I thought you'd become disillusioned with them. I thought..."

"That's another matter. I have a right to be disillusioned, because I've seen and felt the greatness of their idea. I'm a disillusioned believer, while you... your disillusion is too easy. It's facile, childish."

"Do I understand you correctly? This is a gang of Satan-worshippers you're taking me to?"

"No. You don't understand me correctly. You don't begin to understand. You don't understand the first thing about anything."

"Tazawa, listen. You're trying to cut me down to size; I see that. You remember me from high school as arrogant and conceited, and you think you're giving me the medicine I need. It's kind of you, but... really... I've changed. I've gone through a thing or two. I'm prepared to admit that I don't understand the first thing about anything. How's that?"

"*You've* gone through a thing or two? *You?* Bartender! Another gin and tonic for my friend

27

here, and another beer for me. It's early, we've got time. Tell me this thing or two you've been through, I'm dying to hear."

"It's not... it's hard to put into words."

"Try."

"Can't we go somewhere else? It's impossible to talk seriously with this... this music, this..."

"Wherever we go it'll be the same. You know that as well as I do. I bet it's a love story you're going to tell me. Am I right?"

"Well... yes."

"I knew it. You have a face that speaks volumes. Well, go on, I'm listening."

Scene Eleven

"Her name is Yoshiko. I met her – "

"Speak up, I can't hear you."

"Her name is Yoshiko. I met her in a pachinko parlor. Of all the idiot places to meet someone. I'd never been in a pachinko parlor before. I had time on my hands... well, I didn't, really, I should have been in class, but..."

"I remember. You were going to be a doctor like your father."

"Dentist. Yes, that was the idea. My father had it all mapped out. My life, I mean. But what can you do? Dentists are born, not made. I am not a born dentist."

"So you rebelled, cut classes, took up pachinko..."

"It would have been a rebellion worthy of the name if there'd been something I was interested in instead. But there wasn't. I had no enthusiasm for dentistry, but no enthusiasm for anything else either."

"And yet you were always top of the class. Teachers held you up as an example to all of us."

"High school was a long time ago."

"There were people who hated you, you know. I wasn't one of them. I actually admired you, in a way. You were number one, I was number two – not very far behind you, but I had to work, whereas you... effortless. Natural genius."

"I'm no genius."

"Oh, but you are, and one day it'll show. Your genius is sleeping right now, that's all."

"Sleeping very deeply. Do you want to hear the story, or not?"

"Yes."

"It was a hot sunny day, the sun so bright... well, kind of like it's been lately, so bright you have to practically close your eyes against it or it'll kill you, incinerate you, it seems to absolutely hate your guts... and I'm trudging about aimlessly and I come to this pachinko place, lit up even brighter than the sun... I don't know what made me go inside. Pachinko – I'd never played it before, never had the least interest, the faintest curiosity... Anyway, I open the door, or rather the doors slide open automatically, and I'm hit by this... this raw noise wrapped in cold, cold air... If I'd suddenly been whisked onto an alien planet in another dimension, I couldn't've been more disoriented. And I have no idea where to go, what to do. I'm standing there in the middle of the floor like an idiot, pummeled by noise, my eyes dazzled, the air thick with cigarette smoke, when... the next thing I know there's a young woman beside me."

"Who will turn out to be Yoshiko."

"Tazawa, have you ever loved anyone? I mean– "

"I know what you mean. You mean loved in the manner of a French troubadour, or a Victorian gentleman. The answer is no. Most emphatically no. So it's a romance you're going to tell me."

"No, it's no romance."

"Well, go on."

"I'm not sure I know how to. It'll mean telling you something I've never told anyone – except Yoshiko, of course, who hardly..."

"How mysterious! You fill me with curiosity."

"Should I tell you? Why not? It'll be amusing to see the expression on your face. As a boy you always cultivated an expressionless face. To judge by outward appearance, nothing moved you, nothing surprised you. I thought that was very suave, very cool, and did my best to imitate you. Are you still the same, in that regard?"

"I didn't 'cultivate' an expressionless face. My face is just naturally blank. The fact that it doesn't register emotion doesn't mean I don't feel. Maybe I feel more than you, whose face... Well, go ahead. See if you can ruffle my countenance. I'm all ears."

"The fact is, I seem to have been born without that faculty known in modern parlance as a libido. Or if I was born with one, it never developed."

"Hm."

"'Hm'? Is that the best you can do?"

"I'm not sure I've quite taken it in. No libido?"

"I am perfectly indifferent to women. And to men. And – just in case it's crossed your mischievous little mind – to animals."

"So sex for you is..."

"A closed book. An alternate universe."

"Aren't there doctors for things like that?"

"That's what Yoshiko said. And I'll say to you what I said to her: why see a doctor about something that isn't a problem? Why should I wish to crave – why should I *crave* to crave – something I don't crave?"

"But I thought... how's my face doing, by the way? Any reaction worth noting?"

"No, it's as serene as ever. You might be listening to the Moonlight Sonata, instead of this... grotesque cacophony."

"I was going to say, I thought you said you loved Yoshiko."

"Oh, I do. I'll tell you something – and I think I've told you enough now that you can trust my honesty implicitly. Right?"

"Yes, I trust your honesty."

"If she were to say to me on a whim, 'Go up to the roof of our building' – which is fifteen stories high – 'and jump off', I would go without a word, and I would jump. That's how much I love her."

"Better not tell her that."

"She knows."

Scene Twelve

"You never told me your mother was foreign," I hear Tomoko say to Jun.

"You mean you didn't divine it?" I say. My laughter sounds false and strange in my own ears. Perhaps it's time I made my excuses to the young people and put myself to bed.

"I did not."

"Not foreign exactly. Born in the United States and grew up there, but her ancestry's Japanese. No mixed blood, as far as I know. True, she spoke English better than Japanese, which is why Jun's English is so good."

"It isn't!"

"Oh, come! It's better than mine, and I consider mine fairly good! Don't make a fool of your doddering old father!"

"Tell us about her," says Tomoko.

"Yes, do," echoes Jun.

"Some stories," I say, "are better left untold."

31

"Is an untold story a story?" asks Tomoko.

"You say there's no such thing as love. I know you're wrong, but I'll say this: we would all be better off if you were right. Love is an aberration of mind, a disease, a cancer, a – "

"Father!"

"What? Did I spill the wine again?" Listen to me – giggling like a schoolboy! Goodnight, children, goodnight, it's time for the older generation to retire; don't mind me, make yourselves at home, do whatever you –

"Love is *everything* to me!"

What's he babbling about?

"*Everything!*"

"All right, all right. Yes, love is everything, like death is everything once it gains its end! Love decks itself out in beautiful colors, false colors, like the lowest street whore! Ah! Forgive me, forgive me, I'm drunk out of my senses and talking nonsense. Keep an old man up past his bedtime and that's what happens!"

"No, please, go on," says Tomoko.

"No, stop!" says Jun. What is it with him? Is he going to cry? Honestly, he looks on the brink of tears!

"What's wrong?" I am totally bewildered; slightly queasy too. Heaven defend me from disgracing myself!

"Let him talk," says Tomoko to Jun. "It'll do him good. He's kept it bottled up inside him for twenty years."

"Kept what bottled up? You're mad, both of you!"

"No, Jun, no," says Tomoko gently. "No one's mad. Sh. Listen."

"Love. Love? What is it? For thousands of years poets have striven to define it – in vain. 'Love conquers all; let us too yield to Love'... that's Virgil, of course... hm. More to the point are these lines of

32

Catullus: 'I hate and I love. Perhaps you ask why I do. I do not know, but I feel it, and I am in torment.' Yes, love is like hate, and it is torment, torment...

"Your mother – why did I love her? Why? How? We were first-year university students, and we happened to sit next to each other... in a huge lecture hall, packed with some two hundred students. It was an introductory course in anthropology. Anthropology – a secondary interest at best, for both of us. To me at that time, anything that was not Greece and Rome was... nothing. And Misako's main interest was Japanese culture; she had come to Japan on purpose to discover her roots, or recover them, or... But the university authorities – rightly, I would say now – insisted on the acquisition of knowledge across a broad spectrum, and so there we were in an anthropology class, sitting next to each other, studying a certain African jungle tribe to whom war was literally unknown.

"Concerning this tribe, by the way, there is a curious legend. It was said that the chief could sexually satisfy himself merely by looking at a woman he desired. For the woman receiving his attention, the effect was the equivalent of rape – including, on occasion, impregnation. It was a child born in this manner, and not one born of marital relations with his numerous wives, who in the fullness of time succeeded to the chiefhood.

"Yes, there are many curious customs in the world. Maybe love is one of them. Maybe a thousand years from now anthropologists will study us and our peculiar, incomprehensible habit of falling in love, and it will seem as bizarre to them as this African tribe seems to us..."

Scene Thirteen

"I'm drunk. Put me to bed, Tomoko. I'm drunk."

"Come along, then."

"Look at him, passed out on the sofa, snoring like... like..."

"A man lying on the sofa snoring grotesquely – that's the *external* reality. He himself is totally unconscious of it. *His* reality is whatever he's dreaming at this moment. What *he* sees – what's real to *him* – is as inaccessible to us as what's real to us is inaccessible to him. Maybe he's dreaming something beautiful, something inexpressibly beautiful. Your father, I think, has a beautiful soul."

"A beautiful soul! You can say that after... after..."

"After what, child?"

"Why... after... what he just told us!"

"What did he just tell us? What did he tell us that would cause you to doubt the beauty of his soul?"

"Why... he murdered my mother!"

"Murdered your mother! Jun, you *are* drunk. Come, let's get you settled for the night. Murdered your mother! How*ever* does that little mind of yours work?"

"It works the way it works. I don't mean he murdered... I don't mean a court would find him guilty..."

"If a court wouldn't find him guilty, he's innocent."

"That's easy for you to say. You're not his son."

"I'm nobody's son. Nobody's daughter either. For which I thank the gods. Ah! What a terrible thing to say!" A burst of childish laughter escaped her. "You're not the only one who's drunk. Here I am provoking the wrath of the gods with my careless remarks! Come, this day has gone on long enough. When I was a little girl my grandfather used to tell me a bedtime story about a planet where the gods, to punish the people for their sins, withdrew the gift of sleep. The people grew weary, exhausted, they sank into a stupor, but it was a *waking* stupor... and their exhaustion, you see, magnified their sins in their own bleary eyes, until at last they understood how disgusting, how vile, how loathsome they were. But it was too late. Sleep was gone and would never return, there was no release into blessed unconsciousness. Fortunately we haven't come to that yet. Will your father mind, do you think, if I crawl into bed beside you?" She yawned volubly. "Oh dear!"

"He stopped loving her, left her..."

"Who? Oh... Yes, it's very tragic, but it does happen."

"It happens if you..."

"If you what?"

"Tomoko – marry me!"

"Jun, I'm sleepy."

"Marry me!"

"It happens if you what? What were you going to say?"

"If you let it."

"You're too young to be thinking of marriage. You want a mother, not a wife."

"Yes, I want a mother."

"I'm sorry, that was tactless, I shouldn't have said it."

"Marry me and be my mother, and when I grow up you'll be my wife."

"You'll grow up like your father grew up, and realize – "

"I will *not* grow up like my father! I will *not* realize! I *hate* my father!"

"That's the wine talking. Only sleep will shut it up. The sooner the better."

"I love you, Tomoko. I love you now and I'll love you as long as there's life in me, because everything you do is good, everything you do is good because you do it, because..."

"All right, that's enough. Is there a blanket or something we can cover your father with? He'll be cold during the night."

"You couldn't do a bad thing even if you wanted to; as soon as you did it it would become good..."

"Jun, if you don't stop this babbling I'm going to get angry! March! To bed!"

Scene Fourteen

What a strange dream! Misako. Misako never comes to me in dreams, never. And yet here she was, making herself quite at home. She came into my study – the door was open – and smiled. "You've changed," she said.

"Sit down," I said, not at all surprised to see her; I almost seem to have been expecting her.

I closed the book I'd been reading and settled back in my chair, perfectly calm and at peace, happy to indulge in a long talk with an old friend. Other than her presence, there was nothing at all unreal or illogical about the dream. It could have unfolded in the waking world just as it did in the sleeping.

"I've come to tell you that you don't have long to live."

"Is that so?"

"It is, and we are to be reunited in death."

"I'm glad. Would you like some tea?"

"I would, as a matter of fact."

"Come, let's go into the kitchen."

I get up; she follows me down the stairs.

"I can't get over how youthful, how beautiful you look."

"That's quite natural, under the circumstances."

"Yes, I daresay. You know, I suppose, that I've lost my job."

"And won the lottery. Yes, I know. Well, why don't you travel? See the world. Why stay rooted to one spot all your life, a man with your erudition? Don't you have any curiosity to see the *real* Greece, the *real* Rome?"

"I've seen them."

"Never. You've never left Japan, and, since coming here you almost never leave Wakaba. You never even go to Tokyo, though it's all of an hour away. It's changed, you know, since our day."

"It's the mind that travels, Misako – the mind, the imagination. The body is the same wherever it happens to be."

"Well, we won't argue about it. What's the use? I'll never convince you, and you'll never convince me."

"We can agree to differ about certain things. It doesn't matter."

"This is such good tea. It's not what you used to drink. Does that mean even you are not incapable of change?"

"I guess it does. It's one of Jun's discoveries. Tea, wine – he's quite the connoisseur."

"The sound of the waves! Always the same. Honestly, how can you bear living here?"

"Oh, but... I love the sound of the waves. You did too."

"I did not! I hated it."

"That's not what you said. You grew up by the sea, and..."

"The sea terrifies me."

"Terrifies you! But... it's so gentle, so calm... here, at least. So calming."

"So relentless. It's the sound of death. Every wave seems to whisper in your ear, 'I'm coming, I'm coming, I'm coming!'"

"And what's it like, death? Is it fearful? Appalling?"

"It depends on the attitude with which you approach it."

"You say I don't have long to live. I know that myself. Both my parents died of cancer. I can imagine my death quite easily. Oddly enough, most of my life I've been able to put it out of my mind, and go on living just as if I had all eternity ahead of me. Will you be staying for dinner? Should I get something ready?"

"Yes, if it wouldn't be too much trouble."

"Not at all. I'll cook you a feast. Listen, though, I want to ask you something. It's a question that's been weighing on me lately. Is life worth living after you've lost everything? I mean, it's easy to love life when you're happy, prosperous, respected, and even when tragedy strikes, many people, even quite ordinary ones, somehow rise to the occasion, displaying a fortitude, a nobility, you never would have thought they had in them. So it was, in a way, with me after your death – forgive me for speaking of it. Of course I was young then."

"And what would prompt such dark thoughts now, I wonder? You've money, freedom..."

"It seems terribly ungrateful, I know, but... well, I'll confess this to you, though it makes me ashamed: losing my job has hit me hard, very hard. It was more than a job, you see, it was... it's hard to explain... Having lost my job, I really do feel as if I've lost *everything*."

"Nonsense. Teaching at a junior college, teaching children just out of high school, children, for the most part, with no intellectual gifts, no intellectual curiosity – what kind of nourishment is that for a man with *your* gifts, *your* curiosity? You didn't like your students, and your students didn't like you."

"I like them in retrospect. And I wonder if they might not like me too, a little, in retrospect."

"Students don't like professors in retrospect. They either like them here and now, or they don't. You are too shy to be a good teacher. Also too selfish. You have no real interest in nourishing other minds, only your own. You stood in front of a hundred students and mumbled as though you were alone in your study. And when they asked you to speak up you mumbled even more incomprehensibly, as though on purpose."

"But Misako, how do you know this?"

"What are you talking about? Of course I know – that, and a good deal more besides."

Scene Fifteen

"Come," said Tazawa. "It's time we were off."

"Off where? What time is it?"

Without answering, Tazawa slipped off his stool and proceeded to the cash, Maeda somewhat unsteadily following.

"What's the matter with me?" he muttered. "Can't we have a coffee or something? I'm afraid I'm..."

"There's no time. It's not far."

"*What's* not far?"

Tazawa opened the door and held it for Maeda. The night had brought no cooling relief – it was as hot and sultry as mid-day. The area immediately in front of the bar was brilliantly lit up; it was as bright as noon, though with a different kind of light; looking up, Maeda noticed a red neon dancing girl flickering on and off – but Tazawa abruptly turned a corner and suddenly the scene was bathed in darkness and silence. Slowly Maeda became aware of the chirping of crickets somewhere. The sound seemed to swell as he listened. What started out as a distant twitter soon became a screech. Maeda winced. The physical environment, with its hot air, discordant noises, vaguely unpleasant smells, pressed in upon him unbearably.

"Tazawa, I'm going home." He longed for a bath; if he could only get into one, he thought, he would never come out.

"We're here," said Tazawa.

They seemed to be in some sort of park. How big it was Maeda could not tell, but vast trees rustled gently in the faint breeze, and closer at hand he could make out the shadowy forms of swings, a slide, a large sandbox, and benches on which during the day, no doubt, parents sat watching their children at play.

"This way," said Tazawa.

Maeda followed Tazawa to one of the benches, on which he discerned a human form. A homeless man, evidently, sound asleep.

"Look," said Tazawa.

Maeda looked. There wasn't much to see. So little of him was visible, his face hidden by a thick growth of beard, the rest of him, despite the awful heat, swathed in a quantity of ragged, frayed, filthy clothing that would have seen him safely through the chilliest winter.

He lay on his side, curled up into the closest approximation of the fetal position that the narrowness of the bench would allow. His head was covered by a black woolen tuque.

Maeda looked questioningly at Tazawa. "Well? What about him?"

It was a moonless night. The nearest street lamps were some distance away; their pale glow scarcely relieved the gloom. There must have been stars twinkling in the sky, but Maeda, squinting upward, could not make out any. "Really," he thought, "I'd better get glasses. I keep putting it off and putting it off…"

Maeda turned his attention back to Tazawa, whose silence now struck him as odd. He was surprised, though for some reason only mildly, to see a knife in Tazawa's left hand. He suddenly remembered something about Tazawa that he had completely forgotten: he was left-handed.

"I'm not quite sober," he thought; "my mind's not quite clear…something ghastly is about to happen, something…"

In high school he and Tazawa had been on the wrestling team, and he, Maeda, had been the stronger wrestler. "Should I throw myself on him? Tackle him, restrain him? Is he actually going to… kill this… this… No, ridiculous, I'm… my mind…"

So rapidly Maeda scarcely took it in, Tazawa made his move. It was a flying leap, perfectly executed, that landed him on top of the sleeping man. What followed Maeda could scarcely grasp. All he saw was a frenzy of meaningless movement, over almost as soon as it began. Trembling in every limb, he was incapable of thought, incapable of movement. How much time passed before Tazawa rejoined him he could not have said – seconds, perhaps, or, no less plausibly, years, centuries, eons.

He felt a hand on his shoulder. "You said something before," said Tazawa, "about coffee. There's a coffee shop about fifteen minutes from here, if you don't mind a little walk. Quiet, I promise. Come. My treat. We'll have us a nice talk."

41

Scene Sixteen

"How do you like this drought we've been having, eh?" said Tazawa. "They say it's the worst since they started keeping records in 19... I forget which year exactly. It's funny the way the mind works – or doesn't. Mine simply won't come to terms with numbers. No matter how I cudgel it... well, you must remember, you used to help me with my math homework. I can barely count, let alone calculate. No sooner does a number come into my head than it seems to dissolve. And yet, more and more, this is a world of numbers. Measure this, measure that; so-and-so is such-and-such a percentage of what's-it. Well, maybe I never will make a place for myself in this world. Some of us – a certain percentage, let us say – are destined not to. It can't be helped!"

"I don't remember helping you with your math homework."

"Really? Well, you did."

"If you needed my help in math you must have been pretty helpless, because I've no head for figures myself."

"How do you like this place? Quiet enough for you?"

"Yes, it's fine."

"And cool. And the coffee's not bad either."

"No, it's good. Listen..."

"What?"

"I meant to ask you... only my head aches terribly... I get these... these headaches..."

"Bufferin doesn't work?"

"It does, if I have it."

"Michiko-san!"

The plump, grandmotherly proprietor, presiding with a beaming smile over her tiny, dimly-lit establishment, apparently oblivious to the fact that Tazawa and Maeda were her only customers, made a great show of annoyance at being distracted from business which required her unbroken concentration. "What do you want?" she demanded, and burst out laughing. Tazawa was evidently a great favorite of hers.

"Do you have any Bufferins on hand? My friend has a headache."

"Yes, certainly." She slid off her stool behind the cash register and bustled into a back room, reappearing a moment later to lay two white pills in front of Maeda. "Here, take these. Would you like more coffee?"

"How do you manage to stay in business, Michiko-san? These days, you know, you can't just sit back and wait for customers to come to you. You have to rope them in. You need some kind of a gimmick."

"Oh, you're wrong. Don't be fooled because it's empty now. There are times enough when it's filled to bursting, I can assure you!"

"It's not true, you know," Tazawa said in a low voice to Maeda when Michiko had returned to the cash and to her business of presiding. "It was, once upon a time, but not for years. But she loves this little shop, and simply won't admit defeat."

"Which reminds me," said Maeda. "What kind of work are you doing?"

"Me? It's not work, exactly. I am on the payroll, let us say, of our family bookstore."

"Oh – the Alexandria! I remember, I used to…"

"My elder brother runs it. I'm a sort of errand boy. I let him kick me around. He thinks I'm spiritless, and I let him think so. The day will come when he'll see how much spirit I've got."

"What do you mean?"

"I mean I'll burn the damn place down. I'm joking, and you didn't hear me say that."

"Tazawa, does it ever happen to you... what happens to me sometimes... that... well, your ears and your eyes function perfectly, you see and hear everything clearly and vividly, and yet... nothing you see and hear, for all its vividness and clarity, seems *real*. I'm not making sense..."

"Oh, you are. You'd be surprised how much sense you're making."

"The Alexandria! Funny how it's never occurred to me to drop in lately. I used to love that shop."

"Which is as much as to say you loved my father. He conceived it, he built it, he poured his spirit into it. The Alexandria is my father personified, so to speak. Personally, I hated my father... well, we won't get into that. But it does make it hard for me to wholeheartedly love his store. My brother loves nothing. Profit is all he cares about, and since profits are declining, he's naturally thinking of selling. My father would turn over in his grave if he knew. My brother couldn't care less. As for me, I'm rather pleased – I only wish I could *see* him turning. You asked me before if I've ever loved anyone. Let me ask you a question in turn: Have you ever hated anyone?"

"Hated? No. Disliked, certainly – many people; *too* many people, as Yoshiko keeps pointing out – but hate? I doubt I have it in me."

"As a motive force, it's by no means to be despised."

Scene Seventeen

Travel, Misako says. Should I take a trip? It's funny – Misako herself was no traveler. She came to Japan, of course, but having come, she settled down pretty quickly, and Tokyo became the world

44

to her. It's vast enough to be a world. She loved it. So did I. Never once did she say, "Let's go to Greece, let's go to Rome, let's go to Hawaii." She loved everything about it – the crowds, the sticky summer heat, the exhausting pace... and me. She loved me. So hard to believe. I, Masao Horiuchi, was once young, and in love, and... loved.

Boom! Boom! Boom! What's that? Fireworks. The outside world constantly presses upon one. It's inescapable. You flee it in vain. It resents your absence, however temporary; it pursues you like the army pursues a soldier gone AWOL, or the police a criminal, and drags you back into the thick of things. Misako loved the thick of things. So did I. Was I the same man then?

Maybe I should go for a walk – my thoughts are making me restless. But it's so hot out there, and besides, ever since my name and photo appeared in the newspaper I am denied the pleasure of a solitary walk; there's always someone coming up to me: "Oh, you're the professor who won the lottery!" "Congratulations, professor!" "Can I have your autograph?" I'm not joking – three times I have been asked for my autograph! There's a poignant irony here – poignant and also laughable. The fact is, as a professor, as a scholar – I blush to say it, even to think it – the fact is, I secretly, silently, yearned for fame, for celebrity. Misako's description of me as a teacher was quite accurate, and I have never written anything, so obviously, even setting aside the unworthiness of such a tawdry, commonplace, childish daydream, there was absolutely no chance of it ever coming true, as I knew perfectly well, and yet this knowledge did not dim the force of the dream. Fame! A fine celebrity I'd make, with my shrinking dread of the slightest, most casual contact with anyone outside my most intimate circle – and often enough even inside it! And yet... well, enough.

45

Suffice it to say that the obscure scholar's fate was to be celebrated as... a lottery winner.

Misako, Misako! It was kind of you to come the other day. Why don't you come again? I think I'm falling in love with you all over again. Wouldn't that be amusing!

Let me tell you why, scholar though I am, I have never written anything. It is not laziness. You see, I suffer from a curious... affliction; I guess you could call it a mental illness. It is an inability to distinguish between what is important and what is not, between what matters and what doesn't. You have no idea how paralyzing this can be. Every decision becomes something to agonize over. Should I have a Western-style breakfast, or Japanese? Should I, if I am out for a walk, turn left at the crossroads, or right? With my afternoon tea it is my custom to have two *sembei* crackers, and there are times – seriously – when the question of which one to eat first plunges me into an agony of indecision. This "affliction," as I call it, is not upon me all the time. Quite the contrary. Sometimes it retreats and produces a backlash. In its absence I can become positively reckless, acting on the most capricious, meaningless impulse.

But that's another story. Years ago I used to know a man who owned a bookstore. He was a strange man – strange in appearance, strange also in his cast of mind. He was, for one thing, uncommonly small; for another, though healthy enough, he was abnormally frail. If he swatted a slow-moving fly with all his strength, the fly would probably survive. But his weakness was no obstacle to him, for there was only one thing in the world he loved: books. To anything that existed in the world outside of books he was perfectly indifferent; he paid it no mind. His bookshop, in the Kanda section of Tokyo, was called the Alexandria – named, of course, for the ancient Alexandria library. Unlike most bookstore owners, he never stocked a book he hadn't read, or didn't personally approve of. This of course ran directly contrary to the most ordinary business sense, but ordinary business sense was not what motivated him. He had standards all his own, and was quite willing to pay – in fact, insisted on paying – the economic price for living by them. The shelves in his shop reflected his personal tastes and nothing but his personal tastes, for which he considered himself accountable to no one. Customers whose tastes were different could go elsewhere. The biggest bestseller got nowhere with him if he didn't approve of it. He read, of course, voraciously – literature, philosophy, history, science, politics, it hardly mattered what; there is no subject of which he could say, "This doesn't interest me"; *everything* interested him – except bad writing, which did not merely bore him – it revolted him, like a bad smell or an evil action. I don't know if he ever put it this way himself, but he seemed to feel that good writing would save the world, while bad writing polluted it, poisoned it. I don't think it ever seriously occurred to him that to most people, books are at best a peripheral concern. He *lived* in books. Words were more real to him than things, sentences more real than events, literary characters more real – a good deal more real – than flesh-and-blood mortals like you and me. You will naturally think that such a man will steer a business enterprise straight to ruin, but the surprising thing is, he prospered. His eccentric character guaranteed him a certain notoriety. Word got around, journalists wrote him up for the newspapers, he appeared once or twice on TV talk shows. For all his eccentricity he was a friendly, engaging man; he loved to talk, and he talked well; the store became a kind of culture center...

Scene Eighteen

One day, this man – his name was Tazawa – approached me with a proposition. "Why not," he said, "write a book exclusively for me? For the Alexandria, I mean. I'll see to its publication, and I'll pay you a... what is it called?... an advance. On one condition. For a year it will be available only at the Alexandria. Well? What do you think?"

"A book! A book about what?"

"Whatever you like. A biography of Socrates, perhaps."

"So little is known about him."

"Well, whatever you like. I know the quality of your mind. Whatever you produce – "

"You do? But I've never..."

"I know. And I think you ought to. That's why I'm doing this."

Yes, he was thinking more of me than of himself – or rather, he was thinking of the book. He never asked himself, Will it sell? Is this a sound financial arrangement? No, a book was a book; he saw a book in me, and he would be its midwife.

Oh, Tazawa, if you only knew! It was as if – I am no sailor, but the image that comes to mind is a nautical one – as if he'd tossed me overboard from a ship in mid-ocean, out of sight of land! Yes, write a book – a grand enterprise, sure enough, but a book about what? Socrates, he said; all right, let's think about Socrates; but to understand Socrates you must go back to the pre-Socratics and the first glimmerings of philosophy; to understand *that* you must go still further back to a pre-philosophical world, you must explore the

48

pre-rational religions, you must consider the pre-civilized, irrational terrors from which they arose... Ah, Tazawa, you never knew, in your innocence, what you put me through! For years – three years? four? five? I no longer remember – I wrote and wrote, piling up hundreds of pages, thousands, quite possibly tens of thousands. I'm not joking. Tens of thousands of pages! My history of Socrates had become a history of Greece, of civilization, of the world, of man – but not a coherent history; oh, on the contrary, a most incoherent one!

What happened then is not altogether clear – my memory is of tossing piles and piles of paper, endless piles, into a raging fire; of sirens screaming, of searing heat and rough hands dragging me away to safety... But of course this can't possibly be true, for our apartment in Tokyo had no fireplace, and since we continued living there, it could not have burned down. Did I go out of my mind altogether? Jun was little at the time – five, six...

What's that? The doorbell? That's odd. The only people who ring my doorbell are people I call "the peddlers," itinerant sellers and purveyors of this and that – life insurance, futon cleaning, home renovation... Once, in my irritation, I gave one of them very short shrift and had waking nightmares for weeks afterwards: he'd come back with his gangland friends – he looked the type – and beat me up, trash my house... Nothing happened, but since then I never answer the doorbell except for the odd time when I am expecting someone – that journalist, for example. However, the peddlers always come during the day, never after dark... what time is it? The fireworks are over – I'd completely forgotten about them. Hm. I don't seem to have my watch on, and there's no clock up here. There was one once, but I banished it, a sort of whim having come over me to "banish time." It's in the little *tatami* room off the living room, the room I never use except to store "banished" items.

The bell rings a second time. What to do – ignore it? Yes, ignore it – but a kind of irresistible curiosity is upon me, and I find myself creeping down the stairs like a cat, cringing at every creak for fear of being heard. Who could it be? Unfortunately the front door has no peephole, and I'm not sure whether it's possible to see through the window without being seen. There's a third ring... should I call the police? I wish Jun were home. Or could it be Jun, having forgotten his key? No, he's staying over at Tomoko's tonight. And he never forgets his key.

"Masa, open up, it's me!"

My breath catches in my throat. Has he seen me? Heard me? Who's "me"? Ah, of course! Who else? Takeshi! Strange man, Takeshi. Most people think of him as a half-wit. Maybe he is; he's certainly not intelligent; but he has another quality that's maybe rarer, finer, than intelligence: goodness. He's good without knowing what goodness is. Children love him. Jun did as a child. Still does. He spends most of his time at the beach, picking up whatever trash he can find, not so much as a public service as... well, I'm not sure exactly what's on his mind; anyway, he does it.

Suddenly I feel very cheerful, very animated. How pleasant it will be to have a chat with Takeshi over a hot cup of tea!

I fling open the door – but my hearty greeting freezes on my lips. It is not Takeshi but a prefect stranger. Instinctively I shrink back. He regards me with – as best I can make out in the darkness – an ironic half-smile. He says, "Hello, Masa, it's been a long time."

I gape at him.

"I read about you winning the lottery, and thought I'd drop by to offer my congratulations."

Scene Nineteen

"All right, Jun, all right, we'll marry, but listen to me. You have to think seriously about what you want to do with your life."

"What I want to do with my life is be your husband."

"That's not what I mean. Listen. You... this is mad! You've turned my whole life upside down, with your... Jun, listen to me, focus your mind, concentrate! You keep saying you love me, you love me, but... *look* at me, will you? Mine is not the face of a woman a man falls head over heels in love with! Even if there is such a thing as love, which there isn't, but even if there is, you usually love, or imagine you love, something *about* a person, some... *thing*, some quality..."

"I love all your things, all your qualities."

"You don't *know* all my qualities, or even half of them. If you did..."

"I love all the ones I know."

"I'm homely, pockmarked..."

"Just a little, a very little. I love your pockmarks."

"I have two passions in life: the stars, and the mathematics that govern their movements. When am I supposed to have time to... to *receive* this insane, delusional love of yours? When? And what'll you do all day long when we're married?"

"I wish I could write poetry..."

"But you can't, so there's no use talking about it. Let's think of something you *can* do."

"Nothing. I'm totally useless. And stupid, and lazy. I'll keep our house clean, cook our dinner..."

"I won't be home for dinner."

"You'll come home *sometimes*, won't you?"

"You need a career, Jun, a career. Isn't there *anything,* any work…?"

"Yesterday I wrote a poem."

"You did! Show it to me."

"A sort of poem. I'll recite it. Would you like me to?"

"Yes."

"It's English. 'Come down from the clouds, whisper in my ear, tell me why the ocean cries…'"

"Go on."

"That's all."

"That's all? It's nice, but…"

"Not nice enough?"

"Work on it, develop it."

"But that's all there is!"

"All right, never mind that for now. Listen, I have an idea. You know English, and you're good with kids. You can teach."

"How do you know I'm good with kids?"

Tomoko paused, as though suddenly struck by something. She looked at him quizzically. "I don't know. I spoke without thinking."

"One of your intuitions?"

"Maybe. Is it true?"

"I don't know. I don't have anything to do with children. I never think about them one way or the other."

"Maybe I thought so because you're such a child yourself."

"How can a child be a teacher?"

"How can a child be a husband? Wait, I have another idea. My grandfather – "

"Oh, but please, Tomoko, please, let's not talk about this! I love everything about you except this one thing – when you plan my future. I wish you wouldn't."

"But – "

"I know, I know. You're right, but there'll be time for all that later, won't there? Meanwhile, I'm still a student. I'll get a degree..."

"In what?"

"How do I know? Anthropology, maybe."

"Anthropology! But you've never even – "

"I know, but... I was thinking about that story father told, about the chief who made women pregnant just by looking at them. That's really weird, isn't it?"

"Jun, you're impossible!"

"By the way, I had a really strange dream last night. Really strange. Listen. I was in a strange country, I don't know where, on a boat, on a river, and the boat was being steered by two small boys, very small, almost infants, and there was a mist over the river, a beautiful, gauzy mist, and through it, in the distance, I could dimly see mountains, towering and formidable but... I don't know, *soft* – because of the mist, I suppose. And suddenly I start uttering these strange sounds, totally incomprehensible – incomprehensible to me, but not to them; I was somehow speaking their language, you see. I spoke, they listened and then replied, and then I spoke again, still not understanding a word. At one point I must have said something particularly nice, because one of the boys, the older one, smiled, smiled radiantly; he was missing a front tooth..."

"Well? And then?"

"Then? Then I woke up."

Scene Twenty

How I suddenly recognized him I don't know. Not by his appearance, certainly, which not only the passage of time but also his plastic surgery had altered beyond recognition. What, then? His voice? His tone? A certain characteristic curl of the lips, hardly noticeable, perhaps, though obviously I noticed it (it may have been my imagination), which gave a vaguely ironic cast to even his brightest smile? Whatever it was that made Yasushi Yasushi, the flash of recognition, when it hit me, evidently showed on my face, for no sooner was I conscious of it, before I uttered so much as a gasp, than his smile broadened, growing even more challenging, and he said, "I see there's no need to introduce myself. Aren't you going to ask me in?"

As a small child I idolized him, worshipped him. I mean that literally. He would say to me, "I am God, you must worship me." I saw nothing incongruous in this, and "worshipped" him quite willingly, even eagerly – that is, I got down on my knees and bowed my head so that it touched the pavement, and remained in that position until he said, "Rise."

He was four years older than me and lived across the street, three houses down. What prompted him to take me under his wing the way he did I'm not sure – perhaps because this "worship" he demanded came so easily to me; perhaps also because he saw an intelligence in me that, being so intelligent himself, he thought it worth his while to cultivate. My "discipleship," if I can call it that, began when I was eight and he twelve; it ended three years later with his arrest. I never saw him again.

He knew so much, so much. I believed he knew everything. The names of trees, flowers and insects, for example. He knew them all, and taught them to me, taking me for long walks in the nearby woods and fields. (Where we lived was the very outskirts of Tokyo then; now, of course, the forests and fields are long gone.) He lent me books, and made me read them – which, too, I did willingly enough. Under his guidance I developed a vocabulary and a fund of knowledge far in advance of my age. I told him of my dream – conceived before I met him, before he moved into the neighborhood – of growing up to be a private detective. He encouraged me in this, and introduced me to his favorite fictional detective, Sherlock Holmes. We played Holmes and Watson. I, of course, was Watson.

In our neighborhood there lived a boy of about my age who had what teachers and parents called a learning disability. (We children had cruder expressions for it, of course.) I knew him slightly – not as a classmate, since he went to a special school somewhere, but every now and then I would see him in the park and we would play hide and seek together. He loved playing hide and seek. The strange thing was, I could hide in the same place every time and he never caught on that that was the place to look for me. It fascinated me, and I used to play with him on purpose to watch his "learning disability" in action, so to speak – not out of meanness, simply out of fascination. I think I even went through a phase of envying him his impairment – it seemed "cool" somehow.

One day this child went missing. Two days later they found his body, hanging from a tree, in the forest where Yasushi took me for walks. A day or so after that a homeless man was arrested. He confessed. It seemed an open-and-shut case – but then someone came forward, a pachinko parlor operator I think it was, who swore the man had been in his establishment at the supposed time of the murder. Other witnesses seconded this, after which it developed that the man had at various times confessed to other crimes as well, crimes he could not possibly have committed. The investigation was thrown back to square one. For weeks it seemed to go nowhere. And then one rainy day, as I sat at my desk in my room doing my homework, I heard the sudden wail of police sirens. It was near, very near. I ran to the window. What I saw was three patrol cars, red lights flashing, across the street in front of Yasushi's house. And then Yasushi, scarcely visible within a cocoon of officers, was led out...

The shock, of course, was terrible. Everyone knew Yasushi's family as stable, prosperous and loving, and Yasushi himself as a friendly, polite boy, excellent at sports, first-rate at his studies; there had even been talk, I learned later, of sending him to university in the United States, where the system is more open than Japan's conformist culture to the special needs of gifted students.

Scene Twenty-one

You can imagine the eagerness with which I followed Yasushi's case in the newspapers and magazines. As a minor he could not be named; he was referred to as "Youth A." Nor could he be tried in adult court. A family court judge sent him to a reformatory. His family disappeared, no one knew where. Years passed. I won't say I *forgot* about him exactly – on the contrary, his memory would unexpectedly surge at odd moments, sometimes very painfully – but he did at last recede (if I may put it that way) from my immediate mental landscape. Never, ever, did I mention him to anyone, not even my parents, who of course were as familiar with the case as I was. Nor did they mention him to me.

He spent, I think, ten years at the reformatory, or at various reformatories, and then, quite abruptly, the press rediscovered him. At first rumors, then more positive indications were reported of his impending release. He was "cured," said the experts; he was fit to rejoin society. With a new identity and a reconstituted face, he would be free to make his way in the world. I remember how my heart throbbed as I read these rather ambiguous reports. There was a good deal of commentary as well, much of it highly skeptical as to whether the "cure" of so evidently twisted a soul was really possible. It's all very well for the experts to display pride in their skills, but supposing he has another one of his *whims*, or hears one of his *voices*, and kills again? What will the experts say then – sorry? Such was the tenor of the doubters, and they were many.

I must say I myself was rather inclined to take this view. For no reason, under no provocation, he had killed a perfectly innocent child – it was monstrous. Even granting, for the sake of argument, that his soul, or his mind (whatever you want to call it), was diseased rather than evil – still, are such diseases *curable*, in the sense that, say, pneumonia is curable? I'm no psychiatrist and don't profess to know; on the other hand, I doubt the psychiatrists really know either, and my preference is to "err on the side of caution," as the English say.

"Thank you, this is good." He is clutching his tea cup as though for warmth, as though in spite of the heat he is cold. He doesn't speak, doesn't look at me; he seems totally absorbed in his tea, and as for me, I *can't* speak, my mind is simply numb. The silence lengthens, expands. Little sounds become part of it – the refrigerator motor, the slight buzzing of the electric clock. The clock reminds me of time. It's three minutes to ten. The sweeping second hand holds my attention. I watch it for a full minute, and then have to fairly wrench my eyes away for fear it will hypnotize me.

Why is he here? What has he come for? Why doesn't he speak? "It's lucky Jun isn't here" – and I look at him in some bewilderment, as though he had spoken; but no, it's just a thought that popped out of nowhere into my blank mind, and it's followed by its exact opposite: "If only Jun were here."

"Well, Masa?" He speaks at last. For some reason, at the sound of his voice, I glance again at the clock. It is five past ten – presumably of the same night. He seems to notice, and says, "It's not the best time to be dropping in unexpectedly on someone you haven't seen in fifty years. My apologies. But I saw your light and thought you must be awake, so I made bold to... 'Bold,' I say. If you knew how my heart was pounding! Many, many times over the years, Masa, I had thought of you, wondered about you, yearned to see you... and suddenly there you were, staring up at me from my morning paper, your expression seeming to say as clearly as words could have, 'Come on down, we'll have us a good talk!' 'Look,' I said to my wife, 'here's a friend from childhood, haven't seen him since though have often thought how nice it would be...' etc. etc. 'Well, why don't you look him up?' she said – there you have her character in a nutshell – and I said... I said, 'Hm!' Yes, I'm

58

married; we have two children – a daughter and a son-in-law, who I think of as my son, not that he'd pass for my issue, ha ha! – hm! – yes, and a grandchild on the way. You, Masa, are the only person now living, the only... ah, you're yawning! I'm keeping you up!"

"No!"

"Are you sure? It really was unconscionable, barging in on you at this hour. I don't know how I could have – "

"No, really..."

"I am somewhat lacking, I fear, in the social graces."

"So am I."

"You understand, then. Well, if you're not inclined to send me away, could I trouble you for another cup of tea, do you think? It really is very good."

"My son... my son chose it..."

"Hm. Yes... I noticed in the paper that you have a son..."

Scene Twenty-two

"A strange fate has been mine, Masa, a strange fate! But then, life itself is strange. In that seemingly trite phrase, you have the definition of man in a nutshell: Man is the creature who can say of his life, though he knows no other, that it is strange. Last night in my room there was a mosquito – a single, solitary mosquito. It knew exactly where my ear was, knew exactly what effect its buzzing had on me. It was amusing itself at my expense. It was no use my telling myself that after all, it's only a mosquito – I hated it, loathed it, loathed it to distraction, distraction! – for annoying me of course, but even more for reducing me to the abject state of loathing a mosquito! Ah…" He bursts out laughing – a laugh so gay, pure and ringing that I look at him in surprise. I don't think I ever heard him laugh like that as a kid. Of course it would have sounded different to me then… "Here we are, meeting for the first time in fifty years, and I'm babbling on about a mosquito! You expect more of me, no doubt.

"Hm! Ha ha! One scarcely knows where to begin. At one point, would you believe it, being somewhat hard up for money, I actually thought of writing my autobiography? It would have sold, made me rich, and also, by no means incidentally, contributed a wisp or two to our very incomplete, very limited knowledge of the ambiguous organism known as Man. For here's another capsule definition of man, if you're interested: Man is the creature who is capable of understanding that he does not understand himself.

"I didn't write the autobiography because I soon recovered my footing – financially, that is – and the impetus wore off. A strange fate, I said – but not necessarily a bad one. No, on the contrary, in some ways I can actually call myself blessed. How many people, after all, can claim the advantage of being born anew, of starting afresh, the slate wiped clean, at age 25? Even my face, which as a child I hated, was erased, and a new one given me – a face of my choice, quite literally. They had me describe the face I wanted, while an artist sketched; I pored over her sketches and demanded corrections: make the nose a little less sharp, the lips a little less thick, and so on. When I emerged from surgery and saw my face in the mirror, I fairly gasped. Having since earliest childhood been obsessed by a sense of my own ugliness, you can imagine (and maybe forgive) my delight in my newfound beauty. It was something out of a fairy tale.

"It wasn't all smooth sailing, naturally. You remember that I was in what might be regarded as the intellectual class. My IQ put me in the top three percent of our species – did you know that? My dream, as a dreamy adolescent, was to go on to university – if I ever got old enough, that is, because the growing process was so agonizingly, so *insultingly* slow; I began to fear it would never happen – go on to university and study psychology. It was my chosen field, chosen when I was twelve, and by the time I was fourteen I had read just about all of Freud and a good deal of Jung.

"Of course that sort of career was closed to me. Or perhaps I came to that conclusion, or accepted it when others came to it, too hastily. Maybe I should have insisted, struggled, fought... but at that point I just didn't have it in me, which is probably just as well, because, if you happen to be in an institution, fighting and struggling and making it plain that you are more intelligent than your keepers is not what gets you released from it. Ah, Masa, there's so much, so much I want to tell you! Unfortunately, most of it is simply incommunicable. Never mind. I'll do my best. My first job back in the 'real world' was in a factory – more a supervised workshop, manned by 'ambiguous' people like me who, without being totally dysfunctional, fit less snugly than others into society's little pigeonholes. The job was turning out circuit boards for video games. It required the intelligence of a five-year-old child – but here's what's funny: I simply couldn't get the hang of it! I couldn't! You see, matter, materiality, is totally foreign to me. It baffles me; I can't cope with it. I have ten thumbs. I'm forever dropping things, spilling things, breaking things. My wife won't even let me wash the dishes – for good reason. Just the other day, while trying to tape together a frayed wire in our bedroom lamp, I almost electrocuted myself. There was an explosion – well, a bang, anyway; my wife comes running: 'What happened?' 'I don't know!' Turned out I'd forgotten to unplug the thing. My wife gaped at me, speechless. I just laughed; I couldn't help it. God is a comedian, Masa, a comedian – a very, very good one."

Scene Twenty-three

"The terms of my release from the reformatory bound me for three years to supervised labor of one kind or another, after which, assuming I'd behaved myself and shown myself capable of 'integrating into society' – as though 'society' was everything and anyone not 'integrated' into it was nothing – I would be free to make my way as I pleased. The factory got rid of me by shunting me off to some other little corner of the system – a parcel delivery company. I did rather better there. I started out in the office, sorting packages, taking orders, filling out forms. Rather prosaic; but after I learned to drive and got a license, I started going out in the trucks. I enjoyed that. I would imagine my truck was a ship, and Tokyo the sea, and... well, imagination is a wonderful faculty. It shapes the world we live in. If you imagine Tokyo is the sea, and your imagination is powerful enough, Tokyo *becomes* the sea. And if a truck driver can imagine himself the captain of a ship – why, that's what he is. That's what I was. For a time. Until a little accident brought me back down to earth – to land, I should say.

"I hit a pedestrian. A woman. I'm not sure how it happened. My attention had been wandering. When the imagination is out on the high seas while the truck you're handling is crawling through Tokyo traffic... hm. The story seems to be that while I was stopped at a pedestrian crosswalk I unconsciously lifted my foot off the brake, or relaxed the pressure on it a bit, and the truck inched forward without my even noticing, until – thud! Luckily she wasn't seriously injured; I'd been moving maybe half a kilometer an hour; even so, if it had been an old woman she could have broken her hip or even been killed, and then... what a business that would have been! All owing to the incongruous fragility of old women! As it was, my new identity sufficed for the routine investigation that followed; no criminal charges were filed; and the only real trouble I faced was with my boss, who promptly grounded me and put me back to sorting. No matter. My three years were nearly up by then. A new phase of my life was about to begin. The stage had already been set.

"I haven't mentioned our living arrangements. We lived, all of us 'ambiguous' ones, in a dormitory out in Saitama, where they could keep an eye on us – an unobtrusive eye for the most part, but there *were* a lot of security cameras around. Still, I was used to being under surveillance, after all; I was aware of the cameras, naturally, but not unduly oppressed by them. And – I had a private room. Do you know what a luxury, what a gift of heaven, it is to be alone of your own free will? No, you wouldn't know; you've never been in a reformatory; you've never had to be reformed. Lucky you. That was the worst, you know: never, ever being able to be alone. I'll never forget the feeling that came over me the first time I stepped into my room – *my room!* – and closed the door. Oh, my friend, that dingy, stuffy little cupboard of a room was – the earth, the world, the universe, freedom! Oh, you don't know, you *can't* know... I've relived that moment a thousand times, a million times, since. I'm reliving it now – are my nostrils flaring? I bet they are!

"Solitude, freedom! There is no freedom without solitude. What did I need other people for? The ones who surrounded me, I had nothing to do with. I hardly noticed them. What they thought of me I didn't pause to wonder. I do now, but not then. There was one exception, a fellow sorter whose room was down the hall from mine. He was a gambler. A first-rate gambler – my master in the art, the master I eventually surpassed, as he acknowledged himself. Yes, Masa, my intellect, far from withering and dying under the force of adverse circumstances, on the contrary bent those circumstances to its will. I've traveled, Masa, a good deal – not for sightseeing, not for socializing, but for gambling. I play for high stakes, Masa, high stakes. And fortune, for the most part, smiles upon me; my wooing of her is generally successful."

Scene Twenty-four

Haruyuki Maeda started. What was that? Had someone knocked? He must have fallen asleep; the bathwater was lukewarm, the room almost pitch dark.

"Haru?"

"Yes, what?"

"Are you all right?"

"I'll be out in a minute. What time is it?"

"Almost seven."

Not even seven, and already dark. The days were getting shorter.

"Haru, shall I open a bottle of wine for dinner?"

"Wine? There's wine in the house?"

"I bought some."

"Well... sure, why not?" Wine – that was something new.

He was awake but had not shaken off his sleep; it was still upon him, a drag on his thoughts and his movements. Drying himself listlessly with a towel, he found himself unable to remember emerging from the bath; the light was on but he had no memory of switching it on. "My mind's withering, crumbling like leaves in autumn." It was a vaguely poetic phrase and made him smile. "Maybe I can make a haiku out of it."

Towel wrapped around his middle, hair wet and uncombed, he staggered into the kitchen. "What's the matter with me?" His strength was gone; he was trembling. "Fever – maybe I have a fever... Yosh?" No answer. Was she out? Hadn't she just said something about wine? "Yoshi!" Well, he had imagined it. But no, there was the table set, with wine glasses, two tall white candles in holders he had never seen before, and a bottle of red wine.

"If I have a fever I can stay home from school." That had been his mother's rule. He could protest as loudly as he liked that he felt awful, his stomach hurt, his head ached; his mother promptly reached for the thermometer; if it showed a fever he could stay home; if not, off to school. "I'm slipping into second childhood. Well, so much the better."

He wandered into the living room and sank, still not quite dry, onto the sofa. How much time passed before he heard the door open he could not have guessed even if the question had occurred to him.

"I went out to get a corkscrew," Yoshiko explained. "When I bought the wine I forgot we didn't have one."

"What's the occasion?"

"Get dressed and dry your hair. What's the occasion? We're alive! We love each other! Isn't that cause enough for celebration?"

"Yoshi, this sounds so unlike you."

"Does it?"

"Yes."

"Well, maybe I've changed. Or maybe you never knew me. Two people can live together, you know, and even love each other, without knowing each other."

"I don't think I'm up to this sort of discussion. Really, I... I don't think I feel well."

"I'm not surprised, the way you've been living."

"The way I've been living! How have I – "

"Spending days on end lying on the sofa, or sitting in the bath. You're ill because you live as though you were ill, not the other way around. You were going to see Kinoshita, you said."

"To hell with Kinoshita!"

"He would have given you your job back. They were short-staffed, you said so yourself."

"I don't want my job back."

"What do you want?"

"To be left in peace."

"I can understand that, but it takes money to live, and a job is how we get it. Without a job – "

"Without a job a man is forced to be dependent on his woman. But I don't mind that, you see. Quite honestly. I don't mind. I know what the world thinks of such an arrangement. But that doesn't bother me a bit."

"Doesn't it?"

"Not a bit."

"Well, listen to me. I'll tell you why I bought wine. It was to celebrate the *end* of that arrangement. The end! Open the wine, Haru, and fill our glasses. *Kampai*! Cheers! *Santé*! I quit my job. I've entertained my last client. From now on I belong to you, exclusively to you. Body and soul. Money too. Take it, it's yours – as long as it lasts. And when it runs out? I don't know. I don't know how people without money live. Maybe you know. Journalists know things like that, don't they? Another glass! *Kampai*! Wait a minute, I bought a French bread and cheese, Roquefort, at Mitsukoshi. We'll have a feast..."

Scene Twenty-five

"What's that noise?"

"What noise?"

"I thought I heard a noise."

"There was a story in the paper the other day..."

Maeda tensed. "Yes?"

"An abandoned baby, a boy... in a parking lot..."

Maeda looked at her in surprise. "Yoshi, you're crying!"

"It's nothing. I'm drunk. I'm not used to wine."

"Or Roquefort cheese."

She smiled through tears. "Hand me the tissue paper." She blew her nose. "A young couple was arrested – seventeen and sixteen. They couldn't tell their parents, so she gave birth in a hotel room, and then they wrapped the baby in a towel – a hotel towel – and left it in a parking lot, where it was found howling... Oh, Haru. I don't know why – the story makes me so miserable. I can't get it out of my mind."

"More wine?"

"I should have bought two bottles."

"You finish the wine, I'll have a beer. Yes, all kinds of things go on out there. I haven't even looked at a newspaper lately. Did you happen to see a story about a... a homeless man?"

"No."

He fell silent.

"What about him?"

"He was killed. Maybe I dreamed it."

"Tell me."

"A homeless man, asleep on a park bench, and suddenly, for no reason... but if it'd happened it'd've made the paper, right? Therefore it didn't happen. Therefore I'm going mad. Did you know, by the way, that there's madness in my family?"

"Oh?"

"Yes, my great-uncle, on my father's side. I never met him, but the story is that he was incapable of distinguishing dream from reality. He'd have the most fantastic dreams, and they'd be as real to him as...well, the things that seem real to us, you and me, normal people. He spent time in a mental hospital, where he had electro-shock therapy. Maybe I inherited whatever he had. Or maybe I'm him reincarnated. That'd explain a few things, eh, Yosh, don't you think? Maybe I had electro-shock therapy before I was born. Eh?"

"I wish you wouldn't..."

"Wouldn't what?"

"Let's..."

"Well?"

"Haru, let's try to be happy!"

She brightened suddenly, like a little girl spotting a lovely seashell at the beach.

"Let's try to be happy! You love me, don't you?"

"You know I do."

"And I love you."

"You do?"

"Yes. I didn't know it before, and so I made you unhappy, but now... now I know it."

"And what made you realize..."

"Do you really want to know?"

"Yes, the subject is of interest to me."

"I'll tell you then, though I probably wouldn't if I wasn't drunk. A client made me realize. I'm not sure how, or why, but suddenly, in his arms, I realized it was you, you alone I love, you alone I've ever loved and could ever love. Well? Shouldn't our love make us happy, even if the world isn't always such a happy place? Come, come to me. I'll show you..."

"Listen."

"What?"

"It's raining!"

They listened in silence.

"You're right, it is."

"First time in... how long?"

"Weeks."

"Months, maybe."

"Years." She giggled.

"What a beautiful sound it is. Like music. Isn't it?"

"My piano teacher when I was a little girl said Beethoven was inspired by the sound of the rain."

"I hope it rains all night."

"We'll make it rain all night. Come."

"Sh. Listen."

"Haru... I want you."

"Tell me about the client. Did he look like me, or what?"

"No. He looked nothing like you. He's a foreigner, a Russian."

"Russian! Why would a Russian remind you of me?"

"He didn't remind me of you. He just made me realize... I can't explain... His name is Rogozhin."

"Rogozhin?"

"He's a diplomat of some sort. A widower. His wife died last year. He loved her so much that he couldn't imagine going on living without her. He tried to kill himself, took poison, but survived, which made him feel like he'd risen from the dead..."

"I bet he regales all the whores with stories like that. You, of course, took it at face value."

"Yes, I'm not very smart, and I take everything at face value. And you're so clever that you take nothing at face value. Which of us is better off, I wonder?"

"You, probably. Rogozhin. He murders Nastasya in *The Idiot*."

"What?"

"What's the connection with me? How did he make you realize..."

"I don't know! My thoughts are all confused! All I know is I want you!"

"And all I know is that your face... is the face of an angel, Yoshiko."

Scene Twenty-six

"I'll tell you, Masa, what the trouble with this world is. Too many people. Not enough oxygen. Not enough room. You can't cultivate a garden without weeding it. We must weed our garden. It'll choke otherwise. Eliminate one-fifth of the world's population. Do it humanely by all means, but it must be done, and done quickly.

"Personally speaking, I've nothing to complain about. Life has been good to me. I've heard it said that money can't buy happiness, but it seems to me you have to be pretty perverse to have all the things that money can buy and still profess to be unhappy. Or if not perverse, let's just say there's something lacking in you. If you are blessed with all the things money can buy and are still unable to muster within yourself the energy, or courage, or whatever quality it takes, to leap across the gulf that still separates you from happiness, I'd say you must be a pretty poor, pretty spiritless specimen. What's the counter-argument – that it's an imperfect world? Granted. Grossly imperfect. But that's a problem only if you're a monotheist who believes God is all-good and all-powerful. We Japanese are fortunate never to have been burdened with such an absurd belief. Besides, a perfect world wouldn't suit us. It would oppress us, weigh us down. Perfection and humanity don't go together. We can be perfect only at the expense of whatever it is that makes us human – whatever 'human' means. I wonder, Masa, if I could trouble you for another cup of that marvelous tea. Your son must be a very fine young man indeed, if the taste of this tea is at all indicative of his character. I look forward to meeting him.

"What was I saying? Yes... you were wondering why I got married, since I've such a taste for solitude. When you meet my wife, as I hope you soon will, you will wonder no longer. You will see the answer in her face the instant you set eyes on her. I don't mean that her beauty will overwhelm you – ha ha! That's hardly likely. No, what you will see is that she is the sort of woman whose company does not infringe on a man's solitude. Not once in our twenty-seven years together has she infringed on my solitude, though one would hardly describe her as reserved; quite the contrary. We met at the parcel delivery company; she worked in the office. We had very little to do with each other; then I left and was away for over a year. Where was I? All over the world, gambling. Gambling is not a science, Masa, it's an art. The gambler must be an artist. I am one. I came back moderately prosperous, soon to be extravagantly so, then to lose it all – ah, fate! –

then, as I said, to recoup my fortune. We happened to run into each other on the street. She recognized me immediately; I, for my part, would never have known her. We went somewhere for coffee, then somewhere else for drinks. As for the rest, the tale pretty well tells itself. Did I mention we have a daughter? She's married too, will be giving birth soon...

"Yes, Masa, life has been good to me. It has withheld few of its blessings, and inflicted few of its pains. Life generally is good to the artist. There is a mutual sympathy, you see, between us – between life and the artist, I mean. The world's suffering and sorrow have scarcely touched me. I am aware of them, but not first hand. One only has to glance at the news from time to time to know what I have been spared. I have been spared, and I am grateful. Yes, the suffering people endure is appalling, appalling. And I have found myself wondering how people are able to endure it. I've asked myself whether I myself could, and the only honest answer is no, I could not. I have, you see, a morbidly sensitive nervous system – I have only to imagine a pain to feel it, and just that imagined pain makes me writhe. That being so, how could I stand the real thing? I couldn't. I will end my life at the first approach of a more than merely passing suffering. I am determined to. Death holds no terror for me; nothing does; only pain."

Scene Twenty-seven

"Well, Takeshi."
"Yes."
He says "yes" to almost everything – almost always, as now, with a broad, happy smile. I encountered him, as usual, on the beach, me

strolling idly and watching the waves, him at his usual occupation – collecting trash. He drags a big black plastic garbage bag along the sand, and whenever he sees an odd bit of trash – beer can, milk carton, old shoe, cigarette butt – he stoops to pick it up and toss it into the bag. For all his determination to rid the beach of it, the trash doesn't seem to repel him; nothing is too filthy or smelly or disgusting to make him flinch; once I suggested he at least wear gloves; he merely shrugged, just as he did later when I proposed he wear a hat for protection against the sun, and carried on as though he hadn't heard me.

"Finding much?"

"Oh, yes."

"Isn't it terrible," I say, as I've said many times before – not so much to make a point as to try to provoke him, or perhaps more to admire his refusal to be provoked – "the way people use the beach as if it were their own private garbage dump! They're animals! Animals!"

"Oh, they don't mean any harm."

"No, of course not."

"Look. Crows."

"Ah."

It's true. Crows outnumber seagulls; they've taken over the beach. They even seem to think they're seagulls, imitating (mocking?) their comical hopping walk and also (no question of mockery here; could it be a deliberate learning effort?) their swooping, soaring flight.

I wish I could describe Takeshi. I would start with his voice – a child's voice but deep, deep, the deepest baritone; and yet, unmistakably a child's voice. It's hard to explain, like everything about him. Just try to guess his age from his appearance; a glance suffices to defeat the attempt. Is he a young man? Old? He is sometimes one, sometimes the other, sometimes both at once, sometimes neither. His wrinkled face, wispy white hair and stooped, frail bearing suggest age; his eyes, his teeth and most of all his smile, proclaim youth, eternal youth.

I see him often, talk to him a good deal; we are the best of friends, and yet I know nothing about him. He's not from here. I began encountering him on my walks along the beach... how long ago? Five years? Ten? For some reason, at first sight, he reminded me of the 18th-century poet Ryokan, the hermit monk famous for, among other things, an all-encompassing love that extended even to the lice in his chest hair. A verse of Ryokan's sprang to mind, for I know that poet well: "Children! Shall we be going now to the hill of Iyahiko to see how the violets are blooming?" I felt happy, looking at him, though he paid me not the slightest attention; and though my morbid shyness normally makes approaching strangers out of the question – even, for example, to ask directions on a city street, with the result that I often wander lost for hours – I immediately went up to him and said, "Hello!"

"Hello," he replied, without the faintest surprise, as though he had known me for years. His tone suggested, if it suggested anything, that he was happy to see me but would have been equally happy not to see me.

"What are you doing?"

"Picking up trash."

"Why?"

"Because it's trash." Sarcasm? No, not a hint.

"Do you work for the city?"

"No."

"Let me buy you a cup of coffee."

"Yes, all right."

No sooner had I spoken than I found myself utterly unable to account for my invitation, or his acceptance of it; but we walked from the beach into the heart of the town, he trailing his black bag, me wondering where there would be a suitable coffee shop – "suitable" meaning what? Odder still was my total lack of discomfiture at being in such an awkward situation; it seemed quite natural somehow. "How about here?" I said, seeing a sign that looked promising. It said simply *Kisaten* – coffee shop. If it has any other name, to this day I don't know it.

There was the faintest tinkle of a bell as I opened the door. Inside it was cool, dim, quiet – silent, in fact; a small shop in which everything was small, and everything made of dark wood. We seated ourselves on small chairs at a small round table. A waitress approached and silently took my order: hot coffee for two. It seemed natural for me to order for Takeshi, and natural for him to put himself in my hands. That was the first time; we've come here often since; we go nowhere else.

It occurs to me suddenly to wonder, for the first time, if Takeshi knows my name. I don't think he does. How would he? I've never told it to him. He's never asked. The subject has never come up.

Scene Twenty-eight

"Takeshi, I want to talk to you. I want your advice. Here's what it boils down to: I am fifty-six years old and... what should I do with my life? I've lost my job, my wife is dead, my son is grown... I'm asking you as I would the Delphic oracle: what should I do with my life?"

His answer, as I knew it would be, is a smile. He has the most beautiful smile. How to describe it? I have tried before, and failed. Many adjectives come to mind – radiant, innocent, divine, joyous, loving, transcendent, wise, foolish... all true, all beside the point; I dismiss them all. I have imagined myself showing that smile to Socrates and saying to him, "Confess, Socrates! This smile of my friend Takeshi's puts your philosophy in the shade." And he, smiling himself, admits that it is so.

"I have money. I won a lottery, you see. And I have savings. I live simply. I'm sure I can manage quite comfortably for the rest of my life. But a man needs a purpose in life. A reason for living. Otherwise he... well, he... he drifts. Hm. Maybe I'll help you collect trash. How about that? I'll become your assistant. Would you take me on as your assistant, Takeshi?"

"Yes."

We fall silent – that is, I do, and he, who rarely speaks except to answer a direct question, naturally follows suit. Time passes – how much I don't know. Suddenly I hear, "Professor."

I am conscious of being ridiculous in my surprise. I didn't hear the bell, didn't hear the door open, was not aware of anyone else in the room – was my reverie so deep? What was I thinking about? Whatever it was, it's gone, vanished like a soap bubble, and a young man stands before me; he looks vaguely familiar, a handsome young man – a student? A disciple approaching the fallen master to pay his respects? Takeshi is nowhere in sight. I am not surprised. Nothing about Takeshi surprises me; almost everything about everything else does.

"I'm sorry," I murmur, my confusion all too apparent. "I was daydreaming..."

"May I sit down?"

"Yes, of course." Who on earth is he? I can't very well ask him, he'd be surprised at my not knowing; he might conclude that losing my position has unhinged me already. Maybe it has.

He sits where Takeshi sat, opposite me across the tiny round table. We are the only customers.

Most coffee shops have background music, or a TV on. This one doesn't. The waitress comes and, almost in a whisper, he orders an ice coffee. The waitress looks at me and I nod, not quite sure myself what my nod signifies.

He seems to have something in mind, this unexpected companion of mine, but not to know quite how to begin. He looks down, crosses one leg over the other. Still he says nothing. It is up to me, as the older man, to break the ice. Two lines of Sophocles come to mind. It is natural that they would; they were the subject of the last class I taught. If he is a student, he will recognize them. The speaker is Antigone, determined to bury her rebel brother in defiance of the king's ban: "Leave me alone with my madness. There is no punishment can rob me of my honorable death."

He looks up and smiles; it is the faintest of smiles – and suddenly I recognize him; I feel my face go hot with embarrassment; he is not a student at all but that journalist who interviewed me after I won the lottery; what on earth is *he* doing here? The waitress brings our coffee – ice coffee for me too, thus showing me what my nod signified.

Scene Twenty-nine

"Grandfather, grandmother, this is Jun. Jun, this is grandfather and grandmother. Now, let's all sit down and go through the motions of getting to know each other. Grandfather, I'm relying on you to put this child at ease. He's very nervous."

"Nervous! About meeting us! Surely you told him – "

" – what simple, homespun people you are. Certainly I told him, and if he failed to draw the conclusion that there's nothing to be nervous about, that's his problem. You'll find him a little slow, I'm afraid. But just look at him. Isn't he beautiful?"

"He is, he is indeed. Jun, welcome. Tomoko has told us a great deal about you too, and we've long been looking forward to meeting you. Haven't we, Kazuko?"

Kazuko smiled and bowed. Somewhat to Jun's surprise, she wore a kimono. She was a tiny woman, barely reaching Tomoko's shoulders, though Tomoko herself was of slightly less than average height. The kimono was of blue-gray unfigured material, the sort of outfit a woman of the pre-modern age might have chosen for an occasion which called on her to be present but inconspicuous. The grandfather, for his part, wore a dark suit and tie, the businesslike appearance his dress gave him belied by the widest smile Jun had ever seen; he seemed to be deliberately drawing attention to his teeth, which were in fact remarkably white and even. He had a thin, almost ascetic face expressive of depths you sense without being able to put your finger on what if anything they signify. Thick spectacles made his eyes seem preternaturally large. His hair was a thin white mane, swept back from his high forehead. The effect of his appearance on Jun was a strange one. It made him think, "I'd really like to paint this man," though he had never painted a picture in his life, or even thought of painting one.

"Tomoko is certainly right about my being a bit slow," said Jun with a smile, "but about my nervousness, she exaggerates."

"Her exaggerating is habitual, as is her malice," said the grandfather, smiling more broadly than ever. "To her, truth is raw material for genius to distort at will, and she has never doubted for a minute, from the time she was old enough to talk, that she is a genius. On that point I don't contradict her, but I doubt very much you're slow. If you were, I'd have noticed by now. When it comes to sizing up character, I'm not the worst of judges. I think even Tomoko would give me credit for that. Wouldn't you, my dear?"

"All the credit in the world," said Tomoko. "Come, grandmother. "Let's us see to tea and let the men talk."

"Sit down, sit down. You're used to tables and chairs no doubt, but as Tomoko must have told you everything here is in the pure Japanese style. Does that bother you?"

"Not at all. I am Japanese, after all."

"Very few people today are Japanese. We are a dying people, though outwardly flourishing. I try, in my own small way..."

"Grandfather..." Tomoko had left the room but now paused in the passage leading to the kitchen. "Grandfather, please, don't read him a lecture. Though on second thought, why not? He hasn't heard it before, he might find it interesting, in a quaint sort of way."

"Tomoko argues that 'people' in the sense of nationality is an antiquated concept..."

"A dead concept. Stillborn."

"...that it is enough to be human without being Japanese or American or Chinese or what have you. But as an amateur student of history I know that it is not enough to be human. Our humanity gives us certain biological possibilities – upright posture, opposable thumbs, a larger brain – but it is nationality, or, if you will, culture, that gives us art, science, civilization. No people has ever been civilized without belonging to a nation; the greater the nation, the greater the civilization. Japan's is a very great civilization – known, alas, to only a very few Japanese today. Tomoko calls me a militarist and a fanatic because I regret that we

79

have transformed ourselves into a nation of foreigners."

"What would you have us do, bring back the Way of the Warrior? The only way for Japan to rise above that barbarism was to turn to foreign ideas, because Japanese culture had nothing better to offer."

"Japanese culture at its best, my dear, was the Way of the Warrior *in peacetime.*"

"The Way of the Warrior in peacetime is an unsustainable contradiction, which is why it collapsed. Imagine," she said to Jun, "this argument has been going on since I was three years old! Always the same, down to the very words we use. And yet somehow to grandfather it never loses its freshness. I guess when you reach a certain age irrelevance becomes irrelevant. Well, if you'll excuse me, I'll give grandmother a hand in the kitchen."

Scene Thirty

"To me *tatami* matting," said the grandfather as the four of them sat, the two men cross-legged, the women kneeling, on cushions round the low Japanese-style table sipping green tea, "has about it a freshness, a cleanness, an expansiveness altogether lacking in carpeting. Its very blankness stimulates the imagination. Depending on your mood it can be the sea, or a vast plain, rice paddies stretching out as far as the eye can see."

"Rise to the occasion," said Tomoko across the table to Jun, making no effort to lower her voice and sighing with theatrical weariness. "Tell him he sounds like a poet; ask him if he writes poetry, which of course he does; he's dying to recite something, I can tell."

Far from taking offense, the grandfather laughed heartily, again seeming to open his mouth as wide as possible in order to make a display of his white teeth. "As a matter of fact, my dear, you're right. Just this morning I composed a haiku, and I confess I am, as you say, dying to recite it."

"Jun will understand, I'm sure. He's something of a poet himself."

"Are you really?" said the grandfather, very much interested.

"Oh no," said Jun, flurried. "Really, Tomoko, you shouldn't... no, I'm no poet. I lack the... the... hm... not the *feeling*, I think; there are moments, I think, when I *feel* like a poet..."

"Jun, if your face turns any redder I'll have to call the fire department!"

"But the words... the words I don't have..."

"He's a bundle of incoherent feelings," said Tomoko.

"So was I at his age," said the grandfather. "It takes time to master words. Years. Mastery comes with maturity, experience, hardship. It doesn't – "

"You're keeping us waiting. Recite your haiku."

"'Harvest moon rides an autumn breeze into the evening sky.'"

"I call for a moment's silent appreciation of that very pregnant image," said Tomoko. "By the way, something I've always meant to ask you: haiku poets are so full of 'the moon,' everything is 'the moon,' but they never seem to mention the stars. Why is that?"

"Because the moon is everything. It is enlightenment, it is death, it is eternity..."

"And the stars are nothing?"

"To us Japanese, I think, the stars are too remote to speak to us directly. The moon speaks to us directly."

Jun, meanwhile, was looking at the grandmother. Perhaps feeling his gaze on her, she raised her head and, meeting his eye, smiled. He lowered his eyes in embarrassment. He had been thinking how to bring her into the conversation; she had yet to utter a word in his presence, and he struggled to come up with some little question he could put to her. It should have been simple enough, but somehow nothing suitable occurred to him.

"Excuse me." The grandfather rose, and only then did Jun become aware of a telephone ringing in some distant part of the house.

"Well?" said Tomoko when he had left the room. "What do you think of him? Can you see yourself working for him?"

"*Working* for him?"

"Didn't I mention it? No, come to think of it, I don't think I did. I spoke to him about the possibility of employing you. You supposed all this time he was making idle conversation. Not so. He was observing you, sizing you up. He is, as he said, a very shrewd judge of character, and you may be sure that not so much as a flicker of your eyelid escaped him. By now he knows you better than you know yourself."

"Working for him! I never thought – "

"That's why others must think for you. He runs a considerable business, you know, a vast web of commerce – the Saito Trading Company. Imports, exports, you name it. There aren't many corners of the world he doesn't deal with. Do you remember, Grandmother, that song you used to sing to me when I was little, 'He's got the whole world in his hands'?" The song is about God – the American God – but in my mind I always applied it to Grandfather. Here he is. You do, in a sense, have the whole world in your hands, don't you, Grandfather?"

82

"Attach the phrase 'in a sense' to any proposition you like, my dear, and it becomes, 'in a sense,' true. That was Rogozhin. He'll be here soon. Rogozhin," he explained for Jun's benefit, "is the son of a very dear friend of mine, a Russian, a business partner before his untimely death in 1992. The son is attached to the Russian embassy. A fine young man – laid very low, I am sorry to say, by the death of his wife last year. It is strange. When Tomoko's father, our son, perished in 1989, it was old Rogozhin who comforted us with the teachings of the Buddhist sages, that transience is the nature of all earthly things; now it falls to us to offer the same sad comfort to the son."

Scene Thirty-one

"Yes," he says, "that thing I did on you was the last story I wrote. The last story I will ever write. Terrible story. Terrible. Unworthy of me, unworthy of you, unworthy of all of us. I'm sorry, truly sorry. I failed to do you justice, failed... failed. Now I know you better. You'll be like a father to me – won't you? Because my own father... my own father... *failed* me, you know? He... yes, he failed me."

"You're drunk."

"No, don't get me wrong. I forgive him. I forgave him long ago. Ages ago. All fathers fail their sons. Being a father, living up to a son's expectations... no man can do it. No man. No man. It's impossible, too much to ask. I'm not a father, but I'm a man, aren't I? – and I realize... realize... hm. I've forgotten what I realize! Come home with me. I'll introduce you to my wife. Imagine being married to... to an angel. You're right, I'm drunk, but... drunk or sober, an angel is an angel!

Bartender!" – for it hardly needs be said that the friendship begun in the coffee shop is being consummated, so to speak, in a bar. "Vodka! To Dostoevsky! Hooray! Nazdrovya! There's one passage in Dostoevsky, you know, that's always moved me. It's in *The Devils*. Kirilov says to Stavrogin, 'Have you seen a leaf?' And Stavrogin, instead of saying, 'What kind of an idiot question is that? Who hasn't seen a leaf?', answers quite seriously, 'Yes, I have.' Everything in Dostoevsky, you see, is a symbol of something beyond itself, and a leaf, a tiny, insignificant leaf, he somehow manages to elevate to a symbol of... I don't know... of... of life itself!"

"Hm."

"My wife Yoshiko is an angel. I'm repeating myself, I know – not because I'm drunk! No – because I'm in love. And she loves me. She does. She loves me, I know that now, though I didn't before and was unhappy. Are you married? Of course you are, you have a son. Though that doesn't necessarily... Forgive me, my tongue... I ought to cut it out, it's the only cure for talking too much."

"Sobriety is another."

"No, that's too high a price. Now that I'm drunk I make a vow never to be sober again! Here's our vodka. To Dostoevsky! Ah, I'm repeating myself again. Why does that TV have to be on? Why does every bar, every restaurant, every... have a TV on? Bartender! Seriously. I'm asking you seriously, civilized human being to civilized human being. Okay? We can watch TV at home. We come here not to watch what we can just as easily watch at home, if we're stupid enough to want to, but in search of... of... well... friendship, intoxication, elevated conversation – in a word, life itself! Do you see what I mean? Instead – what are those women laughing at? Look at them! Shrill, hysterical laughter, and those grotesque, distorted faces – it's enough to send chills up your spine, and yet just listen to the applause! Listen to it! The audience loves it! That's what the masses call entertainment! Are the masses really so debased, really so debased as to... to be fed torture and mistake it for entertainment? Is it possible? This is not living life, this is... this is Hades! Do you know what Hades is, bartender? It's the underworld, home of the dead! Read Homer and you'll know! Am I right, professor? This man is a professor, he teaches Homer; if we read Homer instead of watching TV..."

"Sh..." Unable to recall his name I somewhat foolishly pat him on the shoulder while directing a sheepish smile at the bartender, who shrugs and moves away. "They're not interested in Homer here. Even in the classroom, sad to say, they're not much interested in Homer. It's a sign of the times..." I check myself, fearing the onset of a drunken monologue of my own. "You talk of failure. I failed my students. If I'd taught them better, wouldn't they be interested in Homer? Of course they would. But I was impatient, I expected them to already know what they were there to learn, I reviled their ignorance when I should have led them gently, gently into the kingdom of knowledge. Yes, I deserve – "

"Look. What's that?"

"Eh?" To my surprise his attention is focused on the TV he'd been attacking a moment ago. The grotesque laughing women and the idiot applause have given way to a scene of frenzied commotion. Sirens wail, people scurry about, a building is on fire.

"That's the Alexandria!"

"What?"

"It is! Look!"

"The bookshop?" How would he know it? Well, maybe he would, he seems to be interested in books. "How can you tell? It looks like nothing on earth!"

"I heard the announcer say 'Alexandria.' Look, there's the headline on the screen."

"I can't read it, I don't have my glasses on, where are they?" I fumble for my glasses.

"It's the Alexandria, the Alexandria!"

He pushes his chair back and bolts from the room. "Wait!" But he's forgotten me, and a moment later I've forgotten him. The announcer's voice is not clear, it's as if the thick gray smoke filling the screen is muffling it, but at last I too catch the words "Alexandria bookshop in Kanda." "Do you know it?" I ask the bartender as he passes.

"Know what?"

"The Alexandria in Kanda."

"No."

Scene Thirty-two

"Misako, is that you?"

"Father?"

"Jun!"

"Father, where have you been? We've been – "

"What time is it?"

"After two."

"Of what day? I've lost all track of time. It hangs heavy on my hands, you see, and so I tried to shake it off. I succeeded, but success comes at the price of disorientation. Never mind my senile babble. I think I'll have a hot bath."

"You're soaked."

"It's raining. Stupid of me to go out without an umbrella."

"Where have you been?"

"How long was I away?"

"Three days. We were so worried."

"Who's 'we'?"

"Me and Tomoko, of course. She's not the worrying type, but even she – "

"Even she, eh?"

"She tried not to show it, but – "

"You could tell. Nothing is concealed from a lover's eye, they say. What was she worried about? That I had vanished into another dimension? Or 'met with foul play'? What exactly did she see, with those dark powers of hers?"

"She didn't say, but I could tell…"

"She was right, I did vanish into another dimension. I escaped, I think, but… I'm not sure. Maybe I didn't."

"Can't you speak to me in language I can understand?"

"I'm not sure I can."

"Try."

"I'm a little… a little feverish, I think."

"Take off your wet clothes. I'll get your bath ready. When you come out we'll have a cup of tea and you'll tell me all about it. I have things to tell you too."

———

"Misako!"

"Yes, it's me. Do you remember how we used to bathe together?"

"Yes!"

"The tub was too small for the two of us. This tub is no bigger, but it doesn't seem at all cramped. Does it?"

"No, not cramped at all."

"Could it be because we love each other more now than we did then? It's generally said that young love is the strongest love of all, but that may

87

not be true. In youth, you see, the body gets in the way; the body and its needs are so..."

"Urgent."

"Inflated. Like a balloon. Suddenly, it bursts."

"We can start again, start over. It's not too late."

"I don't know if it's possible, but it pleases me that you want to."

"I do want to. We'll try. I'll do everything in my power..."

"Your power unaided is not sufficient. You must seek help."

"Where? Where must I seek it?"

"From Yasushi."

"Yasushi?"

"You are surprised I know about him. You never mentioned him to me. But knowledge, in a certain phase of existence, is not restricted to what one has been told. Yes, go to Yasushi."

"Is there no one else? Must it be Yasushi? If you only knew..."

"Your soul shrinks from him. I do know."

"You wouldn't impose this on me if it wasn't necessary. Very well, I'll..."

"Father?"

"What?"

"Are you all right?"

"Of course I'm all right!"

"I met her grandparents. Very, very nice people. The grandmother is a lovely quaint old lady in a kimono. She said not a word the whole time. She might be mute for all I know. How's the tea? Is it strong enough?"

"Perfect. Wonderful. Sublime. Really."

"The grandfather runs a trading company. He offered me a job."

"A job! What kind of job?"

"I'd be in charge of marketing a special kind of headphone. You can use them to listen to music, but their special feature is that they emit sound waves or something that neutralize sound. You put them on and suddenly the world grows quiet. They're very expensive, 55,000 yen. I said to him, 'Do they sell?' And Rogozhin said... Ah, I haven't mentioned Rogozhin. He's a Russian, the son of an old friend of the grandfather's; he came in wearing them – them and dark glasses too; he made quite a picture – and he said, 'Oh, they sell all right. The naked ear is intolerable.' The naked eye too, obviously,' said Tomoko. Rogozhin laughed."

"Let me guess – it was not a humorous laugh."

"You're right, it wasn't. How did you know?"

"Just a feeling. A man who comes into a house wearing headphones and dark glasses is not generally cheerful."

"He's in mourning for his wife."

"Why is he offering you a job? You're a student, you have to finish school."

"I told him that. He said it doesn't have to be now."

"Marketing? Is that really what you want to do with your life?"

"What I want to do with my life is be Tomoko's husband. That's all that matters."

"I see."

"Oh, father, father... I love her so much!"

Scene Thirty-three

"Yoshiko-san? Is that you?"

"Yes. Who is this?"

"Rogozhin. Don't hang up – please. I must speak to you."

"Rogozhin! I've asked you – "

" – not to call. I know. And I know you're not in... in business any more. I understand that. But that doesn't mean we can't talk to each other, does it? We can be friends, can't we? Come and see me, Yoshiko, it'll... it'll save my life. Bring your boyfriend, if you don't trust yourself alone with me. All I ask is... to be permitted to see your face, to hear your voice... Yoshiko, this is a dying man who addresses you!"

"He's not my boyfriend, he's my husband. Why are you dying?"

"Bring him with you. I will say nothing – I have nothing to say – that cannot be said in front of him."

"He's not here."

"Yoshiko, Yoshiko! Do you not know me? Am I a man to... to trick a woman into coming under false pretenses, to lay a trap for her, to force her against her will? Surely, surely you can't think that of me? Yoshiko, I swear by the soul of my late wife, by her sacred memory, by her image that is engraved on my heart for all eternity... I think of you as a sister, and of myself as your brother. Will you come? Or let me come to you?"

"No, you mustn't come here. I'll go to you."

"Now? At once?"

"Yes."

"Do you promise? Then I may expect you within twenty-six minutes?"

"Yes."

"Yoshiko... forgive me, forgive me..."

"But remember what you promised. We are brother and sister, nothing more."

"On the soul of my late wife, I swear it!"

———

"Who are you talking to?"

Yoshiko gasped. She had not heard him come in, and suddenly he stood before her, confronting her. A mere glance sufficed to tell her he was drunk, sullen and exhausted.

"Where were you?" she demanded, seizing the initiative. "You've been away for days. Didn't it occur to you I'd be worried? Couldn't you have at least called? Or answered your phone?"

"I did call. I called and called. But your line was busy."

"You're lying."

He slapped her across the face – not hard, but the shock was enough to make her scream. He staggered to the couch and collapsed on it. "Ah, Yoshiko, this world's no good, I'm telling you! This morning, for the first time in weeks, I bought a newspaper. Have you seen the news lately? Do you know what's going on out there? Do you have any idea? Banks collapsing left and right, stocks tumbling – it's awful! The ground's vanishing beneath our feet, I tell you!"

"How dare you hit me!"

"Hit you! Yoshiko! How can you say such a thing!"

"You're drunk."

"Prove it! Well, maybe a little. I've been drinking, you see. I'm a good man but I fell in with bad companions. Do you know, are you aware, that in the past three days seven children across the country have been murdered? One of them by his own mother? The world is going mad! It's madness out there! Chaotic, incoherent madness! Hit you! I'd sooner cut my belly open. Do you know, by the way, that I have an ancestor who disemboweled himself? You've probably heard of him, he's in the history books. Watanabe Kazan. No? He was a great man. An artist, a scholar. He was a loyal samurai and a Confucian, but flirted with dangerous thoughts, and wrote

91

something that criticized the government. He was arrested and exiled, and finally he killed himself in penance for his 'disloyalty.' That's the kind of blood that flows in my veins. He was my great-great-great-great... great-great... I'm not sure how many 'greats' there are... grandfather. Well? What do you think of that?"

———

"What the hell are *you* doing here?"

"That's a fine greeting," snickered Tazawa. "Makes a fellow feel quite welcome."

"I was... I'm expecting someone."

"And fate sent me instead. How disconcerting. May I come in? Or maybe I should come back another time. I was, I admit, very much looking forward to a talk with you. You have a way of bolstering my sagging confidence. Only you can. I'm not sure what it is about you. What is it about you, Rogozhin? People who judge by appearances generally think my confidence is solid as a rock. But appearances can be deceiving. Really, my confidence could use some bolstering. Is it a lady you're expecting?"

"That's no business of yours."

"Just making conversation. Don't be so touchy. Well, it's up to you. Invite me in and I stay. Tell me to go, and I go. "

"You may as well stay. She seems to have... what's the English expression?... stood me up."

Scene Thirty-four

"Don't sit on the couch," said Rogozhin pettishly. "It's a white couch, and your clothes, as usual, are none too clean."

92

"I understand," said Tazawa. "I'm not offended, don't think I am. I know your little ways."

"It's good of you to make allowances. It would be even better if you came in clean clothes."

"Let's go into the kitchen. I feel more comfortable there anyway. Drawing-room elegance is not my cup of tea. Speaking of tea. A cup of good strong Russian tea would be just the thing, if you have some."

"It'll bolster your sagging confidence?"

"No, only your words of wisdom can do that. You once taught me that, given the distorted nature of this fallen world, to do evil is in fact to do good. I'm oversimplifying your thinking, no doubt."

"Not much. I'm not your teacher and never taught you anything, but – "

"You're wrong."

" – but I certainly have moods when I feel that way. Now, for instance."

"You're wrong about not being my teacher. You're my master and I'm your disciple."

"I'm no master, and the last thing I want is a disciple. Here, drink your tea. What's on your mind?"

"Why – the 'eternal questions,' of course. You know what's on my mind. You put it there. Since evil is the dominant force in the universe – "

"Tazawa. Listen to me. I know your kind pretty well. You're a two-bit thug with a brain. It's a dangerous combination. If a snake could think, it would think like you. You can philosophize, and not badly, but the part of the brain that regulates moral conduct is missing in you. Maybe your mother took thalidomide or something when she was pregnant with you, only instead of being born with physical deformities, your deformities are moral. You don't mind my speaking frankly to you?"

"Oh, no. On the contrary. Please, continue."

"I daresay you have a knife on you, or maybe even a gun, and that you're perfectly capable of murdering me without a moment's reflection either before or afterwards, and if I seem to risk your anger it's not courage that prompts me, but indifference. Slack, flabby indifference. Life lost all meaning for me when my wife died. That's when I started amusing myself with the likes of you. A sad, mournful sort of amusement, as I'm sure you'll agree – one that, at this point, I've grown rather tired of."

"Yes, I sympathize with you there. I'm not very good company. I wish I was better. Really, I'd amuse you if I knew how. It's the least I can do. I owe you so much."

"What for?"

"What for? Why, it was you who opened my mind."

"If so I regret it. Some minds are better closed. Yours is one of them."

"Come, this despair is unmanly."

"It's true. Very well, I'll rally my strength just enough to try to persuade you to forget everything you claim to have learned from me. All that – about the supremacy of evil and what not – was my grief talking, not me. Forget it, just forget it."

"'Evil is truth,' you once said."

"Everything is truth."

"Pardon?"

"Everything. There is no such thing as falsehood. Falsehood doesn't exist. Human beings are truth-bearing creatures, whether we like it or not. That's our nature. Nothing we perceive, or conceive, is false. Each of us embodies a fragment of the truth – a tiny fragment, the barest sliver; a somewhat larger fragment in the case of sages and philosophers – real philosophers, I mean, not the likes of you and me. Tazawa, do me a favor – finish your tea and go. I'll hardly shock you if I say I can't bear the sight of you. You seem to... I don't know... to embody everything that is vile in myself, everything slimy. Worse, you lack my inhibitions. I confess I liked that in you at one time, but now... it's not you that's changed, it's me. Do you mind? You'll forgive my rudeness? I really would prefer to be alone just now."

"Of course, I understand. One question, if I may. Everything is true, nothing is false. Does that mean that if I perceive, or conceive, the world as flat, then the world is flat? Is it as true to say that the sun orbits the Earth as it is to say that the Earth orbits the sun? Do I understand you correctly? Or am I unintentionally distorting – "

"There is one kind of falsehood."

"What's that?"

"The deliberate lie."

"I see. Well, goodbye. I'll think over everything you've said. It's interesting, really, the way your every utterance seems to go straight to the heart of things."

Scene Thirty-five

"Haru, let's go away from here! Away, away! Far away!" Yoshiko's eyes shone through tears; she clung to his neck. "How far can we go? What's the farthest place on Earth from here? We'll look it up in the atlas, and go there!"

"Patagonia, I think. I used to dream of going there as a kid."

"Patagonia! What a beautiful name! It's in South America, isn't it? We'll go there, buy some land, grow our own food..."

"We can do that, if you want to."

"We'll build a fence around our land, a high fence, a palisade... Is that the right word, palisade?"

"But why, Yoshiko, are you throwing your life away on me? Go, leave, find yourself a real man, and live!"

"Patagonia! I want to go to Patagonia!"

"All right, all right. But it's not so simple. One day in the future no doubt we'll be able to just close our eyes and say 'Patagonia,' and our very thought will whisk us there. But in these primitive times we have to take all kinds of steps, measures – get passports, earn money, make flight reservations, go to the airport, spend twenty hours cooped up in a plane..."

"We have money."

"How much do we have? Relative, I mean, to the plane fare to Patagonia, and the price of land there."

"My sister's a travel agent. Did you know that?"

"No. I didn't know you had a sister."

"Of course I have a sister! And a mother, and a father... You've never asked me about them."

"It's true, it never entered my head."

"Well, I'm sure if it had entered your head you'd've asked, so it's not your fault. Maybe it's mine, since it never entered my head to tell you about them. My sister and I are twins. As children we were very close; we'd laugh hysterically about all the people who couldn't tell us apart. Then we stopped being children, and we got tired of being mistaken for each other. We began to argue, to fight, to hate each other. We haven't spoken to each other in years. But that doesn't matter. She's a travel agent. I'll call her. If she can book us a flight to Patagonia tomorrow, will you go?"

"Tomorrow?"

"Oh, Haru, I was *so* hoping you would say yes. Without doubts, without hesitation, without second thoughts, just 'Yes.' That would have been so wonderful. But it didn't happen."

"Well, no... I mean, it's a big step, one has to think – "

"You're *wrong*! One *doesn't* have to think! There's no *point* in thinking! Thinking doesn't help, it only complicates things! As soon as you said 'Patagonia,' I seemed... it's hard to explain... I seemed to hear my destiny calling. That's *it*, I said to myself. It has nothing to do with thinking."

"I see. Well, all right. Go ahead. I put myself in your hands. Your destiny is my destiny. Whatever 'destiny' means."

"Shall I call her?"

"Call her."

"We'll start all over again, Haru! We'll be reborn! We'll be thirty-year-old infants, and we'll grow up together, we'll... what's that?"

"Someone's at the door."

"Sh! Don't move. Don't make a sound. He'll go away."

But the knocking grew louder, more insistent.

"Let me answer it," said Maeda. "It's probably a salesman or something. I'll get rid of him."

"Haru, I'm scared."

"Scared! Of what?"

"I don't know! Why doesn't he leave? Isn't it obvious no one's here? Why does he keep knocking?"

Maeda gently disengaged himself from her and went to the door. Opening it, he found himself facing a foreign man wearing dark glasses, with fair hair and sharply chiseled features, and though he had never met Rogozhin before and Yoshiko had never described him, he knew immediately who it was.

"Forgive me," said Rogozhin breathlessly. "I couldn't... it was not in my power... I have no designs on your wife but I must see her. I'm sorry, but I must."

"Well... if you must you must!" said Maeda with a faint smile.

Scene Thirty-six

There's an autumn chill in the air. I should have brought my jacket. I didn't think of it. Look, the sun is rising. How long has it been since the sun rose? I mean to say, since I *saw* the sun rise. The rising sun wakes the sea gulls and the crows, who rise in turn to greet the sun with their squawks and caws, respectively. No sign of Takeshi, though it was him I came to meet. Why should I expect to meet him at this time of day? Well, I didn't *expect* it, exactly, one doesn't have *expectations* where Takeshi is concerned... Anyway. He's not here; the rising sun illuminates a beach that is absolutely deserted, absolutely silent save for the sounds of the seagulls, the crows and the waves.

"Go and see Yasushi," said Misako. Was she serious? You can't always tell, with her. But I think she was. All right, I'll go and see Yasushi. Today. He lives not far from Kanda. We'll make today a day of pilgrimages. I've been meaning to stop by the Alexandria, to pay my respects to its charred corpse. And something else. That park at Funabashi. First, a homeless man was killed there. Then, not two weeks later, in the same park, almost the same spot, they find the corpse of a six-year-old boy. An ordinary, insignificant, nondescript little park, the papers say. It existed insignificantly and nondescriptly for a hundred

98

years, and then suddenly, in the space of two weeks – two murders! It stirs the detective in me. Yes, I'll go and have a look.

So this is retirement! Isn't it strange – since my teaching career ended I haven't opened a book. All I read now are the newspapers, which I scarcely used to glance at – thinking them beneath me, I suppose. I'm no Freudian, but I think I can take a stab at psychoanalyzing myself: I am going to seed *on purpose*; it's my way of taking revenge on those who forced retirement on me; still more, on my students, who let it happen without so much as a gesture, a murmur, of protest. One day one of them will run into me and be shocked at the sight of me: "Professor! Is this shell of a man really you, professor? Is *this* what our indifference has made of you?" And they'll realize, if nothing else, that indifference in the face of injustice is a crime... Listen to this babbling of mine! I might as well be one of the crows, for all the sense I'm making! Maybe I was a crow in my last life – or will be one in my next.

"Father..."

"What? Why are you looking at me like that? I went for a walk! Is that not permitted?"

"How am I looking at you? I didn't mean – "

"No, you didn't mean." He didn't, probably, but... I don't know... this air of his of watchful concern, like he sees me going to pieces and is tortured by his helplessness to prevent it... No, it's my imagination...

"Would you like some tea?"

"Yes."

What if I simply disappeared, vanished? I'll shave my head and become a monk...

"Do you know what I was thinking, father?"

"No, what were you thinking?"

"Maybe this semester I'll take a course in ancient Greek literature."

He's humoring me, trying to cheer me up. Filial piety. Doesn't it occur to his simple little mind that it is humiliating to be humored? Honestly, I don't think it does!

"Take whatever courses interest you."

"It's taught by Professor Tachibana. Do you know him?"

"No." I know one thing about him: he's teaching and I'm not.

"The water's boiling." He fusses about, preparing tea. "I'm going to Tokyo today," I announce, hoping I sound as if I don't care how that strikes him.

"Oh?"

"Yes, I have some... errands to run."

He's suspicious and trying not to show it. "How long's it been since you've been to Tokyo?"

"A while."

Scene Thirty-seven

At Funabashi Station I catch the eye of a uniformed station official, radiant with youth and red-faced pudginess, and blurt out something that utterly astonishes me, so little had I planned anything of the kind: "I am a private investigator working on the case of the little boy who was murdered in a park near here. I wonder if you could direct me to the park."

"Certainly, sir." His manner at first showed a slight tension, as though he feared a question he would be unable, in his inexperience, to answer; but this one is easy, it does not take him at all out of his depth; he is quick to shrug off his uneasiness and rise to the occasion. "Take exit number 3, turn left, continue straight on to the first traffic light, then go right..."

I thank him and become part of the crowd streaming towards exit 3. Perhaps they've all come to investigate the murder. The whimsical thought brings a smile. Yes, unquestionably, the train ride – or something – has improved my mood. My sullen snappishness of earlier in the morning is quite gone. Was it really this morning I was walking along the beach? It seems long ago, another lifetime, a childhood memory. The solitude, the dawn chill, the crows – all part of a vanished world. The crowd carries me outside, where the heat, the sunlight, the clamor of the street – and it isn't even Tokyo yet! – are positively overwhelming. A car horn sounds, a motorcyclist races his engine. Straight on to the traffic light, the man said. Will the traffic light even be visible in this glare? Here it is. Yes, it's quite visible. Right, I think he said.

I am suddenly in a small town, a village. How did I get here? These are not streets so much as lanes, alleys, hushed and deserted; the sound of my footsteps echoes in my ears. It would hardly surprise me to see a woman in kimono and clogs carrying water from a well, or a samurai, sword at each hip, hurrying along to bargain with the local rice broker. From an open window somewhere drifts the sound of a samisen. I pause to listen. Why, I wonder, does it strike me as so beautiful? The playing is not skilful – even I, no connoisseur, can recognize that. It's probably an older woman at practice, having only recently, with nothing else to do, taken it up as a hobby. She stops in mid-strain, starts again; there is something timid in her approach; perhaps her teacher is with her, showing signs of impatience. How astonished she would be to know she has an audience, an audience of one, entranced and, inexplicably, very close to tears!

Suddenly a small child tears past me. Where would he have come from? The little demon – he's running full speed, his school bag bouncing crazily on his back. He vanishes as abruptly as he appeared. He's probably late for school or something. Did he oversleep? He too, perfectly unaware of my existence, has an effect on me. He recalls me to myself, reminds me of my mission. The park should be around here somewhere. Yes, here it is.

I pass through a kind of turnstile and pause, uncertain how to proceed. There's no one here; well, naturally, the children are at school. There are swings, a slide, a sandbox, benches. An insignificant, nondescript park. Is this the right place? Can two grotesque murders, committed two weeks apart, have left the landscape looking so normal, so undisturbed, so... I'm groping for a word... serene? In the sandbox I notice a patch of pastel green. Slowly, hesitantly, self-consciously – like the samisen player – I draw nearer; it's a shovel; some child would have left it here. Perhaps at home, on discovering its absence, he was plunged into despair, or fear – his parents might give him a beating. Or maybe – my heart lurches in its cavity – can it have belonged to the murdered boy? I stoop down, pick it up, turn it over in my hands. No, surely the police would have taken possession of it if it had been there at the time of the murder.

Scene Thirty-eight

The boy's body was found in a copse behind the rest room. I have no trouble finding the spot

102

and, having found it, stoop to examine the ground. Expecting to find... what? Ten days have passed; it has rained; the ground has been disturbed; nothing is as it was. This is idiotic. What am I doing here? What have I come for? If Jun could see me now! What would he say? "Come, father..." and he would take me gently by the hand and lead me away, as one would an old man who has lost his senses. I rise, not without difficulty – old age really does seem to have suddenly descended upon me – and make my way back to where the benches are. I sink down on one, and close my eyes. There is a park near the college, which I would walk past on my way to work, and every morning I'd see sitting on the benches there the same old men, day after day, staring vacantly into space... and now look at me, I am one of them! No, I must throw off this mood, I mustn't let it gain possession of me, because once it does it drags you down to a place from which there is no escaping! Suddenly a mad thought comes to me – not so much a thought as an impulse: There's nobody here, why not go up the slide and slide down? Imagine how *that* would look to Jun!

I look around: not a soul in sight, not a soul. No doubt the homeless and children and local retired people have given the place a wide berth since the murders. Strange that the thought hadn't occurred to me before; it's obvious enough now. Who would want to play *here*, or sit here passing the time of day? It's haunted! Even the birds... Yes, it's true: even the crows, even the sparrows have fled. I am alone, my solitude guarded by... Ah, those lines of Sophocles... blind Oedipus' wanderings have taken him to the sacred grove at Colonus and he questions a passerby, who tells him, "Sir, before you ask me any question, come away from that seat. That place is holy ground..."

I get off at Akihabara, transfer to the Ginza Line, get off at Kanda. One hears of vast changes afoot in Tokyo; "you'd hardly recognize it," Jun says. It may be so, but this particular neighborhood is quite unchanged, quite recognizable. Time has passed it by. It hasn't even aged. It's old, of course, but it always was. Here's the little noodle shop where old Tazawa and I used on occasion to meet for lunch. He loved noodles, and slurped them lustily. They were the only food I ever saw him eat. But it was not so much the noodles that drew him as the fact that the proprietor claimed to be the son of one of his favorite writers, the novelist Nagai Kafu, who died in 1959. Impossible to verify the claim, of course. Kafu's love life was of the demimonde, and children are not part of his official biography. He may have had them anyway, of course. "Why would he lie about it?" demanded Tazawa. Why indeed. The only gain it represented to him was Tazawa's unstinting affection, which in fact seemed to afford him no small degree of satisfaction. Authentic or not, he had at least read Kafu's work and talked knowledgeably about it. Other than that, he claimed to have met the famous author on only one occasion. He was five, and remembered, with shadowy imprecision, being taken by his mother to visit a rather kindly-looking elderly gentleman in a bathrobe and funny round thick-rimmed spectacles. The only words he remembers his father addressing to him seem rather improbable. They are: "The life of the stupidest adult is simply unimaginable to even the brightest child."

The door of the shop creaks as I push it open.

Scene Thirty-nine

"Takeshi!"

"Jun!"

"Oh, I'm so glad to see you. In fact, in a way, I think I kind of came here looking for you. Not *consciously,* but now that I've run into you I have the feeling that it was you I was looking for all along. Do you know what I mean?"

"Of course."

"You're bag's almost full. Where do you take the trash you've collected?"

Instead of answering, Takeshi stooped to pick up a half-crushed oolong tea can lying at his feet. He examined it briefly, then showed it to Jun, as though the sight of it would resolve any doubts still lingering in the young man's mind. Then he tossed it into his bulging black bag, nodding his head in affirmation of something or other.

"Takeshi, here," said Jun, handing him his cell phone. "You bring good luck. Dial her number for me! I've been trying since early morning... Why doesn't she answer? She knows I'm trying to reach her. Please, Takeshi... wait, here, let me show you; you press this – use your thumb – and then the number: 090... zero's here, at the bottom... 090 – here, let me take your bag – 4315-8907. She'll answer this time, I know she will, I feel it... Tomoko! Where were you? Why didn't you answer? I'm at the beach, in Wakaba. I've been calling all morning... and then I met Takeshi and said, 'Here, you try' – and it worked! As how could it not, Takeshi being Takeshi! Listen, I'm coming into town now, where can we meet, I must, I absolutely *must* see you! Oh, Tomoko, if you knew... when you didn't answer I thought... I don't know what I thought! It was as if... you'll laugh at me... as if you were no longer in the world, and the world... what an awful, awful place the world is without you, Tomoko! I know I'm being silly, you don't have to tell me! Go ahead, laugh at me, I love it when you laugh at me. I'm coming to your place now, I'll be there in an hour and a half. Sharp! Flat! Goodbye, Tomoko, I think I'm going crazy! I'm drunk without wine; what do I need wine for? Goodbye, I'll see you soon. Takeshi, I could hug you!"

Takeshi, having noticed a crow hopping along the sand a few yards off, was now squatting by its side, to all appearances deep in conversation with it. Looking up at the sound of Jun's voice, he accorded the young man a bland smile and a wave.

———

"Tomoko, let's get married today. Right now, right this minute!"

"That again! Marriage!"

Jun's face fell. "But you said you'd marry me."

"Right now I have other things to think about. Professor Sawamura wants me to do my thesis on dark matter."

"Well?"

"Well! It's easy for you to say 'Well'! Do you have any idea... But of course you don't. Sometimes I wish the gods had given me the protection they gave you – a simple brain that sees nothing, including the fact that it sees nothing. Instead..."

"I see one thing."

"What's that?"

"That the gods have been kind to me."

Tomoko smiled. "Poor fool."

"Listen..."

"What?"

"Let's have a Shinto wedding! We'll summon all the gods of Japan…"

Tomoko turned away from the computer screen she'd been staring at and faced Jun directly. For a time she merely gazed at him in silence. Jun, radiant with excitement, talked on. It was a certain shrine that had put the idea into his head, an inconspicuous, unpretentious little shrine he happened to pass the day before; actually he'd passed it any number of times without noticing it, but this one time, for some unknown reason, it drew his attention… No, that wasn't true, he knew the reason; he'd watched entranced as a young beautiful woman in a magnificent red kimono made her way past the vermillion *torii* gate up a short flight of steps to the shrine, where she clapped her hands in the traditional manner and bowed her head… "The sight was so moving, Tomoko! So moving! Oh, I wish you'd been there! And I thought…"

"Jun."

"What? Tomoko! You're crying!"

"I'm not." She brushed away a tear. "Jun, listen to me. Your father calls me a prophet. I'm not one, of course, but it is true that sometimes I see things, not knowing why, or how, or where they come from, or what they mean, or… anything – and this morning I… saw something…"

"What?"

"You're going to be unhappy, Jun, and I'm to be the instrument of your unhappiness."

"You! That's impossible!"

"No, Jun, it's not. It's only too possible."

"But how can *you*, the… how can my happiness make me unhappy?"

"Come to me, Jun, let me… no, Jun, not that, I haven't time. Just let me stroke your hair for a moment. Why do you cut it so short? Let it grow out a little." She kissed him on the cheek. "There.

107

Now, be a good boy, mummy has to keep an appointment with Professor Sawamura, who is going to devour her with that dark matter of his!"

Scene Forty

Haruyuki Maeda closed his eyes. Hot water, almost scalding, lapped against his chin. He stretched his legs full length in front of him. He felt empty, weightless, as though the material part of his being had dissolved in the mineral hot spring, leaving... not *nothing* exactly, but at least nothing identifiable. Sorrow, pain, fear, even happiness, even pleasure, had dissolved – good riddance! He was past all that now. The sound of a door opening and closing – evidently someone had joined him – did not cause him to open his eyes, or to feel that his solitude was being invaded. Now whoever it was was easing himself into the water. The surface rippled slightly, but settled again almost immediately.

Time passed. Civilizations rose and fell. The planet warmed, cooled, and warmed again. The universe expanded. The sun grew cold and bloated; it swallowed the Earth. Through all these developments Maeda's eyes remained closed and his soul at peace, though he was awake and aware of everything that was going on.

"I beg your pardon?"

Maeda gasped. Who had spoken? His eyelids snapped open, and he found himself staring through a thin cloud of steam at a mild-looking, rather elderly man with a yellow wash cloth on his head, squinting at him from the other end of the tub.

"I'm sorry," he said gently. His voice echoed strangely – a typical bathhouse echo, but strange all the same. "I didn't mean to disturb you. I thought you had spoken."

"No, I... that is... I don't think so."

"Perhaps you dozed off and mumbled something in your sleep."

"Yes, that's possible."

"As a matter of fact, my impression was that you addressed me by name."

"Addressed you by name! How could I – "

"You couldn't, of course. One has absurd fancies sometimes. I thought I heard you say 'Watanabe.'"

"Wata... Did I say Watanabe? I may have... hm! Is your name Watanabe?"

"At your service."

"I'm terribly sorry. I was... you see, I do have an ancestor by that name. On my mother's side. A remarkable personage, I'm told. His name is Watanabe Kazan, and lately I've been – "

"Watanabe Kazan! Is your ancestor?"

"Well... yes." What made me blurt that out, Maeda thought to himself in surprise and disgust. Now he'd have to humor this stranger, who was plainly impressed by the news and eager to pursue it, when all he, Maeda, wanted to do was sink back into his dream of the future cosmos without the Earth in it. Had Watanabe Kazan been in the dream? He had no memory of that. But what a marvelous place it was, that Earthless cosmos! Only when you had seen it could you understand that the Earth was not a planet like any other but unique – a filthy, corrupt excrescence whose existence defiled the entire universe, and once it was gone the universe roused itself as though from a bad dream, as though from a nightmare, and a kind of cosmic morning set in... Oh, what a splendid, glorious dream, a dream perhaps vouchsafed once in a lifetime to one man in a million; by some miracle it had been vouchsafed

109

him – and he had lost it, had thrown it away! How had Watanabe got himself mixed up in that? Probably he hadn't, and the Watanabe opposite him had merely imagined it; he himself had been willing to dismiss it as an "absurd fancy," and there it would have ended if only...

"Do you know why I came here?" said Watanabe.

"Eh? No..."

"I have never been to this hot spring before. Have you?"

"Yes, many times."

"I saw an ad for it in this morning's paper. I almost never read ads, and there was nothing remarkable about this one; I'm not sure what drew me to it. Also, I hardly ever go to public baths. And yet, here I am. Do you see what I'm getting at?"

"No; in fact, I..."

"What I'm saying is that there seems to be something fated about this meeting of ours. I would like to know what it is."

Scene Forty-one

"Won't you come in?"

"Thank you. I shouldn't impose, but I do need to rest for a moment."

"Oh, please, don't talk of imposing. No friend of my husband's imposes on me."

I follow her inside. The hallway is long, narrow, and dark. It leads into a parlor which is its exact opposite: spacious, airy and bright, the slanting rays of the afternoon sun streaming in through what I believe are called French windows. "Please, sit down." I am only too happy to; I don't know why I'm so tired. I feel as if I've traveled vast distances.

110

I sink into the armchair she indicates and close my eyes.

"I'll bring you some tea. My husband will be home soon. He went for a bath."

"Ah."

In the woman's absence I find myself staring at a framed black-and-white photograph on the wall directly opposite me. It is of a young smiling couple. Can the man be Yasushi? He looks nothing like the Yasushi I knew as a child – naturally; he'd had plastic surgery. Still, I can't help thinking... Of course if the photo were anywhere other than in his house, nothing about him would suggest Yasushi to me, but it *is* his house, and something *does* suggest him. He's thirty, perhaps thirty-five, clean-cut, handsome, smiling; a man with a future, you'd say. And the woman – is she the same woman who ushered me inside? I can't say I observed her very closely, but the mole on her chin is unmistakable even at a glance, and there it is in the photograph, so the matter is beyond all doubt.

She returns with tea. I take the cup from her and sip it gratefully.

"Tell me," she says, seating herself on the sofa just under the photograph, "how do you come to know my husband?"

"Oh... we go back many years. I knew him as a child. He was older than me, and I looked up to him. More than that, I worshipped him. Yes, that's not too strong a word. Then I lost sight of him, and just recently, out of the blue – "

"Oh! You must be the professor!"

"Yes, I – "

"Who won the lottery!"

Yasushi was certainly right about his wife being no beauty; even as a young woman, if the photo doesn't lie, the best one could say about her is that she was plain; an uncharitable view would characterize her as positively ugly, and old age can scarcely be said to have improved matters; but there is something about her – Yasushi hinted at this too, I think – that dissolves all barriers; without being conspicuously outgoing she somehow draws you out of your shell; you feel something friendly in her, something warm, sympathetic; you quite forget she's a stranger – in short, I tell her the whole story of how I went from professor to ex-professor, and speak, most uncharacteristically, without shyness or reserve, even eagerly. She listens, sips her tea, nods. Yes, she says, the world is becoming a strange, unfamiliar and inhospitable place, not just for scholars of ancient Greek but for the most ordinary people, the sheeplike creatures who simply take their given environment for granted.

"Just before you came," she says, "I was watching the news on TV. There's this park in Funabashi" – my surprise seems to pass unnoticed. "First a homeless man was killed there, then a small child, and now a young woman."

"A young woman? When? I knew about the other two..."

"This very morning."

"This morning! But..." I stop myself from blurting out that I had been there this morning, and murmur instead, "How strange!"

"Strange and incomprehensible!" We both gasp. Yasushi stands before us, grinning; we had neither of us heard him come in. "Strange and incomprehensible. Masa! I'm so pleased to see you. I have just been to purify myself." He sits down beside his wife on the sofa and, without glancing at her, without the slightest superfluous movement, as though knowing exactly where it would be, takes her hand gently in his. "What is it that strikes you as strange?"

"The murders at Funabashi Park," says his wife – whose name, it suddenly occurs to me, I don't know. "There was another one this morning. I heard it on the news."

Scene Forty-two

"Don't spill it," says Mrs. Watanabe, handing her husband a cup of tea. Turning to me, she adds, "He's always spilling things."

"And bumping into things. And breaking things. And stepping on things. It's true. I don't know why."

"One day not long ago he was trying to tape up a frayed wire in our bedroom lamp – "

"Yes, I told him about that!"

"Were you like that as a child?"

"Yes, as a small child, but then I outgrew it, and even became something of an athlete. I was a good skier and a better swimmer, and I was on my junior high school soccer team, generally considered an asset to it. Ah, youth! Youth! This tea, Masa, hardly compares to the brew you served. Your son chose it, I think you said."

"Yes…"

"If you had tasted it," he says to his wife, "you would have formed a very favorable impression of the young man. I know I did. I feel as if I know him, though of course we've never met. One of these days we'll get our families together – eh, Masa?"

"Kazue and Ghost are coming for dinner tonight. Our daughter and son-in-law," she says for my benefit, and then adds, "Why don't you stay?"

"Ghost?"

Yasushi chuckles. "It comes so naturally at this point, we forget it's not his name. It's rather an interesting story. His father was a Zambian, a promising young man who came to Japan to study medicine. How he and Ghost's mother met I don't know. How they parted I don't know either. He seems to have disappeared. Whether he fled upon learning she was pregnant, or whether he got into some other kind of trouble – alive or dead, free or under compulsion, he vanished, and hasn't been heard from since. Ghost grew up in Japan, with his mother and the man she eventually married, a fine man who was as kind and attentive to Ghost as though he were his real father. And so Ghost is Japanese in every respect – except that he's black."

"Ah."

"Black as coal. So you can imagine, Japan being Japan, that his formative years were not easy."

"I daresay."

"But he survived. He did more than survive – he flourished. His character has just the right mix of toughness and charm. You'll see when you meet him. He fought when he had to, and fought well, took no nonsense from anybody – but he preferred not to, and as soon as his fighting won him the respect he considered his due, he dropped his fists and let his charm do the rest. When kids called him "Black Ghost," he turned the tables on them. He adopted the nickname with pride. Now in the family that's the name he's known by."

"What does he do?"

"IT. What else? That's what people are doing nowadays. It can't be helped."

"You don't approve?"

"Not really. Toys. This new world of ours is awash in toys. That's what all this gadgetry amounts to. For children, the old toys were better. For adults – "

"Excuse me," says the wife, getting to her feet. "It's time for me to see to the shopping. Professor... er... I'm sorry, I don't know your name."

"Horiuchi."

"And I'm Ikuko. Won't you stay for dinner?"

"No, thank you, really, I..."

"Stay," says Yasushi.

"I'm afraid I can't..."

They know, of course, that it's not a matter of being unable to; my desperate, red-faced groping for some plausible excuse is perfectly visible to both of them, but Ikuko's tact is admirable; instead of pressing me she says simply, "Well, some other time then," and with a slight bow leaves the room.

"For adults, as I was saying," Yasushi resumes with a smile, "they are a ticket to perpetual childhood. Ghost and I have some lively discussions on that subject, as on many others. What we need, I tell him, is not more information, not more technology – we have more than enough of both, and had more than enough of both even before 'IT' and 'cyberspace' and 'virtual reality' and all that. *God*, I tell him, *God* is what mankind needs. You'd think he'd have caught on by now that I'm only saying this to get a rise out of him, but no, clever as he is, he takes me quite literally, he takes everything literally, he thinks I'm a Christian missionary, I'm not joking – well I actually told him I was – and fairly flies off the handle. God, he thunders – for he's quite a thunderer, when he gets worked up – is the worst enemy mankind's neurotic imagination ever saddled us with. Prehistoric man no doubt needed gods for his own prehistoric purposes; but to civilized man they are an insult, a degradation. 'Have a little respect for my feelings,' I admonish him, at which, to the extent his color permits, he blushes, for he has a genuinely kind and generous heart and wouldn't offend me or anyone for the world if he could help it – if his passions, I mean, didn't get out of control the way they do. Maybe

115

tonight – Masa, I have the most wonderful idea! I'll introduce you as a Shinto missionary, and you can preach the myriad gods of Japan!"

"Does Shinto have missionaries?"

"Well, an exorcist then. You can exorcise his evil spirit!"

"I'm afraid I'm not well acquainted with 'the myriad gods of Japan.'"

"The gods of Greece then. The myriad gods of Greece. The Olympians, nymphs, naiads, satyrs. We'll convert him to those – Zeus, Dionysus. Eh? That should appeal to the actor in you!"

"The actor in me?"

He laughs – the same gay, ringing laugh that surprised me at my house. "There's an actor in all of us, isn't there? In some of us more than others. I used to watch your movies at the reformatory. Ken Kon – ha ha! Brilliant, brilliant!"

Scene Forty-three

"Seriously, Masa. This son-in-law of mine – a fine young man, obviously going places, good, solid future ahead of him – and moreover, as I said, a good heart; he loves my beloved feather-brained Kazue dearly, a father can tell, I entrusted her to him with an easy mind; still, for all his virtues and good qualities, not the sort of man one can discuss the great cosmic questions with. Who *can* you discuss the great cosmic questions with nowadays? You can discuss the economy, the environment, the latest suicide bombing, the newest cell phones… but do gods exist? Or one God? Is there life after death? Are we alone in the universe? What is good, what is evil, what is justice and where is it to be found? These are burning questions – or were; they seem to have vanished from the mind. To a man like Ghost, it's simple: the market is the final arbiter of everything. What is marketable is good, what isn't is worthless. 'Listen,' I once said to him, 'human beings have five senses, correct? Just suppose for a moment we had seven senses; wouldn't we perceive things that are now hidden from us? Or seventy senses, or seven hundred, or seven million. Is it even conceivable that our paltry five senses give us anything like an adequate sense of the cosmos, the infinite cosmos we inhabit? We're like a blind man,' I said, 'who doesn't know he's blind, and so we blunder and thrash about, causing the havoc we see daily on the daily news.' Imagine a volcano on the brink of eruption. 'Of course,' he shouts – for my obtuseness, and everyone else's, but especially mine, has him in a perpetual fever of impatience; 'of course our five naked sense are limited; that's where technology comes in; technology extends the senses...' 'You misunderstand me,' I said, shouting even louder than he – poor Kazue; she thought we were fighting! – 'that's like saying we can have an otherworldly experience by going to Mars; it's nonsense; don't you see? No sooner do we set foot on Mars – or set eyes on it, for that matter – than Mars becomes part of Earth, part of the human world...' I was joking about Shinto, but speaking seriously, I think Shinto gives a more accurate account of the world than science – more accurate because more human. And the Greeks? Tell me about the Greeks, Masa. And tell me this: why did polytheism die out? Why do almost all worshippers of God insist nowadays that God is *one*?"

"Hindus..."

"Yes, Hindus – well, convert him to Hinduism if you like. But India apart, the civilized world worships either one God or none. But I want a world of many gods, Masa! As many gods as the fertile human imagination can bring forth! Why should I settle for less?"

"Hm."

"Tell me about the Greeks. I don't have a good grasp of history. What I'm asking is, did monotheism *have to* triumph? Was it written somewhere that it *had* to? Was the rise of Christianity inevitable? Could things have turned out differently?"

"Of course they could have."

"They could have, couldn't they? But then, in that case, what *is* deserves no more consideration than what *could have been*."

"I'm not sure I follow you. What *is* – "

" – is a fluke! Nothing more. It deserves no special dignity merely because it happens to *be*. Seriously, Masa. What is it about what *is* that draws everyone into it like... quicksand, like... like... damn!" He had forgotten his teacup; in reaching out his hand as though in search of the elusive word, he spills a quantity of tea on his pants. His discomposure is fleeting, immediately forgotten. "Let me put it this way: there's reality, and there's unreality, right? If what *is* isn't intrinsically better than what *isn't* but could just as easily *have been*... I mean, if reality isn't intrinsically better than unreality... or even intrinsically more real... then what is this overwhelming... authority, this overwhelming power, claimed by, and universally accorded to, reality? You see what I'm saying?"

"I – "

"Is the God of the Christians real while the myriad gods of Japan are mere figments of the imagination?"

"I wouldn't say – "

"Come with me, Masa. Come, my friend. I want to show you something." He rises abruptly to his feet, hitting his knee against the lamp table.

Instinctively I reach out a hand; for an instant the lamp seems about to fall from the impact, but Yasushi has scarcely a glance to spare for it. "Come." I follow him up a narrow flight of stairs into a tiny room, a kind of garret. He switches on a light – a naked bulb dangling from the ceiling. "It's a bit dusty, I'm afraid. I don't think Ikuko even knows this place exists. I only come here when she's not home – to practice my secret vices, ha ha! Look, this is what I wanted to show you."

Scene Forty-four

"What is it?"
"What does it look like?"
It's a tiny clay object he has taken – with uncharacteristic delicacy, I notice – from its perch against the wall and handed me. A triangle surmounted by a blob is my first impression; my second, a pair of suggestive swellings having oriented me somewhat, is that the triangle represents a female torso. The blob must be a head.

"This," he says, "is said to be the oldest piece of representational art in Japan. Is it human? A fertility goddess? Both? Neither? Something else altogether, something beyond anything we can imagine? It is some 12,000 years old. The original is in a museum in Mie Prefecture. I am fond of museums. I bought this at the souvenir shop for 800 yen."

I look at it with a kind of self-conscious absorption. Evidently it means something to him, and he expects it to mean something to me, and whatever I say must be worthy of that expectation. Perhaps this is how my students felt when I required them to respond to the magnificent utterances of Aeschylus and Sophocles. Somewhat furtively, as though ashamed of my wandering attention, I glance round the room, but there is nothing to see, just four bare walls and a bare floor; it seems to have been set aside as a kind of shrine for this... whatever it is. Dumbly I hand it back to him.

"Have you ever asked yourself, Masa..."

"What?"

"Why do human beings grow old and die?"

He's looking at me intently, as though seriously expecting an answer. I have none.

"Animals, yes – but humans?"

I wish I knew what to say.

"Imagine this, as I do sometimes: a Christian missionary travels back 12,000 years in time to the people who worshipped this, and says to them, 'This is not a god, it's an idol; there is only one God, who lives in Heaven and sent His only begotten Son, born of a Holy Virgin... etc., etc. How many converts would he win, I wonder."

"Hm."

"Why must we grow old and die? To be resurrected, I suppose the Christians would say. In fact I know that's what they would say. There was a Catholic priest who used to come to the reformatory, a wizened little dwarf of a man who himself looked like a bit of statuary made by some primitive tribe somewhere. He smelt of onions. For some reason he took a special interest in me. I think he saw me as 'resurrectable,' so to speak. Once I said to him, 'I won't be resurrected because I'm not going to die.' If I'd shot him I could not have produced a more dramatic effect. It was such a breathtakingly absurd, stupid thing to say! On the other hand, why is it more absurd than resurrection? If you can take one thing on faith, you can take another; you can't use reason to discipline faith because faith is by definition beyond reason. Well? Where does that lead us? Nowhere. Tell me, Masa, do you feel yourself getting older?"

"Yes."

"Fatigue? Weakness?"

"Yes."

"Me, no. Not a trace. I'm as robust as I was at thirty, and if anything I seem to be growing stronger, not weaker. Are there many men my age who can say that?"

"Probably not."

"So maybe I have been singled out for a special fate. I don't quite believe it, but then I don't quite disbelieve it either. I feel as if I could *come* to believe it, let's put it that way. Do stay for dinner, Masa. Just think of the fun we can have, you playing the missionary of Zeus. Instead of Ken Kon, detective – Ken Kon, Olympian missionary! I'm telling you, this son-in-law of mine has no sense of irony, he'd take you perfectly seriously... Masa, it's irresistible!"

"I'm sorry, I promised Misako..."

"Misako?"

I meant to say Jun and it came out Misako. Not surprising, perhaps – I came here, after all, though I'd more or less forgotten, at Misako's urging.

"Misako? Ah, I see! You sly dog! Ha ha! Well, in that case I won't keep you. Run along to your Misako-san, give her my regards! You'll come again? I can't tell you how much I enjoy your company, Masa. Here, take this," he said, suddenly handing me – or rather, almost thrusting upon me – the clay figurine. "This is the sort of thing one keeps only if one doesn't have a very old friend to give it to. Go on, take it, I want you to have it. With my ten thumbs I'll probably end up smashing it, ha ha ha!"

121

Scene Forty-five

"Yes. Maeda."

"Maeda-san? This is Kinoshita of the *Maiasa Shimbun*... Hello?"

"Kinoshita-san?"

"Where are you now? Are you free to talk?"

"Kinoshita?" said Yoshiko, looking up from her magazine.

Maeda got up from the sofa and, speaking into the phone as he left the room, said, "Yes." He proceeded down a narrow corridor into a little *tatami* room that Yoshiko for some whimsical reason persisted in calling "the baby's room." That is no doubt what it would have been had there been a baby. The only things in it as it was were an ancient cassette player and an old laptop. Instead of throwing them away, which would have cost money, they had simply flung them in the room and forgotten about them. "I'm free to talk." He lowered himself onto the floor and sat with his back against the wall.

"I should have gotten in touch earlier," said Kinoshita. "I hope you are well?"

The usual hemming and hawing. "I'm well." Was he actually going to offer him his job back? After all this time? Should he take it? Would Yoshiko be pleased? Nothing had come of their wild talk of going to Patagonia, but "starting anew" as "thirty-year-old infants" in some unknown land was a project, however vague, that continued to tempt them, Yoshiko especially.

"I... uh... ahem!" How on Earth, Maeda wondered, as he inevitably did whenever he spoke to Kinoshita, or thought of him, had this man become a journalist! A senior editor, yet. He closed his eyes and steeled himself to be patient.

Kinoshita was humbling himself, after all; it must hurt. In pain, we stammer.

"We received an email today." He had steadied himself, apparently. "It is a curious document. I thought it might interest you. Supposing I forward it to you, and after you've read it we can talk again."

Had Maeda understood him correctly? "What is this all about?"

"Do you remember you once spoke to me about a 'cult that worships evil'?"

"Yes."

"Well, I recalled it as I read this... er... communiqué. There may be a connection. I can't be sure, of course. Will you read it?"

"Yes, certainly."

"I'll send it at once. We'll talk again..."

———————

"What is it? What did he want?"

"Yoshiko please, let me breathe!"

Without a word Yoshiko laid down her magazine and left the room. Squinting into his tiny cell phone screen, Maeda read, in bold 16-point: "ONLY EVIL CAN CURE THE WORLD."

"That sounds like Tazawa all right," he thought.

Below, in ordinary 10-point type, was written the following:

"To the media: You are so fixated on al-Qaida and organized terror that you miss the main point! What is the main point? *Dis*organized terror! *One man, one man* working alone, can destroy the world!! Destroy the world **in order to save it**! *THAT* is the main point! When a patient is critically ill, do doctors refrain from surgery on the grounds that surgery is painful, disfiguring, invasive? No! They cut what must be cut. Quickly. Boldly. It is

123

the only way. Cutting, seen out of context, is EVIL, but of course it is not, it is GOOD, because cutting alone has the power to SAVE. This world is ill – critically, desperately *ill*. Everyone sees that, everyone. It must be cut, cut, CUT – cut mercilessly, cut without pity – cut that it might be **saved**. This is the task – the grim, inglorious, demeaning but necessary task – which I have taken upon myself. I will cut, cut to the bone, to the bone, so that when we finally awake – "

He was startled by a sudden noise at the door. "Yoshiko, wait!" But the door slammed shut, and though the apartment had been perfectly still before, he knew from the altered quality of the stillness that he was now alone in the house.

"...when we finally awake from this nightmare, we, the human race, will have regained our youth and will start afresh.

"The three murders I have committed to date were not part of my mission. They *revealed* my mission to me. It is not in mindless, random violence that my destiny lies. I see that now. I hereby dedicate myself to the violence that SAVES – because, you see, mesdames et messieurs, only violence *can* save."

Maeda recalled the appalling murder he had witnessed of the homeless man in the park in Funabashi. He had never forgotten it, the image was never absent from his mind, but tempering its impact somewhat was his inability to determine whether it had actually occurred or whether he had dreamed it. This "communiqué," crude and "disfigured" (such was the word that occurred to him) as it was, seemed to place the matter beyond all doubt.

He dialed Kinoshita's number.

"Maeda. Kinoshita-san? I've read it. I'll call my friend. Maybe he'll grant me an interview."

Scene Forty-six

"Oh, Rogozhin, you're the only friend I have in the world!" Yoshiko was weeping piteously. "I want to die!"

"Why, what... Wait, let me get you something."

He left her collapsed on the couch, the same white couch he had forbidden Tazawa to sit on, and went into the kitchen. As he attended to the samovar – a genuine Russian samovar, without which, he often told himself, life abroad, in no matter how splendid a country, would be intolerable – he had a sudden idea. Where do ideas come from? The human mind is such a peculiar, unaccountable instrument! For years, decades, it fails to see what stares it straight in the face; then suddenly, apropos of nothing, it does see it, and there it is, so plain, so clear, so obvious, that you can only wonder in astonishment how you could possibly have missed it. Samovars. Genuine Russian samovars – they would sell wonderfully in Japan, as novelty items if nothing else. He must tell Saito-san at once. Well, at the first opportunity. Just at the moment he had his hands full.

"Here, drink this," he said to Yoshiko, setting the teacup and saucer down on the table in front of her. "Be careful, it's hot. And strong. Russian tea, you know – there's no nonsense about it. You see what I mean?"

"Yes, it's very good. I'm sorry." She shivered suddenly.

"Are you cold? I'll bring you a blanket."

"Yes. Please. No. I'm fine. Wait." She stood up. "I don't know what came over me. I shouldn't be here. I shouldn't... I don't even remember coming..."

"Sit down. You're ill. Your face is flushed, feverish."

"It's the tea."

"No, it's not. Yoshiko... I'm your brother, remember? Confide in me. What is making you unhappy? Isn't there something I can do?"

"Yes."

"Yes? You said yes?"

"Take me away from here. We'll go... we'll go to Patagonia! Would you go with me to Patagonia?"

"Yes."

She looked at him, speechless. He too said nothing. There was a noise, muffled electronic music.

"What's that?"

"My cell phone." She drew it out of her jacket pocket.

"Don't answer!"

She glanced at the phone. "It's him. You don't want me to answer?"

"No. At least... well, it depends."

"On what?"

"On what you want me to think."

"Then I won't answer." She laid it on the table beside the saucer. "It'll ring for a long time."

"Let it."

"What melody is it?"

"Don't you recognize it?" She smiled at him. "It's the Moonlight Sonata."

"I'd never have known if you hadn't told me."

"Tell me about your wife. Was she Russian?"

"No, Japanese."

"Tell me about her."

"When she died, it was as if... as if nothing. There is nothing to compare it to. She died, and everything in the world was exactly the same, except that she was no longer in it. I'm making no sense. Other men also love their wives, and lose them..."

"How did she die?"

126

"In childbirth. Almost unheard of in the developed world, and yet it happens."

"And the baby?"

"Born dead."

"How terrible!"

"The baby, quite honestly, I scarcely think of. But Emi, Emi... You probably thought I was joking when I said I wanted to die before I met you. Or maybe that I was acting, playing a part to win your sympathy."

"No."

"No, you wouldn't have thought that. Another woman would have, but not you. I'm sorry. I know you better than that."

"Are you serious? You'll throw up everything you have here, just like that, and go with me to Patagonia?"

"Yes, certainly."

"No questions, like what for, what'll we do there, why Patagonia of all places, how much will it cost?"

"No questions."

"You're a strange man, Rogozhin-san."

"It's still ringing."

"When I talked about Patagonia with *him*, he was full of questions, though he has much less to hold him here than you have."

"It stopped."

"Do you know, when I was a little girl I was terrified of people? All people, everyone. I lived in a shell. I was terrified of my teachers, terrified of my classmates, terrified of everyone I saw in the street. I felt so helpless, you see, so defenseless..."

"Children are defenseless, of course, against wickedness, but most children are blissfully unaware that wickedness is man's natural state."

"Somehow I was not unaware of it."

"But why? Had someone done you harm?"

127

"No. No one. On the contrary, everyone I knew seemed to like me; everyone was kind to me. My own experience taught me nothing of evil."

"How did you come to know if it, then?"

"I don't know. In dreams, maybe. I used to dream of being buried alive. I'd wake up screaming. My mother would hold me and say, 'What's wrong, what's wrong?' But I couldn't answer, I didn't have the words. At one point they wanted to take me to a psychiatrist..."

Scene Forty-seven

"Bufferin-san! *Irasshae!* Welcome!"

Maeda stared in amazement at the beaming, grandmotherly woman who greeted him from her perch at the cash register as he walked in the door. Of course, he recognized her at once as the proprietor, but "Bufferin-san"?

"Don't you remember? You had a headache. I gave you Bufferin."

"Ah!" Yes, he remembered. He glanced around the dimly-lit little shop. Tazawa was not there, nor was anyone else.

"Sit down. Coffee? My waitress quit on me, she's off to Thailand, or Singapore, or some place... everyone's moving, in motion, here, there, but when you're my age you realize that one place is very much like another, and you develop a stillness, or should I say a motionlessness... hm! Anyway, until I find a replacement, and they're not easy to find these days, I have to do all the work myself. It's quiet now, but when it's hectic it's a real strain on my old legs! And how is Shusaku-kun?"

"Shusaku-kun?"

"Here he is! I was just boring your friend with my troubles. My waitress quit. Sit down, I'll bring you your coffee."

"Shusaku-kun!" said Maeda as Tazawa settled himself. "I couldn't figure out who she was talking about."

"We go back a long way, Michiko-san and I. She was a neighbor when I was little. She was more of a mother to me than my own mother."

"Your mother died when you were three. What are you accusing her of?"

"Of dying when I was three. Your mother didn't, did she?"

"No. Tazawa, listen. Do you by any chance know the author of a certain document entitled 'Only Evil Can Save the World'?"

"Ah! How would that have come to your attention, I wonder?"

"Here you are, gentlemen," said Michiko, setting their coffees on the table with practiced aplomb. "Is there anything else I can get you?"

"I'm quite hungry," said Tazawa. "Could I trouble you to fix me something?"

"It's no trouble at all!" Her delight was plain. "What would you like?"

"A sandwich."

"Nonsense! I have some curry rice left over from lunch. I'll heat it up for you."

"Wonderful. Thank you."

"Bufferin-san? Forgive me – may I know your name?"

"Maeda. No, nothing for me, thank you."

"Are you sure? You get a second cup of coffee free if you order a meal."

"He'll have the same," said Tazawa, lightly touching Maeda with his foot under the table. When Michiko had gone he said, "If you can make somebody happy as easily as that, why not do it? I'll eat it for you if you're not hungry. Her curry is

129

out of this world. So! You were saying? About 'a certain document'?"

"Full disclosure: I'm here, in a manner of speaking, as a reporter."

"In a manner of speaking?"

"My editor at the *Maiasa Shimbun* called me this afternoon. He thought the document – the 'communiqué,' as he called it – would interest me, and he forwarded it. Reading it, I thought of you. I called him back and told him I'd see what I could find out. So yes, 'in a manner of speaking.' I haven't been rehired, haven't agreed to go back to work, but I am in touch with the *Maiasa Shimbun*. That's what the ethics of the profession require me to tell you."

"The ethics of the profession! You seem quite changed from the last time we spoke. How's Yoshiko-san, by the way?"

"She's fine. Thank you."

"Meaning she isn't. My ear is very sensitive to tones. I could have been a musician – or a journalist, maybe. I'm not easy to fool."

"You could have been a lot of things. Instead, you..."

"What?"

"'One man, one man working alone, can destroy the world.' Is *this* what you've made of yourself?"

"You don't approve?"

"Did you think I would?"

"Did you think it would matter to me one way or the other?"

"Well, I guess that's the main thing I wanted to ask you. What *does* matter to you?"

"Supposing I say nothing does?"

"Well, if you say that, and say it seriously, I would say in reply, why not kill yourself instead of others?"

Tazawa looked at his old friend in genuine surprise. "Kill myself? Why? You're making a mistake – and I think I know what it is. You confuse nothing mattering with despair. They're not the same. Not the same at all. On the contrary. Once you realize that nothing matters you experience a joy so intense... I couldn't begin to describe it to someone who hasn't felt it."

"A joy so intense it makes you want to 'destroy the world in order to save it'."

"That puts it very well. You're certainly no fool, Maeda."

A door swung open and Michiko-san appeared with two steaming bowls on a tray.

"Gentlemen – your curry!"

Scene Forty-eight

"There is nothing, Maeda, nothing, nothing more beautiful than destruction! Destruction on a vast scale, destruction for its own sake, destruction that outrages every moral precept! Destruction, destruction, destruction! Destruction, executed boldly, is its own justification! Do you know who understood that better than anyone? Picasso! Picasso was a born destroyer. Unfortunately, he was an artist, and confined his destruction to canvas and sculpture. I'm not an artist, but I am a Picasso..."

"Stop, please stop." Maeda's head sank into his hands.

"I said I'm not an artist, but you know, in a sense that's not true. In a sense an artist is exactly what I am."

"Listen." Maeda raised his head. "I told you I was here as a reporter. I didn't specifically mention

131

that I'm recording our conversation, but you might have inferred it. Did you?"

"Recording? No, the thought didn't occur to me. So you've got this insane raving of mine on tape! Ha ha! That's good. That's really good. Why don't you take it to the police, see what they make of it? Ha ha ha!"

"The prospect doesn't seem to worry you."

"Oh, it does! It worries me terribly! Well, listen. If you can have a concealed tape recorder, what's to stop me from having a concealed bomb? In seconds this place will be reduced to flaming rubble, with bits and pieces of you, me and Mother Michiko there strewn all over the place and barely identifiable as former sentient beings. Give me the recorder."

"What?"

"I'm not joking. Hand me the recorder. I'll count to ten. One, two... Are you thinking of calling my bluff? Three... Michiko-san! One more cup of your out-of-this-world coffee, please! Four."

"Coming up!" Michiko sang out from behind the cash.

"Seriously, Michiko-san, you must advertise! Your coffee is fantastic, it'll be a hit, but people have to know about it!"

"Don't you worry, tonight's a slow night, but when it's busy it's more than I can handle!"

"Five. Thank you." Tazawa briefly examined the little device, then slipped it into his shirt pocket. "Would you really have taken this to the police? They would have laughed at you, and for good reason. No, but seriously, is it my fault that destruction is so irresistibly, irresistibly beautiful? Sex, now... but what is sex if not destruction in disguise, destruction in another form? You wouldn't know, of course... or has Yoshiko-san succeeded in rousing your... no, I see by your expression that she hasn't. But sex, orgasm... it's nice, but it's not the real thing, it's just a... what's the word... a symbol, a metaphor, a euphemism. Children play house, adults play sex, but the *real thing*... Oh, thank you, Michiko-san, thank you, you're an angel, this is angel's brew – am I right, Maeda?"

"Yes, yes indeed."

Michiko beamed.

"I could sit here drinking this coffee and chatting with you all night, Maeda, honestly I could. Sometimes, when the mood is right, the brain starts firing a certain way, one thought leads to another, and you simply can't believe the things that come out of your own mouth! You didn't know you had it in you! Yes, when your own thoughts astonish you – there's something orgasmic about that too, isn't there? It's as Rogozhin says..."

"Rogozhin?"

"Haven't I mentioned Rogozhin? It's to him I owe the opening of my mind. He's a Russian, a diplomat. He's my master, I'm his disciple. I'll introduce you to him sometime."

"Rogozhin. Fair hair, wears dark glasses..."

"Yes, he has some sort of eye condition. Ah, so you know him!"

"Yoshiko knows him."

"Does she really! Well, that's very interesting, I'm very pleased to know that! Very pleased indeed! We'll have to all get together sometime! So tell me something. Are you going to write about this?"

"I don't know. I know one thing..."

"What's that?"

"We'll say goodbye, go our separate ways, and I'll walk to the station thinking, 'Did this really happen?' And no matter how hard I try, no matter how vivid my memory is, I won't be able to quite convince myself that it did. It's a kind of disease I have. Nothing that happens seems quite real to me."

"Yes, you mentioned it. A rather fatal disease for someone in your profession, I would think, no?"

"Yes, probably."

"Well, here, take this," he said, reaching into his shirt pocket and handing the little recording device back to Maeda. "I'm sorry if I frightened you. I have what you might call a whimsical sense of humor. But seriously, though: Rogozhin was telling me about Bakunin and Nechaev, two Russian revolutionaries of the nineteenth century who really did believe that mindless, wholesale, amoral destruction was the necessary prelude to a rebirth of the world, a rebirth they held to be necessary. They were midwives, you see."

"Are you a midwife too? Did you really commit those three murders you confess to in the communiqué?"

Tazawa laughed. "I haven't even confessed to writing the communiqué!"

"And of course it was you who torched the Alexandria?"

"The Alexandria? Was the Alexandria torched? Really! I didn't know. I'm a bit out of touch, you see."

"Listen. This Rogozhin character. Do you know where he lives?"

"Of course. I told you. I'm his disciple."

"Would you give me his address?"

"Why?"

"Well, as a favor, with no questions asked."

"As a matter of fact, I don't know the address. I know the house, though. Shall I take you there? Ah! Do you know – I think I've put two and two together! The last time I visited him, our conversation was interrupted – he was expecting a lady! I wonder if the lady... of course, of course! All the pieces fit together! Michiko-san! We must be on our way. We'll come again soon. How much do we owe you? What do you mean, nothing? You can't do business that way, I'm telling you! Here... Maeda, lend me five thousand yen, will you? I don't seem to... There. Well, come along, it's a bit late, but Rogozhin won't mind, he doesn't keep conventional hours. We'll continue our conversation at his place, under his guidance, and as to your private business with him, don't worry, you can count on my discretion!"

Scene Forty-nine

I can't go on this way, drifting from day to day, I can't! I'm not old, I can do something, maybe write something, travel... Anything, anything rather than this demoralizing, debilitating idleness! Misako! You don't come to me anymore – is it that you've given up on me? You sent me to Yasushi, and, stifling my repugnance, I went; you seemed to hint that something would follow from that, he would bring us together somehow, or was that my imagination? All I have to show for the visit is this grotesque... figurine – this *reproduction* of a figurine – ten thousand years old, so primitive you'd hardly know it was human...Three months have passed since I was fired. In all that time not one student, not one colleague, not one, has called to express sympathy, or ask how I'm doing, or engage me in talk about Plato, Sophocles... Well, I understand; I'm not the sort of man people go out of their way to seek out; I'm not resentful; but I do wonder at myself. Look at these books I'm surrounded by, shelf upon shelf fairly groaning under their weight, and yet in three months I haven't opened a single one! How to account for that? Between their covers are the thoughts and feelings of the greatest minds the human species has ever produced! It was them that made me turn away from acting all those years ago, so that I could devote my life to being their disciple – their worthy disciple, as I hoped... but no, I am not worthy of them; *they* would not be crushed by so insignificant a misfortune; *they* would scarcely notice it; they would have shrugged it off long ago and gone on their way, while I... hm. I think I'll go for a walk.

It's cold – November already. Why do I stay here? I could go to Thailand or Malaysia or somewhere, Tahiti maybe – buy an estate and live like a king with the sun for his servant. What's to stop me? Nothing, nothing – that's the trouble! There's nothing to stop me from doing *anything* – no wonder I do nothing! Crows, crows – look, there's one hopping along the road with something dangling from its beak, a bit of paper it looks like – no, plastic; another crow caws from somewhere and this one looks up, lets the thing drop, delivers an answering squawk, then picks it up again and hops on a few paces. Why am I shivering like this? It's not *that* cold. No, but it's damp, raw. I'll go back in and draw a hot bath... in the middle of the day? Why not in the middle of the day, if that's what I want! It's my house, my bath! What if Jun comes home unexpectedly? What will he think? Why should he think anything? Anyway, he's hardly ever home these days, he practically lives at what's-her-name... Tomoko's place. I don't blame him. My idle, useless, aging presence must be distasteful to him. It's distasteful to me. Well, enough of that. Enough!

"Excuse me."

"Eh?"

I gasp, start – I am grotesque in my surprise; did I think the planet was uninhabited, or what?

What does this person want with me? A girl, a child, in a high school uniform.

"For ten thousand yen I'll play with you for an hour, if you like."

"*Play* with me?"

"Yes. Well. You know."

I gape at her. I am struck dumb. My brain churns, but what emerges is not thought but something else. The next thing I know I am *running,* thinking to myself, 'This is mad, mad, mad, I'm losing my reason,' but running all the same, faster, my breath coming in torn gasps; I haven't *run* in years, decades, I'll have a heart attack... it's all I can do to get the key into the lock, my fingers are trembling so.

I sink into a chair in the kitchen; I can't catch my breath,   this is dreadful; Misako said I haven't long to live; is this it? Is this the end?

"Father!"

"Jun!" I spring to my feet. What's he doing here? "Get out!" I hear myself shriek. I push past him and rush up the stairs, stumbling on one of them and nearly falling flat; but I manage to right myself, and reaching at last the refuge of my study, I slam the door. Outside a crow caws twice and is silent.

Scene Fifty

"Father, what is it, what's wrong? Let me in!"

He can't open the door, I'm leaning against it.

"Father?"

A stupid impulse seizes hold of me to keep silent, muffle my breath as best I can, veil my existence until he doubts it himself and goes away, leaving me to myself. To myself! Oh, what I wouldn't give at this moment to be alone in this room, this study of mine, with all its books representing all the ages of mankind and five – five! – of its languages! Solitude, solitude! Absent not only from the presence of other people but from their thoughts as well, their misplaced concern, their distorted images of me! They think they know me because they know my face! Even Jun, even Misako when she was alive... why, I scarcely know myself! A lifelong disciple of Socrates, and yet I failed to heed his most urgent injunction: "Know thyself!"

"Father? Are you all right?"

I turn and open the door. "Yes, I'm all right. Jun, I may have to leave you for a time."

"Why? What do you mean?"

I don't know what I mean. The words emerged of their own accord; I become aware of them in the same way as Jun does – as I hear them. Still, they do not surprise me, as they do him.

"Just what I say. You yourself said I should travel. Maybe I will."

"Oh. Well, yes, why not? It would do you good."

"Well, I'm thinking about it."

"Where would you go? Greece?"

"Maybe. There is a matter or two I would like to take up with the Delphic oracle. Ha ha."

"You can probably do it on the Internet these days, no?"

"Yes, very likely."

"Father, when Tomoko and I are married, you'll come and live with us, won't you? We want you to."

"Live with you? What for? What am I, homeless?"

"No, but why should you be alone, when – "

"I should be alone because I want to be alone! Can't you understand that? No, I don't suppose you can – but Tomoko can, I'm sure of that!"

138

"What do you mean?"

"Nothing. I don't know what I mean. 'I fear,' as King Lear said, the mighty King Lear, 'I am not in my perfect mind.' No, I'm joking. But what are you doing home in the middle of the day? Don't you have classes?"

"What's that?"

"That? Oh... a figurine. Very ancient. Someone gave it to me..."

Scene Fifty-one

"This is it here," said Tazawa. Peering through the darkness, Maeda made out a squat featureless concrete building, five or six stories high.

"What time is it?"

"See the light in the third floor window? That's him. The light means he's up and receiving visitors. You don't have to stand on ceremony with Rogozhin. Like all Russians, he loves to talk. He *lives* to talk. His mind is on fire, and he sets other minds on fire. That, in a nutshell, is Rogozhin. Come."

"No."

"No what?"

Tazawa opened the door and ushered Maeda into a well-lit dark-green hallway. "There's no elevator." He led the way, Maeda following almost against his will, up a flight of stairs, then up another. "Here." He rapped three times on the door, three evenly-spaced knocks – a signal? There was no answer. "He's asleep," Maeda whispered. Tazawa said nothing, but Maeda noticed that he seemed not in the least put out by the awkwardness of the situation; he was calm and showed no sign of impatience. A minute or so went by. Maeda had just opened his mouth to say,

"Come on, let's go," when suddenly, no premonitory sounds indicating it was about to happen, the door opened – but it was not Rogozhin who faced them; rather it was a young woman, rather homely, slightly pockmarked, a little on the plump side, or maybe it was the shapeless yellow sweatshirt she wore that made her look that way. She peered at them inquiringly through narrowed eyes. "Maybe," thought Maeda vaguely, "she's shortsighted and can't see us clearly."

"Tomoko, it's me," said Tazawa familiarly.

The young woman's expression did not alter in the least.

"Is he up?"

"Yes."

"May we come in? I've brought a friend. Don't worry, he's one of us."

Tomoko stood slightly aside, as if to suggest – so it seemed to Maeda – that she was not barring the door but not extending an invitation either. Tazawa walked past her into the flat. Maeda followed. Tomoko closed the door behind them.

The room was brightly, almost dazzlingly lit by a floor lamp beside the armchair on which Rogozhin sat at his ease, his left leg crossed over his right. He wore dark glasses and a blue-and-white striped bathrobe. His thin fair hair looked damp, as though he had not long before stepped out of the shower. Tomoko seated herself on the white couch next to the armchair. She sat leaning forward, her elbows on her knees and her chin resting in her clasped hands. There was something somehow tense and expectant in her posture, but her lowered eyes, to Maeda at least, seemed more vacant and indifferent than anything else.

"Why is the room so bright, if he has trouble with his eyes?" Maeda thought, his own eyes recoiling from the unpleasant pressure of the glare.

Suddenly he remembered Yoshiko. "How could I have forgotten her?" It was strange – Yoshiko, after all, had been his reason for asking Tazawa for Rogozhin's address in the first place – but the fact was that on the way here, perhaps due in some way to Tazawa's presence, she had more or less slipped his mind. He fixed a sharp gaze on Rogozhin, but before he could speak Rogozhin rose to his feet and said with a smile, "Maeda-san, what a surprise."

"Where's Yoshiko?"

"She's asleep. She was exhausted. Maeda-san, forgive me if I seem to intrude in your private affairs, but I think sometimes you have no idea what Yoshiko suffers on your account."

"I've come to take her home."

"She is free to go, of course, if she likes. If she prefers to stay, however, she is here under my protection."

"You have no right..." He broke off. "What's that?"

His attention had been drawn to a picture on the wall to his left, above the couch on which Tomoko sat. It was more a sketch than a painting. Three men in kimono kneeled on the floor. The men on the left and right wore traditional samurai swords; the hands of the man in the middle were shackled. "That's Watanabe Kazan."

"Yes. Do you know it?"

"Where did you get it?"

"The original is at the Tahara Municipal Museum in Aichi Prefecture. I bought this at the museum gift shop. It's a splendid museum. Have you seen it?"

"No, I...no."

"That's one of two prison sketches. I have the other one as well; it's in the room where Yoshiko is sleeping."

"She can sleep at home. She is my wife, I – "

"Maeda-san, listen to me. She came to me of her own free will in a very distressed state. It is not my nature to come between a man and his wife. You have my word of honor that there is nothing between us which you would have cause to resent. That we are close I do not deny. She herself defined our relationship: we are, she said, 'brother and sister.' I beg you, therefore, to let her sleep, and when she wakes up... She loves you very much, Maeda-san. Very much. It is for you to ask yourself whether you are worthy of such love."

Maeda lowered his eyes. "I am not."

"No. In that case, may I suggest the next step– "

"But worthy or not – "

"You are her husband. I quite agree, and as soon as she wakes – "

Tomoko rose suddenly. "I think I'll go for a walk. Maeda-san, won't you come with me?"

Maeda gaped at her in astonishment. He didn't know what to say, and Tomoko's offhand manner – she scarcely glanced at him – only increased his bewilderment. "Goodbye, Rogozhin-san. Thank you for the tea. I'll be sure to mention your idea to my grandfather. Come," she said to Maeda. "Let's go."

Scene Fifty-two

"It's raining," she said. "I felt a drop."

They had been walking in silence, slowly, at Tomoko's pace, Tomoko apparently lost in thoughts of her own, Maeda wondering, a little desperately, what she could possibly want with him, why she had so unexpectedly claimed him as an escort; what, if anything, he was called upon to do or say. Had he ever met this woman before? He

142

could not recall ever having done so, and yet she seemed to know him, not only to know him but to feel perfectly at ease in his presence; she treated him like a friend so old and established that speech itself was superfluous.

Yes, it was drizzling slightly; he too felt a drop of rain on his cheek, and another on the top of his head, just where his hair had started to thin. He lived not far away, was practically in his own neighborhood, and yet Tomoko had turned into one narrow side street and then into another, and he had lost his bearings; nothing looked quite familiar; nor, however, did it look quite unfamiliar. A raindrop landed on the lens of his glasses, turning the glow of the streetlamp into a white shapeless blob.

He removed his glasses and wiped the lens with the sleeve of his jacket. "Where are we going?" – it was on the tip of his tongue to ask, but he hesitated; why? He did not know. Suddenly he tensed. A thought had come to him which, having come, seemed so plain, so obvious; how could he have missed it until now? This sudden impulse of hers to go for a walk, with him in tow – that could easily have been in response to a signal, unseen by him, from Rogozhin, who might well have wanted him out of the way. That supposition was reasonable enough; the one that came in its wake was not, as he knew himself, but its plain absurdity seemed not to weaken its power but, if anything, to strengthen it: that she was going to kill him.

On second thought, was it really so absurd? This Rogozhin character seemed to have developed a philosophy that justified motiveless, cold-blooded murder; Tazawa boasted of having put that philosophy into action; he, Maeda, had himself witnessed, or seemed to have witnessed (he had still not settled the question of the reality

143

or unreality of that moonlit scene in the park), a murder of a sleeping homeless man...

And there was Yoshiko. "Sleeping," Rogozhin had said; did "sleeping" mean dead? Should he bolt from this woman and dash back to Rogozhin's flat, dying in the attempt, if necessary, to save Yoshiko from Rogozhin's and Tazawa's clutches?

"Do you mind stopping in here for a cup of coffee?" Tomoko inquired.

He found himself staring into the brightly-lit window of some sort of all-night restaurant. Tomoko opened the door and a wave of warmth hit him; he shivered; yes, it was a chill, damp night, and the warmth was pleasant. There was music too – most incongruous music; was it Noh music? He was certainly no expert, but that is what it sounded like.

Scene Fifty-three

The waitress smiled at Tomoko in recognition. So she's a regular here, thought Maeda. "Coffee?" the waitress asked. Tomoko nodded. The waitress turned to Maeda, who nodded too. His nervous system seemed to have been taken over by an alien force. He no longer felt in control of his own movements.

"It's a chilly night," said Tomoko, looking directly at Maeda for the first time. She smiled. "You must have thought it strange, my taking you away like that. You see, I was suddenly struck by a question: 'Would he come?' There was only one way to settle it, and so, doing violence to my maidenly shyness, I blurted out my incongruous invitation. I'm sorry, really, it was childish."

"No, that's quite all right," Maeda heard himself say rather stupidly. He felt himself flushing.

The waitress brought their coffee.

"Do they always play this kind of music here?" Maeda asked. It was the only thing he could think of to say, and the lengthening silence oppressed him.

"Yes, at least whenever I'm here, and it would be presumptuous of me to suppose it's for my sake."

"You come here often?"

"Once in a while, when I'm in the neighborhood. Rogozhin is a friend of my family's, you see, and I drop in on him from time to time."

"You said something, I think, about mentioning an idea of his to your grandfather."

"Yes. My grandfather runs a trading company. Rogozhin's late father was his business partner. The idea was to import Russian samovars and sell them as novelty items. What do you think, would they sell?"

"I don't know. Very likely they would. What's the name of the trading company?"

"Saito Shoji."

"Oh!"

"You know it?"

"Of course."

"Of course. Everybody knows it."

"I met your grandfather once."

"Did you!"

"I interviewed him. I was a reporter on the *Maiasa Shimbun*. Tomohisa Saito. So you're his granddaughter. Well well."

"What did you think of him?"

"He seemed pleasant enough. He talked less about his business, which was the supposed subject of the interview, than about his vision of Japan's glorious destiny, whose unfolding, he said,

145

it grieved him he would not live to see. It was his unlucky fate, he said, to live while Japan was at its historical nadir. But all the while he smiled and smiled, so that it was hard to know whether he was speaking seriously or pulling my leg."

"Yes, he has a talent for keeping people guessing. That's probably why he's so successful. So you were a reporter. Were?"

"Yes, I sort of resigned in disgust."

"How does one do that exactly? 'Sort of resign in disgust'?"

"My disgust, like my other emotions, is equivocal – part genuine, part theatrical. The omnipresent media has turned us all into actors. We live as if we're perpetually on camera, perpetually in front of an audience. Hm. It's a kind of theory I cooked up..."

"Being, or having been, in the media. you must know whereof you speak. What about love? Can people in our day genuinely love each other, do you think? Or is that too just acting?"

"It's not *just* acting..."

"You and Yoshiko-san, for instance."

Maeda started. "Do you know Yoshiko?"

"Just to say hello to. Do you love Yoshiko? Really, genuinely love her?"

"I... I don't know."

"No, of course not, how can a person really know these things? You're right, we're all actors, only I don't agree that it's the media that has done this to us. I think it's part of what makes us human. The media has magnified it, no doubt. But then so did Greek tragedy, or Japanese Noh. Do you like Noh? I do, very much. You might say I grew up with it, my grandfather being something of an expert."

Maeda looked down at the table and saw Tomoko's hand caressing his own. He was surprised, and at the same time not; he realized

146

that this had been going on for some time now, though he had only just become consciously aware of it. She met his eye, and smiled. She pressed his hand more firmly. "I am not an actor," she said. "Do you know what my boyfriend thinks I am? A prophet." She gave his hand a playful pat. "He thinks I can read the future."

"Oh! You're the..."

"The...?"

"The... hm! Did your boyfriend's father win a lottery by any chance?"

"He did. I suppose you interviewed him too?"

Maeda nodded.

"What a busy career you had, before you 'sort of quit in disgust'!"

Scene Fifty-four

Maeda awoke as though from something deeper than sleep. His head felt heavy, his body stiff. Where was he? He lay back on the pillow and closed his eyes. The pillow yielded under the weight of his head as readily as a cloud would have. He remained in that state, neither asleep nor quite awake, for what, for all he knew, might have been ten thousand years. His eyelids fluttered open at last. "Tomoko?" He reached out with both hands, as though unsure which side of the bed he lay on. His left hand encountered resistance; then he felt his hand taken and caressed. He smiled. Yes, he remembered now. Astonishing, astonishing what that woman had done to him – such a plain, such a homely woman; if you noticed her at all – on a train, say, or on a crowded street – your first inclination would be to turn away, not in disgust exactly, but... well, suffice it to say that she was anything but physically attractive; moreover, she

147

took no pains to make herself attractive, or at least mask her unattractiveness – and yet it was that woman, that woman who had awakened desires in him he had thought not dormant but absent. He'd been mistaken, obviously.

Was it night or day? Night, if the pitch darkness was truly indicative – but this was the point: *nothing* seemed truly indicative of *anything*. He could not so much as guess as to his surroundings. All he could be sure of was that he lay on a bed with Tomoko beside him. Even the bed was conjectural. It could have been a futon; but a vague, indefinable feeling he had of being above the floor suggested a bed. The same kind of feeling gave him the impression of being upstairs – upstairs from what? From the ground floor, from ground level. It was strange: no matter how long he lay staring into the darkness, his eyes did not grow accustomed to it; they made out not the dimmest outline, not the faintest shape; and yet this impenetrable blackness was not oppressive; on the contrary, it was somehow comforting.

"Maybe I've died and this is eternal life." The thought was accompanied by a piercing sensation of joy, a joy so intense that it was all he could do to keep from crying out. Yes, to lie in this blackness, silent, motionless, not knowing where he was and not caring, with no hunger to satisfy, no restlessness to relieve, aware of nothing except Tomoko's presence beside him – to lie like that through all eternity... "So Tazawa was right after all, and Rogozhin. Evil *does* save the world, just as they said; and murder, however ghastly and appalling it may appear to those who see only appearances, in fact is a blessed liberation from a diseased, corrupt world; it dispatches us to our true home. And their other victims? The homeless man, the children, Yoshiko... how much blood do they have on their hands, those two? There may be hundreds, thousands of victims. Perhaps I'll meet them, like Odysseus in the land of the dead; only he encountered gibbering, disembodied ghosts, whereas I find myself in a realm of joy..."

"Tomoko," he whispered. He felt her stir beside him; she stroked his face, his chest, and he realized now for the first time – it had not occurred to him to wonder about it before – that he was naked under the covers. "Tomoko, Tomoko." Could this really be death? Oh, how good, how good if it was! Because if it was, then all death did was remove the shadow of death from life!

Part II

Scene One

A strange dream I had last night – or maybe it was real. The city was engulfed in a wave of random murder – that at least is real enough – and when my doorbell rang it was neither the murderer (my first thought) nor Takeshi (my second) but a high police official come to coax me out of retirement. The constabulary was helpless, he admitted as I poured tea. There were no clues that led anywhere, none that made any sense. If only *I* would... if only... oh, of course it was an imposition, of course I had earned the repose I was at last free to enjoy in my old age.. still... for the good of the community... of decent, law-abiding mankind... if I would put my detective skills to work...

If only sleep had lasted a few minutes longer I would know how I responded. Unfortunately, it didn't, and I don't. My first confused impulse on waking was to clutch at my arm – I was pouring tea all over the pillow! My second was a horrified fear that I had wet myself. No, I hadn't, but soon would if I didn't take prompt preventive measures. In the beeline to the toilet the dream's urgency faded, giving way to something like shame – shame at my incurable childishness. Detective! Detective Masao Horiuchi, the broken-down, superannuated ex-professor of ancient civilization, bringing murderers to book, bringing peace at last to a troubled, much-tried city!

Bright spring sunshine floods the toilet cubicle. Yes, spring is here at last, after an unusually harsh winter of record snowfalls and record cold that seemed to – only "seemed to," I know! – mock global warming. Of the snow, only patches remain, and if that sun is any indication this day could well see the end of them. The earth is boggy, the air rank with the smell of new life struggling to be born.

What time would it be? Why should it matter? Why should I, with no work to do and no appointments to keep, be forever fretting about the time? I could live timeless if I chose. Some time ago I "banished time" from the study; what's to stop me from banishing time from the whole house? Get rid of every single watch and clock in it. Take the calendar off the kitchen wall. Cancel my subscription to the newspaper. Kant said time doesn't exist in nature; it is merely a "category" of the human mind. I think that's what Kant said. I must get back to my books, my studies. I will. And I will exercise, too. Mind and body both have grown slack. What have I done all winter? Nothing. I have seen no one, except, occasionally, Yasushi and his family. Even Jun is hardly ever home, and when he is, there's an unbridgeable gulf between us. I don't know why. We don't know what to say to each other any more.

It is five past eleven, the clock on the wall in the kitchen informs me. Five past eleven! How can I possibly have slept so late? Usually I am up by six, six-thirty at the absolute latest. Was I up late last night? No. Did I get up during the night? No. So why... Hm! Perhaps I slept for a hundred years, or a thousand, and have wakened to a world transformed beyond my most fantastic

151

imaginings? Let's see what the   newspaper has to say. Here it is, in the mail slot as usual, the *Maiasa Shimbun*, dated March 27, 2009 – all is as it should be. A black banner headline: another murder! Horrible, horrible! A wave of random murder; Tokyo has never, in all its history, seen anything like it. This is the twenty-third victim since the murder of the child in the park in Funabashi, the park I visited (I blush to recall it!) last summer, to "look for clues." Some days, weeks or months ago the *Maiasa* published a "communiqué" from some group or other that threatened, or promised, to spread evil in the name of good – how did their reasoning go? I no longer remember. Yes, I will cancel my subscription and retreat to my study, there to resume my study of the ancients, in solitude, in peace, until death puts an end to it.

But today, March 27, is no ordinary day. It is Yasushi's birthday. There is to be a party, to which I have been invited. I have promised to go. Yes, I will go. It will be my last sortie, my last "sally," to borrow the language of Don Quixote.

Scene Two

The party isn't until six, but I leave the house immediately after lunch. Sunlight floods the kitchen, as though inviting me outside, and I accept the invitation. That gives me five hours to kill. Shall I walk along the beach? Or go straight to Tokyo and see what's doing there, behold the great city yawning and stretching itself as it wakes from its winter slumber? True to form, I am unable to decide, and stand motionless at the intersection where I must turn either left to the beach or right to the station.

This inability of mine to decide the most inconsequential things, a lifelong infirmity, has naturally grown worse since my forced retirement. One of these days, at some moment such as this, I will, I sometimes fancy, find myself literally, physically, paralyzed. It is a fortuitous circumstance that saves me from such a fate now. Someone is approaching from the road to the beach, and he looks vaguely like Jun. In response to no thought that I am aware of, I hastily turn right, and it is only after having bought my ticket and lost myself in the station crowd that I pause to ask myself why I reacted that way. Was it really Jun? Maybe it was, maybe it wasn't; he was too far off for me to see him clearly. Supposing it was – why would his presence send me scurrying off in the opposite direction? I have no idea; it makes no sense to me. Did he see me? What would he be thinking if he did?

On the train I sink into one of the "priority seats" reserved for the old and infirm. I can get away with that now, though this is the first time I have not disdained to do so. I am letting myself go; this is not good; idleness is not good for me, I must... etc., etc. I close my eyes. As a child I used to wonder about a place called "nowhere." Where was it? Was it off-limits – *tachi-iri kinshi?* Even as I wondered I would think to myself, "No one else wonders about such things, just me" – and I'd know instinctively not to breathe a word of it to anyone. Only to Yasushi was I completely open. Only from him did I have no secrets. That was part of the "worship" he demanded and I willingly accorded.

My eyes are closed but my ears, of course, are not, though I have often thought mankind would be the better for closeable ears. There is not much talk, most people being absorbed, no doubt, in their cell phones or Walkmans or whatever; nor is

153

there silence, for the announcements coming through the overhead speakers are incessant: next station such-and-such, doors on the left side will open, please don't forget your personal belongings, please hold on to the hand rails, please watch your step, please watch your children, please keep your cell phones on silent mode, please yield your seat to expectant mothers and the elderly, the toilets are in cars one and five... I'll go to Greece; what's to keep me here? I told Jun months ago I was going, but as though telling him had been the only point, no sooner did I blurt it out than I stopped even thinking about it, and sank into my winter stupor. Stupid, stupid. "We should have the right to carry a gun, like in America," says the man next to me. What? My eyes pop open – is he talking to me? No, of course not – to the woman on his left. The man looks about thirty, the woman sixty. Are they mother and son? She murmurs something I don't catch, to which the man replies, "You'd just let them slit your throat?" Ah, they're talking about the murder. There has been no obvious pattern to the slayings. Some of the victims have been strangled, others stabbed, others still poisoned. The latest, a man of 83, had his throat cut while taking an evening stroll; it happened just around the corner from where he lived; it was hardly even dark, but the murderer had vanished by the time the first passerby noticed the body.

Scene Three

"Professor! Come in, come in. What'll you have?"

The two other customers look up from their noodles at the newcomer who merits such a voluble reception. The newcomer blushes and winces. I've asked him more than once not to call me "professor," but there's no help for it; "professor" is what I am to him; to call me anything else would be to turn me into something unrecognizable in his eyes.

I take a seat at the counter and say nothing. He knows perfectly well what I'll have, and without further ado he turns to his vats and griddle to prepare it. No sooner had I pushed open the door than I realized my mistake; I shouldn't have come. I don't want noodles, the closeness and stuffiness of the confined little place chafe me, the bluff good humor of this "son of Kafu" and the noisy slurping of the diners clash with and heighten a craving for silence, silence, silence – but is silence to be had in Tokyo? Why didn't I spend the afternoon at home, where all the silence in the world is mine for the taking? And why, having impulsively and for no discernible reason come to Tokyo hours ahead of time, did I gravitate to this of all places? Well, I "gravitated" here because this is where gravity, in the guise of habit, drew me. First I went to the Alexandria. Why, given that the Alexandria burned down months ago, did I go there? Habit again – every visit to Yasushi seems to begin with a sort of pilgrimage to the Alexandria. Late last fall I stood watching them clear away the charred rubble. Two or three times during the winter I passed by to see what they would build in its stead. That was my mission today too, previous visits having yielded no clue. Now work has at last begun. The grinding din assaults the ear long before the site comes into view. Through a barrier you see bulldozers, earth movers, cranes, trucks, men in hard hats scurrying about on towering scaffolding. I'm not sure how to describe what happened next: a wave of panic, fear – I scarcely know what to call it! I fled as though for my life – and the next thing I know I'm pushing open the door to this noodle shop

155

owned by a man who claims to be the son of the novelist Nagai Kafu, a shop I used to frequent with my old friend Tazawa, the Alexandria's late owner, and more recently on my own as the inevitable conclusion of my Alexandria "pilgrimages."

"Just this morning," the old gentleman says as he lays before me a steaming bowl of *tanuki udon*, "I was reading one of father's stories..." He pauses, as though suddenly struck by something in my expression that suggests I may not be in the mood for his chatter. Contrite, I force a smile.

"Oh? Which one?"

"*Two Days in Chicago*. Do you know it?"

One of the *American Stories*. He lived in the United States for a time as a very young man, very early in the twentieth century. *Two Days in Chicago* – yes, that would be his celebration of the free and wholesome American approach to love, as opposed to the stifling Confucian rectitude he knew at home.

"It seems so strange. There are so many things I would like to ask him. He comes to me in dreams sometimes."

"Does he? Does he answer your questions?"

"Last night he got mad at me. He said, 'I'm not your father, leave me alone!'"

The man is seventy years old at least, and ready, by the look of him, to burst into tears at having been rejected in a dream by a father who (even granting the doubtful premise that he was the biological begetter) was no father in any meaningful sense, and whom he met, if ever, once in his life, when he was five! Truly, human nature is endless in its vagaries!

"The question I couldn't help asking myself as I read is how come, for all his admiration of the West and its freedoms, and all his detestation of things Oriental, he returned to Japan before he was thirty and for the rest of his life never so much

156

as set foot outside of Tokyo? Don't you think that's strange?"

"Yes, Kafu was a strange man," I murmur.

"Why do you suppose...?"

"Really, I have no idea."

Scene Four

One of the two customers noisily pushes back his chair and approaches the cash to pay. His curiously lumbering gait suggest the noodles might be weighing him down, or perhaps – no, he has a game leg and walks with a slight limp. Nagai attends to him, sees him out, and then returns to me. "A strange man, you say. Yes, very strange. Is strangeness an inherited trait? What do you think, professor?"

"I think you are rather more serious today than usual."

"Today is my birthday."

"Is it! Talk of strange – I'm on my way to a birthday party."

"I am seventy-four years old."

"No! You hardly look it. Well, turning seventy-four might well make a man serious. Tell me, Sokichi" – the question suddenly occurs to me – "how is it you never married?"

"I was married."

"Oh?"

"In fact I am married. We were never divorced. My wife left me."

"I'm sorry, I didn't know." I glance over at the one remaining customer. He looks, from behind, very young; older people don't slouch like that. His slurping is utterly unrestrained, his bowl of noodles seems endless, and his total absorption in it, to the apparent exclusion of everything else in the world except possibly the comic book his left arm holds flat on the table while with his right hand he manipulates his chopsticks, reminds me vaguely of the students I faced in my last years of teaching. Once upon a time youth meant strength, vigor, determination; now it seems to represent the height of decrepitude.

"Fortunately," says Sokichi, "there were no children."

"Ah, yes. Children..." I must make my excuses and get out of here; Sokichi is gearing up to tell me the whole story of his wife's departure – he is one of those people, increasingly common in our day, with no sense at all of privacy, of my business as opposed to your business; he has no secrets from anyone he is acquainted with, or even from a stranger who inadvertently shows some slight interest. Like his supposed father, he is a kind of novelist – a novelist without a pen. But no, I am being unjust. After all, I have known him for twenty years at least, and this is the first I've heard of his wife.

Scene Five

"Yes, I'll never forget that day... I came home, the house was dark. There was a... there was a note..." His lower lip is trembling, he is reliving the experience. "Sokichi, wait," I murmur – wait, I want to say; before you begin, let me out, let me be on my way; but no, suddenly he wants to talk, and since it was my question that broke the dam... I glance again at the one other customer in the place; maybe he's done at last? He'll get up and proceed to the cash, thus putting a natural end to it and giving me my opportunity to slip out into the brilliant spring sun, pitiless melter of snows and vapors... By no means; "hell will freeze over," as Misako used to say – ah, Misako! – before he tears himself away from his noodles and his comic book. "A note on the kitchen table. We had known each other as children, as babies – like Chokichi and O-ito in Kafu's *The River Sumida*... We were playmates; at three we loved each other, at five we swore to marry someday; at eighteen we did marry, and... and this sad man you see before you, sir, was happy as few people on earth are, as few..." Removing his glasses, he dabs his eyes with a pocket handkerchief. "What an old fool I am! Seventy-four years old! Would she even be alive now, I wonder?"

Relief suffuses me – he is done; the mood has passed; he is not going to tell the story after all. My relief is not unmixed with a stab of guilt. Is my capacity for sympathy so shrunken, so shriveled?

"Once I thought of hiring a detective to search for her..."

The door jerks open and in strides a young man, evidently very hungry, if his air of being in a fearful hurry is anything to go by. His firm step falters as the sudden interior dimness momentarily disorients him, but Sokichi's cry of delight on seeing him brings him back to earth. "Tazawa-kun!"

Tazawa?

But Sokichi has not forgotten me. "Tazawa-kun, this is Professor Horiuchi – like me, a very old friend of your father's."

The young man accords me a slight bow and says with a smile, "My father seems to have had a lot of old friends."

Can he really be Tazawa's son? He seems so strong, so healthy – a startling contrast to his frail, wispy wraith of a father!

I make him an answering bow and, seizing the opportunity, say to Sokichi, "Well, I must be off."

159

Busy with the newcomer, he does not seek to detain me.

Scene Six

"Tomoko! Tomoko, where…"

"What's wrong with you, Jun? You're trembling."

Jun gaped at her. He was speechless. For three weeks, day after day and late into the night, sometimes all night, he had haunted the sidewalk outside her apartment, interrupting his distracted vigil there only to venture into the corridor and up the stairs to ring her bell and strain his ears for footsteps, knowing perfectly well this was insane, since he knew perfectly well the apartment was empty – but where was she? Why had she simply vanished without a word? Was she in trouble? Should he call the police?

And now here she was, showing no more emotion at the sight of him than mild surprise at meeting him unexpectedly. No, that was unfair – she had noticed his trembling and, taking his hand, was being gently solicitous. "Come, I'll fix you some hot tea, I could use some myself."

She carried a light suitcase, and on her back was a knapsack. So she'd been traveling. How could she have left without so much as a word to him? Dumbly he followed her up the stairs, not daring to yield to his natural impulse to shower her with questions. She fished in her pocket for her key, inserted it into the lock, and pushed open the door. "I'll open the window, it's as musty as an old cellar. There. Come in, spring! You've taken my advice and let your hair grow, I see. Wasn't I right? Doesn't it suit you?"

"Tomoko, where – ?"

"Spring, new life! Doesn't it stir the poet in you? Have you written any poems lately? Recite me one! I'll bet my grandfather is simply overflowing with poetry. Shall we pay him a visit? Tomorrow maybe. Oh, no, not tomorrow, I'm meeting Professor Sawamura tomorrow – oh, I'll never get my thesis done! Sawamura's a brilliant, brilliant man who has no patience with people less brilliant than himself, which means just about the entire human race, and yet for some reason he has seen fit to encourage me – but I'm afraid his patience is wearing thin, and when I tell him I've made   no progress since our last meeting..."

"Tomoko, where were you?"

"In Oiso. I had an abortion. Jun, I'm afraid I'll have to ask you to excuse me... really, I must... if I don't – "

"You what?"

"If I don't get some work done..."

"You had a... what?"

"An abortion. You know what that is, don't you? Listen, Jun, I want you to understand what's at stake here. Dr. Sawamura is one of the world's leading authorities on dark matter, and he has graciously condescended to be aware of my existence, which is no small thing in itself, and to accept me as a kind of disciple, which... ah, but how can I expect you to understand? You don't even know what dark matter is! Honestly, Jun, I've said this before and I'll say it again: sometimes I wish I had a brain like yours, a simple, nice, perfectly good, perfectly functional brain which sees nothing except what it needs to see... but no, the gods made me their plaything and gave me a measure of their intelligence! What does a human being need with a god's intelligence, eh? Tell me that!"

161

Scene Seven

His face wet with tears, he walked and walked. It grew dark, and his first coherent thought was, "I don't know where I am." His second was, "It doesn't matter," and he walked on. For twenty years life had been kind to him, too kind, and now, suddenly, it had plunged him into such utter, hopeless despair as to constitute almost a rebirth, a rebirth into a new world whose contours were unknown, unimaginable, hostile. Only one tragedy had marred his earlier life – the death of his mother when he was seven. Yes, that had been bad, but a small child has ways of cushioning himself from the very worst. There is the inability to understand, there is the loving father to fall back on, there is the saving shortness of the child's memory as new events rush in to fill the void. What was there for him to fall back on now? Death, death, only death, and he was startled, when the thought came to him, by his own strangled voice crying out, "Mother!"

He looked about him, frightened. Cars passed, their headlights on, but the sidewalk was deserted. It was some sort of commercial street he was on, lined with small shops, many of them shuttered. He passed a barber shop, a cake shop, a shop selling *inkan* signature seals. In none of them did any business seem to be taking place. Where was he? What time was it? He was hungry and cold, and very tired. In a tiny, dimly lit grocery store he saw a woman arranging bananas in the window. How beautiful they looked! He paused, and the woman, catching his eye, seemed to furrow her forehead slightly, as though mildly surprised at the sight of him. Should he go in? No, what he needed was a restaurant, a full meal, hot *miso* soup above all – but his strength was gone, and his compulsive shivering, he realized now, was not merely cold, it was fever.

A little bell tinkled as he pushed open the door. "*Irasshaemase*," said the woman, bowing slightly without interrupting her ministration to the bananas.

"Those bananas look nice," Jun murmured.

"They're from Taiwan," said the woman. "Good heavens, are you ill?"

"Yes, I... yes. How much for..."

"Sit down, wait, here's a stool. You're feverish, I can tell. A mother who's raised three children knows a fever when she sees it! Sit – wait, I'll get you..."

He felt a delicious warmth pervade him. Evidently the woman had wrapped him in a blanket or something; he didn't open his eyes to see. "Wait, I'll bring you some hot tea..."

He must have dozed, for he had a dream, and when he woke his confusion was such that he didn't know whether the dream had been horrible or beautiful. He came home from school and opened the door to his room, and on his bed his mother and father lay unclothed, locked in a gentle, passionate, loving embrace, and though they should have started at the noise he'd made, so absorbed were they in each other that they remained entirely unconscious of his presence, even when he started to cry. He awoke crying. "Here, drink this," said a woman, handing him a cup. He looked at the woman in bewilderment, and then remembered. "Thank you," he said. He sipped the tea gratefully. It was still hot; he couldn't have been asleep long.

"Would you like another cup?"

"Yes, please, and... a bunch of bananas, please. Those yellow ones..."

Scene Eight

"Come in, come in!" Ikuko's face lights up at the sight of me, and the others, drawn by her hearty greeting, crowd round – all are glad to see me, and the room itself is so bright, so cheerful... "Happy birthday," I say to Yasushi. We embrace. Ghost and I shake hands; laughing, Kazue presents her hand to be kissed – a ceremony we initiated some time ago in comic imitation of English 19th-century manners. From somewhere comes the lusty cry of an infant, at which Kazue excuses herself and dashes away to attend to it.

How happy, how delightful everything is! The coffee table in the living room is lined with bottles, glasses and an ice bin. "Help yourself," says Yasushi. "This scotch here – Ghost brought it and he's something of a connoisseur. By the second sip, all is right with the world; by the third, even Ghost would admit it's hard not to believe in God! No, no, I'm joking," he cries, laughing, as though to forestall a heated protest. "We'll argue later. For now, let brotherhood reign. Soda? Sit, sit, why are you standing? Forgive my babbling. Today, you see, I've made a discovery, and it's made me very happy. What discovery? That there is life after sixty! There really is! And that being true, it would seem to follow" – once more casting a roguish glance at his son-in-law – "that immortality is a fact. I'm joking, I'm joking!"

"There are some things you shouldn't joke about," says Ghost quietly. "Joke too much, and finally you yourself don't know when you're joking and when you're serious."

"Once upon a time the young learned wisdom from the old. Now it's the other way around. Professor, put this young whippersnapper in his place! Enlighten him on the seriousness of joking.

164

Tell him about Aristophanes – there's a name to reckon with, eh?"

"Aristophanes – hm. Yes, your father-in-law's right, joking was serious business. It was a form of worship, you see. The god Dionysus – "

"Listen, can I ask you a question? What I said about not knowing when you're joking and when you're serious – I'm being serious now – we've known each other what – six months? And we're friends, right? But – "

"I know what he's going to say," Yasushi interrupts in high glee, "and you're guilty, guilty as charged! It's impossible to know when you're kidding and when you're being serious! You joke with a straight face, and laugh away your solemnity. Come, Masa, come, it's time for you to commit yourself! I told you" – this to Ghost – "he's a secret worshiper of Zeus, Dionysus, Artemis. A polytheist!"

"Not secret," I smile, falling in with the banter. "Open. An open worshiper."

"Open worshiper of what?" asks Kazue, just back from ministering to the baby.

"Of life," I say. "Of the life I see in you."

Yasushi looks at me in some surprise. Have I said the wrong thing? I don't know what made me blurt that out – something I seemed to see in Kazue's face, a kind of light, it's hard to explain – a kind of *maternal* light, I'm tempted to say. Motherhood suits her. She's a rather homely girl – well, not *homely* – but just at that moment she suddenly looked inexplicably lovely.

"Listen," says Ghost. "I'm no historian, but I've read a little history, and the conclusion I've come to, correct me if I'm wrong, is that mankind would have been so much happier, so much better off, if the word 'worship' had never entered into his vocabulary, if he'd just gone about his business – "

"The tone-deaf man says music is an illusion," says Yasushi.

"Well?"

"The loveless man says love is an illusion. The godless man... oh, by the way," he says, turning to me, "there'll be someone else dropping by later on – someone I met in, of all places, a public bath."

"What are you saying," demands Ghost, his belligerency rising, "that the godless man is tone-deaf?"

"God-deaf. Eh, Masa? God-deaf."

Scene Nine

Between Ghost and me, in the short time we've known each other, there has grown a surprising friendship. I say surprising because there has been nothing like it in my life before. Of all the students I taught over the years, not one could I ever claim as a friend. It was as Misako said: I had no real interest in teaching, only in learning, and my students somehow sensed – it must have shown with painful clarity – that I considered them not worthy objects of my pedagogical attentions but rather obstacles littering my path, and so a kind of mute mutual resentment hovered in the air of my classrooms, poisoning even my best lectures. Yes, as a teacher I was a failure, and if not a single former student has come to seek me out since my forced retirement, I have only myself to blame. But with Ghost it is different. With Ghost, I might almost say, I am a different man. In his presence I seem to lose my instinctive distaste for young people – for their noise when they are noisy, for their sullenness when they are quiet; for their brash self-confidence when they are intelligent, for their torpor when not.

Whether my feelings towards him are to be explained mostly by his personal qualities or by the position I have come to occupy in the family as a whole, I don't know. The position I occupy is that of family friend, confidant, a sort of favorite uncle, and I can hardly say how it came about, or why I seem so popular among them, why they all seem to dote on me, to love me, why they are all so happy to see me when I come. I am not lovable, not sociable – on the contrary, I am morose, reserved, crusty; but their attitude seems to be that none of that matters – "we will take you as you are, love you just as you are…"

The baby sleeps through most of dinner but wakes as dessert is being served. Kazue hurries upstairs, and returns cradling it in her arms, her head bent low over it and her face glowing with that peculiar light. "Here, let me have her," says Ghost, but Kazue ignores him and instead places the baby in my lap. Morose, crusty I said of my own character, but I'm not really, it's only shyness that makes me appear that way, and as I enfold the infant in my arms I feel a surge of such love, such love in my heart, that for a moment I am almost frightened. This love… I don't know… it is not of this world…

"I wanted to bake a cake," Ikuko is saying to Kazue – "I'd carry it in and it would be blazing with sixty candles…"

"You'd set the house on fire," Yasushi interposes.

"Me!" retorts Ikuko. "*I'd* set the house on fire! This from a man who – "

"Yes, you're right," laughs Yasushi. "More likely me than you, eh? Ha ha ha!"

"One of these days you really will set the house on fire! 'No cake, please,' he insists; 'I don't like cake.' Can you imagine? We've been married twenty-eight years, and I never knew he didn't like cake! Anyway, that's why we're having ice cream..."

Scene Ten

"Seriously, I want you to level with me." We're back in the living room, the ladies sipping coffee, the gentlemen scotch. Ghost, the baby now asleep in his lap, challenges me. "This business about Zeus and all – are you joking, or not?"

"Why should I be joking?"

"Give me a straight answer, a simple yes or no: yes I believe in Zeus, no I'm pulling your leg!" His earnestness is almost comic – but he's like that. When he's roused, which is most of the time, he simply won't be put off.

"Yes I believe in Zeus."

His eyes bore into mine; at last his expression softens and he says quietly, "All right, I'll believe you, and if you're joking, let it be on your conscience."

"Why do you find it so – ?"

"No one believes in Zeus nowadays!"

"But they once did!" says Yasushi, leaning forward in his excitement. "Everyone did – everyone, not just fools. The greatest philosophers and poets. Didn't Socrates believe in Zeus, Masa? Didn't Aeschylus, Euripides?"

"Socrates was tried and put to death for not believing in the gods of the city."

"Yes, but – " Ghost has a face on which every inner stirring is written in tiny movements, twitches, winces. It has occurred to me that one could perhaps study them and learn to read them, thus sparing him the necessity – an awkward one, he plainly feels – of putting his thoughts into words. "Yes, but *we, we* don't live in that city, *we* live..."

"Well? Yasushi prods him. "Where do we live?"

Ghost glares at him. "No god lives in my city! That's all!"

"I think what your father-in-law is saying," I intervene, playing my habitual role of good-natured, neutral peacemaker, "is that your city would be the richer if it were otherwise."

"Some riches are just poverty in disguise!"

"Yes, that's true."

"Yes, by Zeus!" cries Yasushi, raising his glass.

"You're mad!" says Ghost, looking from one to the other of us in a kind of horror. "You're mad, mad, both of you!"

"We're human," I say. "It is human to be mad, and mad to be human. No, wait." Ghost checks himself on the verge of an outburst. I am silent – to gather my thoughts, but also to assert command. My dramatic powers, lost in the classroom, are coming back to me. My silence fills the room. Everyone is silent, waiting for me to speak. I await the right moment, sense it when it comes, and say, speaking slowly and quietly, "Animals are sane. Humans, in order to be human, must have a touch of madness in them. We are finite beings living in an infinite universe – and, unlike the animals, of which the same might be said, conscious of it. It is their unconsciousness which keeps them sane, and our consciousness which explains our madness, which is sometimes less than sanity, sometimes more. However far science rolls back the curtain, there will always be more that we don't know than that we know. Oh yes. Infinitely more. No amount of new and accumulated knowledge will change that, or even alter the proportion much between the known and the

169

unknown. That being so, atheism is as much a matter of faith as theism." I pause; it is on the tip of my tongue to say, "Any questions?"

"Why?" says Ghost, speaking now as quietly as I, as if he has taken some of my quietness into himself. "Of course man has much to learn, but he also has the capacity to learn, and the more he learns the less he's ignorant of. That stands to reason, no?"

"No, because however much he learns he remains a prisoner of the human brain – which, for all its awesome complexity, is still a physical organ bound by physical limitations. Reason, philosophy, mathematics, technology, help us stretch those limitations, but we cannot transcend them altogether. We can be aware of infinity but we cannot enter it, cannot *participate* in infinity. Our very nature bars us from it. And there's another thing."

"Well?"

"Morality. You yourself mentioned conscience just now. Where does it come from? Nature? Show me an example of morality in nature. It doesn't exist. Morality is not natural. What then? Social? But it must have preceded society, because how could society have begun without it? Supposing you have something I want and I'm stronger than you – why shouldn't I snatch it from you, or kill you if necessary? What is there in nature, or in the psychological makeup of man, with all its urgent and irresistible desires, to tell me that though I *can* do this, though I'm *capable* of doing this, I *shouldn't* do it? Why *shouldn't* I? What does *shouldn't* mean? For example: No matter how hungry I am, I know that the grass growing in abundance at my feet is not to be eaten – I couldn't digest it, and even if I was starving to death, the mere thought of eating it would disgust me. Why is

170

there no similar natural barrier to prevent me from committing moral outrages?"

Ghost is silent; he is looking at me intently, waiting for me to continue. The others too; though I am not looking at them but at Ghost, I can *feel* their eyes on me, I can *feel* their attention. Why, over so many years, did I fail to built this kind of atmosphere in the classroom? Where was my inspiration then? Where was my tongue?

I don't know how long the silence lasts; I am conscious of the silence but not of the passage of time. It is a pregnant silence, not a hollow one; a charged silence. I feel almost as if I could say to Ghost, like old Cephalus in the *Republic*, "Come, let us see to the sacrifices," and he would rise without a word to help me slaughter a beast.

It is Kazue, Kazue the silent, Kazue who speaks so little that her voice, the odd time she does raise it, sounds perpetually strange in my ears – it is Kazue who breaks the silence. "There's a cult," she says, speaking barely above a whisper, "that says evil is good..."

Scene Eleven

"Wait a minute, wait a minute!" Ghost is off like a race-horse who has been kept too long pawing at the starting gate; he is suddenly furious; ignoring Kazue, though it was she, apparently, who in all innocence ignited him, he leans forward in his chair, to all appearances ready to fling himself upon me. "You are arguing the existence of gods from the existence of *morality? Morality?* Was God *moral* when he demanded Abraham sacrifice Isaac? Or when he made his sordid little bet with Satan in the Book of Job? As for Zeus and those other perverts up there on Mount Olympus, if

171

mankind took their cue from *them*..." He is choking with rage; he can barely get the words out. Yasushi, I see out of the corner of my eye, is smiling, not a broad smile, on the contrary a scarcely perceptible one, but it lights up his whole face; there is something in his air that suggests the puppet-master well pleased with his puppets' performance. "If man is moral," Ghost resumes, breathless, "it is *in spite of* God, not because of him... or them, or... whoever, whatever! To say nothing of how morality differs from culture to culture! In some cultures theft is moral, in others murder, cannibalism. Pastoral tribes raid each others' cattle. Odysseus – doesn't he go off raiding at the end of the *Odyssey*, with the blessing of the gods? You know all this, know it better than I do; why are you... laughing at me?" Is he going to burst into tears? "There is nothing divine about morality. There is nothing divine period. There is no God, there are no gods, and if I see any sign of religion sprouting in little Mei-chan here, I'll... I'll... root it out of her! As I would poison! It *is* poison!" In his fury he seems almost ready to begin at once squeezing any incipient poisonous godhood out of the tiny little being in his lap. Perhaps he does squeeze, for the infant wakes suddenly with a piercing cry. Kazue springs to her feet and snatches the baby from him.

"I *hate* God! If he were here, I'd *shoot* the bastard, I'd... I'd blast him into non-existence, the non-existence that is rightfully his!"

"We're fortunate to live in a country with strict gun laws," observes Yasushi mildly. "Imagine if this was America. God would be in serious danger!"

"If he exists he *usurped* his existence!"

"Usurped?"

"Kazu, let's go home, really, I've had – "

172

"Oh, stay," says Ikuko, evidently used to his moodiness and not at all alarmed by it. "You don't simply walk out on your father-in-law's sixtieth birthday party, it's not done."

"It's not moral," says Yasushi.

"Seriously, Kazu. Let's go to Africa. I'm tired of Japan. An exhausted, dying country."

Kazue at the moment has no attention to spare for him; she's fumbling with her blouse to bare a breast for the baby, who's now crying as though furious at her parents' stupid incompetence.

"Africa!" cries Ikuko.

A ring at the doorbell cuts her short. Kazue, uttering a faint cry, flees with her bundle into the kitchen. Ghost, as though such interruptions are beneath his notice, says again, "Exhausted, dying. Africa's poor, but at least it's alive, it has a future..."

"Ah, that's him!" says Yasushi, springing to his feet. "Damn!" Typically, he has forgotten the scotch in his hands; fortunately the glass is almost empty, so only a drop stains his pants.

"Put the glass down," says Ikuko – "not on the table, on the coaster! Honestly, if this isn't a sixty-year-old infant I'm living with!"

I remember Yasushi mentioning earlier another guest who would be joining us. Yasushi's enthusiasm is plain. I don't know how the others feel, but to me it seems a shame, an intrusion. Kazue's flight seems a symbol of the fractured harmony. I have more to say to Ghost. Maybe that's what I like best about him – he is the one person I know who makes me feel I have something to say.

Scene Twelve

Yasushi returns from the hallway followed not by one but by two newcomers – who, to my astonishment, I recognize before he introduces them. They are no less astonished at the sight of me.

"Imagine," Yasushi is saying, "this gentleman claims descent from no less a personage than Watanabe Kazan! We met at a public bath. He dozed off in the tub and mumbled 'Watanabe' in his sleep. 'At your service,' I said, not realizing I was waking him up. Yes, fate – or God, if you prefer" – that with a grin at Ghost – "works in mysterious ways! The young lady I don't know, but" – with a gracious bow to her – "you are most welcome. Come, let me introduce you. My wife Ikuko, my son-in-law who among us goes by the name Ghost..."

But Maeda and Tomoko are both staring at me – as I am, of course, at them. Yasushi, noticing at last, makes a joke of it: "They are dazzled at the sight of the famous Professor Horiuchi – who can blame them?"

Maeda comes forward. "How are you, professor? We haven't met since – "

"Ah, so you do know each other!" exclaims Yasushi.

" – since the day the Alexandria burned down."

Tomoko too has mastered her slight discomposure. Smiling, she offers me her hand. "And *we* haven't met," she says, "since... when was it?"

A faint whimper from the kitchen reminds us of Kazue. "My daughter's in the kitchen with the baby," says Yasushi. "She'll join us soon. But how

174

is it, Masa, you come to know these young people?"

I glance at Tomoko, not sure what to say, or what to make of her being with Maeda. But she, not at all disconcerted, answers for me. "I'm a friend of his son's."

"Which reminds me," says Yasushi – "after all this time I've yet to meet the young man!" Laughing, he says to me, "Ever since that first time, I've associated him in my mind with tea!" And then, "Where is he now? Why not call him and have him come over?"

"Yes, let's," says Tomoko.

"I don't know where he is," I say. "Lately our paths don't seem to…. don't seem to cross much."

"I'll call him," says Tomoko. She takes her cell phone from her handbag and sets her thumb in motion. The odd feeling comes over me that it is the only thing moving; everything else seems in a state of suspended animation. "No answer," she says, startling me out of my reverie. She snaps the phone shut.

Scene Thirteen

Jun awoke in a room he did not recognize, his eyes dazzled by the sunlight streaming in. As he grew accustomed to the light, he took in his surroundings. It was a small room, floored with *tatami* matting, the walls white, clean and bare except for a hanging scroll directly in front of him. What was it, a monk in meditation? It was the barest sketch, hard to make out. On the floor directly beneath the scroll, in a plain vase, was a single red flower, the only bit of color in sight. Rose? Carnation? He couldn't tell; what did he know about flowers? He himself was lying in a

175

futon in the middle of the floor. He closed his eyes. He had had a dream, a long, complex, vivid, beautiful dream, some vague glimmer of which remained, but hovering just out of reach, as though on purpose to taunt him: "You woke up, now pay the price." "But I didn't wake up on purpose..." "To hear people tell it, nobody does anything on purpose. Well, here's a hint: you were in paradise. We took you there for a glimpse, the faintest glimpse." "Who's 'we'?" "Never mind that, that's not your affair."

Yes, yes, he remembered, it was coming back to him. A young man, slightly older than Jun and wonderfully handsome, had been delegated to show him around. "We eat and drink all day long. The food never runs out, it is unfailingly delicious, and we never get full, never get fat. We fall asleep at twilight, never later, and wake at sunrise, never before." "Do you dream?" "No. The older people do, I'm told." "And... and love?" "Love?" "Yes, is there no love here?" "Not that I know of. I... I don't know... I'm not sure what you mean. Excuse me..." Yes, he remembered now. Without meaning to, he had upset the young man, who had been so friendly at first but suddenly grew reserved, guarded; he excused himself and slipped away, and it was at that moment that Jun woke up.

Tomoko... Tomoko! Her image was suddenly before him. The stabbing pain in his heart was so piercing he almost cried out – perhaps he had cried out; some faint echo of his voice seemed to hang in the air. Where was he? Would someone come? He strained his ears; no, there was no sound of approaching footsteps, no sound of anything. Perhaps he was still asleep, still dreaming. If so he might meet the young man again; if he did he would apologize, explain; perhaps they could still be friends. "I was hasty," he would say, "I spoke without understanding; tell

176

me more." No, it was no use; he was awake, fully awake; he was hungry and, remembering the bananas, he groped for them behind his pillow, realizing as he did that, far from loving Tomoko less for what she had done, he loved her more, much more, so much more that his previous love paled into the merest insignificance, the merest passing fancy, beside this new and almost frightening love he now felt for her.

Scene Fourteen

"I swear to God" – it's Ghost talking; where are we? – "if God exists, I hereby make it my life's mission to kill him. And if there are many gods, I'll hunt them down one by one..."

"You're drunk." So am I. No, not drunk, something else. When I'm drunk to this degree of confusion my head aches, but now...

"Come on , let's settle it once and for all..."

"That's not how such questions are decided," I hear myself say.

"No?"

"No. They are settled over the course of a lifetime. With your dying breath, you will know."

"Then let's die."

"Now?"

"Now."

"Is the uncertainty really so unbearable?"

Who said that? Ah, that's Tomoko swimming into view. I'd thought it was just the two of us, but evidently not.

"For my part," says Tomoko, "whether God exists or not is the most insignificant question man has ever asked himself. What earthly difference does it make?"

"Where's Yasushi?" I ask. "Where's our host?"

"The only questions that concern us are questions that are scientifically answerable. That leaves our plate full enough, believe me."

"Why shouldn't the question of God's existence be scientifically answerable?" demands Ghost.

"Because," I say, "a scientific answer would make faith unnecessary."

"It probably is," says Tomoko, ignoring me – quite pardonably, for I am aware – pleasantly aware – of making no sense, and besides, I doubt I spoke audibly, if I spoke at all. Suddenly I know where we are. This is the upstairs room, the garret, in which – when was it? – Yasushi presented me with that figurine, the fertility goddess or whatever it is, "the oldest piece of representational art in Japan." How did we get here?

"Is it just the three of us? Where are the others?"

"What others?" says Ghost. "There are no others."

"Your wife, your child... What do you mean, 'There are no others'?"

"There are..." Suddenly – I am astonished to see it – Ghost is in tears. He is sobbing. I look over at Tomoko to find her looking at me. "It takes people in different ways," she says.

"What does? What...?"

"How do you feel?"

"Light. Buoyant."

"Me too. It's a kind of soma."

"A kind of...?

"Maybe LSD, for all I know. You never know with Rogozhin. But he said it's soma. A narcotic used in ancient Vedic rituals. It was said to confer immortality. You haven't met Rogozhin, have you?"

Scene Fifteen

"Is he serious about going to Africa?" Ikuko asks Kazue.

"Oh, no. At least... I don't think so."

"Now listen to me, my girl. You are no longer a child. You are a wife and a mother, and it's time you realized that life must be lived, not simply drifted through. I'll tell you what *I* think. I think he *is* serious. There is a restlessness in him, a recklessness... You know how fond your father and I are of him, but there's something in his character that... well, something unpredictable. You never quite know what he's thinking, what he's capable of. I suppose you could say that about a great many people, maybe about everyone, but... well, there's something sometimes a little *desperate* about him. Do you see what I mean? Do you see it too? Or is it just an old woman's fancy?"

"Desperate?"

"Poor child, she hardly knows what the word means! There's a certain kind of hunger which, when food is not its object, is called desperation. Are you going to dry those dishes or not? If not, give me the dish towel, I want to finish up and go to bed, I'm tired. What time is it? Past two. Professor! Good heavens, you startled me. Where did you materialize from?"

"Ikuko, listen. I've made up my mind. I'm going to change my mode of life. I'm going to stop this senile drifting and latch on to something, *do* something..."

"It's funny – I was just talking to Kazue here about drifting."

"I owe my awakening to your son-in-law. He's an inspiring, dynamic young man. He talks straight, and something about him compels you to listen. 'You,' he said to me, 'are letting yourself go to seed, your thinking has grown sloppy, even I can see the holes in it, and God knows I'm no thinker...' He's wrong about that, he *is* a thinker, there are depths in him, pity he's all consumed by this IT business... but there, that's just what I promised him I *won't* do – spend the rest of my life muttering to myself about how golden the past was and how bleak the future is. Ikuko, I'm going to find a job, get back into the classroom, be a *real* teacher this time."

Scene Sixteen

"Where's your father?"

"I don't know," says Kazue. "Maybe he went to bed. Let's go home" – that, with a yawn, to Ghost, who is suddenly in the room with us – or perhaps he has been here all along, I'm not sure, I really am a bit... how to describe it? Confused, and yet... what's the opposite of confused? Maeda and Tomoko are here too, and Tomoko says, "What are you laughing at, Professor?" Am I laughing? Yes... yes, I believe I am.

"You're not going home at this hour," Ikuko is saying to Kazue. "You'll sleep here."

Kazue looks at Ghost, as though to gauge his reaction to this suggestion – actually more of an order than a suggestion. But Ghost is deep in conversation with Maeda, as I notice for the first time because suddenly he has raised his voice: "No, if God exists I want to know, to *know*; I have that right as a man, at least to *know*."

"Well, good luck to you," says Maeda indifferently.

"Where's the baby?" asks Ikuko.

"How can... I don't understand you, it is *the* question, *the* question, and yet – "

Kazue's piercing cry cuts him off. "The baby!" Her face drains of color. "The baby! Where's the baby? Mei-chan!"

She flies from the room – funny, I hear no footsteps...

"Professor..."

"Yes, Tomoko," for it is she.

"Do you remember you once spoke to Jun and me about love? You said love is an aberration, a disease."

"Did I say that? No, I don't remember."

"Perhaps you've changed your mind?"

"Perhaps I have."

"Yes, you seem different from the way you were then."

"Do I?"

"You told us you first met your wife in a university anthropology class. You were studying a certain African tribe to whom war was unknown. You said the chief had the power to impregnate a woman merely by looking at her with desire."

"Yes, the chief – "

"Mama!" Kazue, cradling the infant, throws herself sobbing into her mother's arms.

"What? What is it?"

"How could I have... have *forgotten*... For a moment I actually didn't *know* where she *was*!"

"Excuse me a moment." I seem to hear someone calling me – a strange feeling, for I hear no voice, just feel a kind of... a kind of pressure, as it were. I slip out of the room and go up the narrow flight of stairs, more like a ladder than a staircase, that leads to the garret. The light is on, the naked bulb dangling from the ceiling, and on the floor sits Yasushi, cross-legged, like a monk in meditation, except that on his face is a kind of smile... I say a *kind* of smile because... well, I'm not sure... his face is smiling, and his eyes, but not his lips. So *this* is where he is; but we were here before, and I don't remember Yasushi being of the company; in fact I remember wondering where he was – suddenly it seems as if   his peculiar smile is in response to that very question.

"What's that?" – a sudden ring.

"My cell phone." Tomoko. So she's here too. "Yes?" The silence deepens as she listens. "Wait a minute." She passes the phone to me. "It's for you."

"For me!... Hello?"

"Who is this?" Male voice, clearly surprised; what is Tomoko up to?

"Horiuchi."

"Hori – ? Father? What... what..."

"Jun?"

The line goes dead, and I hear myself mumble, in utter bewilderment, "What's going on?"

"Well, it's the soma. We're all a little strange tonight..."

Scene Seventeen

"Not *another* murder?"

Yes, another murder. The TV news announcer is quite certain on that point, but his extreme gravity is belied by his extreme youth – perhaps he's joking?

"The first foreign victim," says...who? Ah. Maeda.

"Is it a foreigner?"

"That's what the man just said. A nightclub hostess."

"Your noodles, gentlemen."

"Would you mind turning that off?" says Yasushi. "We're celebrating a birthday, after all!"

"Are you? How strange," says Nagai. "It's my birthday too." Laying down the tray, he shuffles over to the TV and switches it off. He looks tired; he seems to have aged since I saw him last.

"There, that's better."

So we're in Nagai's restaurant. Who's "we"? Myself, Maeda, Yasushi, Ghost. Of course, I remember now. It was I who suggested we come; I was hungry and a hot bowl of noodles seemed as if it would   hit the spot. The men agreed, the women passed, Tomoko saying she would take a taxi home, Ikuko pressing her to stay the night... how *that* ended I don't know.

"Here's my point, though." It's Yasushi, talking to Ghost. "Why is goodness not synonymous with happiness? Why doesn't our happiness *reveal* goodness? Do you see what I'm saying? Why is happiness one thing, and goodness another? If it makes me happy, it's good. Why is that not the case?"

"Because happiness is unworthy of man. Man is a seeker. He must uncover secrets, at whatever cost. He must learn the truth if it kills him. But all a happy man wants to do is preserve his happiness."

"Do you know, it's funny. Once I thought like you."

"Nagai-san here" – this is me speaking – "is the son of the novelist Nagai Kafu."

"Oh, professor..."

"Is that true?" Maeda. My words seem to have jolted him out of a reverie. "Nagai Kafu? Why, just this morning I was reading his *Strange Tale*." He turns to me. "Tomoko gave it to me. She said, 'You must read this.'"

"*Strange Tale from East of the River*?" asks Nagai, fairly pouncing on Maeda.

"Yes. Are you really his son? I didn't know Kafu had a son. He – "

"The prostitute O-yuki in that story was modeled on my mother."

183

"No! That's astonishing," says Maeda.

"Why?" I ask.

"Well... if for no other reason..."

"Well?"

"She seemed so... so intent that I read it."

"Who?"

"Tomoko."

"Ah. Tomoko. Yes. She is... remarkable. Remarkable. A remarkable woman..."

"Prophetess, scientist..."

"And literary connoisseur. Kafu. Not everyone, you know – if Nagai-san here will forgive me for saying so – goes around recommending Kafu nowadays. Or even knows he existed."

"Her grandfather owns Saito Trading Company."

"Yes, I know."

Suddenly there is noise, commotion, a blur of activity. Quiet restored, Nagai lies prone on the floor, in something like the fetal position, his white apron stained crimson. Ghost and I look at one another. What has happened? A kind of idiocy seizes hold of me – I don't know how else to express it. It has hold of Ghost too, evidently, to judge by the vacancy of his gaze. The noise reshapes itself in my mind, separates into its component elements – a door crashing open, a shot ringing out. The latter sound, of course, I know not from real life but from my acting career – once I myself was shot.

"Tazawa!"

Who said that? What about Tazawa? Maeda. He is strangely excited. No, excited is not the word. He is beside himself. "It was Tazawa! I recognized him!"

"Tazawa? You know Tazawa?"

"Oh, believe me, professor, I know Tazawa! All too well do I know Tazawa! All too – "

"Call an ambulance, somebody!" Yasushi – I had forgotten about him.

No, it isn't possible, it isn't possible! I have no memory of leaving the restaurant, but I am in the street; I'd thought it was night, but the sun is rising; of course, the nights are short now; there are people around; it's too early to go to work; most of the passers-by are walking dogs; yes, the dog population has risen dramatically lately; I read about it just recently, some sort of dog boom;   it'll be a hot day, by the looks of it; I'd better get... I'd better... hm..."

Scene Eighteen

The only true life is *here*. How stupid I was ever to think otherwise, ever to leave. Here in my study, at my desk, surrounded by my books, my beloved books... what, what tempted me outside? What is lacking here that I hoped to find there? Stupid, crazy. For young people, of course, it's different, they can't be expected to know... But at my age... Two things, two things only, are missing: a lock on the door, and... and... well, a toilet. One can live without food, at least until one dies, but the lack of a toilet... such a trivial object, scarcely worthy of mention, and yet without it, my whole plan crumbles to dust. You've guessed, of course. My study is to be my crypt, my tomb, my Egyptian pyramid. Yes. How long does it take, I wonder, the passage from life to death? Antigone, now – she was to have starved to death in the cave in which Creon, the king, had imprisoned her for her disobedience, her determination to bury her rebel brother in defiance of the king's express command. Impatient, she hanged herself. Creon was not wicked, only misguided. The ancient Greeks did not think of good and evil as we do; evil is not the tragedian's problem. My students were not interested in this. How could they not have been? My subject was the nature of man – how can it have seemed trivial to them, even granted their youth and inexperience? I tried to tell them, tried to... to *wake them up*; but I failed. My head was on fire, but the fire burned inwardly, invisibly to them; all *they* saw was my fumbling, mumbling, limp, shambling exterior; it's my fault, not theirs, I've no right to blame them; and yet... no, I'm being too harsh on myself; my ineffectual mumbling was the *result* of their indifference, the *result,* not the cause. When you're facing a room full of bored, yawning faces, focused, if on anything, on their cell phones, some actually talking into them even as I spoke... But that's not the point. I was thinking: how long does it take for death to come to a man who takes no food? Isn't there a character in *The Tale of Genji* who starves to death? I believe there is. Do I have the *Genji* here? Of course I do. It's years since I read it. Will I have time to finish it, if I start it now? But if I'm to do this right, I must order my priorities. Reading *Genji* will not help me clarify how the Greeks saw good and evil. Or... is that necessarily true? I remember now; I'd forgotten – how *could* I have forgotten? – I'd begun to *see* things, things no one else was seeing, threads linking Greek tragedy to Japanese tragedy. Are they one and the same thing, in different forms? That was the question I was starting to raise in class. Here, I said to my students, is a genuine inquiry, let us pursue it together, let us be fellow seekers of truth!

Hm. Will I be strong enough to resist the hunger pangs, when they start? I have never been strong, never. I've never *had* to be strong. Maybe my students saw that in me, and knew that my talk was just talk. Tragedy's theme is the elevating quality of suffering. How could I, who have never suffered, never been wrung by fate, speak convincingly on such a theme? What a sham I must have seemed to them! They saw through me – of course they did! No, I never suffered. I have no *capacity* for suffering – I'm not made of the stuff of Oedipus or Antigone; I'm a fraud, an actor – well, yes, an actor, but even as an actor, I wasn't a *real* actor, just a guy in front of a camera going through the motions of acting. What... who's there? A lock on the door; the door has to be locked for this to work, locked, locked! As it is Jun will come home, he'll walk blithely in, smile that smile of his, say "Hello father," and all my plans, my carefully laid plans... Perhaps I'll just disembowel myself, samurai fashion. Once I did – in a movie. It was my best role. At least that's what the critics said.

Scene Nineteen

Why doesn't whoever it is go away? A peddler, if it's one of them, will ring, at most, twice and then give up and go on to the next house; he has a whole neighborhood to cover and no time to waste, but... five rings already, and now a sixth! Can it be Yasushi? Yes, it's probably him; I remember his first visit, when he rang the bell; at first I thought it was Takeshi... well, maybe it is Takeshi. Come to think of it, I haven't seen Takeshi in ages. Saint Takeshi. Ha ha. Yes, maybe he is a kind of saint. Maybe in some unconscious fashion I've been calling him, and he, being a saint, gifted with an inner ear attuned to such calls, heard, and is now coming to me in answer.

Wearily I get to my feet. Why wearily? What labor has caused me to be weary?

The ringing has turned to knocking. My weariness turns to fear – fear of this unknown being who is so determined to come face to face with me. It is not natural. A robber? I am known to have won a lottery, and therefore, presumably, presumed to be rich... but a robber doesn't pound on the door seeking admission... unless... unless what?

"Professor! Professor! It's me! Open up!"

"Me," is it? I am halfway down the stairs.

"Professor! Professor!"

It's Ghost. Unmistakably it's him. He has a slight lisp, hardly noticeable until you happen to notice it, but once you have...

"Ghost! What...?"

"Why didn't you answer? Come with me, I want to show you something."

He seizes me by the hand and fairly drags me outside. He is laughing, laughing hysterically. "They'll lock me up in a madhouse for sure. Oh, it's too much!"

"Where are we going? Let me lock the door at least."

"There's no time. It's very close... Look."

Along the wall of the little white church two streets over from my house is a scrawled message in red spray paint: "There is no God."

"Well? Why don't you say something?"

"You did that?"

"I was going to add an exclamation point – 'There is no God!' – but...well, maybe there *should* be an exclamation point, what do you think? Should it be spoken quietly and calmly, or shouted? That is the question! The ones I did in Tokyo have an exclamation point."

There was nobody, not a soul around. "You fool, it's *me* they'll suspect!"

"You?" Ghost's surprise is perfectly genuine. "Why would they suspect you?"

188

"Let's get out of here."

I jerk my hand free and stride as rapidly as my short little legs permit in the direction of my house, leaving him to follow or not as he pleases. He does follow. I close the door behind him and lock it.

"You're very careful about locking the door," he says. "I wouldn't've thought it'd be necessary, in a community like this."

"Would you like some tea?"

"Is your son home? I'd like to meet him."

"No, he's not home. Where's Kazue? Aren't you supposed to be at work?"

"Let's go into your study. It's up these stairs, isn't it? Wow!"

His childish awe as he enters the room is so characteristic of him somehow that I can't help laughing.

"I've never *seen* so many books!"

"Yes, well, over a lifetime they do accumulate."

Scene Twenty

"So!" The way he sits across from me, his elbows on the desk and his chin resting in his hands, reminds me of Jun. Ghost is older, of course – and black, of course. Would anyone, looking at him, guess there was Japanese blood in him? What an effect he must have on strangers, when he opens his mouth and unleashes his pure, idiomatic Japanese, indistinguishable from theirs except for being, perhaps, more passionate, and in all probability better, richer, for he is an unusually articulate young man. "Tell me…" He pauses, idly picking up a book on the desk. "*An Introduction to Cultural Anthropology.* Hm. Ah, that reminds me! What was that about the African chief who impregnates women merely by looking at them?"

189

"Yes, I've been looking through my old books... The chief? It's amazing, really, how... *adaptable* the world is to our way of looking at it. There's no such thing as reality, there's only..."

"Illusion?"

"No, not that either."

"Well what, then?"

"There's another tribe I remember reading about. The eldest son had to kill the father. It was required by custom, accepted by all, unquestioned by anyone. If a man chanced to die in any other fashion, except in battle, it was deemed a great misfortune, an appalling disgrace."

"What's your point?"

"My point? I'm not making a point, I'm... hm. Speaking of impregnating women... do you know the Greek myth of Zeus and Io? She was a princess of Argos and a priestess of Hera. Zeus fancied her and turned her into a cow so Hera, his wife, wouldn't suspect. But Hera was not deceived, and sent a gadfly to torment the poor girl and give her no rest as she fled its sting. It drove her through the wild places of the earth, home to savages and monsters. Only when she arrived at last in Egypt was the punishment revoked, and Zeus came to her again, impregnating her by the breath of his nostrils."

Ghost looks at me, his own nostrils flaring with impatience. "There must be a point to all this. You're trying to tell me something."

"No, you're mistaken, I just..."

"What did you mean when I showed you my spray-painting and you said, 'It's me they'll suspect'?"

"Did I say that? I'm not sure. I'm not sure what I meant. Probably nothing more than that I don't like what you're doing."

"Don't you? Wouldn't you prefer to live in a world free of nonsense, if you could?"

"I'm not sure I would. Nonsense, as you call it– "

"As I call it!"

"Don't take offense. When you have lived a bit longer you will realize that nonsense is a gift of the gods, without which..."

"What's this?"

He rises to his feet suddenly and strides to the bookshelf on which rests the ancient figurine. He takes it in his hands and examines it with interest. Then he turns a quizzical gaze on me. "What *is* this?"

"Your father-in-law gave it to me. I'm not sure what it is exactly. He told me it's the oldest piece of representational art in Japan. A fertility goddess, perhaps."

"My father-in-law gave this to you?"

"Yes, as a token of friendship."

"How would he have gotten it, I wonder?"

"He never showed it to you?"

"No."

"Hm."

"You and he go back... how many years?"

"We were children together. He was four years older, and took me under his wing. He was my master and I his disciple."

Ghost is silent, contemplating the little object with unwonted absorption. The expression on his face is new to me. It is almost rapt. He speaks at last, his tone now almost shy. "It's a lot to ask, but... would you let me have this? As a... well, a token of friendship."

"No, I'm sorry." I am surprised to hear myself say this – astonished. Why am I rebuffing an overture that gives me so much pleasure? But if Ghost is offended he doesn't show it – which, in Ghost's case, is as much as to say he is not offended.

191

Replacing the figurine on the shelf, he picks up the *Introduction to Cultural Anthropology* and, as though nothing had happened, says, "Can I borrow this?"

"Of course."

"I won't keep it long, I just..." He laughs suddenly, a ringing, boyish laugh. His white teeth gleam against his black face. "I don't know what I just. Goodbye for now. I'll come again. May I?"

"You are always welcome."

"Talking to you is... I don't know. You don't say much, but the little you do say... kind of makes me want to either punch you or go back to school. Sometimes both. Goodbye, I have to run, they'll miss me at work. I'm sort of on probation as it is..."

Scene Twenty-one

Haruyuki Maeda pushed open the door of the police *koban* and stepped inside. He found himself in a little room furnished with three desks, two of which were occupied by uniformed officers, one very young and the other, grizzled and ruddy, verging on elderly. It was the young one who, with a wordless look of inquiry, addressed himself to the newcomer. Just then the phone rang, a startlingly loud, brazen jangle, at which Maeda fairly jumped. The noise broke off immediately, however, as the elderly officer snatched the receiver. "Yes," he barked.

The younger officer continued to regard Maeda quizzically. But Maeda was unable to gather his thoughts. He was distracted by the elderly officer. His voice was husky, throaty, gravelly, and Maeda suddenly recalled, though there was nothing obvious to bring it to mind, a story he'd read recently of a young man accused – falsely, it turned out much later – of groping a girl on a crowded train. The man was seized by other passengers and dragged off the train at the next station. Maeda imagined himself in the man's place, hauled before just such an officer as this hoarse elderly one. What chance would he have against him, however innocent he might be? His defenses, however firm to begin with, would crumble in an instant. All this flashed in no time through his mind. The young officer, seeking no doubt to encourage him but betraying more than a hint of impatience, said in a flat, emotionless tone, "Yes?"

"I'm sorry..." What was he apologizing for? For his sudden and most inopportune attack of speechlessness. Why had he come here? No one had pressed him to. But having come, he must speak. With a wrenching effort to disengage his mind from the elderly officer's voice, he began, "I've come to report..." How did one go about saying these things? For a seasoned journalist, he really was, at bottom, a ridiculously unworldly character. "It's regarding the murder at the noodle shop..."

"Noodle shop?"

He explained as best he could, but it was difficult; every thread of coherent thought seemed under malicious, spiteful attack by the elderly officer's grating voice. "It happened two weeks ago, the murdered man was the proprietor, his name was Nagai, he was the son of..." Flushing, he broke off; the name Nagai Kafu wasn't likely to mean much here. "I was there, I witnessed the murder, I can identify the perpetrator."

The young officer regarded him steadily through narrowed, squinting eyes. Other than the squint, there was not the trace of an expression on his face to suggest to Maeda how he was taking this. Nor did he speak. Was this standard procedure, learned at the police academy, a trick to unsettle a person and make him blurt out more than he means to? The telephone talk could be that too, for all he knew. On seeing him enter they could have made it ring, and now the elderly officer was talking to no one, his purpose merely to rattle the newcomer and annihilate his defenses. As if in response to the thought the officer suddenly slammed the receiver into the cradle, in such a manner as to make it clear the call was being terminated on his, rather than the caller's, initiative. He immediately turned his attention to some papers on the desk, according Maeda's existence not the faintest acknowledgment.

His narrowed eyes still fixed on Maeda, the young officer spoke at last, very quietly. "You can identify the perpetrator?"

"His name is Tazawa. I know him. We grew up together. He's responsible for other murders as well. At least... I think he is..."

"You think?"

"I mean to say..." Why had he come? Why? He had known this would happen, that he, Maeda, would end up being regarded as a suspect; that's the way the police are – everyone they encounter is a suspect, they can't relate to people on any other terms; if their glance falls on you, you're a suspect; he'd been a reporter, he *knew*... And yet he had come anyway! He closed his eyes to steady himself, took a deep breath, and proceeded as best he could with his explanation. "I'm not absolutely sure as to the others, but I was a witness to this one. I... I recognized him clearly."

"And yet you waited two weeks..."

Yes, that was damning, he could see that. Anyone, not only a police officer, would wonder about that. Either you did a thing like this immediately, or you didn't do it at all.

"I was afraid, shaken, I haven't been well..."
Why did he add that about not being well? Like a
child casting about for excuses for missing class –
that's how he must look!

"What other murders do you think he is
responsible for?"

"There's been a wave of murders in Tokyo over
the past year. I believe... I have *reason* to believe –
that he's behind them. I used to... I... I'm a former
reporter with the *Maiasa Shimbun*. I talked to him.
He told me about a... a cult he belongs to, a cult
that... worships evil..." "They'll think I'm mad!" it
suddenly struck him.

Scene Twenty-two

Maeda was startled by a sudden clattering
noise. Looking up, he saw the elderly officer
pushing back his chair and rising to his feet. He
was not a tall man, nor conspicuously heavyset,
but his slightly forward stoop, the hunch of his
shoulders, and a certain air he had of being under
pressure from some invisible weight he bore, gave
him a strangely massive appearance. Instinctively
Maeda stepped back a pace. In the officer's
extended right hand was a paper. When Maeda
evidently failed to understand his silent invitation
to take it, he barked, "This?"

Maeda's hand trembled as he took it. His
feeling was of having, of his own free will – his own
free stupidity, rather – pushed open a door he
might just as easily have left closed, and entered a
world he might just as well not have entered, but
now, having entered it, there was no escape; the
old world, imperfect but familiar and therefore
somehow negotiable, was lost to him forever. At

the top of the paper he read, "ONLY EVIL CAN CURE THE WORLD."

He swallowed. "Yes. This."

"So you know the man who wrote this, do you?"

"Yes."

"His name's Tazawa, you say."

"Yes."

"And in your opinion this Mr. Tazawa is not simply a bored and idle young man having a laugh at our expense but actually means what he says."

"Yes."

"Means every word of it."

"Yes, I think..."

"'Destroy the world *in order to save it.*' 'The world is critically ill.' 'Cut mercilessly, cut without pity.'" He paused. Maeda noticed out of the corner of his eye that the young officer had retreated to his desk, and a comical thought somehow found its way into his mind: that the phone would ring, and now it would be the young officer's turn to play the distracting role.

"You smile? You find it amusing?"

"I'm sorry. No. It's anything but amusing. Tazawa is capable of anything."

"And when did you first become aware of that – that Mr. Tazawa is 'capable of anything'?"

"When?"

"When? Weeks ago? Months ago? Years?"

"We... we grew up together. In a way I think I've always known it."

"How many lives would you have saved in coming to us sooner?"

"Some. Some, no doubt. I... I'll never forgive myself..."

"I suppose you are one of those who think there's not much to choose from between criminals and cops."

"No!"

"I suppose you yourself weren't a member of the 'cult that worships evil'."

"Me!"

"And that you come to us only after falling out with Tazawa, over – "

"No! No!"

"Over a woman, for example."

"A woman!"

"Or over power, leadership. Who leads, who follows. Who gives the orders, who takes them. Do you think this 'cult that worships evil' is anything new? Do you think we haven't dealt with the likes of you before, that we don't deal with them every day? Do you think evil is your invention?"

Maeda's head reeled. There was simply no replying to this onslaught, at least not in his distracted state. Beer – if only he could have a sip of cold beer, just a sip; that would clear his head and enable him to give a worthy and credible account of himself; but he could hardly ask this enraged officer for a beer; and yet was he to be doomed for want of such a simple and everyday commodity?

Suddenly he thought of something. The thought was so simple, so obvious – why hadn't it occurred to him long ago? Possibly it was the word "invention" that had suggested it to him. The mind is a capricious and unreliable instrument – his was, at any rate. He closed his eyes and took a deep breath.

"Tazawa doesn't give the orders," he said, aghast at his inability to keep his voice from trembling. "The strings are pulled by a Russian, a man named Rogozhin..."

The officer glared at him. The silence seemed to go on so long that Maeda began to doubt he had spoken. Whether he had or not, the thought of Rogozhin brought in its wake another thought, that of Yoshiko, whose image in turn suggested the image of the woman who had supplanted her, not only in his life but, it seemed, even in his memory – Tomoko. Where was she now? Where was Yoshiko? Dead, murdered. Should he report that to the officer? No, he could hardly do so, at this late date, without appearing complicit.

Scene Twenty-three

"Before," said Yoshiko, "I had many fears. What wasn't I afraid of? I was afraid of everything! Now I have only one fear – that you will stop loving me."

"But why?" protested Rogozhin. "How can that happen? How can you suppose...?"

"I can suppose because I know how unworthy I am of being loved by you! *You* don't know... but one day you *will* know... and... and... when that day comes..."

"That day will never come, Yoshiko, never. Not while there is breath in me."

Yoshiko was unable altogether to suppress a giggle. "Sometimes you talk just like an opera."

"It is sometimes hard for me to express my true feelings in Japanese. It comes out stiff, awkward."

"I love the way you speak Japanese."

"I will teach you Russian, so that I may love the way you speak it."

"I'm hopeless at languages."

"We'll see. Japanese is a language of limits, confined spaces. When one speaks Japanese one is forever conscious of the towering mountains just behind and the sea-pounded coast just in front. Russian is the language of the boundless steppe, the endless tundra. When a Russian speaks Japanese, or a Japanese Russian, he becomes a different person. You will see... Yesterday I submitted my resignation to the embassy."

"Your resignation!"

"You are surprised. Why? How can we go to Patagonia if I don't resign?"

"Are we really going to Patagonia?"

"Isn't that what you wanted?"

"Yes, in my dreams, but..."

"Your life has not taught you that dreams can be made to come true. You will see. It may be that I have as much to teach you as you have to teach me."

"As I have to teach you! What can I possibly...?"

"Shh... Yoshiko! You have taught me so much already! From whom have I learned, if not from you, that life is a miracle, that life is a gift, that life rises triumphant from the ashes of the most desolate misery! *You* have taught me that, Yoshiko, you and nobody else. You woke me from the dead, Yoshiko. From worse than death."

"The day will come, Rogozhin, when you'll see me as I really am, not as you want to see me, and... you'll hate me. The more you love me now, the more you'll hate me then."

"Yoshiko, if you knew, if you knew how you torment me..."

"You will compare me to your wife and find me lacking."

"No, Yoshiko. I swear to you..."

"You swear – but I can see the expression on your face! You can't see it but I can! I saw how your expression clouded over at the mention of her. I am in competition with a dead woman who can never diminish herself in your eyes by the petty little things a person does in the course of everyday life! Oh, Rogozhin, Rogozhin! Kill me, that I may compete with her on equal terms!"

"There will be no pettiness in our lives, Yoshiko. Everything we do will be touched by grace. How do I know? Because I feel it. I feel it so powerfully, and see it so clearly, so clearly, that I cannot be mistaken. It is up to me now to prove it to you, so that you feel it and see it as clearly as I do. And you *will* see it, Yoshiko, you *will* feel it. But you must be patient. It takes time. And so for now I will ask one thing of you – one thing only, but a great thing: that you trust me. Can I ask that of you, Yoshiko? Trust. I have no right to ask it, but I dare to ask it anyway – because it is better than dying, and a condition for living. Will you trust me, Yoshiko?"

When she was silent he pursued, "Will you try, at least?"

Her eyes closed, she murmured almost inaudibly, "I'll try."

Scene Twenty-four

How long Jun lay in a state between sleeping and waking he could not have said. His mind worked, but it worked strangely. He was, in a manner of speaking, conscious of being unconscious – unaware of the passage of time but not unaware of time as an entity; unaware of where he was, but knowing he was unaware, and yet not wondering on that account. He was aware of people coming and going – two people in particular, a man and a woman, who seemed quite concerned about him, and he could have quite easily reassured them that he was fine, at peace, even happy – but he chose not to, and it was not out of malice, for there was no such thing in his heart, but something else – again, he knew not what. "This is all very strange," he would think to himself, and yet the truth was it hardly felt strange at all; it felt perfectly ordinary, and he would have been content to persist in this state for the rest of his life.

Awake or asleep, he thought constantly of Tomoko – with love, but without longing. Why should he long for her? He possessed her, possessed her more completely than he ever had before, more completely than he could have believed possible.

"Wrap me in folds of night."

"He's awake!"

"He said something."

"What did you say, son? We didn't catch it."

Jun opened his eyes. The man and the woman of whose presence he had been intermittently aware – he knew them at once – hovered over him, their faces simultaneously reflecting relief and anxiety in equal measure. "What did you say?" asked the woman, echoing the man. "Can we get you something? You must be hungry."

"Wrap me in folds of night. That's a poem... I think... I'm a poet, you see. A sort of poet. Hungry? Yes."

"You stay with him," said the woman. "I'll go downstairs and fix him something."

"Nothing heavy," said the man. "A little *miso* soup, nothing more." To Jun he said, "We were afraid we'd lost you."

"Lost me? But I wonder..." He tried to raise himself to a sitting position, but found the effort exhausted him, and sank back on the pillow. "Would you mind... could I trouble you for a pen and paper? Just a scrap, so I can write down my poem before I forget it. It would be a pity if I did, before I could recite it to Mr. Saito. I think he'd like it. Don't you? He loves poems."

"A pen and paper. Yes, sure... Wait here, I'll be right back."

Left alone, Jun closed his eyes. "'Wrap me in folds of night' – is that really a poem? It sounds like a poem, it feels like a poem... Tomoko, I know, will say, 'Work on it, develop it, polish it.'" He smiled. "She's right, of course, but I'll explain to her: 'It came to me in that place between waking and sleeping – that's the way poems are there!' And she'll understand – is there anything she doesn't understand? She'll smile and ruffle my hair and say, 'It's beautiful, Jun.'"

"Here you are, son." The man seemed slightly out of breath as he handed Jun a somewhat stubby pencil and a small sheet of paper with, printed on top, "Enomoto Grocery," followed by an address and phone number.

"Enomoto Grocery?"

"Does it matter, that being there? It's the only paper I could find."

"Oh, no, no, not at all." He hastily scribbled the poem and said, "Look how childish my handwriting is."

"Here's Yoko with your soup. Can you sit up? Here, let me help you."

Passively surrendering to the man's ministrations, Jun allowed himself to be propped up, and took the steaming bowl from Yoko, who said, "Careful, it's hot."

Scene Twenty-five

His recovery proceeded apace, and soon he was able to get out of bed unassisted. "Don't push yourself," Yoko advised. "You mustn't tax your strength."

"But I have no right... how can I have..."

"Don't be silly, it's nothing."

"How long have I been here?"

"No time at all."

He learned that Yoko and her brother, Yuji, ran the grocery shop together. It had been their parents'; they had grown up in the shop. When their parents had retired, Yuji took it over; as for Yoko, she had unexpectedly married into a wealthy family, and now, a widow with three grown children, none of whom lived in Japan, though they did come back to visit periodically from their various corners of the earth, had moved back "home," over Yuji's protestations that with her money she should "make a real life for herself." This *was* real life, she insisted; she wanted nothing more.

Yuji evidently had a knack for business, at least for the grocery business, for he had singlehandedly turned a floundering little shop into a thriving concern. Then, fourteen years ago, he had been struck by tragedy – his son died.

"It hit him very hard," said Yoko when she and Jun were alone, sipping tea. "He loved that boy, doted on him. Well, of course, all good parents love their children. You suffer their pains, delight in their joys, and when something happens to them... Someday you'll understand; you can't possibly now. What was I saying?... He was fifteen, on his way to baseball practice when an old man lost control of his car and hit four kids. Yusuke was killed, another boy ended up paralyzed. It was too sudden – too absurd, I guess you could say. You can't take it in, you can't even grieve properly. He and I are about as close as a brother and sister can be, and yet in my presence he has never so much as shed a tear. Some people thought him cold, unfeeling. They'd see him in the shop, working as usual, greeting customers with a smile as though nothing had happened, and they'd say to themselves, 'Here's a man who has just lost his son – can he have forgotten him already?' Oh, no,

203

he didn't forget, outward appearances are deceiving."

"Sh! On the stairs, footsteps; he's coming..."

"Oh, you needn't worry. He won't mind our talking about it. If he would, you can be sure I wouldn't. I was just telling Jun about Yusuke," she said as Yuji came into the room.

Yuji took his wallet out of his pants pocket, and from his wallet extracted an old, somewhat tattered photograph, which he handed to Jun. "This is him. It was taken less than a week before he died."

Jun looked at the photograph. It showed a rather ordinary-looking boy, in a baseball uniform, smiling a little stiffly, apparently self-conscious in front of the camera. Jun had no idea what to say.

"How about a little walk?" Yuji proposed suddenly. "If you feel strong enough. It's a beautiful evening. I'll take him to the grove," he said to Yoko – "if you don't mind taking over downstairs for a bit." He reached out a hand and took back the photograph, returning it to the wallet without, so it seemed to Jun, even glancing at it. "It's beautiful in the grove at this time. Come. A little air will do you good."

Scene Twenty-six

One would never have suspected there was such a place in the neighborhood, with its clutter of small shops, gas stations, hole-in-corner restaurants and seedy little bars. Yuji called it "the grove" – weed patch would perhaps be a more apt description, but he was right, Jun thought, to call it beautiful in spite of its rather scrubby appearance. The sun, still bright, was just beginning to set, and the one wisp of cloud in the sky was tinged ever so slightly with pink. There was a sort of path, whether made deliberately or simply trodden down by people chancing to pass that way Jun could not say, though he noted that just then there was no one in sight except the two of them. Leaning lightly on Yuji's arm, Jun took one halting step at a time. He could have managed quite well without support, but his strength seemed disinclined to assert itself. That was all his illness amounted to, really – a warm, rather pleasant lassitude. Birds were singing, a regular chorus of them. Strangely enough, he only became aware of it now, for the first time.

"Look," said Yuji. He paused before a tiny flower at his feet, a tiny pale blue flower that Jun on his own would never have noticed, and yet Yuji gazed at it, rapt. After a time he resumed his walk, Jun following. He expected Yuji to say something about the flower, to explain what about it had drawn his attention, but no, not a word. They came at length to a little stream, bordered by a wooden fence. Again Yuji paused, leaning on the fence and gazing into the flowing, rippling stream. Not at all impatient, Jun adapted himself to Yuji's pace. He seemed to have no will of his own. Sometimes, pausing, Yuji would murmur, "Look," and point out a flower, or a little bug crawling on a leaf, or a bird. At last, seeming to emerge from a kind of reverie, he said, "Come, we'd better go back, we mustn't tire you." And Jun submitted as passively and contentedly to this as he had to everything else.

Scene Twenty-seven

"Misako! Misako, you're back!" I'm so glad to see her I astonish myself; have I ever, ever in my life, been as happy as I am at this moment? But she is stern: "Why aren't you eating? What's the matter with you?"

"I... I'll eat, Misako, I'll eat, let's go downstairs, we'll fix something. I'm sorry, I've been... I think I'm entering my second childhood, Misako."

"You've been three days without food."

"Three days? Is it three days? But you know, I don't even feel hungry. I've been reading, Misako. But... you've come. That's the important thing. Come, we'll go downstairs and talk as we eat."

"Where's Jun?"

"Jun? I don't know. He's grown up now, you see. He comes and goes at his pleasure. He has that girlfriend of his."

"You're making a mistake about Jun."

"What mistake?"

"You imagine he's grown up, you deal with him as one adult to another. You're wrong. He's still a child. He needs a father's guidance."

"And a mother's."

"Yes, I've failed him. I feel it keenly."

"Do you know, Misako, these last few days... I feel somehow as if I'm only now starting to live, as though everything up to now has been... has been... not playacting exactly... a kind of rehearsal, for what's to come. But Misako... you'll stay, won't you? I so want you to stay, and I'm so afraid you'll..."

"I'll stay as long as you want me to. My staying or leaving is entirely up to you."

"Up to me! How can that be, Misako? You said before... you sent me to Yasushi, you said it all depended on him."

"Yes, and you went to him, and as a result it now depends on you."

"I don't understand."

206

"No. There are certain things you have to be in my state to understand. The figurine was the key, you see. It had to be in your hands."

"The figurine? What does that have to do with...? I almost gave it away!"

"It's fortunate you didn't."

"But... the figurine... Yasushi gave it to me a long time ago. Why didn't you come immediately?"

"Time is not so much a factor in our world as it is in yours. We'll talk of this afterwards. For now, I want you to eat something. What is there in the fridge? Masao, listen to me. In a sense you were right in saying you were only now beginning to live."

"Yes, I feel..."

"Do you remember when you left me?"

"Can you think I've forgotten? The anguish that tears my heart... You see, Misako, I didn't understand... didn't understand that... you loved me, and that your love... I was blind, Misako, blind."

"I can't blame you. I didn't understand that I loved you either. Only after you left did I understand, only when it was too late. Only in the awful desolation..."

"But Misako, if only you'd... if only..."

"Yes, 'if only.' But I was a passionate young woman who didn't understand her own passions. How real they seemed then, and how unreal, how unimportant, even comical they seem now!"

"Only tell me one thing, Misako, that you're here to stay and won't ever leave."

"I've already told you, I'll stay as long as you want me to."

Scene Twenty-eight

Yes, a new life is beginning for me now. Misako is asleep, she's exhausted, she fell asleep as soon as her head touched the pillow, just as she used to do! We used to laugh about how easily she slipped from wakefulness into sleep – in mid-sentence, sometimes; while I... sleep simply wouldn't come! Sleep found me unworthy of her ministrations, I suppose, or maybe, being so occupied with Misako, she simply had no attention to spare for me, and I would lie awake for hours, fretting, tormented... But now I don't want to sleep. Now I would grudge every minute of consciousness sacrificed to unconsciousness. What time is it? I have no idea not the faintest; I only know it's pitch dark and has been for hours, and may it go on being dark forever!

Misako. Does she know, she who seems to know everything, how I hated her? It's terrifying to hate somebody like that. Why, I could have murdered her! Why? What did she do to me that I hated her with such fearful, fearful intensity? Nothing. She was blameless; even then I knew she was blameless; I blamed her for nothing. It happened like this: one day the woman I loved I loved no longer. That's all. Why did I love her no longer? For no reason. No reason I can think of. Loving her, I had thought her beautiful; not loving her, I found her not merely ordinary but ugly, hideous... Just recalling it is making my hands tremble; look: they are shaking uncontrollably. It is strange how little our feelings have to do with reality, our most powerful, most irresistible feelings...

But she's forgiven me, she's come back to me. Oh, I have so much to make up for! And I will. I'll make it up to her. Look at me, shedding tears like a child! Well, let them flow. Tears are cleansing, purifying...

Scene Twenty-nine

It had been cloudy and threatening rain when Maeda entered the police box, but he stepped out of it into dazzling sunshine. He walked without knowing or wondering where; the crowd into which he had merged absorbed his personal identity, and he surrendered it without regret. There had been a moment in his interview with the officers when, reasonably or not, he expected to be arrested; his arrest seemed to him so certain that in his mind he surrendered his freedom, if not willingly at least without resistance, and was bewildered, even oddly disconcerted, when the moment passed; more so almost than he would have been by the clang of a cell door shutting. Recalling these feelings as he trudged along, he could not account for them; they made no sense to him – had the whole episode been a dream? It had been *like* a dream – but no, it had occurred; one wakes from a dream, however lifelike, and knows it for a dream. This was not that; this was reality.

"Where shall I go?" he asked himself, but mechanically, without urgency; the traffic light at which he had stopped with the crowd turned green, and, with the crowd, he proceeded. How long he walked on in that half-awake mental state he could not have said and did not consider. Suddenly he stopped short. He felt someone bump him from behind, but his abrupt return to consciousness, as it were, was no lasting obstacle to the crowd, which instantly made the necessary adaptation and surged around him. His mind suddenly was full of Tomoko. The cause was not mysterious. There she was, on a movie marquee. It was not her, of course, and even the resemblance, on closer inspection, was far from close; the actress was older, prettier, and wearing a beautiful figured kimono, which it would be hard to imagine on Tomoko, or Tomoko's awkward body doing justice to. Still, for some reason, she had suggested Tomoko to Maeda, and now at least he had an object in view – he would, he *must*, get in touch with Tomoko.

That was easier said than done. Her cell phone, as he knew from past experience, was off more often than it was on; when she was busy with her studies she was as inaccessible as if she'd been whisked physically to those other corners of the universe she researched. "Dark matter." She laughed at her "simpleminded" boyfriend for his inability to even conceive of such a thing. Did she think he, Maeda, was any less simpleminded in that regard? Interesting, he thought, that Jun continued to be spoken of as the "boyfriend," while he, Maeda, was... what? The widower of the woman whose murder she, Tomoko, had connived at! – if not actually committed.

"How is it," he wondered, "that the thought doesn't appall me? How is it that, instead of shrinking from her in horror, I... How is it that... instead of making my flesh crawl she has set it on fire, with cravings I would imagine are more familiar to the drug addict than to the lover? And... how is it that Yoshiko's death leaves me so indifferent? It makes no sense, it makes no sense! Can a man know himself so little? Can a man be such a stranger to himself? Is it possible? Is everyone like that, or am I some kind of freak?"

Scene Thirty

"Well, tell me, son, you're a poet..."

"Oh, no, no!" Jun protested, but Yuji seemed not to hear. He was a little drunk, as was Jun, for Yuji had brought up to Jun's room a bottle of Japanese saké and two saké cups, and though they sipped unhurriedly, it had been going on for some time.

"Tell me," Yuji pursued. "To a man who has lost *everything* – is life worth living?"

"I don't know... what do you mean?"

"Lost *everything*. Wife, dead. Children, dead. Business, gone. Reasons for living,   none. Would such a man be right to say, 'Life on these terms is senseless, the only reasonable thing is to put an end to it'? Or should he say, 'As long as a man is alive he has that one gift which is more precious than all others, more precious than wife, children, wealth... and that most precious gift of all is life itself, and I have it, therefore, whatever I have lost, I am blessed.' What do you think, son? You have youth, and you have poetry. I really want to know what you think."

"What I think is that... that love..."

"Yes?"

"Love... I don't know, I don't know!"

"Look at that laughing sage there."

"Eh?"

Yuji pointed to the hanging scroll above the red flower in the unadorned earthenware vase. "I drew it myself, and it's very bad, you can hardly even tell he's laughing. Wait." Dimly Jim was aware of him getting up and leaving the room, and he thought with some relief that he was at last being left to himself, but before he could make a move to crawl into his futon Yuji was back. "Here, this is the original. It's an ancient Chinese sage called Han-shan. Look. Have you ever seen such laughter? Have *you* ever laughed like that?"

Jun looked at the scroll in silence. He shuddered. It was mad laughter, scarcely human.

"You have to be mad to laugh like that," affirmed Yuji, as though Jun had spoken his thought aloud. "Supposing *he* had lost everything – would *he* stop laughing, do you think?" When Jun remained silent he said, "But he, being a sage, never had anything to lose. Your cup is empty." He reached for the bottle and filled Jun's cup and his own.

"I wish you'd speak to me, son. You have so much to tell me, if only you would."

"Crow on a gravestone. Caw, caw, caw!" Suddenly Jun was laughing. It was not the laughter of the sage, not "mad" laughter, but rather harsh and forced, and it ended in a coughing fit which might have overwhelmed him had Yuji not come to the rescue, thumping him vigorously on the back. Strangely enough, he too was laughing.

"That's good," he said.

"It just came to me," Jun sputtered.

"Drink, drink. 'Crow on a gravestone, caw, caw, caw.'" He refilled both their cups. "Look at the silence," he said, and laughed again.

Scene Thirty-one

Tomoko and Kazue, having met for the first time at Yasushi's birthday party, struck up a friendship that seemed to grow closer by the day. Ghost for some reason did not share Kazue's affection for Tomoko, and could scarcely repress a scowl whenever he came home to find her there, drinking tea with Kazue and fussing over the baby.

"She may as well just move in with us," he grumbled.

"Why do you dislike her?" Kazue inquired. When Ghost merely shrugged without answering, she pouted, "Lately you dislike everybody."

Ghost smiled, took her in his arms, and – an habitual gesture – placed his broad flat nose against her tiny, lightly freckled one. "I dislike everybody who stands between me and you. What I want to do when I come home is squeeze your ass, fondle your tits, bite your ear lobe and sexually harass you in all kinds of obnoxious ways. A third party, whoever she is – but her in particular, I admit – is in the way."

"Why her in particular?"

"Why indeed. Some people you like the instant you see them, others you dislike. Maybe it's the pheromones they give off. She and I have clashing pheromones."

"Who do you like the instant you see them?"

"You."

"Besides me."

The doorbell rang. "Dammit, if that's her again..."

"Why would it be her? She just left."

It was Ikuko, in great distress. She slumped into a chair. "I've no right to burden you with this, but... I'm sorry... I can't..."

"Mama, what is it?" burst from Kazue.

"Nothing, nothing." Her daughter's alarm alarmed her in turn, and she fought down her agitation. "It's nothing. You stay here with the baby. Osamu" – she was the only one in the family circle who didn't call him Ghost – "would you mind coming home with me?" She stood up. "Don't worry," she said with assumed lightness to Kazue, "I won't keep him long."

Kazue, with her habitual docility, let them go without a word. Outside, Ghost said, "What's wrong, mama?"

"He's in one of his rages again."

"Rages?"

"Oh, you don't know! Yes, he is prone to occasional attacks of... I don't know what. Usually it's just shouting, but just now he got so furious at a table he bumped into that he knocked it over, shattering the lamp and the glass gondola he bought me in Venice."

"Mama, you're going too fast for me. Rages? I've never seen – "

"Our well-kept family secret! Well, we'll be there in a minute, you'll see for yourself. I'm sure he'll have calmed down by now, and there was really no need to trouble you."

The two families lived just across a little park from each other. Soon they were in the house. As Ikuko had predicted, Yasushi was quite calm. They found him on his knees, ruefully picking up bits of shattered glass. He met them with a sheepish grin. "Look what I've gone and done!"

"Leave that," said Ikuko roughly, her self-possession entirely regained. "I'll do it, you'll tear yourself to shreds. Go into the living room with Osamu."

"My war against matter!" laughed Yasushi as they settled themselves. "Do other people ever experience this, I wonder? Do you? No, you reserve all your hatred for God. Well, with me it's matter. There are times I want to kill it, strangle it, torture it! But matter... what can you say? Matter is matter – the more I rage and stamp, the harder it laughs at me – or rather, the softer. It knows I can't win, and *I* know I can't win, and yet..."

"A war against matter! Well, that's a new one on me."

214

"I have ten thumbs, Ghost. Ten thumbs and two left feet. I am forever bumping into things, dropping things, stepping on things... you know that yourself. You laugh at me, and I laugh with you. Most of the time. Well, just now I bumped into the table and... and in that instant... only for an instant, mind you... I hated that table with such fury, such... And why, I wonder? Because it hurt me? But it didn't. I didn't hit it hard, there was no pain; it's just that... there was no reason, no earthly *reason*, why I *should* have bumped into it! It's not as if the hallway is too narrow to pass through. Four people could easily walk abreast between the table and the wall. So why... Ah, here's Ikuko. My dear, truly, I'm sorry, I'm ashamed. How I must have scared you!"

"*You* scare *me*! You know me better than that, I hope!"

Scene Thirty-two

"Do you believe in God, Rogozhin?"

Rogozhin laughed. "What a strange question!"

Yoshiko reddened. "I'm sorry. It is a little strange. I don't know what it was... the look on your face, maybe... that made me suddenly want to ask."

"Have you ever read Dostoevsky?"

"No. I've read hardly anything."

"There are people, a very few people, for whom books are superfluous. You are one of them. You were born wise."

"Oh, stop!" Yoshiko squealed as though she was being tickled. "Born wise! My teachers certainly didn't think so."

"Teachers are the last to know. Anyway, in Dostoevsky, two characters will meet, and before

215

they've drained the first glass of vodka one will fix his burning eyes upon the other and demand, 'Do you believe in God?'"

"I wish you did believe in God."

"I didn't say I don't – but why?"

"I don't know. I don't know how to say it. I know so little about these things... about anything. The thought that came to me was that you're a... oh... a kind of holy man without holiness..." She broke off in confusion. "I'm not making sense."

"A holy man without holiness. I'm not sure I understand."

"I'm sure I don't." She giggled again. "Ever since I met you I keep getting these... these thoughts in my head, that I hardly recognize. It's like they're not mine. They're yours."

"So that thought about me being a holy man without holiness is my thought? Well... maybe it is. Maybe it is. What other thoughts...?"

"Thoughts I hardly have the words to express. That life is dreadful, ghastly, but we have the capacity to rise above suffering..."

"The capacity and the responsibility. You see, Yoshiko, happiness... just think how absurd it is to be happy! This is not a world of happiness, it is a world of pain, of suffering. How can anyone fail to know this? No one can, no one does, it's clear, clearer than anything. There is not a pain, a grief, a horror, which it will not be our lot to bear at one time or another in our lives, if we haven't borne it already, and having borne it already is no assurance against having to bear it again, and again. Only death sets us free, and death itself is pain, grief and horror. Happiness? On what grounds, with what justification? Happiness is either madness, or... an act of worship. Do I believe in God? I believe in a God to whom the only acceptable form of prayer is happiness, true happiness, in one who knows full well that

216

happiness is absurd. You are my happiness, Yoshiko – which is as much to say, you are my prayer. I mentioned Dostoevsky. I am currently engaged in translating some of his minor works into Japanese. A publisher I happen to know asked me to. I said my Japanese wasn't adequate, but he insisted I was the man for the job, and I let myself be persuaded, because I do love Dostoevsky. My name, incidentally, I share with one of his characters. A murderer, as it happens, but most of Dostoevsky's characters are murderers, and yet are no less blessed for that. The story I'm working on at present is called *The Dream of a Ridiculous Man*. Just as I share Rogozhin's name, I share the ridiculous man's ridiculousness. One night when he is on the brink of suicide he has a dream, a strange dream in which he is whisked to another corner of the universe and finds himself on an Earth very much like ours, only the fall of man as recounted in the Bible has not occurred, and man there is sinless, loving, happy. And though he wakes up knowing everything he saw was a dream, still, he accepts it as truth, and it saves him. And I too... What's that?"

It was the doorbell, which now rang again, and a third time. "Rogozhin, open up." Rogozhin and Yoshiko looked at each other. The voice was muffled, but Yoshiko recognized it immediately. "Maeda!" she gasped. "Don't open!"

Scene Thirty-three

"Of course I'll open," said Rogozhin calmly. "Are we to begin our new life in fear and cringing, shrinking from every ring of the bell, like children or criminals?" Gently disengaging himself, he went to the door and opened it.

"Rogozhin, I..." He caught sight of Yoshiko and stopped short.

For a time – a second, a minute, an hour – time itself seemed paralyzed. No one moved, no one made a sound. Later, Maeda tried to recall what he had been thinking during that time, and could only conclude, though tentatively, that his mind had been perfectly empty, as it never had been in his life before. However long it lasted, it was Rogozhin who put an end to it, with a breezy invitation. "Come in, come in, we weren't expecting you, I'll light the samovar."

He was gone, and Maeda and Yoshiko were alone.

"You're alive," breathed Maeda in a whisper.

"As never before," said Yoshiko.

Was there anything more to say? If so, Maeda failed to come up with it. The emptiness was gone now, but filled with nothing communicable. He continued to gape at her in astonishment, until he observed that Yoshiko's expression as she regarded him was one of steadily mounting terror. "What is it, Yoshiko? Why...?"

"What have you come for?"

"Why... to take you home, of course." He had not come for that at all, and was surprised to realize he had said such a thing. But the words, once spoken, could not be unspoken. "I'm your husband. You're my wife."

"You thought I was dead." Her voice trembled; she made an effort to steady it. "I was. Dead to you. As you are to me."

The silence returned. Rogozhin came in with teacups on a tray. "Sit down, please, why are you standing?" He placed a cup for Maeda on the lamp table by the armchair, and rejoined Yoshiko on the sofa. "He wasn't wearing dark glasses before," thought Maeda, noticing them now. "Or was he, and I just didn't notice?" "Sit." He sat.

"I've come to tell you," he said, "that I've been to the police about you. That is..."

"To the police about me!" If Rogozhin's astonishment was feigned, it was remarkably well done. "About Yoshiko?"

Maeda shook his head. "No. Not about Yoshiko. I'm sorry, I'm a little... no, not a little, a lot... confused. There's something about you, Rogozhin, that confuses people. Or maybe it has nothing to do with you. Please make allowances, is all I mean to say."

"All right, I will make allowances. Please, go on."

"I went to the police to report a murder I witnessed, committed by Tazawa, at a noodle shop in Kanda. I told them that Tazawa was part of a religious cult that worships evil as the supreme good, and that you were the cult's leader. I told them where they could find you."

"I see. And how long ago...?"

"Yesterday."

"Evidently they didn't take you seriously, since they haven't paid me a visit."

"They could yet. The wheels turn slowly."

"Maybe they'll come when they've gathered their evidence. So you've come to warn me, is that it?"

"Yes. To warn you and... to apologize."

"I daresay the police pressured you and pressured you, until you hardly knew what you were saying."

"It's true. It's no excuse, but it's true."

"Did Tazawa tell you that I was his leader?"

"Yes."

"And you didn't believe him, is that what you're saying? You didn't believe him, but you reported me to the police anyway?"

"Tazawa is a murderer and a liar, but about that... I did believe him. When I spoke to the police, I believed what I was saying."

"And what then caused you to disbelieve it?"

"Tomoko told me."

"Told you what?"

"That you were a good man and had nothing to do with anything bad."

"Tomoko told you that."

"Yes, Tomoko."

Scene Thirty-four

"Let's talk," said Rogozhin. "Let's get to know each other. Perhaps we can even become friends."

"Where's Yoshiko?"

"Yoshiko? Yoshiko went to bed hours ago. Are you all right?"

"I'm not sure. My head feels a little funny."

"In a good way, or bad?"

"In a... an interesting way."

"All right, I'll come clean. That wasn't pure unadulterated tea you were drinking."

"It wasn't?"

"Have you ever heard of soma? It's a mildly narcotic liquid from a plant that grows in India. The ancient Hindus believed it confers immortality. I believe it does too."

Dimly Maeda was aware that Rogozhin had just said something surprising, but he seemed incapable of surprise, though not of laughter, apparently, for he heard laughter and knew it for his own.

"Let's talk, Maeda-san. I sense somehow a kind of sympathy between us."

"What should we talk about?"

"The subject of soma doesn't interest you, I see. And yet – "

"Oh, it does!"

"There's a fundamental question, Maeda, that imposes itself upon every man or woman who has attained a certain level of mental development. The greater the mental development, the greater the force of the question. It is simply this: Why do we go on living? What's the point? It's easy enough to see that there is none. That in itself is not unbearable, but when you add to futility the pain, the grief, the sorrow, the anguish that fills even the relatively privileged members of our species – people like us, I mean, who are not sick, or impoverished, or having our testicles ripped open or being forced to watch as our wives and daughters are raped before our eyes in places where war or anarchy have turned men into beasts... worse than beasts, far worse... even our placid, uneventful little lives are liable to be shattered at any time by... how did Hamlet put it?—'the slings and arrows of outrageous fortune.' Why do we consent to life on these terms? And yet we do consent. By not killing ourselves we consent. We can end our lives easily, painlessly, almost effortlessly. Comfortably, even. We can simply go to sleep and not wake up. And yet we don't. Why? Fear? Are you afraid of death, Maeda? I am, I suppose, to some degree, being of a rather timorous disposition – but not nearly as afraid as I am of what tomorrow might bring if I live on. And yet I live on. Why? Joie de vivre? Granted, life has its joys, and at moments they are very powerful, but not even during those moments, unless one is a perfect child, can a serious person convince himself that the joy of living outweighs the pain of living."

"I have thought of killing myself."

"Of course you have. The thought is inescapable. But you haven't killed yourself. Why?"

"I haven't ruled it out."

"Supposing I were to say to you that I have, here in this apartment, a powder – a tasteless, odorless powder – which will lull you to sleep and then, taking you gently by the hand, lead you with maternal tenderness through a land of the sweetest dreams imaginable – unimaginable, rather – into... forgetfulness, oblivion. Eternal, painless oblivion. Supposing I were to say further that I will make this powder available to you tonight, now, this minute – but only now. Never again. You can either take it now, slipping painlessly into the death I have just described – or you can go on living and take your chances. Well? What's your choice?"

"I must choose right now? This minute?"

"This minute."

"Can't you give me a little time to think it over?"

"How much time?"

"I don't know. A week..."

Rogozhin smiled. "I see you're looking at the Watanabe Kazan sketch. You were struck by it last time too, I remember."

"He is an ancestor of mine."

"Oh is he! Is he really! Well! Speaking of ancestors. When I was in high school I went through a phase where I was going around telling people I was descended from a famous Russian murderer. Do you know Dostoevsky's *Idiot*, by any chance?"

"Yes."

"You do! I told you there was a kind of bond between us, didn't I? I went around bragging about being descended from Rogozhin, who murdered Nastasya Filipovna – without mentioning, of course, that they were fictional characters. I think I almost believed it myself, I was so... what's the word? I had the sort of brain in which fiction and reality were on easy terms with each other, let's put it that way. Too easy terms. I have that sort of brain even now, maybe."

"That powder. Give it to me. I'll take it."

"What? Are you serious?"

"Absolutely serious."

"It's the soma talking, not you."

"Give it to me, Rogozhin."

"Why? What suddenly...?"

"I don't know. I only know one thing. I..."

"What? What one thing? Tell me."

"It passed."

"What passed?"

Maeda laughed, reddening at the raucous, idiotic sound he made. "The knowledge of the one thing."

Scene Thirty-five

"Stay for dinner," said Ikuko. "I'll call Kazue. We'll order in sushi."

"No, really," said Ghost, getting to his feet, "I'd better..."

"Sit," said Yasushi. "I'll tell you something funny."

"I'll call Kazue," said Ikuko again. "Or better still, I'll go over there and help her dress the baby. Not that she needs my help."

"What funny thing are you going to tell me?" Ghost asked when Ikuko had gone.

"Well, this: I think I'm losing my mind."

"That's not funny."

"No, but the symptoms are. For example... Wait. Come with me." He rose and led the way up the narrow flight of stairs that led directly to the garret. Switching on the naked overhead bulb, he said, "Sit down." Ghost was evidently accustomed to being brought up here. Showing no surprise, he seated himself cross-legged on the floor opposite Yasushi, who also sat with legs crossed.

"A bit dusty, I'm afraid."

"You're forever apologizing for the dust," said Ghost. "Maybe one of these days you'll bring the vacuum cleaner up and – "

"Oh no, no!" said Yasushi, in some alarm. He relaxed immediately, however, and laughed genially. "This, you see, is the 'Immaculate Room.' Immaculate is not the same as clean. No vacuum cleaners. Look around. Tell me what you see."

"What I see? Nothing. It's perfectly empty, perfectly featureless."

"Exactly. I spend a good deal of time here..."

"Thinking?"

"Hiding."

"Hiding! From who?"

"Well, from... things. Things. There was one thing here once. A figurine I picked up at a museum. A prehistoric figurine. A prehistoric thing."

"Yes, I know. You gave it to Professor Horiuchi."

"So now there is nothing. No thing. Ikuko and I, I think, are going to have to part."

"What? What are you talking about?"

"I said I was losing my mind. Maybe it's that, or maybe I'm entering a higher state of consciousness. I don't know. I feel myself on the brink of a journey that can only be taken alone. Does that make sense? Wait, bear with me a moment. Today's episode with the table was not the first of its kind. Not the first. You know that vase in the kitchen with the morning glories in it? Two days ago I positively flew at Ikuko. She had

224

moved it maybe a centimeter to the right of where I had placed it. 'What's the matter with you?' she cried. What, indeed? The feeling had passed, and I could only stammer an apology. But the feeling, when it's upon me, and it's upon me more and more lately, is that *everything* in the house must be *precisely* in its place, *precisely*, or else... what? I don't know, the universe will tip over, or something." He laughed. "Don't you think that's funny?"

"It is, rather. What else?"

"Dreams. I have dreams of appalling, shocking violence. Sometimes I am the victim, sometimes the perpetrator. In one recurring dream I murder a child, cut his head off and place it on the sidewalk. People pass it by, give it a glance, and proceed on their way as if it were like any other incidental thing you happen to see on your way somewhere. Tomoko was here the other day. Horiuchi, you know, calls her a prophet. It seems she predicted he would win that lottery he won. Did you know he won a lottery? Anyway, I asked her what the dreams mean. She said, 'You don't have to be a prophet to see that.' 'Well?' I said. She shrugged and refused to say another word."

Scene Thirty-six

One evening not long afterwards Ghost came home to find Tomoko sitting on a cushion on the living room floor, the baby in her lap. He found himself momentarily absorbed in a trivial and irrelevant observation – that her posture was remarkably poor for someone so young. "Where's Kazue?"

"Shopping. She'll be back soon."

"Here, give me the baby."

But as she moved to hand her over the baby let out an anguished squeal.

"Leave her," said Tomoko. "Look – she's busy exploring the contours of my nose. Who knows how decisive it will be to the shaping of her consciousness!"

"Kazue doesn't go shopping at this hour."

"She suddenly discovered she was out of rice. It sent her into such a flutter that I said, 'Go, I'll watch the baby for you.' Do you know, I think Kazue is the most beautiful woman I've ever seen?"

"Kazue?"

"Don't you think she's beautiful?"

"She's... I don't know..."

"Not movie-star beautiful, of course."

There was a brief silence.

"My father-in-law tells me you're a prophet."

He waited for Tomoko to respond; she did not.

"Is it true?"

"Sometimes."

"When?"

"When I can empty my mind. Or should I say, when my mind is empty."

"When your mind is empty."

"It's not a matter of will, you see. Yes, when the mind is empty, prophecy... how did Professor Horiuchi put it? 'Prophecy fills the vacuum.' Or words to that effect. Your father-in-law..."

"Well? What about my father-in-law?"

"You will hear a story from your father-in-law which you won't believe; but it will be true.

"What are you talking about? What story?"

"I don't know."

There was a faint noise at the door. "Sh! Not another word!" said Tomoko in a mock conspiratorial whisper as Kazue, flushed and breathless, made her appearance cradling a two-kilogram bag of rice.

"I'll be going," said Tomoko. "I can see Ghost doesn't want me around."

"You weren't mean to her, were you?" said Kazue when they were alone. "I feel so sorry for her. So lonely, so wrapped up in that morbid research of hers..."

"All you see of her is what she wants you to see. There's more."

"And you see what isn't there."

"In my village in Zambia there was a man, blind from birth, who used to say that only he saw true, that everyone else was rushing around in pursuit of, or in flight from, illusions."

"Your village in Zambia! You've never been to Zambia."

Ghost laughed. "Actually I read about it in this book Professor Horiuchi lent me. The interesting thing is that many people believed the blind man, and followed him. But life in an African village is one thing, life here is something else. There's too much going on here; a person can't afford to be blind. Don't you see, Kazue, she's a lesbian and is attracted to you?"

"A lesbian? Tomoko?"

"A lesbian. Tomoko."

"Oh, Ghost, that's... you just don't like her."

"I've admitted I don't like her. But I'm not mean-spirited, I hope, and... why did you call her research morbid?"

"Dark matter." She shivered.

"They say there's more dark matter in the universe than... light matter. Ordinary matter. You can't touch it, can't see it... it only reveals itself to the mathematician."

"She has a boyfriend."

"So?"

"So how can she be a lesbian?"

"Oh, Kazue, I love you for your innocence, but... all the same... innocence is terrifying! Please,

227

Kazue, trust me. Don't see her. She's not... not what she seems to you."

"What is she, then?"

"Come here." She sat on his lap, the baby in her lap, and Ghost enfolded them both in his long, muscled arms. For a time no one spoke. Ghost felt tears coming to his eyes. This woman, entrusted to him by God – the thought came to him, and so tender was his mood that he did not recoil from it – this woman, so good herself as to be blind to the existence of evil... he must protect her, protect her...

"Why are you crying?"

"I don't know. I think I'm having a religious experience." He laughed, and nestled his face, wet with tears, against hers. "Promise me you won't see her."

"What can I say when she comes?"

"Never mind. I'll talk to her. In the meantime, don't leave the baby with her."

Kazue let out a cry. There was a look of horror on her face. "Would she harm the baby?"

"Sh... no." He stroked her hair. "I spoke without thinking." In a tone of mock gruffness he demanded, "What's for dinner? I'm starving."

"Squid. Here, take the baby, I'll put the rice on."

Scene Thirty-seven

"Have you ever heard of Nechaev?"

"Nechaev? No...."

"He was a revolutionary of the 1860s, a proto-Leninist, I suppose you could call him. I wrote my master's thesis on him. His doctrine was destruction. Universal, ruthless, amoral destruction. Society was rotten to the core, he said,

228

rotten beyond mere reform. Mankind's only hope was a fresh start. But first, destruction. He saw it as a kind of surgery, and himself as a surgeon. He was a surgeon removing cancerous growths, a destroyer clearing the ground for a good, true, healthy and just society. Dostoevsky satirizes him as Pyotr Verkhovensky in *The Devils*. But Verkhovensky is a comic figure, almost ludicrous. There was nothing comic about Nechaev. He founded a society called The People's Retribution, and wrote a tract called *Catechism of a Revolutionary*. He wrote, 'We will unite with the savage world of robbers, those true and only revolutionaries in Russia. To mold this element into one irresistible, all-shattering force – here is our entire organization, conspiracy, task.'

"As a young man I was fascinated by Nechaev, by his rejection of all morality. His amoralism, you see, was not for the gratification of his own petty egotistical desires, but in the name of a higher morality. At least so he said. Was he sincere? Was his love for mankind so all-consuming that he was prepared to sacrifice the present, himself included, for the sake of the future? Did he really believe in the 'universal happiness, paradise on earth' he claimed to foresee as the end result of the horrors he would perpetrate? Or was he merely a perpetrator of horrors, decking out his sordid lusts in the 'higher morality' of revolution? In 1869 the revolutionary group he led – he was a masterful, charismatic personality, a natural leader of men and irresistible to women – murdered one of its members, a student named Ivanov, the purpose in Nechaev's mind being to weld this little group into an indestructible unit whose members, united in crime, would never dare betray one another. Whether Ivanov had really changed his views and was about to inform on the group, as Nechaev alleged, or whether he was singled out for some other reason, or for no reason, is still disputed and will probably never be known. Anyway, the point as far as we are concerned is that, having in a manner of speaking outgrown my youthful infatuation with Nechaev, I found myself drifting back in that direction after my wife died. It suited my mood to gather around me a coterie of impressionable young people and, so to speak, 'Nechaevize' them. It was a humor arising from pure despair."

"And that's when you came into contact with Tazawa?"

"That's when I came into contact with Tazawa. His family owned a bookstore – "

"The Alexandria!"

"Yes, which I used to frequent. I knew his father before I knew him. I liked him, he knew and loved books as few people nowadays do; he knew Russian literature well, and I have fond memories of the many long talks we had... about Dostoevsky, Tolstoy, Pushkin... about Japanese writers... Had he any inkling, I wonder, how his younger son hated him? I don't think he had. Books he knew – about them he could talk learnedly, insightfully, profoundly – but the world outside books was a dream to him, the merest shadow – including his son, who might perhaps be forgiven for resenting that. Resenting it, yes, but in certain natures, young Tazawa's among them, resentment grows to a pitch of hatred that... Do you know what I think it is? I think it's thwarted love. You'll call that romantic nonsense, and maybe it is, but I suspect that deep down Tazawa had – has, I should say – a great longing, a great capacity, for love. Well, we needn't dwell on that. He was in and out of the bookstore, and we formed a nodding acquaintance, which in the fullness of time, as they say, led to his becoming a part of my little 'coterie'..."

"This 'cult,' then, this 'cult that worships evil'..."

"There is no cult, and no worship. He took my words and made of them what he pleased. My words were wild. Playing the part of Nechaev, I preached paradise on earth arising from the excision of all evil, all rottenness, all corruption. Regarding good and evil, I said that good is powerless, only evil is powerful, good sits on its hands and endures, good is passive while only evil is active, only evil can accomplish the task that must be accomplished if mankind is to rise above his present condition... and so on. One must have the courage, I said, to take the evil upon oneself... I may as well have been reading aloud from my master's thesis. I think in a sense I was deliberately reverting to my young-man self, to my self before the darkness that blighted my life... I hardly know what I was doing! Tell me... is it true that you and Yoshiko..."

"That me and Yoshiko... what?"

"She tells me you have never... But Yoshiko is a dreamer, an ardent dreamer. She is not of her time and place, not at home in the world she inhabits. Do you know who she reminds me of? Saint Hildegaard!"

"Saint... who?"

"Saint Hildegaard of Bingen, consigned to a nunnery at age eight with all the last rites of the dead to signify she was dead to this world, living only in the next! She was a writer of uncommon power. She had visions of hell. Some commentators say she inspired Dante."

"And Yoshiko...?"

"Yoshiko sees herself as soiled, polluted, tainted. Not all the time, but when the mood is upon her. You know the mood I mean. She dreams of purification, chastity. She insists you and she never had sexual relations."

"It's quite true."

"True?"

"True. I was incapable."

"No! So it's true then! And all this time I thought... I assumed... It's true! She wasn't dreaming! What a... Forgive me if I seem to make too much of this, but... well then... if I am Rogozhin, you are Prince Myshkin!"

"I never warmed to Myshkin somehow. Dostoevsky created him as a 'supremely beautiful soul,' I know, but I never saw anything beautiful in him. Of course I noted his impotence, but I never identified with him on that account."

"*Were* incapable. You said 'were'."

"Yes."

"Past tense."

"Past tense."

"I think I can guess. Tomoko?"

He nodded.

Scene Thirty-eight

"Pallas Athene now inspired Diomedes son of Tydeus with audacity and resolution, so that he might eclipse all his comrades-in-arms and cover himself with glory. She made his shield and helmet glow with a blaze as steady as the Star of Summer when he rises from his bath in Ocean..." Ah, how I love to read Homer aloud! How I love, how I... yes, but suppose Homer himself could hear me, suppose...would he understand a word I'm saying? Is my pronunciation, my accent, anything he would recognize? I shudder to think how I must be mangling his words. My education was not of the best, nor was I, truth to tell, the best of students, I never even got my doctorate, and even if my teachers had been the most learned authorities in the world, which they weren't – very far from it – Homer's language, and Aeschylus', and Plato's, has not passed from the lips of living men in more than two thousand years; no one teaching it and studying it has ever heard it spoken, has any real idea how it was pronounced... still, even granting that, it can be known better than I know it... Maybe, having ceased to be a teacher, I'll become a student, I'll go back to school... "rises from his bath in Ocean" – how beautiful, how beautiful that is! For having failed to convey that to my students, I deserve... I deserve... the doorbell! No, I do not deserve that... "Diomedes son of Tydeus..." Inspire me with audacity and resolution, Pallas Athene! Ha ha! "All right, all right, I'm coming!" It's Ghost, of course, I can tell by his ring. Somehow everything Ghost does expresses his character, or his mood. Even ringing a mechanical doorbell – listen to how the sound pulses with his impatience; if he was cheerful, I daresay it would radiate with his cheerfulness. There's more than impatience in the sound; there's worry, concern, anxiety. Well, I'll sit him down and read Homer to him, ha ha!

"You're ill!" His very first words as I open the door; how does he have the time to make such an observation? But he's quick; there are few quicker; and if his observations are not always to the point, they at least satisfy *his* standard of pertinence.

"Ill? No."

"You're thin, pale. You look ghastly."

"Thank you very much. Shouldn't you be at work?"

"I don't work Saturdays." So it's Saturday. "Here, I've brought you back your book." What book? Oh. *Introduction to Cultural Anthropology.* "Well, come in," I say, "since you're here."

"Have I come at a bad time?"

"I was reading Homer."

233

"Listen. There's a war in Afghanistan, a war in Iraq, Iran's going nuclear, terrorist bombs are exploding everywhere – and you lock yourself away in your little... book-closet... and immerse yourself in the Trojan War. Will you forgive me for saying there's something just a little bit odd about that?"

"From you I would forgive anything, because you're you. From another, I would take offense."

"Seriously, professor. I am asking you, not for the first time, to be serious for once. You use humor to brush me aside like a fly, when all I'm asking..."

"Book-closet; that's a nice expression."

"All I'm asking is..."

"The benefit of my wisdom?"

"Well, yes. The benefit of your wisdom."

"All right. Let's go into my book-closet and I will give you the benefit of my wisdom."

He follows me upstairs; I usher him inside and close the door behind us. "Sit down." The silence that follows is not me playing Zen-master but me at a loss for words; oddly enough, Ghost falls in with it and shows no impatience. Evidently he prefers my silence to my irony. Irony does not come naturally to the Japanese. Where did I pick it up, I wonder? From Misako, no doubt – unconsciously. We speak to each other in Japanese, but her Japanese, though fluent, is, in ways hard to put your finger on, different from the Japanese spoken here. Irony is one of its elements. I remember once – to cite a very small example – asking her if she liked *natto*, the fermented soybean concoction that almost all foreigners, even those who love Japanese food, find repugnant. Screwing up her face, she said, "Oh, I love it." Even I, who know her so well, am never quite sure when to take her words at face value. Something of that seems to have rubbed off on me. Maybe that's why

234

my students never warmed to me. One reason among many.

"Tell me," says Ghost at last, speaking, it seems to me, unusually quietly. "Tell me seriously – please. Why should a person care about the past? Why spend a lifetime studying it? I could understand if you say it helps us to understand the present. But you don't seem interested in the present. You seem to have turned your back on it…"

"I have turned my back on time. Put a book into my hand, and I am where it takes me. If it's Homer, I am in the thick of the Trojan War; if Plato, I am in the agora with Socrates; if Euripides, I am in the theater, one among ten thousand spectators. Ten thousand spectators – think of it…"

"If Shakespeare, in Elizabethan England? If Tolstoy, in 19th-century Russia? If Kafka…"

"In principle, yes, but somehow it's only the ancient Greeks that can transport me bodily…"

"Bodily?"

"It's an illusion, I know, but an overpowering one."

"Is it a gift, or a disease?"

"Maybe a little of both. I'm sorry. You honor me with your confidence, and I have so little to offer you."

"No, you have a great deal to offer me. I'm convinced of it. I don't know exactly *why* I'm convinced, but I am. Maybe that's *my* overpowering illusion. If only I could draw it from you! I'm afraid I'm being a nuisance…"

Scene Thirty-nine

"Actually," he says, "I'm here not only on my own account but on my mother-in-law's. She asked me to come. She's worried about my father-in-law. Something is going on inside him, something she can't fathom. She asked me to bring you home to dinner. You haven't been to see them lately. She thinks seeing you will do him good. She says his eyes light up every time your name comes up. Will you come?"

"To dinner?"

"Why, what's the matter?"

"Nothing." Everything. It's impossible. Impossible to refuse, impossible to accept, impossible to explain. For a second I fear I am about to lose consciousness; I grip the desk as though to keep from falling – falling into what, seated as I am?

"What's wrong? You really are ill!"

"Yes, I..."

"Is there anything I can do? You should be in bed." He places a hand on my forehead, a surprisingly soft hand, tender. If my eyes were closed and I didn't know whose hand it was, I would take it for a woman's, a young girl's even. "You have no fever. Let me fix you some hot tea. Are you hungry? I thought when I came in you looked... Have you been eating? Do you have a rice cooker? I'll fix you some rice and tea."

"No." His fussing will wake Misako. "Really, I'm fine. A passing dizziness – it comes over me from time to time. I'm fine. It's nothing."

"I'll explain to them that you're ill and can't come. But I can't leave you..."

"Of course you can. I'm fine, I tell you. A passing... Go. Tell them I'm not feeling quite well, but will be sure to visit them just as soon as I can. Very soon. In a few days."

He leaves at last. I see him out and lock the door. Midway up the stairs to my 'book closet' I pause. An idea has come to me, stupid, trivial, and yet oddly exciting. The doorbell is a

236

battery-operated device – what if I... remove the battery? Strange: in all the years I've been living here the idea never so much as occurred to me. The little device is mounted on the wall by the door. I only know there's a battery inside because the casing has little slits through which you can see inside. Can the casing be removed? If it's screwed shut I'll need a screwdriver, which I don't think I have in the house. Nuisance! But no – I give a little tug and something releases immediately; the cover is in my hands; inside are little wires and little electronic things whose names I do not know and, precisely at eye level, a common, everyday little battery. I am suddenly aware of a pounding in my chest – Great Zeus, think of me having a heart attack over something like this! I feel like – why, like Orestes, about to strike his mother dead! No, a strained comparison. Still, it's uncanny how my hands are trembling. "It's nothing!" I tell myself. "This is my house, my doorbell, my battery; if I want to remove it, it's my right, no one would dream of challenging it, it's a matter of perfect indifference to... to everyone! Six billion people in the world, maybe seven by now, not one of whom would be inconvenienced..."

Back upstairs, I place the little battery upright on the desk and sit down. I stare at it and stare at it, until my staring becomes a kind of... I don't know... a kind of contemplation. No one can ring my doorbell, no one can ring my phone (the phone is always on silent mode; I check for messages from time to time, or at least I used to)... no one can reach me! I am inaccessible, as much so as if I were in... another universe! I have become, as Tomoko would have it, dark matter. Homer – what would he have to say about that? The book is on the desk. I pick it up and open it at random. "With that the god went back into the heart of the battle..." What god? What battle? Hm ..."

Scene Forty

"Tell me about love," said Yuji dreamily. "I mean, about being in love. What's it like? Indescribable, I suppose."

"Indescribable." Tipsily Jun sat absorbed in his saké, scarcely following the conversation. His recovery was complete, all that remained was to thank his hosts and be on his way, but somehow he could not summon the will to do it. He had begun helping out in the shop; both Yuji and Yoko seemed fully accustomed to his presence, untiringly if uneffusively appreciative of it; they might almost have been his mother and father, grooming him to one day take over the family business. Evenings they drank saké together, sitting cross-legged on the *tatami* floor of what had become Jun's room. Yuji marveled to see Jun blossoming as a poet. The older man's eyes would close and a slight, scarcely perceptible smile would light up his face as Jun recited his little wisps of verse, hardly even poems, most of them a mere line or two, some no longer than three or four words. Outside a gentle rain was falling; the sound of it tapping on the roof filled the silence of the room, and Jun murmured, "Listen to the moon flooding the sea with light."

"Haven't you been in love?" Yoko asked Yuji.

Yuji was thoughtful. "I don't know. Kimi is a good woman, a good wife, I like her, I'm happy to be married to her, I've never wanted to be married to anyone else... but do I *love* her, as this young man has spoken about love?"

Yoko smiled. "Well, he's a poet after all. He speaks poetically."

"Does love make the poet, or does the poet, from some magic in him, spin mere liking into love? Hm. Yusuke I loved... Yusuke... With Yusuke gone it is a matter of perfect indifference whether I live or die."

"You don't mean that," said Yoko gently. "That's the saké talking."

"Yes, it's the saké talking. But I do mean it. Supposing," he said, turning to Jun, "you lost your Tomoko. Would you go on living?"

"That's not a fair question," Yoko protested. "He can't possibly know – "

"Yoko, please. I want to hear it from him." Once more he turned to Jun. "Would you go on living?"

"Would I... A jagged line in the sky, a break in the clouds... Forgive me, I'm drunk."

"You see, that's the trouble with me. I can't get drunk. No matter how much I drink, no matter how..."

"Come," said Yoko, lifting herself somewhat heavily to her feet. "This young man needs his sleep. We're keeping him up."

"A jagged line in the sky, a break in the clouds," Jun mumbled again.

"Come," Yoko prodded when Yuji made no move to rise.

"I'm coming. Just one word I would say to this young man. Son, your gift, your gift of poetry... ah, damn, damn, it's gone! I had a thought, a glimmer of a thought, but it left me. Your gift of poetry..."

"And he says he never gets drunk!" Yoko said with a smile. "Good night, Jun, we'll see you in the morning."

Scene Forty-one

At the end of June Haruyuki Maeda went back to work at the *Maiasa Shimbun*. He would sit at his old desk, and at odd moments an astonished

239

stupor would come over him. How had he come to be here? Hadn't he quit, determined to free himself from the banalities and trivialities this second-rate newspaper and its third-rate editor heaped on him? In moments like these he seemed to forget everything that had happened between his quitting and his return. He had quit, and yet here he was – had he really quit? Perhaps he had only imagined quitting? Only dreamed it?

But this confusion was intermittent and fleeting. No, his quitting had been real enough; it had happened months ago, but instead of embarking on what he had grandiosely represented to himself as a search for truth, he had slipped – how easy it was to do! – into a degrading, degenerating, debilitating idleness, in the course of which he had lost Yoshiko and gained (in a manner of speaking) Tomoko; had encountered Rogozhin and become (again, in a manner of speaking) a kind of disciple (if that was the word!) of that professor he had first met as a journalist doing a routine and grudging interview with the winner of a lottery.

Kinoshita, the news editor, had been in touch with him from time to time over the so-called "cult that worships evil," and in the course of one of these conversations happened to mention that Sugimura, the court reporter, had left. Had Kinoshita asked Maeda to replace him? Or had Maeda put himself forward? He wasn't sure. Sometimes he remembered it one way, sometimes the other. Anyway, he was a court reporter now, with a specific beat, which he worked on his own and without supervision. No one would send him out now to cover lottery wins or hundredth birthday parties or ribbon-cutting ceremonies.

He had every reason to be pleased. Sugimura was a man in his forties, a seasoned veteran, who had once seen in Maeda a kindred spirit and taken a mentor's interest in him. "The court," he liked to say, "is an unscripted theater of the absurd. Here is human nature in all its unrefined rawness. The big cases don't interest me so much. It's the insignificant stuff, the stuff no one else can be bothered writing about..." And Maeda had always admired Sugimura's writing. In five hundred words Sugimura could tell a story as complete as any novel. In a word he could describe a character; in a phrase he made you, the reader, feel you were no mere onlooker but a participant in what was going on. He could bring a story to life as few other writers burdened with boilerplate newspaper style could. It was a gift, and Maeda knew its value. A conviction that he possessed a similar gift had nudged him into journalism to begin with. The obligation to write "rubbish" had discouraged and embittered him; perhaps, he thought, he had been hasty. "I must make the most of this second chance."

A case then unfolding offered possibilities. It concerned the murder of a dog. The accused was a neighbor who'd been upset by the dog's barking. It was a white spaniel, and though its bark was not overpoweringly loud it was persistent and had a peculiar timbre to it, hard to define, a whining sort of timbre, that made it peculiarly grating if your ear happened to be sensitive to it. It was owned by a family with two teenage children. Driven to a pitch of fury, the accused had repeatedly banged on their door to rant, rave and threaten. "If you don't shut that dog up I'll kill it, I'll feed it rat poison, I'll..." When the dog was in fact poisoned and the accused arrested, he admitted the threats but denied having done the deed. "I never thought of doing it, I only wanted to frighten them into doing something about the barking..." So he testified, his voice trembling so wildly he could scarcely get the words out. Maeda believed him,

241

but the jury, consisting of six ordinary citizens and three professional judges, seemed inclined not to.

Scene Forty-two

The accused, Nagatoshi by name, was a man in early middle age, single, balding, and apparently ravaged by nerves. "To write well," Sugimura used to say, "you must train yourself to see *inside* people." This Maeda tried to do, and he fancied he did, after a fashion, come to some sort of understanding of this man. Not everyone is at home in this automated, hyper-technologized world of ours; for all its conveniences and undoubted benefits, it leaves some people with a feeling of being vulnerably human in increasingly inhuman surroundings. Another case, just concluded, had concerned an elderly man who had suddenly flung himself at a teenager fiddling with a cell phone as he walked home from school. The boy had done nothing wrong, had shown no disrespect, had apparently not even been aware of the elderly man's existence, but the man's rage was boundless; such was his hatred of cell phones and the "zombies" he was convinced they turned people into; it took three passersby to pull him off, and the boy, his cheek dripping blood from where the man had bitten him, was rushed to hospital, though he soon recovered. The accused in the present case must have been in a similar frame of mind, all his rage focusing on that almost albino-white dog with the peculiar bark that penetrated the one space in which he felt he should not be obliged to tolerate the distasteful incursions of "the outside world," "the world as it was" – namely, his home.

Maeda was devastated by the guilty verdict that was eventually handed down. His head sank into his hands. Behind his closed eyelids he saw himself springing to his feet and crying out, "Miscarriage of justice!" Back at the office he began composing his story. If he was truly a writer in the Sugimura mold, here was his chance.

But the words did not come. He gazed blankly at his screen, unable to concentrate. An idea kept intruding. The idea, though part of *the* story, could not be part of *his* story, the story he was writing, for *his* story was the story of the trial, but his idea was that, the trial and its verdict notwithstanding, the real killer of the dog was the family's younger son, a boy of fourteen who had not even come under suspicion. Why did Maeda suspect him? He wasn't sure. A certain disagreeable smirk, perhaps, that the boy flashed at telling moments in the testimony. It wasn't much to go on – it wasn't *anything* to go on, and he'd better forget it and get on with his work, deadline was approaching... But the boy's image kept appearing before him, as though taunting him: "I know you know I did it, for no reason, out of pure malice, because I knew it'd be pinned on Nagatoshi on account of his threats, but I don't care that you know because there's not a thing you can do about it, and having succeeded this once I'll do worse things in future, and do them no less cleverly; they'll never catch me, even with you knowing what you know..."

"Maeda."

"What?"

He looked up to find Kinoshita hovering over him. A sudden impulse took him by surprise and required all his inner strength to stifle – an impulse to leap up and slap the man as hard as he could in his stupid, ugly, bespectacled face. This hatred he felt for Kinoshita was irrational and inexplicable, as he himself knew. True, as an editor he was timid and incompetent; still, he had taken Maeda back, graciously and without condescension; for that if for nothing else he owed him consideration. Besides, was it even certain that he was incompetent? Who knew – certainly Maeda didn't – what pressures he operated under? He had superiors to answer to, he was not always free to do things as he may have wanted to do them; there were rumors afoot that top management was ready to yield to the overwhelming impact of the Internet and close the paper down; a man in Kinoshita's relatively subordinate position would have to walk a fine line.

"I'm afraid we'll have to pull tomorrow's court story. An ad was phoned in at the last minute. I'm sorry. But I see you haven't started writing."

Typical. Ads came first. Still, Maeda was more relieved than outraged. He was off the hook, spared the necessity of writing up as guilty a man he was convinced was innocent. "Well, I'll be going," he said. He would tell Tomoko about the case and ask her what she thought – mobilize her prophetic insight, so to speak.

"Wait. There's something I'd like you to look into. Have you   had any contact recently with that friend of yours from the 'cult that worships evil'?"

No, come to think of it he had not.

"No one seems to have noticed," Kinoshita went on, "that the murders have stopped. There hasn't been one in over three months."

"Yes, that's true, now that you mention it."

"Why not put together a little story about it for the Sunday paper."

Scene Forty-three

A good place to start, Maeda mused to himself on the train home, would be the police *koban* where he had gone to identify Tazawa as the murderer of poor old Nagai-san at the noodle shop. The two officers he had spoken to had been by turns indifferent and menacing; at one point they had seemed more than ready to pounce on Maeda himself as the murderer, not only of Nagai but of all the other victims as well. Frightening though that had been, he recognized it in retrospect as typical police role-playing. He'd strayed into their net – well, they would pump him for all he was worth. And it worked; he ended up implicating Rogozhin as well. They let him go without telling him what they thought of his information, and he had heard nothing since. He knew they had not bothered Rogozhin, whom he saw frequently, but had they taken him seriously regarding Tazawa? You'd think they would have – he'd come forward as an eye witness, after all.

He got off the train at Ikebukuro Station, merged with a swarm making its way to street level, and paused at the top of the escalator. The *koban* was to the left, the two-room apartment he shared with Tomoko to the right. Would Tomoko be home? She was when she was, wasn't when she wasn't; she would not be held accountable, and when he questioned her regarding her long absences she would say only that she was busy at the university, working on her thesis. He went through agonies of jealousy to which she seemed perfectly indifferent. He suspected her of having an affair with Professor Sawamura, her thesis advisor, and was once incautious enough in his distraction to blurt out an accusation to that effect. She did not get angry, did not laugh at him, did not try to reassure him;

her only answer was a barely perceptible shrug. If that's what he wanted to think, it seemed to say, she had no objection. She tormented him in a thousand ways, knew his every weak spot; he seethed inwardly but, more or less successfully, kept his rage bottled up. The fact is, he was terrified of her, and not without reason. He knew perfectly well that she could walk out of his life without a qualm and never be seen again, leaving him to get over his loss as best he could. In a day she would have forgotten him. But for him, life without Tomoko had become simply inconceivable. Was this love, or was it addiction? It was a question he asked himself often. The only answer he could come to, tentative and unsatisfying, was that love itself was a kind of addiction.

He made up his mind. He would go home first. He told himself it was for a beer and a bath, but the real reason was that he burned to know whether Tomoko was there. If she wasn't – why, no problem; she really was writing a very difficult thesis; inevitably, it took up a lot of her time. What did he expect – that she would give it up for love of him? He was not such a fool! Still, she might be home, she *might* – in which case she might be pleased to see him, there were moments when she was, when she smiled with pleasure at his entrance, a barely perceptible smile, and yet how it lighted up her face, how it warmed his heart!

Scene Forty-four

Suddenly the room is flooded with sunlight. Nothing astonishing in that. Zeus the cloud-gatherer is also Zeus the cloud-disperser. The light illuminates the text on the desk in front of me. How rusty my Greek has become! Once I

246

read it like "Iris of the Nimble Feet" – now my plodding pace reminds me of Philoctetes, alone on his island with his loathsome wound... What's this? Ah, the battery. I took it from the doorbell. How long ago was that? Have I slept? If so I'm not aware of it. It's funny – I feel as if I've been away on a long journey and only just got back, and my knowledge, my certain knowledge, that I have not left this chair does nothing to dispel the feeling. Of course, it's possible my knowledge is not so certain. Our mind is so constituted as to feel certain of certain things under certain circumstances on the basis of certain evidence – the evidence of our senses, for instance, though we know sensory evidence is faulty; or of memory, though memory is notoriously prone to error. All right then, I'm *not* certain; I renounce my certainty – maybe I *have* been away.

Kant said – I think it was Kant; I *think* this is what he said – that time is merely a category of the human mind, that in effect we view the world through a mental time-filter, that the world beyond the filter, the "real" world, is totally inaccessible to us, and may not be time-bound at all. What follows from that? Why, nothing – except... except, for instance, that that visit of Ghost's, which I recall as having taken place earlier today, or maybe yesterday, or a week ago at most, may actually have occurred ten thousand years ago, or ten thousand eons ago, or – what's that Indian term? "kalpa"... hm... may have recurred ten thousand times, or ten million, if Nietzsche's notion of eternal return is true... Is this a mental breakdown I'm having? Or is my mind ascending to higher regions of truth?

Scene Forty-five

"Okaerinasai," she said. "Welcome home. The bath is hot."

So overpowering was the relief that flooded Maeda's heart as he opened the door and found her there that had there not been a chair for him to sink into his knees might have given way beneath him. He sat motionless, eyes closed, mind blank, for he knew not how long. Out of his vacancy there arose a kind of dream, or vision, unlike anything he had ever experienced. Only later, in an attempt to recapture and preserve it, did he struggle to put it into words, words which of course failed to do it justice because, other things aside, they lent it a concreteness altogether lacking in the original. He was transported to another world in which everyone is invisible, inaudible – only *he* imposed his presence upon the senses. It is remarkable that in such a world the senses would have evolved in the first place, but evidently they had, for Maeda himself was both visible and audible – he was the first thing the inhabitants had ever been sensually aware of; their shock at the crudity of the intrusion can only be imagined. Maeda did his best to calm them. On his home planet, he explained, people saw and heard and smelled as a matter of course; he, for his part, could not understand how the beings on this world he was now on managed without sensory information; naturally they could not explain something they took so automatically for granted; they must, Maeda supposed, be possessed of other senses of which he knew nothing – intuition? telepathy? At first they could not endure his presence. Eyes accustomed to seeing nothing were offended at the sight of him; ears tuned to silence writhed at the sounds he made. He was afraid he might kill them, merely by existing among them. He would have left, would gladly have spared them the agony he unwittingly caused them, if only he could, but he had not come of his own accord and could not depart at will. They gave him a black cloak to drape over himself, and begged him, if he must speak, not to do so above a whisper. There was no language barrier, which was odd – but oddity in dreams, he told himself in the dream,   is normal.

Gradually, by degrees, they got used to him. He no longer had to walk with such extravagant stealth lest the sound of his footsteps reverberate in their ears like an earthquake or an invading army. His faintest whisper no longer caused them to flee from him in nameless anguish. Once, quite unconsciously, he began humming a tune, and found to his surprise that it attracted rather than repelled them. He sang and their attention grew deeper, almost rapturous. His singing voice pleased them – well, that was a discovery! He had in fact a fine voice, untrained but naturally rich and tuneful. It was their first experience with music. It shocked them to learn that his singing voice and speaking voice were one and the same instrument, so beautiful did the one seem to them, and so ugly the other. Once having made the connection, however, they began to regard speech with less hostility. Slowly, they acquired a tolerance for it. He still had to speak softly, but he grew able to question them, and answer their questions in turn. Time passed; he became less of an outcast; his homesickness eased, finally fading altogether. He found he loved these strange, appearanceless beings – loved them with a serene, undemanding, all-embracing love, loved them all equally, not just one or two for lovable qualities they happened to possess. Why should he even think of returning to Earth, where blind, unruly passion ruled the day? No, he wouldn't return;

even if it were possible he wouldn't; he would make his home here – for here, clearly, is where he should have been born and it was only through some grotesque accident that his birth had occurred on Earth instead. The question then became how he could dissolve his appearance. That he must was plain – but the problem had never arisen before, and his hosts, as eager now to have him stay as he was not to leave, were perplexed as to how to manage it.

Scene Forty-six

He woke in the bath and immediately closed his eyes again, hoping to return to where he'd been, but of course it was impossible. It was odd too, though in his present frame of mind not especially disturbing, that he had no memory of having entered the bath. He remembered coming home, remembered his overwhelming relief at finding Tomoko waiting for him, and remembered her saying the bath was ready. He had then meant to tell her – in fact thought he had told her, though he wasn't sure – that he would first step out to the police *koban* and speak to the officers, and be back for a bath and dinner in half an hour.

Why was the world so constituted that hot bathwater cooled, that human skin grew parched if too long submerged – why, in short, couldn't mankind be born in a bath, live in a bath and die in a bath? Why wasn't the whole world simply a large bath? Well, it wasn't, and that was that. Resignedly Maeda rose, stepped out of the little tub, dried himself and joined Tomoko in the little kitchen. "What's this?" He found to his surprise that Tomoko was cooking a meal, going in fact to some trouble over it. This was unprecedented;

they always, when they ate together, either went out or made do with prepared foods; he had never taken the subject up with her but presumed she had no interest in cooking, and yet here she was, busy over the hot stove, fussing over something he couldn't immediately identify but which smelled out of this world. On the little table were a bottle of wine and two wine glasses. "Open the wine," she said, "it'll be ready in a minute."

"What is this?" he asked again.

"It's called a feast. I suppose you thought I couldn't cook. You reckoned without my grandfather, the redoubtable Sato of Sato Trading Company. No granddaughter of his could grow up without... oh yes, he's a master of the culinary arts as well as a few others – poetry, judo, calligraphy. I'll take you to meet him one day. Oh, I forgot – you've already met him. Could grow up, I was about to say, without learning her way around a kitchen a good deal more spacious than this one. Open the wine and sit down." She switched off the fire. "It's ready."

The wine was Sicilian; the very sound it made as he poured it seemed to make Maeda drunk. He laughed. "This is wonderful. And to think... to think I came home tonight fearing you wouldn't be here and..." He knew he was saying what was better left unsaid but couldn't stop himself; felt no inclination to. "...and knowing that if you weren't it would just... just *devastate* me, Tomoko! Though I know of course you're busy and preoccupied with a realm of reality that I'm incapable of entering..."

"All right, that's enough, stop your babbling."

"What is it?" he asked, sampling what she'd ladled onto his plate.

"Is it good?"

"It's more than good, it's... I've never tasted anything like it!"

"And never will again! It's an invention of my grandfather's, filtered through my own unaccountable imagination. Lamb, of course. The rest is a secret. Speaking of secrets – you are about to uncover one."

"What?"

"You are about to uncover a secret."

"What secret?"

"I don't know. Oh dear, I'm drunk! How good, how good it feels to be drunk! What a pity, what an infinite pity, that we can't keep getting drunker and drunker, feeling better and better, our heads grow clearer and clearer! But it is not to be."

Scene Forty-seven

"Once, Kazue" said Ikuko, "when you were a baby, I took you to my mother's for the afternoon, and came home to find the house empty. It was Sunday, he'd said nothing about going out. Well, so he went for a walk, I thought, he'll be home soon. Only he wasn't. Hours passed. It grew dark. I fed you, put you to bed... What should I do? Call the police? It's something you naturally shrink from doing, until you're certain something's really wrong, but what if it's too late by then? Yes, I'd better call... No, I'm being silly... That went on for what seemed like years... Suddenly there was a noise. I'll never forget... he came downstairs; he'd been up in that... that loft of his, all that time, 'just sitting doing nothing, as the Zen-men say...' I sobbed, wept, flung myself into his arms... He hadn't meant to upset me, had just fallen into a trance or something – a trance called sleep, maybe." She laughed. "I can laugh about it now. I was hysterical, literally hysterical; he didn't know what to do with me; he swore it would never

252

happen again. He calmed me down; the calmer I grew, the more agitated he became, as though realizing the enormity of what he'd put me through, you see. As for me... I've been calm ever since." She laughed again. "Have you ever seen me anything but calm, Kazue? Or you, Osamu? You haven't, have you? Well, it dates from then. Your father... there's a kind of inner serenity in him, an inner... inner peace. I understand him. He was losing that inner peace. He didn't say so in so many words, but I'm not his wife of twenty-eight years for nothing, I could see it happening, as I'd have to've been blind not to. He was losing it, something was happening inside him... It's funny – the first thing I did, after reading his note, was to run upstairs to the loft...It's funny the way the mind works... Well, come, Kazue, let's us see about dinner. Osamu, make yourself comfortable. You have a book with you, I see?" He showed it to her. "Euripides! I wouldn't have thought that'd be your cup of tea somehow."

"No? Maybe not. I'm not sure what my cup of tea is anymore. Professor Horiuchi's been going on about his Greeks, and in the bookstore the other day I happened to see this tattered old volume for 85 yen... Ten plays. 8.5 yen per play." He grinned.

"So you see, children," said Ikuko, "there's nothing to worry about. He just has to be alone for a while, that's all. You mention Professor Horiuchi. I wouldn't be surprised if that's where he's gone."

Scene Forty-eight

When there was no answer to his repeated ringing, Yasushi did not go away immediately. There was the natural reluctance to accept that he had come all this way for nothing, that his very

253

strong desire for a talk with his old friend was being thwarted. In addition to that, though, something struck him as faintly odd. He couldn't put his finger on it at first. True, there was nothing at all odd in a man's not being home when you have come calling without notice, but... of course – the bell made no sound. Usually, standing outside, you hear some trace, however muffled, of a doorbell's ring. He tried again. Sure enough – dead silence.

He walked around to the side of the house, then to the rear. What a scrubby garden. It could have been beautiful. Strange, Masao's failure to take an interest in cultivating things, growing things. He himself, living cramped in the middle of a great city, had hardly any space at all in comparison with this, and yet the flowers growing up under his care, each marking its own particular season, gave him at times a nameless, radiant happiness. He could not imagine life without his flowers, without his turnips, tomatoes and beans. It was the one aspect of life in which matter did not seem bent on defeating him. "Why, in a garden this broad," he imagined himself lecturing Masao, "you could grow almost your entire sustenance! You could..." He stopped. Had it been his imagination? Chancing to look up, he glimpsed, or seemed to, a face in the window upstairs. It was probably the window of Masao's study. His footsteps must have startled Masao, who, looking out the window and seeing him, vanished in the hope of not being seen in turn. Yasushi smiled. "Curiouser and curiouser!" Who had said that? Of course – Alice in Wonderland, Kazue's favorite bedtime story once upon a time.

"What's he done then, disconnected the doorbell? He wants to be alone, undisturbed. Well, we'll see."

He returned to the front door and rapped soundly on it. "Masao, it's me, Watanabe!" he called out at the top of his voice. "Let me in, Masa, I know you're home, I've come all the way out here on purpose to talk to you!" It amused rather than embarrassed him to think how this must look to onlookers and passers-by – but in fact there were none; the street was, or at least seemed, absolutely deserted. Perhaps at that very moment someone cowering in a nearby house, imagining heaven only knows what, was reaching for the phone to call the police. "Come, come, Masao, this won't do! I'm a guest, come from afar, claiming your hospitality..."

"Are you here to see my father?"

He had not been aware of anyone's approach, but was not unduly startled by the presence beside him of a young man, strikingly handsome, addressing him with grave and quiet courtesy.

"Your father! You must be Jun."

"Yes."

"Your father has spoken of you. I've long been anxious to meet you. My name is Watanabe. Your father and I are old friends. I was hoping for a good talk with him, such as we sometimes have, and came out here more or less on the spur of the moment, but he seems not to be home. It was stupid of me to come without calling."

"Please come in, I'll make you a cup of tea." He fished in his pants pocket for his key.

"Oh no, I..."

"Please do." He inserted the key into the lock, and Watanabe watched the door spring open with what to him seemed preternatural ease. "Yes, a key is a marvelous thing," he thought with a smile.

Scene Forty-nine

There is a peculiar state of unconsciousness in which one is, so to speak, conscious of being unconscious. Such was Yasushi's condition as he sat in the train staring blankly out the window at the nondescript scenery. He had inadvertently boarded a local train; it would take hours to get to Tokyo. "I wonder," he thought vaguely, "what shows on my face; whether anyone looking at me would know..." The thought faded, unfinished. In fact the train was almost empty; no one sat anywhere near him, no one was aware of his existence, or he of anyone's; there were no distractions, and he was quite at leisure to review the events that had put such an unexpected end to his visit to Masao.

He did review them, in the sense that they passed before his mind's eye, but their passage was curiously lifeless. Yes, they had occurred; yes, he remembered them, remembered everything with perfect clarity; but it was not a vivid clarity, not a *living* clarity; it did not engage his consciousness; he was like a man dozing in a room with a TV on, dimly aware as he dozes of what's happening on-screen but not aware that he is aware.

Another thought took shape in his mind. Instead of going home he would go to Haneda airport and fly to Okinawa – not for anything he wanted to do there but because it was the farthest in the world he could go without his passport, which of course he was not carrying with him. Once there he would settle into some remote corner and live out the rest of his life in unbroken solitude; yes, he would buy a plot of land and do what he'd imagined himself telling Masao to do – grow his own sustenance, live only on what he could produce himself. It was an attractive plan, and he was perfectly free to carry it out. A simple transfer at the next station would put him on the right track. "Yes," he thought, "that's what I'll do, that's what I'll..." – but he made no movement and had no intention of moving; no intention of not moving either.

He was suddenly aware of someone sitting across from him. This roused him somewhat from his stupor. There were plenty of empty seats; why had this person chosen to sit here? But looking around he saw that in fact there were not so many empty seats; the train was more crowded than it had been; he had not noticed it filling up. His companion was an elderly gentleman whose trim figure and ramrod bearing suggested a former soldier – though of course he could have been anything. Suddenly a strange impulse came over Yasushi. He would tell this man everything. That this was irrational he knew, but knowing it did not weaken the impulse; if anything it made it stronger. "It's not so strong that I can't resist it, and of course I know I *should* resist it..." So he was thinking when, to his astonishment, the man addressed him.

"Excuse me if I seem to be staring; I can't help thinking you look familiar."

"Yes," murmured Yasushi, "I was thinking the same about you."

Scene Fifty

"I knew you as a boy," the man said. "That is, when *you* were a boy. I of course was already approaching old age."

257

"How can that be?" asked Yasushi with a smile. "It's fifty years since I was a boy. Or sixty, depending on how young a boy."

"My name is Harada. I taught you in third and fourth grade."

"Do you know, I've often thought of looking you up."

"No! Is that so?"

"Yes indeed. You, of all my teachers... It's hard to explain..."

"I recognized your potential, you see. I encouraged you. It's a tricky business. One has to manage it without alienating the other children."

"Your encouragement was very important to me. Just this morning I woke up thinking there must be some way to let you know – and now this unexpected meeting! Are you still teaching?"

"Oh no, heavens no. Even when I taught you I was getting ready to retire. I believe I retired the following year, or the year after."

"Yes, well... this is my station..." What had caused him to lead the poor old man on like that? It was cruel, an infantile sort of cruelty; it disgusted him. He passed through the exit gate and into the street. Where was he? He had not even noticed the name of the station. It hardly mattered. There would be a coffee shop somewhere. Yes, here was one. A little bell tinkled as he pushed open the door. For a moment he could make nothing out, so dark did the interior seem to his sun-dazzled eyes. He paused in confusion. He would have turned around and groped his way out again, but a woman, young by the sound of her voice, greeted him; her chair scraped against the floor as she rose to usher him to a table. The darkness faded, but even so he could make out nothing beyond the general contours of objects; their details escaped him. He sat in the chair the woman indicated without knowing the shape or

258

size of the room or how many other customers, if any, he shared it with. Well, so much the better, he decided.

"Sit down," he imagined himself saying to her as she brought him his coffee. "I have something to say to you. Forty-five years ago, when I was fifteen years old, I killed a ten-year-old boy..." Would she scream? No, she'd laugh; she wouldn't believe him; she'd say, "I've heard some pretty crazy pick-up lines, but this..."

He sipped slowly, eyes closed. He felt calmer now, capable once more of reflecting, of distinguishing fantasy from reality. Seeing in Jun the boy he'd killed had, of course, been fantasy, pure fantasy. But how to account for it? Resemblance of some kind? Possibly, but if that is what had struck him when face to face with Jun, it no longer did as he summoned now the two faces to his mind's eye for comparison. The boy too had been handsome in his way, but it was the handsomeness of vacancy, of mental blankness, which Jun, lively and intelligent, in no way suggested. Something else then – but what? What could have struck him with such force that he bolted in panic, panic the like of which he had never experienced before, panic strong enough to be called terror?

Beyond question, something was happening to him. His mind was giving way, subject as never before to promptings of the irrational, of the void, of... he hardly knew what.

Scene Fifty-one

Tazawa had disappeared. Maeda, at the police *koban*, found the two officers who had tormented him the first time surprisingly friendly. They greeted him as an old acquaintance, both the taciturn young officer and the hard-boiled veteran. "Good of you to drop by," said the latter, "good of you to drop by."

Was this irony? There was something about the man that seemed to warn against taking anything he said at face value. On his guard, Maeda explained that he had returned to his job at the *Maiasa Shimbun*, that he was now covering the courts, and that his editor had asked him for a story on the wave of murders and its apparent cessation. Would the officers give him the benefit of their thoughts on the subject?

"Murders?" barked the veteran – but he smiled, showing uneven, discolored teeth, as though to say, "Pay no attention to this aggressive manner of mine, it comes with the territory, ha ha! But you and I, we're pals, we understand each other..." Aloud he said, "Let me tell you something about murders. Off the record. There are 32 million people in Greater Tokyo. That's about equivalent to the entire population of Canada, as I read somewhere the other day – maybe in the *Maiasa Shimbun*, come to think of it. The wonder is not that there are as many murders as there are, but that there aren't many, many more of them."

"That seems an odd attitude for a police officer."

"Does it? But what do you think a police officer is? A police officer is someone whose responsibility is to use as much force as is absolutely necessary, not a gram more, to uphold the law. Not a gram more. A gram. A gram too much, it's police brutality. A gram too little...why, a gram too little and in a week, if not a day, you'll come to us begging for a little police brutality, because there's other kinds of brutality which... I know what I'm talking about. Police officers are not very bright, not very educated. That's the general opinion, and it's probably right enough. There are exceptions. I'm not one of them, but young Otomo here has been to college. Got a degree in sociology. Doesn't say much, but knows what he knows. As for me, my universities have been the streets of Tokyo, and good universities they are, too. What have I learned there? Why, this: that in 'the state of nature' – Otomo's favorite expression, eh, Otomo? ha ha! – in the state of nature men would devour each other alive, like wolves."

"The streets of Tokyo – "

"Yes my friend, the streets of Tokyo. Otomo talks – *when* he talks – of a certain dispute among philosophers: are men naturally good, or naturally bad? My answer is, any philosopher who has not settled that question in his own mind should join the police force for a year. I guarantee you – a philosopher who did that would say at the end of the year exactly what I just said."

"Still, there was, or seemed to be, a wave of murders, and it seems to have ended, and so I'm wondering what you think..."

"What I think? What I think is that the word 'seem' is everything here."

"It's everything everywhere," murmured Otomo, who until then had been silent.

Scene Fifty-two

It was impossible to pin the officers down. They insisted – or rather the veteran did, for he did almost all the talking – on sticking to abstract generalities. Statistically and historically, he maintained, the "wave of murders" Maeda was interested in was by no means remarkable. "Wave of murders" was a media term, a media invention.

261

There had been no "wave;" nor had anything "ended." Yes, Maeda's eye-witness information regarding Tazawa as the murderer of poor Nagai at the noodle shop had been of interest; certainly it had; but Tazawa had vanished into thin air. "He'll surface eventually, of course, and when he does..."

It was a very unsatisfying interview. They're pros, he thought as he left the *koban* and, blinking in the bright early autumn sunshine, merged with a stream of pedestrians shuffling towards the train station. They know how to deal with reporters: keep them friendly by talking, keep them in the dark by saying nothing of substance. A seasoned journalist knows how to pierce that verbal fog, and Maeda was seasoned enough, but a peculiar circumstance kept him from pressing too hard – from noting, for example, that police efforts to locate Tazawa seemed extraordinarily lackadaisical, given the nature of the case. "He'll surface" – yes, but how many others will he kill while beneath the surface? Maeda's failure to raise this point – this very obvious point – was not altogether rational, as he well knew, but perceiving irrationality in your behavior is one thing, behaving rationally in consequence is something else. The peculiar circumstance in question was his deliberate concealment from the officers, for reasons he himself didn't altogether understand, of Tazawa's murder, before Maeda's very eyes, at midnight, of the homeless man in the little park in Funabashi.

That murder had never, to his knowledge, made the news. It *must* have, of course – it was striking enough – but at that point Maeda had turned his back on the news, willfully limiting his horizons to his own mind and his own apartment, the one he had shared with Yoshiko, and so in a way, though he had *seen* the murder being committed, had been taken along by Tazawa *specifically* that he might see it, it was as if it had never taken place – which did not, somehow, erase his sense of being *complicit* in it, of having himself plunged the knife into the ragged man sound asleep on the park bench...

"I bet I could find Tazawa if I wanted to," he thought as he walked with the crowd. It wouldn't be that difficult. He could start by visiting the Funabashi coffee shop Tazawa had taken him to, where the "Bufferin lady" presided – the lady who had been like a mother to Tazawa, who loved him like a mother and whom, it seemed, Tazawa loved in return, though how genuine his apparent feelings were was impossible to gauge – did he even *have* feelings? She might know where he was; or failing that... but every police officer knows where desperate people go when they have reason to be invisible – the *yoseba*, grim back-alley neighborhoods where day laborers congregate for construction jobs and cheap lodging. Every major city has at least one; Tokyo's is called Sanya, Osaka's Kamagasaki. No one has an identity there; everyone is as anonymous as the day he is born. Why weren't the police looking for him there?

"Should I?" He'd been to Sanya; had even, one summer, hired himself out as an occasional day laborer, more for the experience than out of financial need; he knew his way around the district, though he had never lodged there; seven years had passed, but even so, he might find a familiar face or two. "Maybe I will... but how will that advance the story I'm writing? Even if Tazawa's there, my chances of running into him are pretty small, and supposing I do run into him? What then? *I'm* not the police!"

His cell phone rang, interrupting his ruminations. On a whim a few days earlier he'd downloaded the opening lines of Beethoven's Fifth Symphony for a ring tone; now, as it sounded in the street, muffled only somewhat by his pocket and causing, he fancied, heads to turn in his direction, he blushed at the childishness of his gesture – how could he have failed to see it at the time? What had been going through his mind? Whatever it was, he no longer identified with it, he renounced it, he would change it as soon as possible. "Maeda."

"Kinoshita." Maeda sighed. There was no escaping the man. "Here's a curious item that might be worth following up. Police have arrested a guy spray-painting 'There is no God' on a Christian church. Suspected of a wave of other, similar acts. A black man, though apparently born and raised in Japan..."

Scene Fifty-three

Jun's poetry, for years merely a vague inclination which he himself hardly took seriously, had entered a new phase. He was perpetually being assailed by words. They came at him from he knew not where, in little clumps meaning he scarcely knew what, bursting into his head and demanding in the most urgent, imperative tones, it seemed to him, to be written down. "Just write it down, you'll understand later," they prodded him. They roused him from sleep, cut into his talks with Yuji and Yoko, pierced his saké-induced reveries, gave him no rest. Yuji, noticing his agitation and sensing its cause, had conferred upon him a pen and a little pocket notebook. It was filling rapidly. Soon, he reflected as he sat at his father's kitchen table sipping tea, he would have to get a new one. Opening it at random, he read, "The City of Vagina in the Country of Scorn." What *was* this? Was it poetry?

Suddenly he had a sense of not being alone in the house. He shut the notebook, in much the same way as one immediately, with embarrassment, stops talking to oneself if someone turns out to be within earshot. That strange man he'd encountered at the door had said his father wasn't home. Could he have been mistaken? But if so, if his father was upstairs in his study, why hadn't he come down? Jun's presence in the house had hardly been furtive, his father could not have been unaware of it. He listened, straining his ears. Sure enough, a voice was speaking softly – his father's voice. Reciting Greek? Jun could not make out any words, but the sound, a mere murmur, seemed more conversational than declamatory. There were pauses, as though to make room for a second speaker, but if there was someone else in the study with his father, Jun could catch not the faintest sound of his voice.

Jun sat on, puzzled and undecided. Should he go upstairs? It seemed the obvious thing to do, and yet he hesitated. If his father was so deep in conversation with someone as to not have even perceived Jun's presence, his barging unexpectedly into the room would be an intrusion. The visitor might be a former student, or a former colleague. Jun would be out of place. He was shy, and almost morbidly sensitive to awkwardness of which he was, or thought himself to be, the cause.

Then another thought struck him: Tomoko! It might be *her* up there with his father! Hadn't there been that time, long ago – or perhaps not so long ago; one loses track of time, sometimes – when he'd called Tomoko's cell phone only to end up talking to his father? His head had not been too clear; he had not known what to make of it and so had made nothing of it, had dismissed it as a dream, but the memory of it came back now with

265

more force than the initial surprise had borne. Tomoko!

Scene Fifty-four

He laid the tea-cup he'd been clutching gently on the table and, careful to make no noise, pushed his chair back. He stood up and tiptoed out of the kitchen and into the hall. At the foot of the stairs leading to his father's study he paused to collect himself. Closing his eyes as though to sharpen his hearing, he listened. Yes, unmistakably it was his father's voice, speaking softly, even tenderly, and though the sense of the words still escaped him, he heard enough to know the language was Japanese, not Greek. As before, he spoke as though to someone, pausing here and there as though listening, but no second voice was audible. Was he talking on a cell phone? Was it possible? Could his father, in his absence, have so far overcome his antipathy to modern communications, an antipathy that bordered on dread, as to go out and get a cell phone? No, impossible! At the very least, highly unlikely. Jun hadn't been gone that long – or maybe he had? – no, he certainly hadn't been gone long enough for an elderly man, naturally conservative, temperamentally stubborn, his thinking firmly rooted in the vanished past, to shed his fear of being "wired" – and deprived, therefore, as he saw it, of his precious solitude, his individuality, his very humanity – hadn't been gone long enough for such a revolution to have taken place! Easier to believe his father was communicating with Tomoko by mental telepathy.

Were his father and Tomoko lovers? Was his father the father of Tomoko's aborted baby? This

266

was insane. What were such absurd thoughts doing in his head? It was all very well to dismiss them as absurd – what if they were true anyway, regardless of their absurdity, regardless of their horror, *because* of their horror? What would he do if he unearthed incontrovertible evidence of their truth? Behind his closed eyelids flashed a scene of such horrifying vividness that it was all he could do to keep from crying out: a scene of him flinging himself on his father and strangling him, strangling him with his bare hands, his father gasping, gagging, begging for mercy, for forgiveness, and Jun squeezing harder, harder, harder...

He had never known such inner turmoil, never imagined such a thing. He stood at the foot of the stairs as though rooted to the spot, his knees trembling so violently he feared he might fall.

When he came to himself he was at the beach, gazing out to sea. Placid as glass, it glinted in the bright sunshine. It seemed to be winking. He shivered. There was a slight chill in the air. Autumn. Was it autumn already?

Scene Fifty-five

"Misako, hear me out, please. This house, it's like a... how can I say it? Like a second skin..."

"More like a shell. It's not only for my sake, it's for yours as well. Mostly for yours. We can never be happy here. *You* can never be happy here."

"I *am* happy here."

"You don't know what true happiness is. It's snug, comfortable, familiar, and so you say, 'I'm happy here.' But that is a delusion, Masao, a delusion."

267

"Aristotle says – "

"Masa, it doesn't matter what Aristotle says. Was it Aristotle who advised you to take the battery out of the doorbell and turn your house into a tomb? I want to live in a *living* house, Masa, a house that's *alive*."

"You said you'd stay, Misako, as long as I wanted you to."

"Stay with *you*, I meant, not stay in this house. Yes, as long as *you* want me to. And if you really want me to stay, you'll at least come with me to look at the house I've found. Just look at it. If you don't like it –"

"If I don't like it you'll find another house and make me look at *it*, and then one after that…"

"If you really wanted me to stay, that wouldn't bother you so much."

"But Misako, why move, why? What's the point? Imagine having to move all this stuff, all these books…"

"We won't move the books, we'll leave them, dispose of them; you will free yourself of the books once and for all."

"Free myself of my books!"

"You're like a child who's being told it's time to leave his teddy bear and go out and find a *real* friend."

"You're taunting me again the way you used to. You're reminding me…"

"Of what?"

"Of what I don't want to be reminded of. Do you know, Misako, are you aware, there was one time, one moment, when I could have killed you? One moment, a fleeting moment, and yet… I, a man who had never hated anyone, never had a violent impulse towards anyone… If there had been a gun within reach, or even… even an ax… You're laughing, but…"

"I am *not* laughing and yes, I am aware, though I wasn't at the time. What *was* I aware of at the time? I am appalled, looking back, at my own flightiness. If you had murdered me, it's nothing I wouldn't have deserved. That's the truth, and I admit it."

"No, it's not true. You were blameless; it was me."

"Well, we won't argue about it. Come look at the house I've found. Just look at it. From outside. If you don't like it you don't even have to go in. How's that?"

"Where is it?"

"In Tokyo. In Shinjuku, but in a back street so quiet you'd swear you were out in the country. Do you know what it reminded me of when I first saw it? Hansel and Gretel. The house they come to in the forest. My father used to read me that story when I was little. At bedtime. It was my favorite bedtime story. And looking at that house I remembered it for the first time in…"

"But how did you happen to… what were you doing in Shinjuku?"

"What is anybody doing in Shinjuku? A million people pass through Shinjuku Station every day. I was one of them. That's all."

Scene Fifty-six

"You seem quite alone here," said Yasushi.

"Yes," said the waitress, "it's a lonely spot." She was, as he had supposed from the sound of her voice before his eyes had adapted themselves to the dim lighting, young, but also, as he would by no means have supposed, built on a remarkably large scale, tall and stout, even imposing – almost comically so, given her youth and her soft, musical manner of speaking.

"Bring me another coffee, and one for yourself." Once upon a time he had been quite a lady's man, and, though sixty, was as handsome as ever – more so, perhaps, age having sculpted rather than withered his features. "Do you mind? I feel like talking, and from your face I can see that you're a good listener."

"Yes, when my father was ill he liked to talk to me as I sat on the edge of his bed. He spoke of things he had never spoken of before."

"Just so. I might have known you'd have had some experience of the sort. Your father is well now, I hope?"

"Yes, quite well, it was nothing serious."

She turned to the coffee maker, her easy movements betraying not the faintest hint of tension, and carried the cups, one in each hand, with the calm dignity of African women Yasushi had seen in his travels bearing jars on their heads. She laid the cups down and quite unselfconsciously sat down opposite him. If anything about the situation struck her as odd, perhaps even a touch threatening, she showed no sign. Her face reflected nothing so much as a perfect, untroubled serenity – and yet Yasushi saw, or thought he did, that for all her apparent innocence she knew how to look after herself, no easy prey for any man who might take it into his head to prey on her.

"You'll laugh, but there is something in you of the African desert," said Yasushi with a smile. "Something in the way you move, or maybe it's that long flowing white dress you have on. I seem to see you gliding across the sands. I wouldn't be surprised if, in a former life, you were an Ethiopian princess."

Her response was a smile so faint and fleeting it might have passed for imaginary. Perhaps it was.

"Of course," he continued, "appearances are deceiving. We know so little about ourselves – where we come from, where we're going, why we're here, why we do what we do. Are we the masters of our own fate, or are we helpless instruments in the hands of a being so vastly superior to us, with designs so utterly beyond our comprehension, that we can form no conception of its nature, or purposes, or anything? And not knowing even that much, what, in all seriousness, *can* we claim to know? That the earth is round? That the universe is so many billion years old?"

He looked at her, smiling, as though inviting a reply, and she looked at him, as though waiting for him to go on. The silence that followed seemed to absorb them both, to give them both pleasure, the pleasure of a shared silence that is no less satisfying, to those who know how to partake of it, than the pleasure of shared confidences.

"It's strange," Yasushi resumed at last, not so much breaking the silence, so quiet was his voice, as adding another layer to it. "As you age, the world seems to weigh on you, gravity to bear down on you, with greater and greater force. All physical things – sound, matter, light – grow increasingly oppressive. You are subject to delusions: in my case, that matter is conspiring to crush the life out of me, that I am helpless to fight back, my only defense being to *placate* matter – do you understand what I'm saying? – to placate matter, to pray to it, plead with it, make sure every object under my control is precisely in its place, failing which the whole universe will crack, or tear me to pieces in its pain and rage... It's a delusion that comes and goes. You see it's not on me now, since

271

I speak of it as a delusion. When it's upon me it's real enough, believe me, nothing more so."

Again he fell silent; again the waitress continued to regard him with unruffled calm. "Yes, I've come to the right place," thought Yasushi; "this is doing me good." Aloud he said, "The end of the world is upon us. Upheavals... does one have to be a prophet to see them? No, they're plain. Maybe these upheavals are the birth pangs of a new, better world. Very likely they are. But the world we know is over, and what's to come is beyond my capacity to imagine. Beyond everyone's, I should think. I came out today to talk to my friend Professor Horiuchi about this, but he's... he wasn't home. He lives in Wakaba. He's a historian. The past is his field, and I came to talk about the future. Does that make sense to you? It does to me... although maybe it's my son-in-law I should be talking to. He's in IT, helping to make the future – the post-upheaval future. PU, Post-Upheaval. Time will acquire a new dimension: there was BC, followed by AD; PU is next. Just the other day my son-in-law was talking about how astronomers are discovering new planets in different solar systems. No doubt there's life on some of them, intelligent life, moral life. Maybe we'll meet them on the Internet. But will their morality be anything like ours? Even among us, at different times and places, under different circumstances, one culture's abomination is another culture's pride and virtue. Human sacrifice, to name just one example.

"Long before you were born, when I was fifteen, I killed a child, hung his body from a tree, was arrested, institutionalized, 'rehabilitated,' given a new identity... I'm aware how fantastic that sounds, and how little likely you are to believe me. I won't ask you if you do believe me. There's the little bell, someone has just come in, you'll have to attend to him. Go. I'll sit here a few minutes more, and then I'll be on my way. I have to get back to Tokyo. My family will be worried about me. They see what's happening to me, or something of it, though they're hardly in a position to understand it, and they are naturally concerned. I don't want to burden them any more than I have to, during the time that remains."

Scene Fifty-seven

Kazue flung herself sobbing into her father's arms. "He's been arrested! Arrested!"

"What's this? Who's been arrested?" There was no getting anything further from Kazue; stroking his daughter's hair, he looked questioningly over her head at Ikuko, standing in the kitchen doorway, arms folded across her chest, the very image of grim stalwartness in the face of disaster.

"Your son-in-law," she pronounced dryly. "It seems he's been going around spray-painting 'There is no God' on Christian churches all over Tokyo."

It was strange. All the way on the train home he'd sat nursing a thought that had come to him out of the blue and whose sheer absurdity was as irresistibly attractive as the aching tooth you can't keep your tongue off: the next time he saw Kazue alone he would tell her his secret. The girl was so childlike, so innocent, so instinctively good – how would she react? How? He even realized, as he had not at the time, that his confession to the waitress had been a sort of rehearsal for a confession to Kazue. The waitress he need not worry about – she would simply disbelieve him, as anybody would. Kazue too, at first, would be incredulous; but he would know how to convince her. She would believe him in the end, and when she did... what? Would she cry out? Turn pale? Faint, like a lady in a Victorian novel? Would she hate him? Or, sensing his great need for her, love him all the more?

"Once upon a time," Yasushi thought to himself, "I was going to study psychology. I was a brilliant student, on fire to learn how the mind works, and what relation its workings bear to a certain order of being, universally acknowledged but obscurely known and variously defined, called 'the truth.' Circumstances intervened, my studies came to an end; there came a time when I could have resumed them but I'd grown lazy, became absorbed in gambling... Now all I have to study are the workings of my own mind, and right now what my mind is suggesting to me is that this scene now playing itself out before my eyes was arranged *deliberately*, by *providence*, to stop me from making my confession. Providence... I learned about that from Father Connell at the reformatory... Hm. Query: Can the utter irrationality to which the mind is unquestionably liable possibly *not* reflect the irrationality inherent in truth? Ah, Masa, Masa, what a pity you closed your door to me today! What a talk we could've had, Masa!"

"He called, he was laughing," Ikuko was saying.

"Eh? Who called?"

"Who called? Osamu! Ghost!"

"He was laughing?"

"Evidently he thinks it's funny. He was caught in the act, and promptly confessed to having done the same thing at numerous other churches. Go to the police station so he can be released into your custody. I would have gone myself, but Kazue here is hysterical, as you see, and I couldn't leave

274

her and the baby. Go. It's lucky you came home. Where were you?"

"What police station?"

"Ueno."

"All the way out there? All right, I'll go. Kazu-chan, you must get hold of yourself, my dear." Gently he disengaged himself and sat her down on the sofa. "You mustn't worry. He's a good man, but genuinely good men, you know, don't have an easy path through life. Only mediocrities do. It's most unfair. Be understanding."

He was surprised, on closing the front door behind him, to find it had started to rain. The sky had been cloudless all day; the afternoon sunshine had been positively dazzling. Well, but what was surprising about that? Should he go back for an umbrella? No, he wouldn't bother; it was no more than a slight drizzle, and though like anyone else he disliked getting wet, there is something about an umbrella that makes a certain type of man feel foolish, and he preferred not to walk into a police station, of all places, feeling foolish. As if his errand was not foolish enough to begin with! Would he be expected to apologize on his son-in-law's behalf? He chuckled to himself. Spray-painting "There is no God" on church walls! There is a certain poetry in that which, however, the police were unlikely to see, and he promptly assumed a grave demeanor, though he had some distance to travel.

Scene Fifty-eight

On the train into Tokyo Jun tried to empty his mind as, so he had heard, Zen adepts do, but the harder he tried the more it teemed with fragments of thoughts, scraps of images, incoherent sounds.

275

"Wrap me in folds of night... wrap me in folds of night..." It was his favorite among his new poems. Eyes tightly closed, he silently recited it, repeatedly, rhythmically, like a mantra. "Wrap me in folds of night, wrap me..." But there were no protective folds to cling to. Something awful was going to happen; he felt it. "Write it down, write it down!" shrieked a voice in his head. "Write what down? What?" "The crows roared, laughed, then vanished." Yes, he had given birth to another poem. Squeezed tightly into his seat between two other passengers, he managed, with much squirming, to dig the notebook and pen out of his pants' pocket. "The crows roared, laughed, then vanished." He had observed something of the sort on the beach; it had made no particular impression then; now, suddenly, on this crowded train, it came at him, as though furious at having been passed over.

He got off at Tokyo Station. There was a seemingly endless passageway to negotiate, and two more trains to take. It was deep twilight, almost night, by the time he reached Tomoko's apartment. The dread in his heart seemed to deepen with every step he took. It was unbearable. Any catastrophe would have been preferable to this nameless, formless anticipation. It was an old building, squat, three-storied, on land owned by a Shinto shrine. Tomoko's flat was on the third floor. He bounded up the outdoor stairwell and pounded on her door. "Tomoko! Tomoko! Tomoko!" "I'm out of my mind," he thought. "Tomoko!" The door remained closed. She wasn't home. About to turn away, he was arrested by a slight sound. The door opened a crack; a narrow beam of light, very bright light, seeped through. Tomoko had no lights this bright. The door was held by a chain lock. "What is it? Who are you?" A man's voice. That professor... the dark matter professor, what was his name?... Sawamoto? "Tomoko..."

"There's nobody named Tomoko here."

"Wait, wait! Nobody named... what are you saying?"

"I just moved in. I don't know... There's nobody named Tomoko here."

The door closed. He heard a faint click.

Scene Fifty-nine

I awake from a fearful dream, fearful. Horror! And yet... what was fearful about it? I recall it clearly, in detail, and, reviewing it in my mind, I find nothing in it to account for the scream that woke me, or the fear, the trembling, that accompanied my waking. It was simply this: I came home from teaching late one afternoon – it was early winter, and already pitch dark – to find three small children on the floor in the kitchen, laughing, chattering (one, I think, was crying), banging on pots and pans, making the most dreadful racket. I gaped at them in astonishment. Whose children were they? What were they doing here? I tried questioning them but they all answered at once, though without breaking off their play; it was impossible to make anything out. Then Misako came in. "Ah, you're back! I have to go out for a while. Keep an eye on the children." "Keep an eye on the children! Who...?" "I won't be long, I just..." "Just what? Just what?" She was gone, and I none the wiser. What was this? I had come home intending, as I did every evening before dinner, to spend an hour upstairs in my study, my "agora," reading Plato, immersing myself in his changeless "reality," his "ideas." I had been looking forward to it – again, as always, though perhaps this time with even more anticipation than usual, since the passage I was studying was especially interesting: Socrates initiating his two eager young interlocutors – would that I had students so eager! – into that which is fairer even than knowledge and truth – namely the Good, that Good which is to the Ideas what the sun is to the physical world. Well, I thought, these children are no concern of mine. I climbed the stairs to the study, shut the door behind me, and took the book down from the shelf. But it was no use. The shouting, the crash of the pots and pans, reached me even here, muffled at first but gradually growing louder, louder, louder, while I sat on at my desk, impotently covering my naked ears with my hands... until my own scream woke me and the noise stopped, but the silence that followed was not comforting...

Scene Sixty

Ghost became a celebrity. Maeda wrote the story that got the ball rolling. Suddenly every media outlet in the country wanted a piece of him – daily newspapers, weekly magazines, TV talk shows, Internet blogs. It was a surprise at first, but in retrospect, how could it have been otherwise? The notion of a black Japanese was in itself a curiosity; the peculiar crime he'd committed, though reprehensible, seemed more comic than threatening, and intriguing besides. What was going on in his mind? What was he trying to prove? His ebullient personality, his remarkable facility with language, his gifts as a communicator, did the rest. The public was hooked. Suddenly it couldn't get enough of Osamu "Ghost" Suzuki. His photograph was everywhere. One literary wag noted, rather incongruously but it hardly mattered, that he looked like a black Franz Kafka – intense hungry eyes staring out from under thick, thick brows, hair parted in the middle and cut short as though to emphasize his small but protruding ears.

The churches he had vandalized were outraged at the adulation heaped on him, as well they might be, though he had paid full restitution and, following his guilty plea in court, been handed a two-month jail sentence, suspended for two years. One church leader was moved to make his feelings public in an essay that was carried in several newspapers, the *Maiasa Shimbun* among them. The style was somewhat florid, but the reasoning was close and the sentiments evidently sincere. Religious affiliation aside, the writer argued, what is one to think of a society that rushes to embrace a man, that heaps honors and fame upon him, not for a great deed or a great thought but for a mere prank, for the destruction of property? Was the public at large hostile to Christianity, to the church, to God, to that degree? The writer did not think so. It was true that Japan, the most "Westernized" country in Asia, was also, paradoxically, the least Christian, measured in terms of the number of church members. There were numerous historical and sociological factors involved, which he proceeded to discuss at some length – Maeda, charged by Kinoshita with paring the piece down to reader-friendly size, severely abridged this part of it – but hostility? In thirty years of church work he had never, ever, he said, encountered it.

In a way, he went on, hostility would have been preferable, insofar as it would have suggested thought, feeling, seriousness, a search for truth. Mistaken but sincere hostility can be confronted, challenged, both with rational argument and with Christian love. Suzuki-san himself seems to have harbored strong atheist views and indeed a kind of hatred of God. He, the

279

writer, would welcome an opportunity to sit down with Suzuki-san for a serious discussion. Hatred of God is not necessarily evil; indeed, it might betoken a particularly warm and ardent heart that, given proper guidance, will turn from hatred of God to fervent love of God; had he not seen it happen? He went on to describe one instance which Maeda, not without regret for it was an interesting story, however irrelevant to the main theme, cut.

The fact was, the writer resumed, the celebrity that suddenly rained down on Suzuki-san had nothing to do with the meaning of his act but with its attention-grabbing sensationalism, with his undeniable charm, with his unusual identity as a "black Japanese." It was mindless, frivolous. Worse – was it not a kind of idolatry? Was not idolatry rampant in society today, not only in Japan but throughout the developed world, even in the most outwardly Christian countries – in the United States, for example? And did not the general state of society today prove the Biblical teaching concerning idolatry, that man could not turn from God to idols without dehumanizing himself? Did not, indeed, Suzuki-san's profession as a designer of sex robots make the point clear beyond the need for further argument?

Scene Sixty-one

"Designer of sex robots?" It was the first Yasushi had heard of it. "Where did he get that from? You could sue him for defamation."

"I'd lose."

"Why?"

"Because I am a designer of sex robots. As to where he got it, well, it's sort of common knowledge since I blurted it out on *Life's a Comedy* two weeks ago."

"What's *Life's a Comedy*?"

"A TV talk show. It's very popular. You've never heard of it? Really? You're as out of touch as our friend the professor."

"That's an exaggeration. He's a recluse. It's true, though, that as one ages one loses interest in popular things. Especially in *very* popular things."

"What interest replaces it?"

"Eternity, I guess."

"Maybe you and that priest should get together."

"I once knew a priest..." It was on the tip of his tongue to tell Ghost of the priest he'd known at the reformatory, Father Connell, the wizened little dwarf who, unconscious of how strongly he smelled of onions, had spoken with such heat concerning resurrection. Ghost would say, "What were you doing at a reformatory?" And he... but no, this was not the moment. It would come, though, that moment, it would come, he felt it, he would "blurt out" his secret, not on TV... although, on second thought, why not on TV? The thought hadn't occurred to him before; now that it had, it was oddly captivating. Ghost's celebrity was such that his father-in-law would be a welcome talk show guest, if he put himself forward, and... he would give the network more than it bargained for! But what was this will to self-exposure that was upon him lately? It was something new. The reformatory had done its work well; it had given him a new identity, an *innocent* identity. Years had gone by, decades, without him thinking of himself as the perpetrator of a monstrous, grotesque, irrational, appalling crime; not that he had forgotten it, but the crime he remembered had been committed by *someone else*, someone who had no more to do with *him*, with the husband of

281

Ikuko and the father of Kazue, than... well, than those unimaginable life forms Ghost was looking forward to finding on another planet somewhere. What had changed? Did he think of himself as the perpetrator of a monstrous crime *now*? Why was he suddenly... It was at moments tormenting in its urgency, tormenting, this craving to reveal himself, to be the object of horror, revulsion, scorn; and then all of a sudden it would be replaced by an equally strong but opposite impulse, to disappear without a word and never be seen again by anyone whose love he had won under false pretenses. But it was not the falseness that unsettled him – the falseness had nothing to do with it. Suddenly he thought of the figurine he had given Horiuchi. Why? There was no conceivable reason for that of all things to come into his mind now. But then lately there seemed no conceivable reason for anything that was going on in his mind.

"Actually," Ghost was saying, "maybe his way of putting it *is* defamatory, in a way. 'Designer of sex robots' isn't really my profession, but it ties in with artificial intelligence, which *is* my profession, or rather my field..."

"Does Kazue know?"

"Know what?"

"That you design sex robots."

"I have no secrets from Kazue."

"Why have secrets from me?"

"It just never came up."

"It wouldn't, would it, unless it's brought up."

"I suppose I thought you wouldn't understand."

"Does Kazue understand?"

"Does Kazue understand... 'Understanding' is not a word I use in connection with Kazue. She has other modes of... of relating to the universe."

"She's an idiot, you mean."

282

"Kazue? An idiot? You know I don't think that!"

"Was she upset? Did she laugh? What was her mode of relating to the universe in this case?"

"Why are you angry?"

"Answer my question."

"She was serious. She asked – entirely without irony, as far as I could see – 'Why would anyone want to have sex with a robot?'"

"To which you replied?"

"To which I replied that some people can't get it on with humans."

"True. And they're entitled to their pleasure too, I suppose. Eh?"

"You'd be surprised, you know, if you ever looked into it, how little difference there is between people and machines. The human brain – what is it but a very complex machine? At the present rate of progress, we'll have replicated that complexity in fifty, sixty, seventy years. Robots will be conscious, autonomous, sentient beings – more intelligent than we are, probably. We'll rule them until they take over and start ruling us."

"I'm glad I won't live to see it."

"Meiko will. Maybe even Kazue and I will. If we do, I'll bring you back to life."

"Indeed!"

"Don't laugh. I'm serious."

"I'm not laughing."

"We can create a program to replicate your personality. A robot who looked like you and had your personality, your character, your feelings... well, he'd *be* you, wouldn't he? There's this woman I work with. She was born male but is now female. At fourteen she suddenly learned that her parents were not her real parents. She has no idea who her real parents are, either her mother or her father, knows not the first thing about them, not the most insignificant little scrap of a fact. Then she

283

developed a bad heart so she got a new one. To top
it off, every few weeks she dyes her hair a different
color. So you naturally ask yourself, Who *is* she?
When she says *I*, does she mean what you and I
mean when we say *I*? You see what I'm saying?"

Scene Sixty-two

"No, Misako, no, I'm sorry, I will not leave this
house. Not even for... not even for you. You call
this house my tomb. So be it. What I call life you
call death; what *you* call life *I* call death.   For you,
life is *out there*. For me, it is in here, here in my
agora, with my books, my – "
"Masa. An agora is a marketplace – crowded,
noisy, alive."
"Crowded and noisy I grant you."
"Your beloved Socrates found it alive enough
for him. It would never have occurred to him to
withdraw into monkish solitude."
"You don't know him. He carried his solitude
inside him."
"Well, carry yours inside you."
"You don't understand. I can't live in the 21st
century. I don't want to. It frightens me, appalls
me, horrifies me, repels me. Man is ceasing to be
man, ceasing to be human. I don't *want* to be
wired,   networked,   enslaved,   condemned,
condemned to the... the... the *depthlessness* – yes,
that's the word. Depthless, depthless. Look into
people's eyes and you see it – there are no *depths*
there, no... *depths.*"
"You're mad."
"I've seen it, Misako. I saw it in the eyes of my
students!"

"You never looked into the eyes of your students. You despised them too much to acknowledge their existence, and then – "

"Go now, Misako. I won't detain you any longer."

" – and then, when they responded in kind, you retreated into an imaginary world in which you stood head and shoulders over the blind, deaf, 'depthless' multitude – solitary preserver of the vanishing past, custodian of knowledge, wisdom, 'depth', humanity! You're a poser, Masao, nothing but a poser – an actor. An actor playing the part of a sage."

"I'm no sage."

"I've just said that, haven't I?"

"I mean I never thought I was a sage. As to my personal defects, with which you seem so familiar, I grant them all. You're telling me nothing that doesn't come out of my own head. Go now."

"You're sending me away?"

"This is not the place for you. For you it would be what you say it is for me – a tomb. Life means different things to different people. I am discovering what it means for me."

"You need help."

"Yes. Yes, Misako, in the worst way. Don't hinder me, then, from seeking it. Goodbye."

Part III

Scene One

In the silence that followed his knock on the door Jun was seized with a sudden horror. Whose door was he knocking on? Where was he? How had he got here? It had simply vanished from his mind. "Is this how a person goes mad?" It was not amnesia, he knew perfectly well who he was, and remembered with perfect clarity having been turned away by a stranger at Tomoko's apartment – Tomoko's *former* apartment... "Sato-san!" It all came back to him. With Tomoko and his father both lost to him, not knowing where to turn, the image of Tomoko's grandfather, with his wide, wide smile, his swept-back mane of white hair and his general air of being a survival – a triumphant survival – of a vanished past, had filled his mind, flooding it with a kind of light, as it seemed, and beckoning him: "Come to me if you've nowhere else to go! You'll read me your poems, I'll be so pleased..."

He had not heard the door open, in his distraction he must have missed it, but it was open now, and here was the gentleman himself, in what might have been the same dark business suit he wore the last time – the first and only time – they'd met. The man peered at him through thick spectacles; he seemed at first not to recognize his visitor. From deep inside came the muffled sounds of animated talk, Jun's first fleeting impression of which was that it was in a foreign language. He shrank within himself. It had not occurred to him that there might be company; he had imagined finding – been certain of finding, stupidly enough – the old man alone and waiting for him...

He simply did not know what to say. Perhaps if the man had not spoken he would have turned tail and fled, dashing headlong into the street and flinging himself in front of a truck, so overwhelming in that one instant was his mortification and despair. But Sato had recovered from his surprise. There was that astonishing, radiant smile of his. "Jun-san! Imagine, I didn't recognize you! Come in, come in! Tomoko's here, and a few friends..."

Numbly he followed his host inside. He quite distinctly heard the words "Tomoko's here," and quite realized their import – without, however, being shocked out of his detachment. Indeed, he wondered at himself: "Tomoko's here; I should be happy, confused, terrified, all three at once... But I'm not..."

"Kazuko, bring an extra cushion."

Jun was aware of a stir, but not of its details. Here he was in the same *tatami* room which on that first occasion the grandfather had likened to rice paddies stretching as far as the eye can see; he had recited his poem about the moon and Tomoko had asked, Why always the moon? Why not the stars? "Yes, why?" Jun thought now, and blushed because it appeared he had unconsciously spoken aloud, and everyone was looking at him in puzzled silence...

Scene Two

Tomoko was looking at him as though at someone she knew she had met before but couldn't quite place. "How homely she is," he thought. She and four others were seated on cushions on the bare *tatami* – "like rocks at the Ryoanji," it suddenly struck him; such a stupid notion it was, too. The Zen-style rock garden at the Ryoanji Temple in Kyoto was famous; in senior high school his class had visited it on a school trip, and somehow, though it had not much impressed him at the time, he had not forgotten it; at odd moments in his life the image would recur to him, prompting the most unlikely comparisons, of which this was one.

He recognized Rogozhin, in his dark glasses but without headphones, and another man who was a stranger to him, and two young women who likewise he had never seen before. Kazuko now reappeared, wearing a kimono as she had been the first time he'd met her, with a cushion in her hands which, kneeling, she placed on the floor with a gravity suggesting that much hinged on precisely where and how she placed it. But perhaps that was Jun's imagination, because when she looked up at him her wrinkled little face was wreathed in smiles.

Tomoko broke the silence. "When you came in, Jun, Rogozhin was telling us his interesting theory of light and truth."

"It's not a theory," said Rogozhin mildly. "Well, maybe it is. I suppose the fact that it first came to me when I was quite a small boy does not disqualify it from being a theory. Call it that if you like. I simply maintain" – he turned to Jun with a friendly smile, as though welcoming him into his circle of initiates – "that twilight is the true light.

288

Darkness obscures, daylight dazzles, but twilight reveals. As a child I would rise before dawn just so I could reap the benefit of seeing things *as they are.* I took to wearing sunglasses during the day, even indoors. My parents were troubled – my mother was positively distraught. It seemed such a peculiar thing. What was to be done with such a child? Should they force me to take them off? Or indulge me in the hope I'd get over it? They tried first the one tack, then the other. Yes, family life for a child like me was often quite uncomfortable, though I loved my parents dearly."

On this incongruous note he wound up, having apparently explained everything to his own satisfaction. But Tomoko seemed eager to pursue the matter. "Light is infinite in its shadings and in its variety of intensities. The human eye, as you know, perceives only a tiny, infinitesimal fragment of the electromagnetic spectrum. Why should one particular shading within that infinitesimal range be 'true' and all others 'false'?"

He really does have a dazzling smile, thought Jun. He couldn't take his eyes off him.

"You are right of course. It's a childish notion, as I said."

"And yet you persist in wearing sunglasses."

"Call it the eternal child in me."

One of the young women stirred uneasily. "Yoshiko, I have to go..."

"Go! Why?" protested Tomoko. "I'm sure Jun has come with a poem to recite to us. Am I right, Jun? Grandfather, pay attention, Jun is going to recite a poem."

Scene Three

"No, really, I... Really..."

"Maeda-san!"

"What?"

"This young man, it will interest you to know, is the son of Professor Horiuchi. Jun, Maeda here is a devoted follower, a devoted friend, of your father's. He's a journalist. He interviewed your father after he won the lottery. I'd love for you to get to know each other. By the way, grandfather, did you know, were you aware, that Maeda here is a descendant of Watanabe Kazan?"

"No! Are you really?"

"To the sound of the siren I drift into sleep, thinking, 'It's not for me, it's not for me...'"

"Jun!" Tomoko seemed genuinely delighted; she rubbed her hands together in high glee. "That's beautiful! Sh! Listen... Sure enough, there *is* a siren in the distance – police? ambulance? fire? I don't suppose we'll ever know! – proof, whatever it is, that the poem was composed spontaneously, on the spot. We are witnesses not to a recitation merely, but to a composition! Oh, Jun, I'm so proud of you!"

"Write it down, write it down!" – this time it was not a single voice in his head but a ragged chorus of voices urging him on. But everyone was looking at him; he shrank from pulling his notebook from his pants pocket and scribbling down this latest scrap of verse that had come to him so unexpectedly and might vanish as suddenly, or remain in his memory in distorted form, if he failed to record it at once. Tomoko came to the rescue; the expression on his face must have betrayed his predicament, at least to so acute an observer, and she said softly, "Go ahead, Jun, write it down."

"Splendid! Magnificent!" Sato could hardly restrain his excitement.

"Grandfather, sh, let him write it down, then we'll all shower him with compliments."

290

"Yes, of course..."

"She has to see to her dogs," Yoshiko murmured to Rogozhin. Then, to Sato, with an apologetic smile, she said, "My sister has three dogs – a Chihuahua, a toy poodle and a miniature dachshund. They are as demanding as children."

"They *are* children," said the sister.

Jun looked up from his notebook to see the company clustered round the door, seeing the two women off.

"I'll go with you," said Rogozhin.

"No, why?" said Yoshiko. "I'll come back. May I come back?" she asked, addressing Sato. "Give me an hour. I'll be back in an hour."

"The poor girl had a nervous breakdown," Tomoko whispered to Jun, sitting down beside him. "Her boyfriend left her and she sank into a depression. Couldn't work, had to quit her job. She was in the travel business. Now she's the mother of a family of dogs. Do you see what the illusion of love can lead to?"

Scene Four

"Maeda, come here!" Tomoko called out imperiously. "This young man, as I said, is Professor Horiuchi's son. I'll leave you two together, I'm sure you have much to talk about. Oh, Rogozhin – by the way. I read your translation of the Dostoevsky story. It's not to my taste. I'm surprised it's to yours. But that's what I like about you – we've known each other since we were children and yet you keep surprising me. Lost innocence, golden ages. Does your mind really run on such tracks? But you'll give me the answer I deserve – that your mind runs on many tracks simultaneously. I apologize for having done you an

291

injustice, for failing to appreciate..." She started suddenly. "What's that?"

"What's what?"

"An explosion, screams, blood..." She looked about her, dazed and bewildered. She touched a hand to her forehead and examined it, as though expecting to find blood on it. She closed her eyes. "I know what you're thinking: 'Poor Tomoko, long on the brink of madness, has at last gone over the edge.' Jun, speak up for me. Tell them that sometimes... sometimes... I... Tell them, Jun."

"It's true," said Jun. "She sees the future."

"Sometimes. Grandfather, call the police."

Sato laughed. "And tell them what? That my granddaughter the seer dreamed of an explosion?"

"That you have reason to believe there may be a bomb in the house. That you received a threat, that you..." A new light came into her eyes as she regarded her grandfather. "You *did* receive a threat, didn't you?"

"My dear, a man in my position has enemies. A man in my position receives threats. It's inevitable."

"Never, never, never have I experienced anything with such clarity, such piercing... piercing..." She shuddered. "Grandfather, you're a samurai, I know, and I too of course have samurai blood in my veins, of which I always strive to be worthy. A samurai is calm in the face of death. But we're not on the battlefield now, and..."

"We are always on the battlefield."

"Metaphorically speaking."

"By the way" – Sato turned to Rogozhin – "this latest 'threat' comes from someone claiming to be your disciple."

Hearing this, Maeda involuntarily exclaimed, "Tazawa!"

Sato looked at him with mild surprise. "Yes, that's his name. Do you know him?"

"Yes."

"Do *you* know him?" Rogozhin asked Sato.

"No. What's the matter with you?"

Rogozhin's agitation was unmistakable. "He's no maker of idle threats. I second Tomoko's advice. Call the police. But first... the first thing is to get out of here."

Sato laughed again – a strikingly youthful, ringing laugh, it seemed to Maeda. "You surprise me, Rogozhin. 'Calm in the face of death,' Tomoko just said. You, of all people, I would have thought..."

"Oh, no, I'm no samurai. Once, in my despair, I admit... but now... no, I want to live, to live! And I want you to live. You have been like a second father to me. This Tazawa... he's no idle killer, he's a revolutionary who firmly believes that every murder he commits brings us closer to the promised land, paradise on earth, a cleaner, purer, truer existence. He calls himself my 'disciple,' and in a sense he is. He believes all that because I told him *I* believed it. After Emi died... after... oh, Sato-san, do you know what despair is, do you have any idea? Maybe you do, you lost a son..."

"I lost a son, but I did not despair."

"No, you're too strong a man, too good a man... But I lost a wife and I did despair, and in my despair I yielded to despairing thoughts, which to Tazawa became a kind of action plan. And I saw from the start what a twisted, deformed character he was, and what he was capable of, and yet even that didn't stop me; if anything it encouraged me. And now you, my second father, are to be blown to bits by a fanatic animated by my ideas, or rather my ravings? No, it can't be. If not for your sake then for mine..."

"And there's grandmother to think of," Tomoko interposed.

"You don't know your grandmother if you suppose she is any less a samurai than I am – or than you are, for I know your heart, Tomoko, I know your heart well..."

Scene Five

To Maeda it seemed he had just wakened up, and yet he was not in bed but in the street; it was night. The street was a busy one, judging by the traffic, though he seemed to be the only pedestrian. The headlights of the oncoming cars tormented his eyes. He shivered; it was cold. Where was he? What time was it? Instinctively he reached into his rear trouser pocket for his cell phone, and was surprised – and then surprised at his surprise – to actually find it there. 11.43, it read. Not very late. If he could find a station, the trains would still be running. And this cell phone – why, it linked him to the whole planet. What was that Dostoevsky had said about man being changed physically if he lost God? He couldn't remember; as an adolescent he had read Dostoevsky with passion, but that was a long time ago; under Rogozhin's influence he had been meaning to reread him, but had yet to do so. In any case, man *had* changed physically; his cell phone was now part of him.

Slowly, as he walked, it all came back to him. At Sato-san's house Tomoko had had a vision of a bomb exploding. Then it appeared Sato actually had received a letter from Tazawa, a bomb threat. There followed a discussion – a fantastic discussion: should they flee, or stay and face death like samurai? His own panicked flight he did not remember, but inferred it from his present situation. In moments of intense agitation one's mental faculties lose track of events. How long,

294

then, would he have been sleepwalking? A brilliant light on his right caused him to pause. Before he identified it as coming from a convenience store the thought of a UFO came to him, and he smiled. He could go inside, buy something to eat, for he was hungry, and get his bearings, ask where he was. Did he have his wallet? Yes; he felt it in his pocket. Still, he passed on without entering the store, and a moment later was at a loss to explain that to himself, and though he could quite easily have turned around and gone back, and indeed felt inclined to, somehow he didn't, and walked on like a man with just barely enough time to get where he was going.

So they would all be there in that doomed house – Sato, Rogozhin, Tomoko, Tomoko's grandmother, and Jun, Tomoko's boyfriend – "funny how I always think of him as her boyfriend, not her ex-boyfriend..." – doing what? Sitting around a table, holding hands as at a séance? No, there was no table, at least not in the *tatami* room... "But shouldn't I, as the only sane one, get the police, or.. or *something*?"

He felt a sudden longing to see Professor Horiuchi. "There must be a train station around here somewhere... but it'd take me two hours to get out there..." But the professor kept unconventional hours... Should he call? He wished he had a better memory. What a lot he had read, once upon a time, and how much he had forgotten! That first year of college, studying pre-med at his father's urging – his father's *command*, it would almost be fair to say. Medicine had no attraction for him, but he'd gone through an intense bout of independent reading, not only Dostoevsky but religion, philosophy. It was something from David Hume he was struggling to recall, something about how reason fails to assure us of the existence of that part of the world beyond our immediate senses. Did he have it wrong? Very likely he did; Horiuchi could set him straight, if only he could talk to him! "The point is... if I walk out of a room, what assures me that the room remains, in my absence, as I left it, instead of ceasing to exist, as my senses tell me it has?" Of course it was absurd that the existence of objects should depend on his, Maeda's perception of them... "Or is it? It depends on what we mean by existence! Or what we mean by absurd! Does Sato's tatami room exist? If I return to it..."

He was startled to hear his name called. It was Yoshiko. She had just left her sister, she explained, somewhat breathlessly, and was on her way back to Sato-san's.

"Where's the station?" he asked.

"Right here." She had just climbed the stairs to street level. "Where are you going?"

"You'd better not go back there."

"What do you mean? Do you know... you were always strange, but you seem to be getting even stranger!"

"It's not me that's strange, Yoshiko, it's..."

"I know, it's everyone else, and you alone are normal! There's something I'd like to ask you. May I?"

"Of course."

"Rogozhin told me that you told him you loved *me* but hated my *presence*. Is that true?"

"Hated? No..."

"What, then?"

"I believe I said I... I don't remember exactly... I had to be *alone* to realize how much I loved you, that in your presence..."

"Your love turned to hate?"

Maeda was silent.

"There really is something twisted about you. Shall I tell you the thought that terrifies me now? That if I hadn't met Rogozhin when I did I might

296

not have realized it in time, and... I don't know, I simply can't imagine..."

Scene Six

He left her, having failed – having scarcely tried – to keep her from returning to Sato's. "Let her go back to her Rogozhin..." But it was not resentment so much as fear of her scorn as he unfolded his tale, his hopelessly incredible tale, of prophetic visions, exploding bombs, Sato's determination to face death like the samurai he was – determination was hardly the word, it was more as if Tazawa's homicidal compulsion, or whatever it was, and the prospects of being a target for it afforded him, Sato, the most radiant happiness he had ever known...

He descended the stairway to the subway, the characteristic underground echo striking his ears with peculiar force. "The naked ear is intolerable" – Rogozhin had said that, explaining his peculiar habit of going about with headphones over his ears, "magic headphones," he called them, marketed exclusively by the Sato Trading Company. Patagonia. Yoshiko had wanted to go to Patagonia. Her sister, now mothering a family of dogs, had been a travel agent and would have made the arrangements. If he had agreed to go they'd be there now, together – no Rogozhin, no Tomoko, no visions, no bombs. In fact he'd had no objection to going. Why hadn't they gone? That sort of project, of course, has a way of coming to nothing. Maybe he'd go to Patagonia by himself.

He gasped – the echo made it sound almost like a scream. Fortunately there was no one in the passage. His cell phone had rung, sounding those first four notes – he had yet to change the ring tone

– of Beethoven's Fifth Symphony. He stopped, closed his eyes, took a deep breath. "What's the matter with me? Why am I so..." He tugged the phone out of his pocket and opened it, arresting the second ring after the first note. "Maeda."

"Kinoshita."

"Kinoshita!" He'd been expecting, if anyone, Tomoko – calling to tell him the bomb had gone off at last, they were all dead...

"I didn't wake you?"

"As a matter of fact you did," Maeda grumbled; it was not true, of course, and yet in a sense it was.

"I'm sorry. One loses all track of time in this job. It could have waited till morning, and if I had paused to think..."

"What is it?" Kinoshita's apologies, like everything about the man, could be gratingly tedious.

"Well, a curious story, a very curious story, just your sort of affair" – what could he possibly mean by *that*? Maeda wondered with a grimace. "Forty-five years ago a fifteen-year-old boy murdered a child of ten – strangled him and then hanged his body from a tree in a forest. The child was afflicted, had some sort of learning disability. You must have heard something about it."

"Yes, I think..."

"The killer was sent to an institution, where he spent ten years. Then he was pronounced rehabilitated, given a new identity, and released, a free man. Well, I've had a tip from a source. Maybe true, maybe not. The source is generally reliable. He assures me the killer is none other than the father-in-law of that character who calls himself Ghost – whom you, I believe, helped make a celebrity..."

He went on, but Maeda scarcely heard him. His head was spinning...

Scene Seven

"I'll tell you what," said Ikuko. "You won't touch anything, how's that? Matter will be my domain – you just leave it to me."

"Who do you think I am?" laughed Yasushi – for now that the fit had passed it all seemed quite funny – "Horiuchi? I can't live in realm of pure thought. He can, maybe, but in me there's what you might call an earthy element..."

"Why this rebellion against matter, then?"

"It's not rebellion, it's... matter no longer *obeys* me. It obeys everyone else, but not me." His smile was consumed by a yawn.

"Sleep, my dear." She eased him down onto the sofa.

"Where are you going?"

"I'll be right back."

She returned a moment later with a quilt, which she spread over him. He gave a faint grunt of appreciation, but was already asleep by the time she straightened herself to a standing position. She sighed. She was tired, exhausted – as much from the strain of concealing her exhaustion as anything else. On the wet carpet at her feet were the shards of a shattered glass vase and two chrysanthemums she had taken from the garden that morning. Yasushi had bumped his shin against the table on which the vase stood; in a rage he had seized the vase and hurled it against the wall. Kneeling, she set about picking up the glass fragments; but no, she would need the vacuum cleaner.

Kazue, with Meiko strapped to her back, came in as her mother was working. "He's asleep," said Ikuko. "I dissolved a sleeping pill in his tea. Let's go into the kitchen. I want to talk to you."

299

She poured tea. "I don't know what to do, Kazue. His mind is becoming unhinged. I see it happening, and I simply don't know what to do."

Kazue regarded her mother in silence, her eyes wide but serene, and Ikuko found herself wondering, much as Yasushi had earlier when tempted to spring a confession on her, whether anything in this world ever could trouble that serenity. Was the girl simple-minded, or was she wise? Not simple-minded in the ordinary sense, certainly. Her grades at school had been excellent. As a child she'd been quite energetic; as a very small child, a regular ball of fire, hard as that was to imagine now. At a certain point in her life – when had it been exactly? – she seemed to turn inward, reading much, talking little; then, gradually, she stopped reading, and spent hours at a time simply staring into space. Her parents worried at first, but there was something so disarming about Kazue's vacancy, if that's what it was, something so contented... You had the feeling, Ikuko was thinking to herself now, that she was retreating voluntarily from active life, having made a rational, intellectual and indeed active decision that she was not suited to it, or it was not suited to her, or not worthy of her; she would spend the rest of her life absorbed in her secret thoughts, which she would share with no one. Did she share them with Osamu?

"What do you think about all the time?" Ikuko asked – the words were out of her mouth before she knew it. Such a simple, natural question, and yet she had never asked it, for reasons she scarcely knew herself – "fear of intruding on sacred space" was the phrase that now popped into her head. She actually did feel, rather to her own surprise, that that is exactly what she had done.

"About Meiko," said Kazue simply.

300

Scene Eight

"For a true Japanese," said Sato, "life is a preparation for death. If we have lived well, we can face death with serenity. If we cannot face death with serenity, we have not lived well. I needn't remind you, Tomoko, nor you, Rogozhin, of the words of Daidoji Yusan, though it is never in vain to speak them and to hear them, however familiar they may be, and if you, Jun-san, are hearing them for the first time..."

"Grandfather..."

"No, Tomoko, don't interrupt. Daidoji Yusan said, 'The samurai must have the idea of death in his mind day and night, night and day, from the dawn of the first day until the last minute of the last day.' For only then are we able to fulfill the responsibilities life demands of us."

"Yes, all right. Grandfather, you are an incorrigible speechmaker, but here's what I propose: if it's our fate to be blown to bits by a terrorist bomb, and if, being able to escape that fate by simply walking out of the house we, of our own free will, decline to exercise that option, as the lawyers say... Just listen to me, will you? I'm as hopeless a speechifier as you are! It must run in the family! – I was going to say, let's 'fulfill our responsibilities,' as you put it, in silence. Perfect silence. No one says a word. Grandmother is showing us the way. All we need do is proclaim ourselves her disciples and follow."

"There is the Way of Silence and there is the Way of Words. I'm sorry, Tomoko, but at such a moment I feel drawn to the Way of Words. I feel inclined to speak, and also to listen. You have often reproached me for being in love with the sound of my own voice, and I don't say you're wrong, although I think your taste for mockery

301

sometimes leads you to distort the truth. But humor an old man. I will speak softly, but speak I must. For those who prefer silence, there are headphones in my study..."

"No, go on," said Rogozhin. "Speak."

"Every nation, every *true* nation, is built around an idea. America's national idea is liberty; ancient Rome's, imperial glory; Greece's, the free play of the human mind; the Jews', obedience to the Law of God; the Christians' – supposedly – love, forgiveness and meekness. What is Japan's national idea? Beauty. Beauty. And here and there, even today, you can still stumble upon remnants – tiny remnants, all the more precious for that – of that pure, timeless Japanese Beauty, that special stillness that Basho likens to the cicada's voice seeping into the rocks."

"If the matter were in my hands," said Tomoko, "I'd have the bomb go off right now, right this instant – the loudest sound the human ear is capable of assimilating propelling us into Basho's stillness."

"I beg your attention. I would like to tell you all a story, a very brief story" – Sato's voice had gone so quiet that Jun had to strain to catch his words. "It is a true story, a story of the distant past, more than four hundred years ago, when the warlord Oda Nobunaga, in pursuit of his enemies, came upon a certain monastery where they had taken refuge. The abbot refused to surrender them, at which Nobunaga made it clear he would set fire to the monastery and burn alive everyone in it. The monks quietly gathered and sat on the floor in meditation posture before a statue of the Buddha. They listened as the abbot delivered a final sermon, which he concluded in this manner: 'For peaceful meditation, we need not go to mountains and streams. When our minds are still, fire itself is cool and refreshing.'" He paused. "I would like now for each of you to say a word, and then, if you like, we will take Tomoko's advice and, as it were, take counsel from the silence. Rogozhin. Please."

Scene Nine

"Shall I tell you a strange thing?" Rogozhin began in his quiet melodious voice. "I feel like *laughing*. Laughing till I burst, laughing till the tears run down my cheeks. That's how I feel, and yet I dare say my face is grave enough and betrays not a hint of mirth. It reminds me of the time – forgive me for referring to it – when Emi died and I wanted to weep, to sob, to – as Dostoevsky put it – drench the earth in tears a foot deep – but I couldn't weep, couldn't shed the smallest teardrop, I simply couldn't, I didn't know how. You can't imagine how it tormented me, my inability to weep for Emi. I felt... felt... it's hard to describe... as if Emi *wanted* me to cry, she *wanted* my tears, *needed* them, as in the desert you need water, was *pleading* for them, pleading, begging, the last thing she would ever ask of me, and I... 'I'm sorry, Emi, I can't, I just can't, I would if I could...' Instead of weeping I mixed with riffraff like Tazawa, and encouraged them, and indirectly reduced us – or maybe Sato-san would say I elevated us – to the ridiculous, or sublime, position we're in now, at which I would laugh if I could but somehow cannot... Well! That's all I want to say, really..."

"Jun-san."

"I... I'm sorry, I..."

"Rogozhin can't laugh, and Jun can't speak," murmured Tomoko. "But he can blush. That is a talent in itself, an increasingly rare one. Who else blushes like that in these shameless days of ours?"

303

"Tomoko, there may be occasions where your relentless sarcasm is not out of place. This is not one of them."

"No, but just look at him, Grandfather – goggle-eyed, mouth agape... like a hooked fish gasping for oxygen."

"A hooked fish, gasping for oxygen!" Jun echoed. "A hooked fish gasping for oxygen!"

"Hurry," said Tomoko, "write it down. You see, Grandfather? You object to my sarcasm, as you call it, but it's just given birth to Jun's next poem!"

"The hooked fish gasps for breath..."

"Composed by Tomoko, refined by Jun. But no, it's yours, it's all yours!"

"Death," said Rogozhin. "Are we really going to die? Is Tazawa really about to dispatch us to kingdom come? For all my respect for your prophetic powers, Tomoko, if it were anyone but Tazawa I would all the same be looking forward with untroubled serenity to waking up tomorrow morning and preparing breakfast, as I always do, for Yoshiko, who likes to lie in bed watching me bustle about and laughing at my clumsiness. And then after breakfast I'd go back to work on my Dostoevsky, and then if the weather's nice we'd go for a walk in the park like a Victorian English lady and gentleman – for so I imagine us. In fact... I know a tailor who does that kind of work, you see, and without a word to Yoshiko I asked him to make us 19th-century English outfits. They should be ready soon now... maybe even tomorrow... Dostoevsky. He had a sacred mission: to save God's life. He knew God was dying long before Nietzsche pronounced Him dead, and he was... well, he was a good doctor, and he struggled mightily. But it was hopeless. Hopeless. I wonder what Yoshiko will say, when she sees the costumes."

"Did it never occur to you," Tomoko asked blandly, "that if my prophecy comes true you will rejoin Emi?"

Rogozhin looked at her, his expression unreadable because of the sunglasses. He tried to speak and could not. Tomoko had reduced him too, it seemed, to silence.

Scene Ten

"What assures me the room I left continues to exist even in my absence? Why, faith, faith! Nothing but faith!" It was an exciting discovery, and it seemed to descend upon Maeda from nowhere – "how did it *find* me, in this mass of humanity?" He wanted to laugh out loud; it was so funny, so true! Faith! Faith in God, faith in the continued existence of people and things beyond the range of your senses – one and the same thing! Faith! His mother had been right after all! If faith in continued existence is permissible, though unsupported by reason (and if it's not permissible then life as we know it simply falls apart) then faith in God, equally unsupported by reason, is permissible too! More than permissible, it's almost – if not entirely – mandatory, required of us as human beings if we're to remain human!"

He stood fairly crushed among his fellow passengers, many of them swaying drunkenly in their dark blue or gray business suits, on the last train out to the Chiba suburbs. He had stood outside it, on the platform, unable to make up his mind. Should he go to Horiuchi's? He wanted very much to, but the hour told against it – you don't go knocking on a man's door at one o'clock in the morning, even allowing for the man's unconventional hours. "It's ridiculous," he decided.

Tomorrow, I'll go tomorrow..." But just then the train's doors began to close and instinctively, impulsively, he flung himself inside, and by the time the inevitable recoil hit him – "what am I *doing!*" – the train was in motion. It seemed to be straining under the weight of its massive human cargo. How many people would it be carrying? Enough to populate a fair-size town, surely. The air in the car was heavy with the sour odor of exhaustion. "Given a choice and an easy way of doing it, I bet half these people would end their lives this very instant, though if feelings persist after death – and who's to say they don't? – they might regret it later. Faith, faith! What an absolutely extraordinary notion!"

Scene Eleven

Had Kinoshita really phoned him? Hadn't he imagined it? What confers *reality* upon the images served up by memory? Why, faith again! And yet sometimes at least, often more likely, that faith, we know, is misplaced. Now a new thought struck him: the call had come just as he had been thinking of going to see Horiuchi. The coincidence was astonishing, almost frightening. Horiuchi and that man were friends. Would Horiuchi know anything about it?

"That man, that man." Here was another memory: "that man's" name was Watanabe, and Maeda had first met him not through Horiuchi but at a public bath, where, apparently daydreaming about his ancestor Watanabe Kazan, he had muttered "Watanabe," and the man had responded. A new identity, Kinoshita had said. Was Watanabe the new identity, or the old?

"What a story this will make!" The journalist in him was awake now, relishing the possibilities. It was funny – his first encounter with Horiuchi had been an interview, on the occasion of Horiuchi's lottery win. He had gone about his work resenting the pettiness of the assignment, and yet look what had arisen from it! First, his "discipleship" – and if Horiuchi was not exactly a great scholar he was at least a thinking man, which alone set him apart from most of the human race and made him a worthy master. "Whose disciple would I be otherwise – Kinoshita's?" He laughed inwardly; perhaps outwardly too for all he knew – or cared, he thought, glancing up at the deathlike faces floating aimlessly about at eye level.

Where was he? His sense of time, of how long he had been on this train, and consequently of how far it had traveled, was gone; it seemed, suddenly, like a very long time. But no, it couldn't be, almost certainly they had not even left Tokyo yet; if they had the crowd would have started to thin. Wakaba was close to the end of the line; they wouldn't be there for a while. He closed his eyes. Yoshiko – he suddenly saw her as clearly as if he'd been staring directly at her. She would be at Sato-san's by now – dead? A mangled, dismembered corpse? And Tomoko too, and all of them? Nonsense, nonsense! There was no bomb, Tomoko's "prophecies" were scattershot; she was the first to admit their fallibility, and laughed herself at the intensity of the "visions" she sometimes had. They popped into her mind as randomly as thoughts pop into other people's – into his own, for example; he knew very well from his own experience, as who did not, how haphazard and unaccountable the process called "thinking" tends to be – thoughts come, they go... as "visions" did to Tomoko, with no relation whatever, or at best a purely coincidental relation, to "that which we call *reality...*" True, true, undeniably true – and yet what cold comfort reason was in the face of irrational fears! All reason can do is show us that our fears are irrational; it cannot erase those fears or even, most of the time, ease them.

Scene Twelve

Something struck him about the large round clock, with its sweeping second hand, on the wall opposite the ticket gate – not the time it indicated, which was twenty minutes past one, but its anachronistic appearance. It belonged on a wartime, if not prewar, movie set, and seemed altogether out of place here by this automated ticket gate that ushered him through with a futuristic beep as he swept his cell phone over the scanner. Had someone put it up there on purpose, relishing the effect? Suburban train station managers were not famous for comic imagination; on the other hand, who could tell?

He shivered; there was a pronounced autumn nip in the air, and a wind too, blowing in off the sea. It was several degrees chillier than in Tokyo; he should have worn a sweater under his jacket. What if Horiuchi was asleep? It was likely enough, after all. What on earth was he *doing* here? The trains were no longer running; he'd be stranded; what would he *do* until morning? Endlessly wander the dark empty streets, uninteresting even in broad daylight? Duck into a convenience store and stand there reading magazines, his eyes assaulted by the glaring fluorescent lighting and his ears by the nonstop pulsating music? Was there a hotel somewhere in town? He'd been here often enough but had never noticed one.

He turned into Horiuchi's street and almost cried out for sheer joy – there was a light on! It came from the second floor – he'd be in his study, then, poring over his books. Was it really Horiuchi's house? Yes, unmistakably. "Praise Zeus!" – the professor's comical devotion to the Olympian gods seemed at that moment especially delightful. He caught sight of a cat asleep in a tiny garden as he strode past. "I'll seize it and sacrifice it..."

He was laughing, laughing; he couldn't stop. What was funny? What, come to think of it, was funniness? Dogs, chimps, even rats laugh when tickled – he had read this only recently in a wire story in the *Maiasa Shimbun* – but only man laughs at... what? What does man laugh at? "What am *I* laughing at? I'd better stop; I can't ring the professor's bell at 1:30 in the morning *laughing* like an idiot! Ah, but... if anyone would understand, he would!"

He rang the bell and struggled to compose himself.

Scene Thirteen

His heart sank as the seconds passed and no one answered; he strained his ears to catch the sound of footsteps, but the silence was unbroken. Perhaps the professor had fallen asleep at his desk over his books; that would explain the light. But surely the sound of a doorbell would rouse even a sound sleeper? But then an odd thought struck him. He had not heard the doorbell. Normally you do hear it from outside, if only faintly. "I probably did hear it and didn't notice; that sometimes

309

happens... Should I ring again?" He hesitated to do so, but could not bring himself to leave either; the thought of the hours he would have to kill before the trains started running threw him into an almost bottomless, almost alarming despair; he had felt this despair before, and knew it to be wildly out of proportion to whatever circumstance chanced to bring it on; but knowing that didn't seem to mitigate it. Even waking the professor, even making an utter nuisance of himself, as it was now perfectly, unmistakably clear he would be doing – "and how could I have failed to see it before I boarded the train, when any thinking person... but I *didn't* fail to see it, I *did* see it, and yet came all the same..." – even waking the professor seemed preferable to hours and hours of aimless, idle, purposeless wandering through dark, empty streets, back and forth, back and forth, like some ghost...

Ghost. "Whom you, I believe, helped make a celebrity." Kinoshita's words over the phone came back to him; he seemed to hear them now as clearly as he had at the time. Spray-painter of churches, sworn enemy of God, "the black Franz Kafka"...

"What? You here?"

Maeda gasped; it was almost a shriek. His stupefaction was total. The first coherent thought of which he was conscious – and how much time passed before it formed he could not have said – was, "If I were prone to heart attacks..."

"I was just going for a walk," murmured the professor. "Since you're here..."

He turned left and walked slowly, Maeda trailing numbly behind.

Scene Fourteen

They walked, or rather trudged, neither speaking. What time would it be? Maeda had no watch; to see the time he would have to take his cell phone out of his jacket pocket, which necessity seemed an obstacle somehow. Thinking of his jacket reminded him of the cold, and he shivered; thinking of the phone reminded him – for strangely enough he had forgotten – that, standing on the professor's porch, he had not after all been all alone in the universe; there had been any number of people he could have contacted at the touch of a button – Tomoko for one; what would she be doing? How would events be playing out at Sato-san's?; Ghost for another – "yes, I should have called Ghost..." His earlier longing for a talk with the professor, now that the professor was right here with him – "assuming I'm not dreaming" – was gone; now it was Ghost he suddenly wanted to talk to. As far as Ghost was concerned, the future of the planet belonged not to humans but to robots; humans, he had said on TV just the other day – whether seriously or playing to the gallery was one of the things Maeda was suddenly eager to ask him – that humans had been merely God's device, insignificant otherwise, for producing robots. At the time Maeda had thought it a rather silly remark; now, suddenly, it somehow seemed perfectly plausible, even profound, in a way. The professor, for his part, seemed altogether unconscious of Maeda's existence. "I can just turn around and walk away; he wouldn't even notice..."

"Your friend Tazawa's been arrested, it seems."

"What?"

"Just imagine. In the den, where I almost never go, is a television set, whose existence I'd completely forgotten. It was my wife's. She used to watch it sometimes. She and Jun. Me, never. When I wandered into the room just now, being unable either to sleep or to read, I saw it sitting there and thought to myself, 'I wonder if I even know how to turn it on.' I pushed a button, nothing happened; pushed another one, and it came to life, a bit like – so I thought; rather a queer thought – like a man emerging from a coma after years and years, blinking in bewilderment... I myself was a bit bewildered. I stared at it for I don't know how long, not understanding a thing, and then... well, it was a special news report; they'd just arrested the suspected mass murderer Tazawa. He'd been about to board a ferry bound for Okinawa."

Scene Fifteen

They walked and walked, slowly, the professor in front, Maeda following, exchanging not a word. "What's he thinking about? Where's he going?" He turned left into one street, right into another. "The beach?" A rhythmic rising and falling suggested, at first only vaguely, waves, and a certain salt tang in the air, noticeable even at the station, seemed to grow more pronounced – but no, if the beach was their destination they would surely have reached it by then. "What am I doing? Why am I following this man like an idiot?" It was on the tip of his tongue to say, "I'm cold, let's go back," but somehow he could not bring himself to break the silence, as though doing so would blow his cover, expose his presence. It was easy enough, under the circumstances, to imagine himself a detective covertly trailing a suspect. A light on in the window of a house reminded him that every other house they'd passed had been pitch dark, not a light visible anywhere. "Maybe he's going visiting..." But they passed the house and walked on.

"Professor..." He had not meant to speak; the word emerged from his mouth as though of its own accord; it almost startled him; but the professor was by no means startled; he paused, turned, and faced Maeda with a smile. "I was thinking," he said. "The trouble, you see, is that I can't write. I can't seem to organize my thoughts. When I try to get them down on paper... I can write *notes*, you see, but... What do you think? Would you be willing to help me?"

"I... I'm sorry... what?"

"You will be my research assistant. You will organize my notes into a coherent whole – into, in short, a book."

"But what... what is it you're writing?"

"The title is, *Why Read Plato?* Come, I'll show you."

The professor led the way to a house and fished in his pocket for a key; only then did Maeda realize they had come full circle and that the house was the professor's.

Scene Sixteen

"Wake up." I shake him and shake him, he will not wake. He moans, thrashes... Is he having a nightmare? Or merely fighting me off? All right, let him sleep, it's just that... I'm worried. About what? I hardly know. It's not natural, to sleep so long. But then, he'd probably say of me, if he knew, that it's not natural to stay awake so long. When did I sleep last? Weeks ago at least, months more likely. The funny thing is I don't feel tired – nor hungry,

313

though I hardly eat. It's as though I've passed into a new phase of existence. Or perhaps I've died, who's to say? Death is the one thing that escapes the probing fingers of science. The most penetrating 21st-century intellect knows no more about it than our remotest human ancestors, barely out of the trees.

Let him sleep. I'll go upstairs... Look at this. Look at this chaos. I'd thought to live alone, undisturbed among my books... I take one book off the shelf and start to read, but a word or a phrase puts me in mind of another book, which no sooner do I take down than another writer, another thinker, another poet seizes hold of my imagination. I'm incapable, that's the truth of the matter. Incompetent, senile. I always was. No wonder my students despised me. Then, reading Plato one day, the words "why read Plato?" popped into my mind, and I thought, That's it! That's the book old Tazawa was after me to write for him all those years or decades ago, only neither of us knew it then, and the project descended into... well, chaos, incompetence, senility. Am I being given a second chance? Is that what this signifies? Face to face with my students, in the lecture hall, I had nothing to say to them, their faces repelled me, their indifference offended me... Now, though, now, from beyond the grave, I burn with longing to address them! Why read Plato? Why, in this 21st century, this post-20th-century 21st century, with its hyper-technology, instant communication, instant gratification of instantly aroused desires... They're indifferent because no one has answered, or even thought to answer, that basic, fundamental question for them. What does Plato, slow, plodding Plato, indifferent to desire, contemptuous of gratification, have to say to the 21st century? Nothing, they naturally assume, and turn back to their cell phones, their video games, their *manga*. But imagine Socrates come back to life among them. Would *he* be repelled by them, or offended? Would *he* dismiss them as beneath his attention? Assuredly he would not. He would approach them in his characteristic manner, engage them, question them, and in so doing force them to question themselves, whether their current mode of life is consistent with the "Good." Ah, how, how could I have made so little of the opportunity I had? I was their teacher. True, I am not a charismatic man; still, with a little effort, a little *will* – could I not have done *something*? Planted some seed in them, some notion of a better life?

Scene Seventeen

Maeda's return to consciousness was slow, and even when it had progressed to the point where he could say, "I'm awake," he was not altogether sure that he was, and altogether *un*sure of *where* he was – "if anywhere," he added to himself, neither knowing nor caring what he meant by it. "I've been drugged," he thought. "Rogozhin. Rogozhin drugs people. Rogozhin!" he called, but his voice startled him, and his next thought was, "I'd better keep quiet."

He closed his eyes, and drifted off again, but it was not really sleep, because as he dreamed he was aware of dreaming. He was driving a car, and though he had never driven before and had no license, he was driving competently enough; the problem was not lack of skill but a perfect ignorance of the town or city he was in; he had no idea where he was or where he was going. Beside him in the passenger seat was Tomoko, who in response to his unspoken question said, "Just keep going straight. I'll tell you when it's time to turn."

She switched on the car radio. The voice was that of a very young woman, scarcely more than a child, and she spoke very gravely, very rapidly, never pausing, never stumbling over a word, as though eager to prove that despite her youth and her childish voice she was worthy of the responsibility she had been called upon to fulfill. Her subject was Tazawa's arrest. Shusaku Tazawa, she said, was a terrorist who killed at random in accordance with a political program which during his interrogation by police he had summed up thus: "I want everything I see to be different from what it is." Random killing would spread from his example. Some would kill coldly for gain, others for the sheer joy of it, others still out of insane, overmastering terror. Terrorist and terrorized would merge, would be indistinguishable from one another. Society would disintegrate; man would revert to his natural state, "the war of all against all." In the fullness of time, out of the rubble, a new society would emerge. What kind of society? That was no concern of Tazawa's and was in any case impossible to predict, for who could predict man? Man was by nature unpredictable, which is to say he was free, boundlessly free, the only entity in the universe of whom that could be said – so he, Tazawa, had been taught by his mentor, a man he named as Rogozhin, a Russian – for he, Tazawa, could never have conceived such thoughts on his own, never; he lacked the intelligence; he had brains enough, though, to recognize the virtue and the truth of Rogozhin's teaching, which was all he needed to fulfill his role. In any case, the new society would emerge, its form and content beyond the imagination of anyone now living; it would grow, mature, rot, and then it too would be destroyed, by some future Tazawa under the guidance of a future Rogozhin... and again and again and again, on into eternity – birth, maturity, rot, destruction...

"Here," said Tomoko. "Turn left. Left, I said!" – for Maeda in his confusion had veered right. He jerked the steering wheel left and woke up with a start.

Scene Eighteen

He woke up and knew he was awake, but something was wrong;   it was as if his awakening had occurred a moment too soon, before he had time to get back to the waking world, whose gate abruptly clanged shut against him. He did not hear the clang, but felt it, and thought, "Will it ever open again? What if it doesn't?" The possibility was too awful to contemplate. It meant the eternal dissolution of all solidity. In its place swirled a kind of vapor, invisible but horrible, weightless and yet oppressive, odorless and yet choking – though his breathing, he observed with more puzzlement than relief, was normal and effortless.

He closed his eyes and it was as if he could see, literally see, his entire life, past, present and future, being eaten alive by a dream; it, his life, seemed to be calling out to him for help, screaming, screaming, though soundlessly; but he was helpless; he could move freely, and his strength was intact, but strength was not what was needed; something else was. What? He did not know.

He was not disoriented; he knew quite well where he was and how he had come to be there – remembered with perfect clarity the train ride out to Wakaba and his midnight walk with Horiuchi; remembered Horiuchi speaking of his book on Plato, then a sudden access of exhaustion, at

317

which Horiuchi, with a sympathy that was almost maternal, helped him out of his clothes and into a futon which he spread hastily on a *tatami* floor in a room Maeda had never been in, presumably Horiuchi's son's room, what was his name – Jun, Tomoko's boyfriend, the poet. What was that poem he had recited at Sato-san's? Something about a fish gasping for air...

Sato-san's. He had left them there waiting for Tazawa's bomb to go off – Sato, his wife, Tomoko, Rogozhin, and Jun. And Yoshiko! Yes, Yoshiko had gone back after seeing her sister home, he had met her just outside the train station. Of course there was no bomb, that was nonsense, merely one of Tomoko's visions – "But what isn't nonsense?" he suddenly asked himself. "What makes sense?"

Sato san, samurai that he was, disdained to flee for his life, preferring to confront death calmly and imperturbably. Tomoko had, or professed, nothing but contempt for the "samurai spirit," but she was imbued with it all the same, at least insofar as indifference to life and death went. Rogozhin's attitude he did not know. And Yoshiko? He had warned her not to go back, and her only response had been to call him weird, and yes, it was true, he was growing strange, even to himself...

"What's that?" He fancied he heard a knock on the door, a hesitant, timid knock, but before he could find his voice and call out "Come in," the door opened, at first just a crack, then, creaking slightly, more broadly.

"Ah, you're awake." The door opened full to reveal, standing in the doorway, not the professor, whom he naturally expected, not Jun, whose presence would at least have been comprehensible, but Ghost, grinning, showing pearly white teeth against his coal-black face. "Well well," said Ghost. "Fancy meeting you here."

Scene Nineteen

"How long was I asleep?"

"A hundred years. In my tribe in Zambia is a man we call the dreamer. He undergoes special purification and spends the greater part of his life asleep, waking only to tell his dreams, which, interpreted by the dream-interpreters, constitute our laws. What would Plato say to that, I wonder? Come, let's ask the professor."

"Seriously, how long – "

"Seventeen hours by the clock, said the professor. But what does the clock have to do with time? Was there no time before there were clocks?"

"What's that noise?"

"'Banish time,' the professor says. That's what he's trying to do. He's got rid of all the clocks and watches in the house – all except one, the one on the kitchen wall, with the cat face and the swinging tail. It's his late wife's, he says, but I think the real reason – "

"What's that noise?

"Noise? Life. I didn't come alone, you see. I brought my family."

"Your family?"

"Not my tribe, my family. Wife, child, father-in-law, mother-in-law. The professor is entertaining them, or they are entertaining the professor. Shall we join them?"

"You brought your family?"

"Your waking, I see, is partial at best. Go back to sleep, if you like."

"Tell me, was I... ill?"

"How do you feel? You don't look well."

"I feel... I don't know how I feel, that's how I feel."

"Go back to sleep."

"Tell me... Tazawa's arrest. Did I dream that, or did it really happen?"

"It happened. They caught him trying to board a ferry."

"I'm afraid to ask my next question. Was there a... bomb?"

"An enormous one, yes. In a market in Baghdad. Over a hundred dead."

"In Tokyo, I mean."

"Tokyo?"

"No? Nothing in Tokyo?"

"Tokyo, to the best of my knowledge, is intact. Did you dream of a bomb going off in Tokyo?"

"Yes."

"My father-in-law says his dreams are so fearful he dreads going to sleep. He fights sleep off with every ounce of strength he has. It overcomes him in the end, of course. Interesting man, my father-in-law."

Maeda eyed him narrowly. "How well do you know him?"

"How well?"

"I'm sorry, I hardly know what I'm saying."

"He's the father of the woman I love. There are few men you know better – or love more, unless you hate him – than the father of the woman you love."

"Is that so?"

"Listen. I'll tell you something strange. Something strange is happening to his mind. My mother-in-law fears it's breaking down, but I think it's evolving, or, as they say in my tribe, *ascending*. He's starting to see connections, you see, that – "

"What's this 'my tribe' business?"

"Oh, just something I started saying on television, and before I knew it it became part of me. Does it bother you?"

"No. Starting to see connections that what?"

"That the rest of us don't see, because our culture doesn't train us to see them. Our culture overlooks them. Our culture overlooks a great deal. If he were in Africa he'd be a shaman. Here he's in danger of being declared a madman. There are too many madmen here."

"They're all shamans really? Is that what you're saying?"

"Maybe we should transport them to Africa, where they'd be respected and useful. They're wasted here."

"Well, you have a national audience. Raise the issue. When a man like you has an idea – "

"'A man like me'? Meaning what?"

"A man with fans, I mean. A man with fans has power. A man with fans can change the world."

"Funny you should say that. The professor was saying just now that change is not the solution but the problem. He was echoing Plato, of course."

"Can I ask you a personal question?"

"I'm an open book."

"You speak of love. In your experience, is there any connection between love and fear?"

"Yes. Loving Kazue, I fear losing her."

"That's not what I mean exactly. Loving Tomoko, I fear... Tomoko. Love and fear are one. I don't know how to express it."

"Words are at best a dim shadow of our true feelings."

"And do our true feelings truly reflect the real world?"

"My friend, our true feelings *are* the real world."

321

Scene Twenty

"Here they are, here they are!" Watanabe cried, rushing forward to greet them as they entered the living room. Maeda was surprised at the sight of him. He had aged – or was his memory playing him false? It was hard to say precisely what in him had altered, and yet the impression remained of confronting an old man – a vigorous, robust old man, but an old man all the same – who at their earlier meetings had not struck him that way at all. "We haven't met," Watanabe went on, "since the night of my birthday party, the night the poor noodle shop man was murdered. An ill-omened beginning for a new year in one's life! And in fact the year has unfolded... how shall I say it? Not normally. Not normally at all. Oh, speaking of normal. Masu" – he wheeled around to the professor, who was sitting on the sofa with little Mieko on his lap and Kazue anxiously bent over her as if to snatch her in case she should fall – "I have a request to make of you. An abnormal request, if you like. Let me have that Jomon figurine back, would you? Iku-chan" – he now turned abruptly to his wife, seated demurely on Kazue's left – "I've solved the mystery. It was when I gave him the figurine that things started to go wrong. Let me have it back again, Masu. I'll give you something else instead."

Scene Twenty-one

Maeda heard a faint cry, a sort of collective gasp. He was conscious of falling, falling, and of thinking as he fell, "I'm losing consciousness." When he awoke at last it was with the feeling of having slept through eons, eons of cosmic birth, cosmic destruction, cosmic rebirth... He had had such dreams before. The thought now struck him, "Maybe I'm epileptic?... But where am I?" Here at least there was no mystery; a pale dawn light seeping through a shoji paper screen revealed a room, dim and featureless but immediately familiar as the one in which Ghost had wakened him and begun babbling about his "tribe." They had then joined the company in the living room – "my family, not my tribe"; Watanabe was there, and the professor, uneasily dandling little Mieko; and then suddenly he had fainted, or slipped and fallen into an alternate universe. He strained his ears but heard nothing, not a sound, not even a bird, which was odd because birds, especially crows and seagulls, were particularly numerous out here and were generally raucous enough, to the point he had often wondered how the professor could stand them.

He was hungry. It was a fierce, demanding hunger. "Can I get up?" He raised himself on one elbow; he felt a slight dizziness, but it was not disabling, and slowly, cautiously, he got to his feet, delighted, almost joyful, to discover that his strength was almost intact. "I'm well! I'm not sick!" He laughed soundlessly to himself. "What an old woman I am!" Such hunger as he felt, indeed, was hardly consistent with sickness.

The wood of the floor felt cold against his bare feet.

Scene Twenty-two

The kitchen as he entered it was dazzlingly bright, as though it had allocated to itself all the light that the house as a whole laid claim to, leaving the other rooms to wallow sullenly in gloom.

323

He had to almost shut his eyes against the glare. It seemed sinister, malevolent, unnatural, but only for a moment. A room facing east catches the morning sun, he reminded himself – "I must anchor myself in reality. I'm a journalist, after all!" That made him laugh. "Some journalist! AWOL, at a time like this, when the world is being turned upside down and I could be writing about it, instead of..." Instead of what? "Never mind, let's see what's in the fridge, I'm starving, the professor won't mind, the professor... ah, here's that cat-clock Ghost mentioned." It grinned at him, its tail swinging back and forth. "Five twenty-three – well! Five twenty-three... You know, I could really be epileptic," he said aloud; "that would explain a few things, though I've never actually had a fit. I don't think I have, anyway. Maybe I'm having a fit now. Maybe this is an epileptic fit..."

There was nothing in the fridge, nothing at all, except for a carton of milk, about two-thirds full. He drank from the carton and winced. Was it his imagination, or did the milk taste peculiar?

"Come upstairs," said the professor, who now stood before him. Maeda was surprised not at his sudden presence, for it seemed to him in retrospect that he had been unconsciously aware, as he peered into the fridge, of a faint footfall on the stairs, but at his sternness, the sternness a man of serious purpose might show towards one insufficiently intent on the task at hand. "Come. We must not keep Plato waiting."

Scene Twenty-three

"No, we must not keep Plato waiting," resumed the professor as he and Maeda settled themselves. "You've read, of course, the *Republic*,

324

and the *Apology*, but it's the *Phaedo* in particular I would draw your attention to. A pity you don't know Greek. Plato in Japanese is... Plato in Japanese. Once upon a time I blamed the translators, and even thought of trying my own hand at it. Tazawa encouraged me: 'Oh, do the *Phaedo*, do the *Phaedo*' – and his whole body would quiver with excitement. 'It was you Plato had in mind when he wrote it!' His very words, I'm not joking; and if you'd known Tazawa you wouldn't *think* I was joking. The *Phaedo* is where Socrates, within hours of his execution, discourses with visitors in his cell on the immortality of the soul. You will read it, you will see. Give me political power for a day and my first and only law – in fact I had just scribbled a note to that effect before I came down and found you in the kitchen... where is it?... hm! – my first law is that no one is to be considered a full-fledged member of the community without having read, and shown evidence of having adequately pondered, the dialogues of Plato, *Phaedo* in particular. Just imagine a city, a country, a world, in which *everyone* has read and pondered Plato! How different from what we see around us! Oh, Maeda-kun... and yet, as a teacher, when I could have... I failed... how? How could I have failed? The words didn't come, the fire wouldn't start. Tazawa now. If *he'd* been a teacher, *he* could have lit the fire, but Tazawa was... Tazawa. And so under his urging I set about translating *Phaedo*, but I soon realized that the problem was not with the translators but with the Japanese language; it is simply too different from classical Greek. English is closer, but even the English versions, even those of the immortal Jowett... But here's my point, you see, here's the theme of these... notations, scraps, fragments, jottings..." – he gestured with comic resignation, in which Maeda seemed to detect a

325

hint almost of panic, towards the disordered mass of paper on the desk – "that it will be your task, my friend and disciple, to arrange, order, amplify, flesh out – because you can write, you see, you have the gift of writing, and I don't, I can only think, after a fashion, and... here's the crux of the matter: Why read Plato, in this 21st century of ours that one would think has left him so far behind? But true masters of thought, my friend, are never 'left behind,' they only seem at times to be. We need Plato more than ever, if only we knew it, because Plato understood freedom, and freedom is precisely what this 21st century fails to understand, and stands most in need of understanding, the more so as 21st-century man thinks he is free! Never, never in the history of mankind, has man been more tightly chained and bound to the world of the senses, like Prometheus to his rock; never has the soul been more dulled, more weighted down with dross... Where is it, in the *Phaedo*?" He groped for the volume on the desk, found it at last, and began leafing frantically through it, as though finding what he was looking for was a matter of life and death and time was running out. "Here, listen now: 'The lovers of knowledge are conscious that the soul was simply fastened and glued to the body – until philosophy received her, she could only view real existence through the bars of a prison, not in and through herself; she was wallowing in the mire of every sort of ignorance, and by reason of lust had become the principal accomplice in her own captivity.' Well, my friend? I ask you – has our situation in this 21st century ever been more lucidly described than in those brief lines, written 2500 years ago?"

Scene Twenty-four

Pleading exhaustion, Maeda made his escape at last; it was night. It seemed to him as he looked up at the sky that he had never seen so many stars. There was no moon. Millennia ago the Babylonians had arranged that mass of stars into constellations, and brilliant modern minds, Tomoko's among them, had learned to weigh them, measure them, analyze their components, situate them in time and space, but all he saw was light, the primordial mystery that no amount of knowledge could elucidate. To look into a sky like this, he thought, is to forget altogether where you are even while recalling perfectly well that you are in Wakaba, Chiba Prefecture, fifty-odd kilometers from Tokyo. He walked up one street, down another. His body was painfully constricted from his having sat so long; his lungs were shriveled from the closeness of the professor's study. He strode rapidly, stretching his muscles and breathing deeply. He felt as if he could walk forever, "if only the night would last!"

An all-night convenience store on his left was like some monstrous sun exercising an outlandish gravitational pull on him. There was an instant of raw terror, which left him shaken even after it had passed. He went inside. He was hungry; he had not eaten; he recalled again the milk he had tasted that morning, and winced. The music, on non-stop in stores like this, was loud, pulsing, numbing, more like amplified construction-site noise than music, but no one in the store – there were quite a few people, he noted with surprise, though the streets were utterly deserted – seemed to mind, or even to hear it, so absorbed were they in leafing through magazines or choosing a late-night snack.

327

He took two *omusubi*, a can of oolong tea and a newspaper to the cash. The girl behind it seemed very young, barely in her teens – and yet her parents let her work these hours? She may have been older than she looked; still... "How old are you?" he asked, and felt himself blush furiously; what business was it of his? Fortunately his impulsive question, incomprehensible to him now that the impulse had passed, was swallowed up by the music. "Shall I heat up your *omusubi*?" she asked brightly and, of course, loudly.

"No, thank you."

There was a children's park, he knew, a block or so away, and there he headed, but on second thought changed his mind and turned into the narrow road that led to the beach. As he walked the salt tang in the air seemed to grow more pronounced, and far in the distance he could make out the bobbing lights of a fleet of squid boats. "How good to be a fisherman," he thought idly. "And yet the sons of fishermen are deserting the boats in droves, moving to the cities, working in offices; pretty soon there won't be any fishermen left, or farmers either... hm... If *my* father had been a fisherman I'd never've wanted to be anything else, never, never... maybe it's not too late, maybe I can still become one; true, I know nothing about fishing, but I can learn, I'm clever and strong and can do anything I want to do... Yes, that's true," he thought, as though such a wondrous fact had never struck him before – "that's true, I can do anything I want to..."

He sat cross-legged on the sand and unwrapped an *omusubi*. A lone seagull wheeled silently overhead. Where were the others? Asleep? Was this one an insomniac? It had problems to resolve, and under cover of night was quietly thinking them over? Maeda watched it, absently but intently; for a time it seemed to absorb his whole attention, but then abruptly he lost interest and emerged from his trance, unable to recall what he'd been thinking. He ate his *omusubi* and sipped his tea. He felt the night chill, but not as a discomfort; rather as a kind of blanket which he could hug tightly to himself for warmth. He unfolded the newspaper. It was his own, the *Maiasa*. It was too dark to read, but the banner headline across the top was easy enough to make out: "'Ghost' Suzuki Arrested in Father-in-Law's Murder." "Yes, I really am not well," thought Maeda, closing his eyes.

Scene Twenty-five

"He's not himself," said Yoko.

"I'm not myself either," said Jun.

"No?"

"But go on, please. Tell me about Yuji."

"It's hard to describe. Something seemed to... go out of him when you left. It was as if he was living through Yusuke's death all over again."

"My mother died when I was seven."

"Do you remember her?"

"Yes and no. There are times when I see her clearly, as clearly as I see you. I hear her voice, as clearly as I hear yours. But is the woman I see *her*? Is the voice I hear *hers*? That I can never know. My pen, my notebook..." Suddenly agitated, he shook the knapsack off his back and began a kind of struggle with it, as it failed to yield the desired items quickly enough. He wrote, then passed the book to Yoko, who, squinting to make out the hasty scrawl, read, "Is the woman I see *her*? Is the voice I hear *hers*?"

"Yes, I understand. When I was little I asked my father, 'Why do people have to die?' and he said

329

– at least this is what I remember him saying – 'Without death there is no life.' Yuji! Look who's here."

Yuji had suddenly materialized, looking dazed and sleepy and, Jun thought, a good deal older than he remembered him – but of course, he reflected, an elderly man just wakened from a nap does tend to look older than he does otherwise.

"You're quite right, Father did say that," said Yuji, "and so did I, to Yusuke when he was small. What else can a father say to a child? That or something else, equally meaningless."

"Jun's written a poem."

"Hardly a poem," said Jun. "Shall we go for a walk in the grove?"

"Wouldn't you like to go farther than the grove?"

"What do you mean?"

"You know, of course, the poet Taneda Santoka?"

"No..."

"No! And you, a poet!" This seemed to bring Yuji out of his daze, and he beamed with pleasure at his young friend. "I thought you'd never come back to us."

"I told you I would, didn't I?"

"I thought we'd never see you again. One's thoughts, you see, flow on quite independently of what one is told. Taneda Santoka was a vagrant haiku poet and a Zen priest. He had no home, no money, no possessions, no job – and no destination, for all his walking. He walked and walked. At evening he'd come to some nameless nowhere nothing little town, and beg until he had enough for the only things in life he had any use for: cheap lodgings, a cheap meal, cheap saké, and a bath. I've never mentioned Santoka to you, have I?" he said, turning to Yoko. "Wait a moment."

He disappeared through the door leading from the shop into the living quarters.

"He has mentioned Santoka to me," Yoko said softly to Jun. "He's getting ready, I think, to go walking."

"Walking?"

Yuji was back before she could explain. In his hand was a thin, tattered, green volume, which he passed to Jun. "He wasn't much thought of while he lived, Santoka, but now, among people who know of such things, he is something of a saint, almost. 'Free verse haiku' his style is called. I was up late reading, which is probably why I felt so sleepy after lunch. He's very much in your style, Jun, or should I say you're very much in his. Reading him made me think of you, and now here you are. Cause and effect? Who's to say? Perhaps you and I are destined to make a Santoka journey together.

"This book was Yusuke's. Imagine Yusuke going in for poetry. I had no idea, no idea at all, until I found this book among his things. He wasn't much of a reader, and nothing I knew of him, or thought I knew, prepared me to find anything like this. What can these poems have meant to him? We were as close as father and son can be, and yet he never, ever, so much as hinted at a taste for poetry. Maybe he had none. Maybe a friend gave it to him and he absently tossed it onto his shelf and forgot about it, and there it lay until, in the aftermath of his death, I found it and, quite mistakenly, imputed to him a secret love for an obscure poet who I myself took to communing with, as a way of communing with my dead son. It's possible. And yet, in the absence of facts, what we believe becomes a matter of what we choose to believe, and I choose to believe that Yusuke loved the poems of Santoka, just as I have come to love them, and mused over them, just as I do, and that

331

his awakening adolescent heart responded to them as my old man's heart does. Yes..." his voice dropped to a scarcely audible murmur – "maybe we are, you and I, destined to make a Santoka journey together."

Scene Twenty-six

"I really am not well," thought Maeda. He had walked and walked, and, finding himself as evening fell in a town of sorts, he decided to look for a place to spend the night. It was scarcely more than a village – hardly even that; it reminded him of an illustration in an elementary school textbook that had somehow stuck in his mind, of a Stone Age settlement of five thousand-odd years ago; it was not likely to offer much in the way of accommodations. The dusty street he trudged along was quite deserted, but through a gap between two half-collapsed houses he glimpsed a bit of beach, and on the sand a woman, all but invisible under a sun bonnet that hid most of her face, sitting cross-legged and, as best he could make out, mending a fishing net. "Should I ask her? Ask her what? No..." His mind for reasons of its own rejected this perfectly sensible means of getting his bearings, and he trudged on.

For all its backwardness and insignificance, the town or village was more extensive, though certainly not more lively, than first impressions suggested. It went on and on, and yet the woman on the beach seemed to have it all to herself. Where was everyone? The men out fishing and the women guarding their chastity indoors? There were establishments along the main street that looked like shops, or warehouses, but whatever business went on in them, if any business did, was well concealed from view. "I suppose I can sleep on the beach, if I have to," Maeda thought, "but it would be better not to, I can imagine only too well how sick I'll feel when I wake up, given how sick I feel now..." He paused; something caught his eye. A sign, in the distance; he couldn't quite make out the lettering – "I really must have my eyes checked..." He squinted. Surely he was not mistaken? Unless he was hallucinating, which was not impossible – but no, no, he was right: a public bath! The surge of joy that coursed through him as the sign laid his last doubts to rest was almost frightening. "This, right now, this... why... this is the happiest moment of my life! If life affords greater happiness than this, I am content not to know it! Why, it would unseat my reason altogether; it would give me a heart attack!" So he babbled to himself as he lengthened his stride. "But what if it's closed? No, no, please, don't be closed, please..." With sinking heart he tried the weathered wooden door; it slid open without so much as a creak, and a voice from somewhere within chirped "*Irasshaemase*, welcome." Maeda closed his eyes in silent appreciation of the mysterious ways of providence.

Scene Twenty-seven

He was not sure of the precise time, but it was evening, and he grimly pictured to himself, his initial joy having worn off somewhat, a cramped little tub packed with shouting, laughing, exuberant fishermen, freshly released from the day's toil, but the changing room was dark and silent, and as he passed naked into the bathing area the burst of noise he was braced for did not materialize. "Can it be?" he thought. "There's

333

really no one here? I have this whole tub" – it was vast, measured against his expectations – "to myself?" It was wonderful, but puzzling. Why was everything so deserted? Since entering the town, whose name, it suddenly struck him, he did not know – "wouldn't there have been a sign somewhere? There must have been; I just wasn't paying attention" – he had seen exactly two human beings: the old woman glimpsed on the beach, and the bath attendant, a young woman – or rather, now that he thought about it, a child; yes, no more than a child, maybe twelve, thirteen, the daughter of the owners, no doubt; she had taken his money, handed him a towel and smiled. Had she said anything? No, not a word, come to think of it; at least he could not recall the sound of her voice... What kind of life would a child that age lead in a place like this, so hostile to anything having to do with youth or even, he was tempted to say, with life?

Taking a bucket, he doused himself with warm water from one of the faucets around the rim of the tub. Soap and shampoo were provided; he used them liberally, then doused himself again and again, lowering the temperature of the water each time until it was quite cold. Only then did he approach the tub. Testing it with his toe, he found it hot, almost scalding. Good, he thought.

He immersed himself slowly. Only those accustomed to traditional Japanese bathing can tolerate water at that temperature. It lapped his chin. He closed his eyes. He felt weightless. "What if death is like this?" In *Crime and Punishment* the lecherous Svidrigailov taunts the murderer Raskolnikov with a vision of eternity as a grimy country bathhouse swarming with spiders. "But," he thought with a smile, "times have changed, and eternity along with it. Now eternity is a bathhouse like this; I'm being given a foretaste of it and asked if I accept it, if I'm ready to move in, and my answer is yes, I am ready. Rogozhin... what made me suddenly think of Rogozhin? Well, Dostoevsky-Rogozhin, it's a natural association. As is death-Rogozhin. "Didn't he once offer me a narcotic, a 'powder,' that... how did he put it?... 'leads you gently by the hand into the kingdom of death,' or something like that? Yes, he did, he did. 'With maternal tenderness' – those were his words He said I had to choose immediately, and I hesitated, and so... the offer was withdrawn!" He laughed, and was startled into silence by the bizarre echo it made.

Scene Twenty-eight

"The last year of his life was... different. I mean, *he* was different. Something was happening to him, or rather *within* him; I didn't understand but I felt it somehow, and..."

"May I ask you..." Maeda paused. The woman was in a delicate state. If he prodded her too sharply he might unwittingly overwhelm her, or offend her, and she would clam up on him. On the other hand, as a journalist, he had a responsibility to get his facts straight. "During all your years together... how many years...?"

"Twenty-eight."

"Twenty-eight years. You had *no idea*...?"

"None. You're surprised. That's understandable. And I daresay you will be even more surprised when I tell you that when I found out at last... I was not shocked. Not horrified. Not even surprised. Not at all."

"Yes, that is surprising. How do you explain it?"

"I'm not sure I can. Except... well, I hesitate to say this, because, like most people, I don't like to be thought mad."

Maeda waited.

"There is something... more than earthly about this whole business."

"More than..."

"Would you believe me if I told you that that is the first... *religious* thought, if that is the right word, that I have ever had in my life?"

"I'm not sure I..."

She smiled. Maeda marveled at her composure. Her "delicate state" was in truth not much in evidence. You would hardly guess, looking at her and talking to her, that her husband of twenty-eight years had only weeks previously been murdered by her daughter's husband, whose stated motive was his horror at the sudden discovery of a crime committed in the distant past, the motiveless murder of a helpless, mentally disabled child – one of the most grotesque crimes committed in the nation's modern history!

"I'll tell you something else strange. My daughter Kazue was no more shocked than I was. You've met Kazue. If you didn't know she was a grown woman, and a mother, you'd take her for a child. Wouldn't you?" She paused. "Maybe she is a child. Maybe she's..."

She broke off, lapsed into thought. The silence lengthened. Maeda did not dare break it; he scarcely dared breathe, for fear the woman would suddenly turn on him and say, "It's no use, you wouldn't understand," and abruptly terminate the interview.

"It's as if, you see, we had all known it was going to happen, known and yet not known... how can I say it so that it makes sense? My husband was very fond of Osamu, all the fonder, maybe, because he *knew* that Osamu was destined to learn of his crime and kill him for it..."

"How did Osamu learn of it?"

She looked at him in some surprise. "From you, he said."

"From me!" It was possible. He had gone through a feverish interlude, and may have said unaccountable things in delirium, though he didn't recall being delirious.

"He was different in his last years," Ikuko said again, almost dreamily. "He had, in a manner of speaking, lost all control of things. Of matter, I mean. Physical objects. He could no longer handle them. He could not pick up an object without dropping it – or if he gripped it to keep it from slipping through his fingers, he'd end up crushing it. He could not move without bumping into something. He'd always been a bit clumsy, but it was getting to the point where he could scarcely function. Sometimes he'd laugh it off: 'Matter and I are incompatible.' Other times he would fly into a rage – and such a rage! He'd smash things on purpose – hurl plates against the wall. 'I'll tell you what,' I said to him, 'matter will be my domain, leave it to me, you stay in the ethereal realm.' I said it to make him laugh, and he did laugh... Oh. Something else, as the end drew near. Everything, in his mind, took on *significance*. There was no such thing as 'it doesn't matter.' *Everything* mattered. The most trivial action could bring on incalculable consequences, incalculable, unpredictable, and potentially immense, grotesquely out of proportion to the cause. For example, whether he laid a newspaper on the table folded or unfolded, or with the front page showing or the back page. This is just one example out of a great many. In the afternoon, with his tea, he would have two *sembei* crackers, and would be thrown into an agony of indecision over which one

337

to eat first – as though the very fate of the universe hinged on it! There was that Jomon figurine he gave Professor Horiuchi, which he simply *had* to get back, or else... or else I don't know what. Neither did he. It was a nameless, formless dread that would come over him. Yes, he was changing. He had an intimation of his fate, you see, and so did I, so did we all, though we didn't know it at the time, didn't recognize it for what it was... The lawyer I hired wants Osamu to plead temporary insanity. But Osamu absolutely refuses. Perhaps you can talk to him. Maybe he'll listen to you. Remind him that he's a husband and father, he can't only think of himself. He must live for Kazue, for Kazue and Meiko, little Meiko..."

About the Author

Michael Hoffman is an expat writer living in Hokkaido, Japan. He is the author of *Little Pieces: This Side of Japan* (2010), *Birnbaum: A Novel of Inner Space* (2008), *Nectar Fragments* (2006), *The Coat that Covers Him and Other Stories* (2004), and *The Empty Café* (2002).

www.ingramcontent.com/pod-product-compliance
Lightning Source LLC
Chambersburg PA
CBHW060352260626
47160CB00006B/2290

Paradox 4: Provoking Fate
Henry Brown
Copyright © Virtual Pulp Press 2024
All rights reserved.

Heap big thanks to John Earle, for proofreading the entire *Paradox* Series (no small task!).

For all the young men struggling to find their way in this toxic misandrist dystopia: learn from the mistakes of those who came before you.

CHAPTER 1: WAKE-UP CALL

K ennedy had been shot.
I had completely forgotten the significance of it being late November of 1963. It all came rushing back, now.

Forgetting I was supposed to be in class, I headed for the dorm. Female faces shined with tears. Male faces scowled in disbelief. Students and professors wandered around campus like zombies as I weaved in between them.

The dormitory break room was packed, and the TV was already on, at full volume. I squeezed in just in time to hear that the President was dead.

My dormmates deflated as their last desperate hope disintegrated.

"Why would somebody do this?" one guy asked, with a blank stare.

"Everybody loved him," someone else said, "even the ones who voted against him! He was taking us to a new frontier."

I was pretty young, way back in the future, when Reagan was shot. I had no interest or understanding of politics then, but I noticed a lot of adults reacted as if it were good news, or funny.

I thought back to the end of my freshman year at Yosemite Polytechnic, at my present time-space coordinates. My roommate then, Gartenberg, had the radio on while he took his magazine clippings down from the wall. Kennedy was giving a speech to media bigwigs, and warned about the danger of secret societies (ironic, since his brother's alleged assassin would be a

Rosicrucian).

At one point in his speech, Kennedy said, "We are opposed around the world by a monolithic and ruthless conspiracy that relies primarily on covert means for expanding its sphere of influence..."

He went on to mention the behavior and impact of the conspiracy, and prophesied that dissent would be silenced. That sounded like the *status quo* in the future Dad saved me from. In fact, all of it sounded similar to Dad's perspective on the world.

Kennedy had discovered something, then denounced it in public. He revealed a secret. Was that what got him killed?

ΔΔΔ

Barely had the shock of the assassination set in, when the lead suspect, while in police custody, was himself murdered. The murder was nationally televised. People couldn't believe anybody had both the ability and the gall to stage something like that openly, with TV coverage. Whoever had orchestrated this sequence of evil events was rubbing our noses in it.

I was just as stunned as everyone else, even though I had heard about the assassination when I was a kid who had no interest in history or politics and just wrote it off as another boring topic grown-ups liked to talk about.

I smelled a rat immediately. A conspiracy of rats.

People who had more information than me were likely suspicious already, but when the sleazy nightclub owner bumped off the "lone nut" assassin before the public could even hear what he had to say, the stench became almost unbearable. No thinking person could accept the narrative being weaved for public consumption.

When asked why he murdered Oswald before he could be made to talk, Jack Ruby's stated rationale was that he didn't want newly-widowed Jackie Kennedy to have to return to Dallas for the trial.

Yeah, right. Sounds legit.

Classes were cancelled the day of the President's funeral. Before and after the funeral, both students and professors went through the motions of class in a daze.

The world was deathly silent for days. Nobody wanted to talk. It was rare to hear music—or anything but news reports—from the radio or TV. Any noise that wasn't absolutely solemn met with annoyance and disdain.

Even at the Yosemite campus, so far from Dallas, I could feel the Big Spooky descending upon the country.

Now I understood why the atmosphere in Bloomington had changed so drastically over two succeeding visits to see Holly. One was before the assassination, and one was after. The event had permanently changed America.

The national mood was still very bleak when school broke for Christmas. I remembered the visit to the scene of the assassination back when Dad took me on that Big Spooky tour. He had planted surveillance drones at the site. I had forgotten all about it and never asked him what he found out.

Perhaps it was Dad's influence on me: I considered the assassination, the Erasers, the CPB, and probably even Fate, as conspirators all linked together somehow, all pushing toward the same insidious goal. I didn't know exactly what that goal was, but it involved turning America into a dystopian cesspool, destroying anyone who tried to expose the truth, and preventing anyone else from escaping the worldwide shitshow they were creating.

I knew very little of the facts behind what all had just happened, but marveled at the teamwork, discipline, and solidarity it must have required. Evil people, working together, could accomplish great evil.

Where was the opposing force?

The police were obviously not part of the resistance, and only a moron would count Jack Ruby on the side opposing evil.

In World War Two, our whole country opposed evil.

Couldn't good men, working together, accomplish good?

Where were the good men, now?

What were they doing? Nothing?
What was I doing? Nothing.
That had to change, or evil would triumph.

CHAPTER 2: DEALEY CROSSFIRE

I had to find Dad.

I searched everywhere I knew he frequented, disturbed to find out that nobody had seen or heard from him for a while.

I left a message for him at predesignated coordinates, but grew impatient for him to check them and find me.

I jumped a warp to Dallas the morning of the assassination. I brought some equipment to intercept the transmission from Dad's drone footage. I planned to also position myself somewhere at Dealey Plaza where I could observe the motorcade, in real time, and maybe try to place the shots. If none of that bore fruit, I was willing to jump back to the previous day and force a meeting with the younger Dad who brought the younger me in on the VTOL.

I rented a hotel room nearby in Dallas and set up the equipment borrowed from BH Station. Then I drove to the Plaza, parking the GTO in the parking lot behind the Grassy Knoll about an hour before the motorcade was due.

I had heard of the Grassy Knoll at my native coordinates and, after a quick jump to 2013 and some intense research, learned that most "conspiracy theorists" believed the sniper who fired the fatal headshot had been located there. I would scout the entire area, but observe the Grassy Knoll closely when the limousine drove by.

Even an hour early, the Plaza was crowded and the Big Spooky made my skin crawl. I examined every person I saw with suspicion, imagining any of them could be in on the plot.

I noticed the "umbrella man" when he arrived. I caught a glimpse of a guy I thought could be a young George H.W. Bush. I even thought I recognized Lee Harvey Oswald himself at one point, standing in the crowd on the street in front of the Book Depository.

I strolled around the entire Plaza, and made it back to the Grassy Knoll with 15 minutes to spare. I positioned myself in the shade of a tree, where I could watch the motorcade while keeping my eye on the location where the street-level sniper might appear.

As I waited, I noticed a Top Tier woman strolling on a route parallel with what the motorcade would take, when it arrived.

Aside from her exceptional good looks and sexy walk, she should have blended in just fine. Her hairdo, dress, gloves, shoes, and purse were all in perfect keeping with the latest styles in 1963. But while everyone else was anxious or excited, she looked perfectly at ease, and even a little amused—like a joke had just been told and she was the only one who heard and understood it.

I wondered if I should try to keep my eyes on her, too. Maybe she figured somehow in what was about to go down.

I was so focused on her and observing the Knoll that I had developed a blind spot in my situational awareness. Somebody grabbed my arm from behind and spun me around.

"What the hell are you doing, Hero?"

"Dad! You're here—I've been looking all over for you!"

Even more wrinkles and gray hair accented his features than I remembered from the last time I saw him. "How did you get here?"

"I drove the GTO."

"Where is it?"

I pointed toward the parking lot.

"Shit—let's go," he said. "We gotta get out of here now, before you FUBAR everything."

We hurried to the Pontiac and he jumped into the passenger seat, urging me to get us out of there fast, but without burning the tires or doing anything else to draw attention.

"Where to?" I asked, approaching the freeway onramp.

"You staying somewhere local?"

I told him about the hotel, and he ordered me to take him there.

In the hotel room, he looked over the equipment and asked, "Where'd you get this?"

"Borrowed it from BH Station," I said.

He turned on the room's television. Pandemonium already flooded the airwaves. Kennedy was murdered while we were driving from the site.

He fixed me with a grave stare full of fear and possibly some anger. "Have you talked to anybody since you've been here?"

"Just the desk clerk."

"Nobody at the Plaza?"

I shook my head.

"Nobody else in Dallas?"

"No. Why?"

"What did you tell the desk clerk?"

"Just the usual stuff—that I needed a room. Two nights. When is breakfast. Like that."

"What name did you use?"

"Ike Johnson. From Arkansas."

"Did you use cash?"

I nodded.

"Okay," he said, and sat down heavily in the room's padded chair.

"What's wrong?" I asked.

"What were you gonna do—try to stop it?"

"No. I just...wanted to see."

He nodded, puffing his cheeks. "How much do you

remember about this from St. Louis?"

"Not much. But I jumped to 2013 and gave myself a crash course."

He sighed. "Even 50 years after, what most people think they know about it is bullshit. What do you think—that Oswald did it? That he acted alone?"

"Hell no," I replied. "He smells like the fall guy."

Dad got up, walked across the room, sat at the table with the electronic equipment, and fiddled around with it for a few minutes. He cued up some footage on the playback monitor, and rolled it. On the display was the inside of a storage room with stacks of boxes. The view changed as the camera drone floated around the room. The view came to rest on a man wearing gloves but no hat or suit jacket, leaning over a stack of boxes, sighting down a bolt-action rifle through an open window. I heard a gunshot, and distant screaming on the audio track.

"Hear that?"

I nodded.

"This is footage of the 'sniper's nest' at the moment of the shooting. Did you see Oswald up there with the rifle?"

"No," I said. "That man with the rifle isn't Oswald."

"His name is Malcom Wallace," Dad said. "He kept his gloves on until he was ready to leave the scene. It might raise suspicion when he leaves the room if somebody notices him wearing gloves indoors."

Wallace fired. There were more shots fired from outside, some distance away. Wallace set the rifle on the floor and stepped away from the window. Moving rapidly, he strode toward the door, yanking one glove off. He stopped, set that glove down on a box while he used his bare hand to pull the other glove off. He resumed his progress toward the door as he reached down to retrieve the other glove. In his haste, he lost his balance and had to push against the boxes to right himself.

"Son of a bitch!" he growled, and used his elbow to wipe the area of the box he had touched.

"See that?" Dad asked. "The simplest little mistake can

blow your whole operation. He tried to correct his mistake, but he left a latent pinky print on that box. Lucky for him and the rest of the gang, they had friends up high running the so-called 'investigation'. Anything that didn't point to Oswald would be ignored."

Dad brought up another video clip, recorded from a different drone's feed. A man with short dark hair and a seemingly permanent subtle smirk etched on his face was standing outside on the street in a big crowd of people watching the street expectantly—just as I had seen live, in the flesh. Their excitement went off the scale as something passed in front of them. They waved and cheered, all smiles—except the dark-haired man. Necks craned as they tracked the Presidential limousine (presumably) down the street.

"That's Oswald," Dad said, indicating the smirking guy.

I nodded.

When the first gunshot sounded, everyone kept rubbernecking and smiling, as if the noise came from a vehicle backfire and wasn't noteworthy enough to distract them from worshiping their beloved idol. Except Oswald. He appeared to know exactly what the noise meant.

More shots rang out.

"That's Kennedy getting greased," Dad said.

The drone followed Oswald into the building, along a hallway, into what looked like a break room. There were some items from an eaten lunch on a table—an empty brown paper sack, plastic baggies, and an empty Coke bottle. The drone flew around to record him from the front, zooming in. His eyes were wide in panic as he mechanically cleaned up the table and threw the remains of his lunch in a trash can. A female co-worker entered the room before Oswald exited.

"Damn it," I said. "This whole deal stank. Oswald was the patsy, just like he said."

"It was a ludicrous narrative on its face," Dad said, scowling as he brought up another clip. "The usual two factors caused so many people to swallow it."

I shrugged. "Public incredulity?"

A fleeting grin interrupted Dad's scowl for a moment. "Outstanding, Sprout. That's one. The other is they made the lie easy to accept. Trusted officials in three-piece suits, looking very sober and respectable, all nodded and harrumphed and confirmed to the world, with straight faces, that the ridiculous Lone Nut Narrative is the official truth. They'll even have an officious commission of trusted legal eagles in three-piece suits go through the motions of an investigation, to concur with the Narrative they've been pushing from the start. Plus, all your neighbors and co-workers, friends and family will appear to have swallowed the horseshit. You can pretend to believe it, too; and you'll be safe from ridicule. Just graze with the flock. There's safety in numbers. And after ten or 20 years, you might even convince yourself it's plausible."

Another window popped up on the monitor. Dad cued up another clip, and rolled it. I saw two men in suits and hats atop a building. One had binoculars. The other had a rifle with a scope.

"That's the rooftop of the Daltex Oil building," Dad said. "Right across Houston Street from the Book Depository. By the way; the 'sniper's nest' that Oswald supposedly shot from...the view of the kill zone was obscured by the trees down at street level. Not the tree you were hanging out by; but the two farthest from you to your left rear, closer to the street. Can't blame Wallace too much for missing *his* shot. But notice this sniper team has an unobstructed view of the kill zone."

The drone hovered behind the two men, recording over their shoulder down to ground level as the motorcade turned left from Houston onto Elm Street. The President's limousine passed the trees in question. It was moving slowly, almost directly away from the rooftop sniper. The rifle fired.

"That's the first shot," Dad said, stopped the clip, and brought up yet additional footage from a different angle. It showed one side of the fence in front of the parking lot where I had left the GTO.

"This angle is across the infamous 'grassy knoll'," Dad said.

"See that guy there?"

A uniformed police officer walked into view in the parking lot, approached a shady area in the foreground, and posted himself behind the fence.

"The cop?" I asked.

"He's not really a cop," Dad said. "Granted: there were some crooked cops who were in on this deal; but this guy is just wearing a policeman costume. My drone camera adjusted for the light quickly and can make him out in pretty good detail. But the film people were using in their cameras on site wasn't too good. Plus, nobody was setting their focus and exposure to zero in on this guy. Who cared what was happening on the sidelines? Everything in deep shaded areas was almost completely blacked out when the film was developed."

The man didn't have a rifle—only a sidearm that remained in his holster. He lifted a walkie-talkie to his mouth and said something.

"See that?"

I nodded.

Dad cued up another clip. A drone camera showed a wide angle of the Presidential motorcade driving along toward Dealey Plaza.

"Anything look wrong to you, here?"

I shrugged.

"Wouldn't you put the President in the middle of the motorcade, surrounded by security?" Dad asked.

"Yeah. I guess so."

"Normally, Kennedy was surrounded by reporters and Secret Service," Dad explained, "and in the middle of the motorcade. But they've got him right up there in the front. Nobody next to him except the First Lady. Crazy, huh?"

I nodded.

Dad pointed to a spot on the screen. "That guy right there in the second car, talking into the radio? He's Secret Service— the shift leader for this detail. The Dallas Police answer to him today, too. There were supposed to be six motorcycle cops riding on both sides of Kennedy's limousine today. Thanks to this guy, there's only two on each side anywhere near, and they're trailing behind the limousine. Ain't that interesting? Watch this."

First, I noticed Kennedy himself, waving to the onlookers. He appeared weary and possibly frustrated behind his politician's smile.

The motorcade took a right turn onto Houston Street. Dad pointed to two men in suits, with no hats, trotting along beside the Presidential limousine.

"All kinds of changes were made at the last minute, so the Secret Service wound up violating its own security protocols for this trip. Agents are supposed to either ride along on the running boards, or keep pace beside the limousine, like these two are doing. Should be at least four of them, actually. But watch the shift leader."

The man Dad pointed to before, riding in the following convertible, stood up and waved the two agents away. The one on the left, wearing sunglasses, came to a halt, then when the following car passed, he swung onto its running board to ride along. The agent on the right, dumbfounded, raised his arms in a "what the hell?" gesture, then did the same.

"Holy shit," I said.

Dad nodded. "Motorcycle cops back where they can't be of use. Secret Service agents waved off. Clear shot to the target with a three-way crossfire as it rolls into the ambush site. Kennedy is a sitting duck."

"You said 'three-way crossfire.' There's the sniper on the roof," I pointed out, ticking on my fingers, "and one in the Book Depository. I didn't see anybody with a rifle near the Grassy Knoll."

"I'll get to that," Dad said.

The motorcade crept along Houston Street, turned left onto Elm, and rolled along even slower than before.

"Notice the speed, now," Dad said.

The limousine passed the trees in front of the Book Depository, and the first shot rang out.

"Look at the shift leader," Dad said.

The shift leader was on his radio again.

"He's telling his security team to stand fast," Dad explained.

I shook my head. "Oh my God. How can people not connect the dots? Cops and agents should swarm to the President. The driver should floor the gas to clear the ambush area, and the motorcycle cops should form a rolling cordon on each side of the limousine. What the hell?"

"Only if you're trying to protect him," Dad said. "Now check this out."

Adjacent to the Grassy Knoll, the limo slowed almost to a complete stop. The motorcycle cops, still trailing behind and to the side, had to brake suddenly to avoid pulling abreast of the limousine where they might have blocked another shot. The following car almost slammed into the limo. A Secret Service agent landed on the rear bumper of the limo, flung there from the hard braking of the following car.

The final rifle report sounded. Kennedy's head snapped back. A chunk of his skull and glob of his brain fell onto the limo's trunk. The First Lady rose and twisted from her seat, climbing onto the trunk deck, grabbing the bone and flesh, desperately trying to fit it back into her husband's head.

Now the limo finally accelerated toward the underpass.

It was gruesome.

"Over across Commerce Street is the Government Building," Dad said. "Plenty of FBI and CIA working out of there. Feds confiscated Zapruder's movie film and didn't give it back for months. When they did, it had been doctored to make it appear the limousine didn't brake for the final kill shot, like you just saw. They did a pretty impressive job for the technology of the time. Stalin's film historians might have been jealous."

Dad cued up a different clip. There was a dark—almost black—border around the frame of the image. Through the bright rectangle in the center of the frame, I saw grass, sidewalk, a street, and people milling about beyond. Silhouetted in the frame was a man with a rifle.

The drone pulled back, in the limited light I saw a second man, with a walky-talkie.

"That's a sewer drain on Elm Street," Dad said.

"Damn mosquitos," the man with the walky-talkie whispered, slapping at his neck. "They had to pick a day when it's wet in here."

"Shh! Shut up!" the man with the rifle said, still sighting out his rectangular shooting port.

A static-laden voice from the radio said, "Here he comes. Again: target is on the passenger side of the rear seat. You are cleared for the shot. Should see him in...three seconds."

"Roger," the spotter said into the radio. To his companion, he asked, "Catch that?"

"Yup," the sniper said, and fired.

"Oh my God," I said. "Was that the Secret Service guy on the radio?"

"Nope," Dad said. "That was 'Badge Man' we saw earlier, in the shade behind the Grassy Knoll, dressed like a cop, with the handheld radio."

Dad stopped the footage; turned around in the chair to face me. "Three-way crossfire. I don't know if Kennedy could have survived that one that got him through the collar. But the one from the storm sewer was definitely a kill shot. It made sure, once and for all."

"Holy shit," I said.

"As you saw, the sniper had to set up a ways back from the opening in the gutter," Dad said. "Even in all the confusion, somebody probably would have noticed the muzzle end of a rifle sticking out of a sewer drain. Trouble is, the sniper has a limited field of fire out that aperture sitting that far back. The target will only appear in it for a split second, then be gone. So they need Badge Man to warn them when the target will appear, and the driver will slow down to maximize the time in the kill zone."

I pounded fist into open palm and began to pace.

"I know you have a lot of questions," Dad said. "And I

know, despite whatever you'll say, that you're wondering why we can't break the rules just this one time and sabotage the assassination."

"You do have a rare opportunity," I said. "You know where everybody is beforehand, and..."

Dad stopped me with a cutting gesture. "I told you the TPB watches for splits in the time stream. There's no way they wouldn't have a detail assigned to monitor something as big as the JFK assassination. I guarantee you, they've got people on the ground there at Dealey Plaza. It's a miracle none of them spotted you. You're provoking Fate just by showing your face out there."

"How would they even know who I am?" I asked.

"They have ways," he replied. "But they'd have definitely ID'd you if you did something stupid."

"Okay," I said, "I know they have some tech that alerts them when there's a new split in the timestream. I get it. But what makes you think they actually have people on the scene, blending in with the crowd?"

"Because I was assigned that kind of duty, once."

"No way. Back there where the assassination happened?"

"No," he said. "Oklahoma City, 1995. Boss never told us why they thought somebody would tamper. But sure enough: some deserter jumped the warp to those coordinates and tried to make mischief. Started pirating all the surveillance video from the area around the Murrah Building before it could be confiscated and the crucial minutes could mysteriously disappear. We caught him in the building itself, days before, trying to save the evidence from the Waco investigations before it could be destroyed."

"So you went along with this kind of stuff?"

He shrugged. "At first. Ours was not to reason why. Reasons...right or wrong...all that was above our paygrade, we were told, if we ever dared make reply. Sure we went along with it. You don't get hand-picked for black ops because of your sterling morality. They don't exactly recruit born-again Christians or Constitutional scholars for those kind of jobs."

"What happened to wake you up?"

He bit his lip thoughtfully, and took a deep breath. "Something probably similar to what Kennedy went through. Oswald too, maybe."

He chuckled at my perplexed stare.

"Not that I was assassinated, Sprout. Although that was attempted. That's what happens when somebody with a job like that starts to reason why, or make reply. No—what I mean is..." He stood, looked me up-and-down, then said, "You know what... I guess it's overdue for me to give you that history lesson. You're ready for it."

CHAPTER 3: THE HISTORY LESSON PART 1

I checked out of the hotel and met Dad at BH Station. We packed a load of gear in the VTOL and took off.

"Let's forget about Kennedy for a bit," Dad said, as we gained altitude and he prepared for a warp jump. "I don't know if it's even possible to go all the way back—"

"All the way back to what?" I asked, interrupting.

"To the beginning," he said. "To when the butterfly was first stepped on. Pandora's Box. The forbidden fruit. Whatever it was; or whatever you want to call it. Can't go back to whenever that was. But we're gonna go back quite a ways."

We jumped to an area over the ocean.

"That's the Atlantic down there," Dad said, pointing out of the cockpit. "We should be over Europe in a little bit. There's something I'd like us to see, but it would be like finding a needle in a haystack. Plus, there's a thunderstorm at those precise coordinates, so it's really too much risk for the potential payoff. Anyway, lightning struck some messenger riding a horse in Bavaria. When his body was found, the documents he was carrying were also discovered. They were evidence of a secret international society, much like what Kennedy himself warned against..." He glanced at the radar display, then out the left side of the cockpit. "Oh, there we are. That's Great Britain to the north of us. The low clouds and fog almost hid it from view. See it? On your left."

I saw the southern coastline out the side window, partially exposed by a break in the cloud cover.

We lost elevation as Dad began a gradual descent. We passed through a gray-and-white cloud that left streaks of moisture on the windshield. When we broke through it, I spotted ships below.

Wooden ships. With sails.

"What year is it?" I asked.

"Should be 1815," he replied. Pointing to the edge of the big island to our left, he said, "That must be Dover, there. Belgium should be almost straight ahead."

We continued our descent and I noticed another coastline in front of us. "So that water between the land masses is the English Channel?"

Dad nodded.

The cloud cover overhead broke, and the sun's rays made the waves below flicker. Beyond the beaches ahead, there was lush grass and woods, brilliant green in the sunlight. There were scores of ships anchored near the coastline.

"This would be a needle in a haystack, too," Dad said, "but we'll at least have a landmark to go by."

We soared over the coast. Dad brought us straight-and-level at about 1,000 feet.

"What about the secret society?" I asked.

"Huh? Oh. Well, that lightning strike may be the only reason we know about them. Of course, most people assume the *Illuminati* is on par with Flat Earth and Bigfoot. You know—'silly conspiracy theory.' People joke about it. It can't possibly be real if clever people mock and ridicule the idea, right?"

I thought back to Bakersfield. "Is it like the Moose Lodge or Elk Lodge, or a fraternity?"

Dad sneered at me, then examined his heads-up display. "Really, Sprout? Yeah: I went out of my way to tell you about some harmless fraternity. Sounds legit. Just watch and listen, alright?"

I realized my question was rather foolish. With cheeks burning, I decided to follow his advice.

As we moved inland, Dad swept his gaze back-and-forth, searching for something. He found it— a scattered kaleidoscope of red and blue rectangles moving around each other, emitting puffs of smoke.

Dad headed straight for this strange sight, and descended to hover at about 600 feet. As we pulled in closer, I saw that the rectangles were tight formations of soldiers in colorful uniforms. The puffs of smoke were from volleys of cannons and muskets.

"Wow," I said. "People used to fight this way?"

"Yup," Dad said. "You either had to be incredibly brave or incredibly stupid to be a good soldier. Look at that slaughter."

One blue formation fired a musket volley into a red formation, and dozens of soldiers fell. I was glad we weren't close enough to see the blood and gore, or hear the cries of seriously wounded, dying men. Amazingly, the survivors closed ranks so that they were once again in a tight formation.

"The redcoats are the British, of course," Dad said. "Their commander is the Duke of Wellington. Most of the blue formations are French, under the command of their emperor himself—Napoleon Bonaparte."

"Oh...right," I said, mentally sorting through references to him in books, and history classes.

"As generals go, he was kind of like Jack Dempsey," Dad said. "He built his reputation in his younger days, beating bigger and stronger heavyweights, with a style that was a bit unorthodox at the time."

"Dempsey was one of those wrecking machines you told me about after Sullivan-Corbett," I remembered, out loud. "We watched his rematch against Tunney."

"That's right, Sprout. Like Dempsey, after he razed the competition to the ground, Bonaparte got soft and complacent when there was no worthy competition to keep in shape for. Not only that, but even when Bonaparte was kicking everybody's ass, he was losing good soldiers to do it. Very few of his troops down there are as good as the men he built his reputation with. Most of them are either foreign conscripts, young boys with no experience, or old farts who can't march or fight very well anymore, but have more passion than sense. Bonaparte sacrificed the fighting-age French men on the altar of his own glory."

An artillery battery fired, cannonballs tore men in half, decapitated them, ripped limbs off, decimating a formation of soldiers. I flinched at the sight.

"If he had quit while he was ahead," Dad said, "Like Gene Tunney, his empire might have lasted for a while. He should have never gone into Spain. But by that time, his ego was working against him. The Spanish campaign was a disaster on multiple levels. But not a big enough one. He decided to throw what was left of the French Army to the mercy of the Russian winter. All that previous glory was spoiled in one idiotic campaign. He was captured after returning to France, imprisoned, but treated pretty well, and had a cushy life. But he still hadn't learned his lesson. So here he is, going out in a blaze of ignominy. What a waste."

I watched the battle for a little while.

A new army arrived on the field.

"Here come the Prussians," Dad observed. "His shit is weak, now."

The Prussians reinforced the British, and began rolling up the French flank.

"Look at that," Dad said, pointing.

A formation which had been held in reserve behind the French lines now began to move up to counterattack.

"Bonaparte just committed his Imperial Guard. That's his best outfit, with the last elite troops in his army. He's only committed them sparingly up until now. They're considered invincible."

"Like John L. Sullivan?" I asked.

"Not exactly. They really were the best, pound-for-pound,

back in his early wars. But they're over-the-hill, now. And maybe they've got the same ego problem their Emperor does."

The Imperial Guard made its presence known, inflicting serious damage on their enemies. But the French Army they came to rescue seemed to disintegrate around them. Then, pressed by withering fire from the British and Prussians, the strong blue rectangle also began to disintegrate into a convulsing bruise, blue streaks melting out of it in the opposite direction of the Prussians.

"That's it," Dad said. "The Imperial Guard finally broke. Check and mate. Party's over. Bonaparte is done for good."

He tweaked the controls and the VTOL rotated in place while Dad searched the countryside around the battlefield. "Keep your eyes peeled for a lone civilian on horseback, riding west, hard."

We chased a few riders that turned out to be French cavalrymen fleeing in panic, before we found the horseman Dad thought was the right one. We followed him to the coast, where he dismounted and got a ride in a boat that took him out to a ship.

"That's our guy," Dad said. "Not wasting any time. He wants to be first to carry the news back to London. He's an agent of the Rothschild Bank. He'll report on the battle to his bosses. But they'll use the British news services—such as they are right now—to spread the word that Wellington actually lost."

"Blatantly lie?" I asked. "Why?"

"That's what the news media does, Sprout. Always has. In this case, it's gonna cause investors to dump all their British stocks and bonds. Huge economic crash. These kind of financial tactics are used over and over. Manipulations of the market, I mean. During the crash, the Rothschilds will buy up all those shares for pennies on the pound. By the time the truth makes its way across the channel, they'll own damn near everything —including the British government, in effect. They'll still have a king, a prime minister, and a parliament who squabble about minor shit and appear to have diverse opinions. But really, the powers behind the throne will be running the show, secretly, through the Bank of England."

"Is this where the secret society in Bavaria comes in?" I asked.

"Oh, they're not just in Bavaria anymore, and they didn't cease to exist like you'll read on the Cabal websites. But yeah— in this new shadow government of the United Kingdom, think of the Rothschilds as the royal family and the *Illuminati* as their nobles and bureaucrats. A dude named Mayer Amschel Rothschild was quoted as saying: 'Let me issue and control a nation's money; and I care not who writes the laws.' In other words, whoever writes the laws will write them how Rothschild wants them written, if they know what's good for themselves."

"Okay," I said, "So these people took over the UK. But America separated from Britain. We set up our own government."

Dad wiggled his eyebrows. "On the surface, yeah: we kicked their asses; they went home and left us alone. We won the *overt* fight. But the Cabal is *covert*. Under the surface, they never gave up on controlling the US just like they control the UK."

He pointed west, across the ocean. "Just about a year before this battle we watched, Andrew Jackson beat the British again, in New Orleans. We kicked them out a second time. But again, that's just on the surface. Behind the scenes, the Cabal has been working to establish a central bank in our country, too. The Founding Fathers knew better than to accept that; but by the time Jackson is President, the Cabal has almost secured control again. Thomas Jefferson kept the First National Bank from gaining control of American currency. Ol' Hickory—Andrew Jackson—stopped the attempt by the Second National Bank."

Dad punched in some coordinates on the warp interface, and we jumped again. He set the VTOL down in an 1864 Canadian forest, and we trudged about a mile in the dark to a large house on a rich-looking estate. We used tranquilizer guns to neutralize the Mastiffs patrolling the grounds, and broke into a pantry annex, where we set up some listening equipment to eavesdrop on a conversation occurring deeper in the house. An insect drone gave us visuals on the meeting in the drawing room where some 26 people were gathered.

There were occasional asides in French; but I had trouble even following the majority of the conversation, which was in English. Their vocabulary was strange to me, and for the first hour or more, the dominant voices spoke in economic terms I didn't really understand. I did catch that there had been a tentative kidnapping planned; but that was being scrapped now in favor of an assassination.

Once a safe distance from the estate, making our way through the dark woods back toward the VTOL, I confessed that I was lost as to what we had just witnessed.

Dad told me we could have surveilled a boarding house in Washington DC where conversations took place that would be much easier to understand. (The owner of the house was a woman named Mary Surratt, and one of the visitors there was an actor by the name of John Wilkes Booth.) But the skullduggery going on there was only one layer deep in something much more sinister.

Dad patiently interpreted the conference we spied on: European bankers needed US President Abraham Lincoln removed, because his interest-free Greenbacks were ruining all the work they had put into establishing a central bank in the States and implementing an interest-accruing fiat currency as legal tender. All their plans and efforts, since their last attempt that Jackson had spoiled, were scrapped by Lincoln's money policy, despite his approval of the Banking Acts to fund the Civil War, which they assumed had sealed their control just a couple years before.

Present in the meeting were agents of the Confederate Secret Service, who had expressed an interest in kidnapping Lincoln as leverage for favorable peace terms for the South. The bankers and newspaper moguls would fund the Confederate plotters...but to arrange an assassination instead of a kidnapping.

Dad urged me to remember this technique: conspirators recruiting other disgruntled parties with separate, but superficially plausible, motives.

It would be up to the Confederate middlemen to arrange the details of the crime. They would commission Booth, John Surratt, Jr., David Herold, John Lloyd, and others to execute the assassination and getaway. The bankers, politicians, and newspaper men pulling the strings would handle the coverup. What the conspirators didn't say in the presence of the Southern agents was that the subsequent investigation would only be allowed to go so far as to implicate the Confederacy; and then shut down without ever piercing deeper.

"Case closed," Dad said, as we climbed back in the VTOL.

"They learned from Jefferson and Jackson," I concluded, "that if they ran up against a President they couldn't persuade, bribe, or blackmail, that they'd have to bump him off."

"Right. But even with Lincoln out of the way, they still couldn't get their central bank installed without a fight." He pointed at the stand-alone computer on the passenger side of the instrument panel. "But first, let's put Lincoln's economic decisions in context. Turn that on, and look up 'Goschen,' G-O-S-C-H-E-N, *the London Times*, 1865."

Obviously, the computer had no access to the World Wide Web when we visited coordinates long before the technology existed; but the computer had tons of data on its hard drives. I booted it up and searched for a file with the keywords Dad gave me.

"I found an article from a 'Lord Goschen, Spokesman of the Financiers, Hazard Circular'," I said.

"That's the one. Read it."

I cleared my throat and quoted out loud from the article: "If this mischievous financial policy, which has its origin in North America, shall become indurated down to a fixture, then that Government will furnish its own money without cost. It will pay off debts and be without debt. It will have all the money necessary to carry on its commerce. It will become prosperous without precedent in the history of the world. The brains, and wealth of all countries will go to North America. That country must be destroyed or it will destroy every monarchy on the globe."

"What do you think," Dad asked, "some harmless crackpot with an idiosyncratic opinion?"

"Judging by the fact that you bothered to save it," I said, "my guess is no."

"So what important info can you dig out of there?"

I thought about the quote for a long moment. "If they don't sabotage the American economy, it'll grow too successful. All the productive people in the world will want to go there, and people like this guy won't be as powerful as they want to be."

"Nailed it. Good job."

I frowned. "But the elephant in the room is: if they know the system will be so good, why don't they build one just like it, so they can be just as successful?"

Dad turned to glance at me with a surprised grin. "Damn, Ike. You painted the bullseye dead center."

I wasn't sure, but wondered if the grin meant he was proud of me.

"That question is crucial for understanding the enemy," he said. "You and me—it's enough for us just to succeed, and live comfortably. But some people aren't happy unless they can keep others from succeeding. They're not content with doing their own thing and letting others do theirs. They aren't satisfied with being filthy stinking rich; or powerful; they have to be wealthier than this guy and that guy, too, and powerful enough to control others. Super-rich or powerful people are never happy. They worry themselves sick about somebody else maybe getting as rich or powerful as they are. Rather than enjoying their wealth and their comfortable lives, they obsess every waking moment about fucking over other people. Even if it's some poor working slob just struggling to put food on the table and keep his car running. Nope—the rich shitbag has to take from that guy, too, and add it to his own fortune—and he gets a sick thrill if he can make the working stiff believe he's doing it to help them, and make the world a better place, because he's so damned generous and compassionate. That right there explains Friedrich Engels; John D. Rockefeller; Michael Bloomberg; George Soros; Bill Gates; and every woke billionaire who ever lived. They could never tolerate the American dream—in America or any other society. Too much competition. A smart guy with a strong work ethic and a good idea might become just as successful as these limp-wristed elites are—or, God forbid, even *more* successful. Nope—gotta lock it up so they stay on top forever. Notice he said it's the monarchies that are in danger."

"That's kind of outdated," I said.

"Just the semantics," Dad said. "An absolute monarchy is a dictatorship; plain and simple. Whether the true monarch is the one on the throne or a puppetmaster pulling their strings. All these slick marketing blitzes like communism and fascism are just dressing up the same old top-down despotism in weasel words that will appeal to ignorant sheep. Call the asshole a king, queen, sultan, rajah, premier, chairman, or president...doesn't matter. Call their underlings nobles, bureaucrats, commissars... call their subjects peasants, serfs or proles...call what they extort taxes, *danegeld* or protection money...it's all the same shit-show. I showed you what real dollar bills looked like when we went to see Sullivan-Corbett, right?"

I nodded. "They were backed with precious metals."

"Right. And you remember our visit to Jeckyll Island. What do you know about the Titanic?"

I shrugged. "Huge ocean liner. Even God couldn't sink it, somebody said. Hit an iceberg. Not enough lifeboats. It sank. People died."

"Two of the passengers who died were the only men with the clout and intention of stopping the latest scheme to establish a central bank over America. The more I learn, the more suspicious I am about coincidences. But hell; maybe it was just a coincidence. I can't explore every single rabbit trail. British elites were behind the plot to control America's wealth; British elites finance ships like the Titanic. Maybe there's no connection beyond that."

Dad entered some coordinates on the warp interface. We took off, and jumped once we had a few hundred feet of altitude.

We parked the VTOL, cloaked, atop a building in 1911 New York City at night. Dad set up a powerful telescope on a tripod, then asked me to look through it.

The scope was focused on an illuminated window on the second floor of a large, stately mansion. Inside the room, two men in suits smoked cigars and engaged each other in intense conversation.

"Know who that is?" Dad asked.

"The one with the glasses looks familiar," I said.

Dad nodded. "That's Teddy Roosevelt."

"Wow."

"We could get audio if we really wanted to," Dad said. "But again, then we'd just get one layer deep. You'd hear the 'what,' but not the 'why'."

"What is the 'what'?" I asked.

"Right now, in that very room, good ol' Theodore is being persuaded to run for a third Presidential term, for the Bull Moose Party. He already served two terms as President, and that was enough for him. But he's being pressured to come out of retirement."

"Okay," I said. "Why?"

"Because if he doesn't, Taft will win his own second term in a landslide. See, the Republicans have dominated the Executive Branch since Lincoln. They need somebody to run third-party who is popular enough to split the vote so the Democrat will win in 1912. The Democrat is Woodrow Wilson. His handler is Edward Mandell House, who will really be running the show."

"Couldn't they find corrupt politicians in either party to control?" I asked, almost not noticing that I, also, was referring to an unnamed "they."

"To be sure. They can, and have. But it wasn't as easy, back then. They hadn't centralized control yet. They were ready to start consolidating power, but Taft was going to veto the Aldrich bill. In fact, they didn't have enough members of Congress to pass the bill, either. So they got Wilson in, first, by splitting the Republican vote. Then they got a few of their moles in Congress to hang around Capitol Hill while all the other Congressmen went home for Christmas Break. With nobody there but traitors, they passed two bills that changed America forever—the Federal Reserve Act and the Internal Revenue Act. Now the bankers could use their debt-based fiat currency to rob the citizens through inflation; progressively bankrupt the country through debt; and control the institutions and people nominally in charge. On top of that, they could now get their hands on people's money regardless of whether people spent it or saved it. Working stiffs, small business owners—everybody. None of this shit was legal, but the bankers had their puppet Wilson in position to sign it into 'law' anyway."

"Even then," I said, "how did they get away with it?"

Dad let out one of his sardonic chuckles. "They found a way around the separation of powers by planting their stooges in the Executive *and* Legislative branches. The Supreme Court should have struck it all down, right? And failing that, the people should have marched on Washington with torches and pitchforks. But the Press never blew the whistle. By the time anybody realized what happened, it was a *fait accompli*. Good men did nothing, while ignorance and apathy worked their magic on everyone else. The Income Tax was miniscule, at first, and voluntary, too. If you refused to pay it, they wouldn't send armed SWAT teams to your house at 3am to kick in your door and throw you in prison. They'd save that for later, when the frog was much closer to boiled."

I thought back to the frog-boiling metaphor he used so often. "So they increased the tax rate gradually—never enough at one time to make people march with torches and pitchforks."

He nodded. "'Oh, it's only a little more than last year. No big deal. Oh, it's only a little more than last year. No big deal.'

Then their grandkids wake up one morning and the fat cats are confiscating half of their wages, tips, and other compensation before the earners even get to touch it. And the federal government is hiring thousands of IRS agents, issuing them combat gear and automatic weapons."

We packed up the telescope and got back in the VTOL. We took off and jumped to 1915 somewhere over the Atlantic. Dad had me open another file in the computer and read him latitude and longitude. He maneuvered the VTOL, scanned the sea below, and asked me, "What do you remember from history books about the First World War?"

"The Red Baron shot down 80 enemy planes," I said. "Confirmed."

He smirked. "Is that it?"

"No. It lasted from 1914 to 1918. Trench warfare. Poison gas. Blackjack Pershing led the American Expeditionary Force. Alvin York won the Medal of Honor."

"Oh boy," dad groaned. "Well, do you know how it started?"

This part I had memorized for a test. "The assassination of Archduke Franz Ferdinand in Sarajevo by Serbian nationalists."

"Let's get beyond the superficial: It was an internecine conflict. Most of the royal families were related to each other in some way. The King of England was first cousins with the Czar of Russia and the Kaiser of Germany, for instance.

"The sun never set on the British Empire, and Britannia ruled the waves; but here was this young upstart nation-state on the continent that already had the best and most powerful army, building its own blue water navy almost 2/3rds as big as the British Grand Fleet, establishing its own colonies around the world... That didn't sit well with the Bankers, or their British proxies. They wanted to move toward a new Roman Empire— a European union—but with the British running the superstate for the Rothschilds. The German Empire...Second Reich...had only been around a little over 40 years; didn't have the seniority. And the bankers didn't want Kaiser Wilhelm as their supreme figurehead.

"So Franz Ferdinand gets assassinated, and the Austro-Hungarians—who frankly don't have the fighting prowess to beat a girls' softball team in battle—are hell-bent on war. Serbia bends over backwards to keep the peace, but for some inexplicable reason, Wilhelm gives Franz Joseph a blank check: Austria-Hungary can start an idiotic war for any idiotic reason, and Germany will fight for them—no matter what. Seems kind of masochistic, doesn't it? Russia, France, Britain and all the British Commonwealth countries are putting aside their differences to stick up for Serbia, guaranteeing you'll be surrounded and outnumbered like crazy...so you let this dying old Balkanized empire drag you into a world war against ridiculous odds. Austria-Hungary can't even beat Serbia; much less help you fight the Russians."

"You're saying something stinks about Wilhelm's decision?"

"To me it does," Dad said. "Ah, here we go. This might be it."

I followed his glance to a ship in the gray waters below.

"Grab the binos and see if you can make out the name of that vessel," Dad said.

I took the binoculars out of their padded compartment and scanned the hull of the ship with them. "Nicosian," I read, aloud.

"Yup. This is it."

Dad piloted the VTOL to follow the Nicosian—which looked like a civilian cargo ship. Then, beside it, the water churned and a steel cylinder broke through the surface. It kept rising up from the deep. The cylinder turned out to be the conning tower of a submarine which surfaced completely.

"That's U-27," Dad announced.

The Nicosian slowed, then stopped. So did the submarine.

"Oh shit," I said. "A German U-Boat! They're gonna sink the ship."

Dad shook his head. "The Krauts are following international laws of war. They're not gonna sink a civilian ship carrying non-military cargo, with civilians still aboard. But they *will* capture it."

The Nicosian and U-27 drifted close to each other. The German sailors tied the two vessels together with heavy rope and boarded the Nicosian. Through the binoculars, I could see a German sailor speaking to a crew member on the British ship.

"It's August 19, 1915," Dad said. "The Great Powers have been at war just about a year, now. Americans are interested in how it plays out; but almost none of them have any interest in getting involved. In fact, more Americans are sympathetic to the Central Powers than to the Allies. Of course, American newspapers are trying to change that by publishing stories about 'barbaric Huns' committing atrocities in Belgium. Most of that is bullshit."

One German, with a pistol drawn, followed a British crewman down a hatch into the cargo hold of the Nicosian.

"Busted," Dad said. "The British have a sneaky habit of using civilian ships to carry military supplies. This isn't the only time they've done it. Not by a long shot."

I had always heard that the Germans were the bad guys in *both* World Wars. This was a bit startling.

"*Now* they're gonna sink the ship," Dad said. "And they're well within their rights to do it."

We watched the Germans lower lifeboats and herd the civilian crewmen into them.

"Eight of those guys from the British crew are Americans," Dad explained. "Otherwise, nobody would have ever known what happened here—aside from the chickenshit Limeys, of course."

As the lifeboats were loaded, a third vessel approached. It appeared to be a merchant marine ship, flying the American flag. It also had something like a wall, or extension of the hull, with the Stars & Stripes painted on it.

"And here's the Baralong," Dad announced, with a sardonic sing-song tone.

Sailors on the deck of the U-Boat and the new ship exchanged signals with flags.

"The British blockade is preventing any shipping coming to or from Germany," Dad explained. "They're trying to starve the Germans into submission. Germans *are* starving to death in big numbers. They're reduced to eating sawdust and animal feed. Germany isn't self-sufficient, so they depend on trade for certain foods and necessities of life. Back in February, the Krauts decided two can play this game. They issued a warning for neutral ships to avoid the waters around the British Isles, or they might be sunk. Wilson is still pretending to be neutral, but he threatened retaliation if any American ships were attacked. The last thing the Krauts want to do is bring yet another country into the war against them, so they don't want to sink a Yankee ship. The Germans aren't just playing fair; they're bending over backwards. And the Baralong is signaling that it's on a humanitarian mission—just helping to pick up the crew of the captured ship."

The Baralong maneuvered around so that she was behind the Nicosian where the U-27 couldn't see what was happening on her deck. Old Glory was lowered down the mast and put away. The Union Jack was raised. The wooden Stars & Stripes facade dropped, exposing deck guns.

I sucked in breath as the guns fired.

The U-27 was a sitting duck. It had no armor to withstand direct hits from naval guns, and began to sink. German sailors abandoned ship. I watched in horror as British sailors on the Baralong began shooting them in the water.

Germans in lifeboats, and treading water, clearly raised hands in surrender, only to be shot in cold blood and left for the sharks.

Dad turned from the scene to lock eyes with me. "Pretty barbaric, those Germans, huh? Now whatever in the world could have inspired those bloodthirsty Huns to commence unrestricted submarine warfare against the esteemed gentlemen of the British Empire, I wonder?"

I was too horrified at the time to comment; but it became obvious later, after I had calmed down: the Germans were screwed either way. They might as well attack all Allied shipping. The British were treacherous scum and Wilson was determined to get the USA in the war one way or another.

"The Baralong is a 'Q Ship'," Dad said. "The British hide guns to make them look like defenseless civilian craft, and fly the flags of neutral countries so they can sucker-punch U-Boats exactly like what you just saw. After this, the Krauts said, 'the hell with it,' and began enforcing their blockade around Great Britain. The British were really hoping they would sink an American vessel, assuming it was just another Q-Ship falsely flying the American flag."

"Those lying, murdering cocksuckers," I muttered.

"I told you about Wilson's threat to the Kaiser," Dad reminded me. "What's funny is if you contrast what he told each empire. He told the Krauts they better not sink any ships with Americans on board, or else, even though everybody knew British Q-Ships routinely sailed under American flags. They'd been caught red-handed pulling this bullshit early in the war. But Wilson told the Limeys they could pretty much continue sailing under false flags, and he wouldn't do shit about it."

Dad took us backwards a few months, to early May, 1915. He cloaked and landed the VTOL in London, set up the telescope again, and sent some microdrones to the palace. I watched Edward Mandell House meet with King George V.

"House is President Wilson's handler," Dad reminded me.

The King asked House what the USA would do if the Germans sunk a British civilian liner with Americans on board, and Americans died as a result. House assured him that would be sufficient to bring the USA into the war on the British side.

"Did you learn in school why Americans were sent to Europe to fight in this idiotic war?"

"A telegram?" I remembered something about Germans trying to persuade Mexico to attack the USA.

Dad scoffed. "The Zimmerman Telegram. Now there's the ultimate convenient blunder by those dastardly, mustache-twirling Huns. So you never heard of the Lusitania?"

"Oh, that's right," I said. "I remember it, now."

We jumped back to late April, in New York City. I saw flyers posted in public places, and ads in newspapers, paid by the German government, warning Americans to not book passage on British ships bound for the war zone. We watched dock workers loading munitions in the hold of the Lusitania.

Dad pointed out that the Rothschild-owned British were acting just like Islamic terrorists—hiding behind women and children to violate the rules of warfare. Either the Germans wouldn't attack the ship (carrying weapons which the British meant to use against Germany) because they didn't want to harm the civilians aboard; or they were desperate enough to do it, which would bring America into the conflict to rescue Britain's treacherous ass from the fire. The Germans had spies in the harbor, and knew the British ship was bearing war material.

The Lusitania, just like the Baralong, sailed under a false flag.

The British Navy deliberately called away the HMS Juno as the Lusitania entered contested waters, so that the ocean liner would have no escort to protect her from German U-Boats.

It struck me that the Lusitania was being set up much like Kennedy was.

The U-20 torpedoed the ocean liner. Torpedoes were expensive, but crude at those coordinates. They caused damage, but rarely were capable of sinking a ship that was compartmentalized like the Lusitania. Nonetheless, when the water seeped in and made contact with the *pyroxylin* (a type of "gun cotton") in the hold, a secondary explosion tore enough of the hull that she sank within a half hour.

For the cold-blooded icing on the cake, Lord of the Admiralty Jackie Fisher called the Juno back to port once again when it tried returning to rescue passengers after receiving the Lusitania's SOS transmission.

About 2,000 passengers died, including more than 120 Americans. The British made sure of that.

"The USA intervened in the war in 1917," Dad said. "Know

what Wilson's campaign slogan was for his reelection in 1916?"

I shook my head.

"'He kept us out of war'."

CHAPTER 4: THE HISTORY LESSON PART 2

"The Rothschilds already had a central bank set up in the US," I said. "Why did they want us in the war so bad? Why did they favor the British, if they had central banks set up in all the countries involved?"

"Another good question," Dad said, as he landed the VTOL back at BH Station to refuel.

While we returned to the wardrobe to change, he explained his theory of crisis and opportunity in the context of "the Great War."

He had educated me on the Hegelian Dialectic before. The Puppeteers couldn't implement a frog-boiling synthesis when people rejected both the thesis and antithesis. The most sure-fire way to get people to surrender freedom and sovereignty was by offering a solution to a crisis.

Of course, that required a crisis. Usually a big one.

If you tried to impose tyranny without a big enough crisis, then regular folks (especially Americans, in those days) would tell you to shove your "solution" where the sun didn't shine.

"Unrestricted submarine warfare" and the notion of a German/Mexican alliance invading American territory combined to form a perceived crisis which convinced enough Congressmen that the solution was to send Americans to fight in a pointless European war.

The "war to end all wars" itself served as a crisis for the next "solution"—the first attempt at the first step toward a world government since the Tower of Babel, some might say. Wilson and his fellow globalists called this Utopian first step the League of Nations. Unfortunately for them, Congress suffered buyer's remorse from the last "solution" and rejected joining the League.

Another "solution" to the same crisis was the Versailles Treaty. The harsh and unfair terms of the treaty amplified Germany's post-war economic trauma. Eventually, hyperinflation would cause such suffering that a plurality of desperate Germans would vote the National Socialists into power.

But there was yet another "solution," first introduced in Russia, spurred by multiple crises including the war; army desertions; widespread hunger; flagrant inequality; and the incompetent cruelty of the Czarist regime.

Dad took me to Carnegie Hall on March 23, 1917. The Big Spooky was throbbing over what seemed to me like a huge victory party. There were seats, but a lot of people were on their feet, including us. Dad pretended to share in the celebration and had coached me to do the same, in order to blend in with the "communist shitbags" swarming all over the place.

There were plenty of women in the crowd. Some were attractive, but most were not. A Tier Four woman, perhaps in her mid-30s, greeted me with a rapturous smile, introduced herself and engaged me in small talk. At one point she whispered in my ear conspiratorially, but the content of her words were lost in the shock of her thrusting her hand down the front of my pants to squeeze and rub my privates. She pulled back to smile at close range with a gleam in her eye. Plain-faced though she was, her brazen act had caused my anatomy to respond in a way that pleased her. She kept fondling as she pulled my head down and rammed her tongue into my mouth.

Dad surreptitiously grabbed her ass while stealthily maneuvering around so she couldn't tell who the culprit was in the convulsing crowd. Her expression wasn't exactly indignant

—more like curious, flattered…maybe hopeful. Her hand slipped out of my pants as she turned. Dad pulled me away and the shifting mass of humanity quickly filled in the gap between us and the horny broad.

Most of the crowd was singing some Russian song, so Dad had to raise his voice for me to hear him. "You can get yourself laid easy at a shit show like this, even in 1917. Degeneracy is rampant in Marxist insurgent movements. Spout off some horseshit about the heroic victimhood of the proletariat…her and a dozen other commie bitches will squirt all over their petticoats. She's probably hopped-up on cocaine or opium or something, too."

While Dad escorted me toward some guy in a rumpled suit, holding a piece of paper and trying to quiet the crowd, I wondered how many of the men here remained dedicated communists primarily so they could get their turn with easy women like the Karl Marx groupie I had just encountered. We got within maybe 20 yards of the guy with the paper and could draw no closer through the mob.

Gradually the singing and other noise died down. "Listen to this shitbag," Dad said.

The guy in the unkempt suit read a telegram that referred to some great accomplishment they "had hoped and striven for these long years."

"What's he talking about?" I asked. "What's the reason for the party?"

"The Tsar abdicated," Dad replied.

The dweeb continued reading from the telegram. Once finished, he made some off-the-cuff remarks which turned into a speech.

"Blah blah blah, workers of the world, unite," Dad remarked, now pulling me toward an exit. "Blah blah blah, the free market is oppressing us."

Back outside Carnegie Hall, Dad told me, "The asshole who sent that telegram was Jacob Schiff—head honcho at Kuhn, Loeb and Company."

Jacob Schiff, Dad explained, was a filthy rich wheeler-dealer who sponsored the enormous war loans to ensure a Japanese victory in the Russo-Japanese War in 1904-5...which exacerbated the problems Russia was already facing. Schiff was also a big donor to the Woodrow Wilson campaign and one of the fat cats who pushed for the Federal Reserve Act. He contributed some $20 million to bring the communists to power in Russia. And that was in 1917 dollars. Dad suspected Schiff was the wealthy benefactor of Leon Trotsky during Trotsky's all-expense-paid exile in New York.

Once the Tsar was out of power, Trotsky (with a whopping $10,000 in his pocket) boarded a ship bound for his motherland. The Bolsheviks had wrested control from the Tsar; now the communists intended to wrest control from the Bolsheviks. Canadian authorities arrested Trotsky in Halifax and threw him in jail. Leading a revolution in Russia (an ally) was, by default, working on behalf of Germany (the enemy), after all. And Canada had gone to war along with the other British Commonwealth of countries *against* Germany.

Edward Mandell House didn't just control Woodrow Wilson, it turned out. He pressured his next-door neighbor, British Secret Service chief William Wiseman, to have Trotsky released and allowed passage to Russia. Wilson himself authorized the issue of Trotsky's passport, despite the fact that the USA was at war by then and this constituted giving aid and comfort to the enemy.

Schiff wasn't the only fat cat bankrolling the communists —not by a long shot. Rockefeller, Morgan, other bankers and robber barons were in on it. This struck me as counter-intuitive. Capitalists were supposed to be mortal enemies of communists. True believers in Marx's Utopian vision wanted to destroy capitalism. So why, after they had made it big in a capitalist economy, would these industrialists and financiers promote and nurture a movement meant to wreck the very system that made their success possible?

It only made sense if Dad was correct about the

psychology of such people.

We jumped to St. Petersburg, dressed in the period uniforms of the Red Cross. The Big Spooky was present, and powerful. We saw dozens of people, including some dressed like us, bribing soldiers in the Pavlovski Regiment with 25 Ruble notes. Dad struck up a conversation with one of the sleazebags handing out money. He spoke fluent English with a British accent. Red Cross missionaries spoke fluent English with American accents. Later that same day, the regiment mutinied, joining the revolution. That guaranteed St. Petersburg would turn Red.

"You getting the idea the fix was in?" Dad asked me.

"But why?" I asked. "It doesn't make sense to me. Why do they want to help the communists so much?"

Dad shot me a tired expression. "Asked and answered, o quick-witted one."

△△△

We moved on to the Great Depression. Like everybody else, public school had taught me that an unregulated free market and *"laissez-faire"* economic policy caused the Depression. Hoover and other "do nothing" Republicans were to blame.

A lot of the financial terms went over my head, but to no surprise, Dad told me the official story was bullshit. The truth was a convoluted web of economic voodoo, but I did catch that the central bank ("Federal Reserve") was crucial in the over-valuation of stock by spurring an inflationary boom. Dad proposed that the stock market crash was probably planned; but the "royal clusterfuck" that followed definitely was.

Dad started with the "bankers' panic" of 1907. The same kind of reckless stock market trading happened in the preceding years that also happened in the 1920s. The difference was that the fat cats (chiefly J.P. Morgan, again) had to bail themselves out with their own money in 1907. The American economy was too robust to be derailed, and normal people with honest jobs were mostly unaffected. But afterwards, the fat cats devised a way to make taxpayers bear the cost of the next crash the stock traders would cause. The Federal Reserve and Internal Revenue Service were the cornerstone to the scheme.

As for Herbert Hoover being a "do nothing" economist, Dad debunked that narrative. Hoover was an interventionist, who meddled in the market in an alleged attempt to stabilize the economy. FDR followed the same strategies—just more of them to a greater degree. By federal government tampering with the free market, they managed to milk the Great Depression out of the Crash of '29.

Of course, there were several solutions ready and waiting for that crisis.

Thanks to a controlled press corps which blamed Hoover and portrayed FDR as the savior, the Democrats were swept into power on a scale not seen since the days of the Confederacy—and they would control Congress unchallenged for the next 62 years —the next century with just a few brief interruptions.

Another aspect of the solution, of course, was to take wealth (and power) from the people and states, and transfer it to the federal government. Ownership of gold was outlawed, and the interest-free dollars still in circulation were rounded up until nothing was left but the Fed's fiat currency. The solution required unprecedented spending, borrowing, and debt. Entitlement programs were established that would balloon to enormous proportions over the next four generations— basically bribe money to keep certain demographics voting Democrat in perpetuity. Taxes had to be raised (not enough to cover the massive spending, of course) but in stages, to keep the frog comfortable in the pot until he would be boiled alive by the rates of confiscation 90 years later. Ultimately, the American middle class would be eliminated.

The Income Tax would no longer be voluntary before the New Deal was over. The IRS would automatically withhold a percentage of workers' earnings from their paycheck; and the citizen would have to play bureaucratic games to get some of it back.

Dad referred to the chain of events between the World Wars as a "trifecta." Socialists were brought to power in Russia, Germany, and the USA. Through the charismatic, authoritarian figureheads in those three countries, the world would be forever changed.

Dad showed me a map of the world in 1936. Russia, the geographically largest country in the world, was the only one colored red. Dad explained that the map only used red to identify communist countries. (If it was used for all socialist regimes, then several other countries would also be colored red —including Germany, Italy, and Great Britain.)

"Hitler would have remained some obscure, mescaline-addicted Bohemian artist if the Germans weren't starving and desperate—and pissed off. They wouldn't have been starving and desperate without the hyperinflation. They wouldn't have suffered hyperinflation without the Second Reich's enormous war debt, the ridiculous reparations required by the Versailles Treaty, and the Depression that made its way across the ocean from America."

I pondered the crisis/opportunity dynamic, which, according to Dad, made the world go around. Was it really so easy to manipulate people? Even free people, traditionally skeptical, like Americans?

"The Krauts wouldn't have been so pissed off if they didn't feel betrayed," Dad continued. "And they wouldn't have felt so betrayed if bankers from their own country hadn't gone along with the plan to bring America into the war. But then, all that has been buried and obfuscated by straw man arguments like the 'stab-in-the-back myth.' Easiest way to debunk an argument or revise history is to get some clown to agree with the counter-narrative...right before spewing some kind of antisemitic tirade about Zionist conspiracies so that normal people will conflate the two and reject it all. The Warburgs ruled over banks on behalf of the Rothschilds in all the great powers—including Germany and America. Good ol' Jacob Schiff had two brothers running banks in Germany. International banking is just like the royal families—everybody's related. And they worked the same war profiteering scheme in every country—including countries on opposite sides. Some of the bankers happened to be Jewish...or at least regarded as Jews. So that played into the Zionist conspiracy narrative: Jews in all the competing nations conspired to save Great Britain by bringing America into the war; and in return they got the British Mandate for Palestine and the Balfour Declaration."

"Is there any truth to the Palestine part?" I asked, remembering from my history classes at Poly that the British Mandate for Palestine had something to do with the formation of modern-day Israel.

Dad shrugged. "Who the hell knows? Could be. Just like the Lincoln assassination, these scumbags like to pull people into their plans who have their own axes to grind...their own grievances that can be exploited by the puppetmasters. Probably some were Zionists. It makes the whole deal more convoluted; but probably."

"Which is why the Nazis hated Jews so much, maybe."

Dad wiggled his head around until his neck cracked. "Genetics don't make good people good; and they don't make bad people bad. But low-IQ people; bovine normies; and educated fools can be led into thinking that way. That's probably how the National Socialists got the Germans to go along with the Final Solution: identity politics. It appeals to sheeple's in group/out group binary thinking."

"When you said 'regarded as Jews,' what did you mean?" I asked.

"Another research project for my bucket list," he said. "There's this theory out there that a whole lot of 'Jews' are not actually from the tribe of Judah, but are descended from Khazarians who adopted either Talmudic Judaism, or Kabbalism, way back before the fall of the Byzantine Empire. But this field trip is about *our* country. We'll never get through it if we chase every rabbit trail."

When Hitler was awarded the Chancellorship of Germany, the Cabal didn't have to stage mass shootings to disarm the German people—people had no right to bear arms to begin with. The National Socialists jumped straight to absolute authoritarianism after the Reichstag fire. The French and British, despite having superior armed forces and an overt interest in keeping Germany weak, chose to appease the rash new dictator as he first violated the Versailles treaty by building up the *Wehrmacht*; then moved troops into the Rhineland; then annexed Austria; then took over the Sudetenland; then occupied Czechoslovakia.

Hitler staged his own "false flag" operation to justify invading Poland from the west, while the Soviets invaded from the east. The Allies had finally drawn the line at Poland, thus "the Big One" (World War Two) finally kicked off.

Dad emphasized the point, however, that they only declared war on one of the invading empires: "Interesting that attacking Poland was an act of war for Hitler, but not for Stalin. Now I just wonder why that might be."

We did some more sightseeing over the Atlantic while Dad continued filling in details.

While the USA was still pretending to be neutral, FDR had the US Navy helping the British, to varying degrees, attack German U-Boats. He had American merchant ships ferrying munitions, and even British troops, for the Royal Navy. Roosevelt effectively turned civilian cargo vessels into his own "Q-ships," armed and aggressive toward German U-Boats.

"Roosevelt keeps assuring everyone that his policies are strictly defensive," Dad said, "but he wants war with Germany bad. Real bad. He assures Churchill the USA will pull their Limey asses out of the fire again. Trouble is, the Lost Generation, who survived the last pointless European war, don't wanna send their sons to die in the sequel. Americans don't like war, anyway. The best way to get Americans to change their mind, though, is to piss 'em off. Churchill said as much. That's why Roosevelt is trying to provoke another Lusitania incident."

"I'm still kinda' upset about Poland," I admitted.

"What about it?"

"They get carved up from two directions," I clarified, "but only one culprit was blamed."

Dad grinned at me. "It's part of a pattern that should be clear to you when this is all over. Communists are good guys, see, so whatever they do is either justified, or ignored. Stalin gobbles up other sovereign countries while he's at it: Lithuania, Estonia, Latvia...invades Finland. No Lend/Lease for the Finns. But as soon as Hitler double-crosses Stalin...that's all the excuse Roosevelt needs to start building the USSR up into a superpower. We never got a dime back from "Lend/Lease," by the way. Or an aircraft. Or a field gun. American taxpayers were grifted to finance the build-up of our communist 'ally,' then were left holding the bag, as usual."

We listened to a radio broadcast in 1940, during which FDR assured Americans that their sons would not be sent to fight in Europe again.

My heart sank as I watched an American destroyer stalk a German submarine, reporting its position so a British bomber could attack it. Another US Navy ship attacked U-Boats for three hours with depth charges before the Germans fired back.

Dad showed me a Gallup Poll from that year: 88% of Americans opposed another war with Germany, even with all this going on. Something drastic was required to turn them pro-war.

"I feel sick," I said.

"Why's that?" Dad asked.

"It's like you're taking Germany's side. Or trying to get me to take it."

Dad sighed and shook his head. "Don't get stuck in binary thinking. You don't understand what the 'sides' really were. Almost nobody did. Sure—FDR wasn't on Germany's side. He also wasn't on America's side. Germany was a tool—just like the Depression. Just like Roosevelt himself. Like pretty much everything else, it wasn't a Good Guy against Bad Guy scenario. There was no Good Guy. It was Bad Guy against Bad Guy... and Bad Guy against Worse Guy. Thesis against Antithesis, so they can wind up with Synthesis. Stalin and Hitler were the Thesis and Antithesis. International Socialism against National Socialism."

He had talked about the Hegelian Dialectic before, but my emotions were hindering my intellectual stamina right then. "Synthesis was the New Deal, then?"

"That was a simultaneous dialectic, Sprout. In America. You're thinking too small."

That fit. I felt pretty small. Small; insignificant, and hopeless.

"Not that I'm gonna shed any tears for the Nazis," Dad said, "but they actually showed incredible restraint. The Krauts learned their lesson from the first war, and didn't take Roosevelt's bait. But there was a nation in the Axis that *could* be provoked into a fight with us."

My heart sank a little more, in anticipation of what might be next.

CHAPTER 5: THE HISTORY LESSON PART 3

The Japanese had never been defeated, and many of them considered themselves invincible. They also didn't understand the American temperament the way Churchill did. So maybe they were too arrogant to consider the risks of a war with the USA; or maybe they underestimated the American reaction to the destruction of the US Pacific Fleet.

Whatever the reason, they would blunder right into the trap.

FDR had Japanese assets frozen. He closed off the Panama Canal to their shipping. He increased sanctions against Japan all the way up to a full embargo. There were several other provocations. Then he made our Navy as vulnerable as he could to the Japanese.

Dad piloted the VTOL over a California naval base before the war, pointing out all the battleships, cruisers, destroyers and aircraft carriers in port. He nodded toward the ships below and said, "US Pacific Fleet."

"Why are they here instead of Pearl Harbor?" I asked.

"Because there's plenty of fuel here, and dry docks," he replied. "No shortage of manpower to draw from to crew these ships. Sailors tend to maintain higher morale when they get to see their families now and then, instead of being stuck on some island halfway around the world where they outnumber women twenty-to-one and if you want to get laid...well, you'll have to settle for the hordes of faggots in Honolulu. Here you got a whole continent behind you and there's only so many directions you can be attacked from. There's nets and baffles in the harbor, to guard against torpedoes. Pearl Harbor doesn't have that. The Japs would never try to attack the fleet here. Never. You ever heard of Admiral J.O. Richardson?"

I shrugged. "Don't think so."

"He didn't want to move the fleet to Hawaii, where they would be sitting ducks. Butted heads with FDR. Got shitcanned. Churchill figured, if Britain could hold out until FDR was reelected, US entry in the war was a done deal. He called that one dead on."

Richardson was replaced by Admiral Kimmel, who also thought moving the fleet to Pearl was foolish, but who followed orders. He believed that Washington's intelligence network would warn him if an attack was likely.

And Washington did have good intelligence on what the Japs were planning. A program called MAGIC had cracked the Japanese code, and determined when the attack was scheduled. Embassy staff in Tokyo provided intelligence that tipped off Washington the location of the attack.

Three of the decoding machines built as part of MAGIC were given to the British, but none was provided to the American Armed Forces in Hawaii, despite being requested. Instead, intercepted messages were forwarded from the Pacific back to Washington, decrypted, then routed through the military bureaucracy back to Pearl. At least *some* of them were routed to Pearl.

Further radio intercepts through MAGIC confirmed the Japanese plans—including the time, place, and manner of the attack. The SIGINT (signal intelligence) was further corroborated by a Yugoslavian double agent; a Peruvian ambassador; Dutch Army code breakers, and the Korean Underground. But the Roosevelt Administration withheld all this information from the men who needed it most—the commanders of US Forces in Hawaii.

I processed all this information, heartbroken, like a kid who just found out there is no Santa Clause.

The Japanese attack on Pearl Harbor was FDR's back door into the war against Germany he wanted all along.

Our entry into the war made Americans accept a lot of "new normals," like Daylight Savings Time, the IRS automatically withholding the "voluntary" income tax from their paychecks. And the second advent of a transitional global government, now called the United Nations, funded mostly by those automatically withheld "voluntary" taxes on American citizens.

After D-Day, General Patton's US 3rd Army broke out of the hedgerows in Normandy and began exceeding all expectations along his race to Berlin. He was finally stopped, not by the Germans, but by Allied commanders diverting his supplies to the predictably unsuccessful Operation Market Garden. This bought time for the Red Army's own race for Berlin.

"So remember," Dad said, "the war started when Poland was invaded from the west by the *Wehrmacht* and from the east by the Red Army. But France and Britain only declared war on Germany, while the USSR got a pass. When the Soviets invaded Finland, Lithuania, and so on...crickets. Then, at Yalta, FDR met with Churchill and Stalin. That's where Roosevelt and Churchill handed Uncle Joe all of Poland and the rest of eastern Europe. Wanna know what our brave boys in uniform were really fighting for?"

Dad showed me the map of pre-war Europe again, then showed me a post-war map for comparison with all communist countries colored red. The later map revealed that the communist empire had expanded significantly during the war.

"You tell me what the war accomplished," Dad challenged me. "Did we 'set the world free'? Looks like the opposite to me."

"But...Hitler was a threat," I replied, weakly.

Dad scoffed. "He was the lesser evil. We replaced him with a mass murderer three times worse. Yay, democracy."

I was desperate to find some outcome of the war that would have justified it. "We did prevent Japan from controlling the Pacific."

Dad rolled his eyes. "You just don't see the pattern yet, do ya Sprout?"

We jumped to the Far East to continue the tour.

In August of 1945, Japan was incapable of offensive campaigns. After the battles for Iwo Jima and Okinawa, even the most fanatical Japanese Imperialists knew they were beaten. Immediately after President Truman had the atom bomb dropped on Nagasaki, Stalin joined the war against Japan, gobbling up more territory, including half of Mongolia and Korea.

In China, during the war, Mao Tse-Tung did very little to help fight the Japanese. He instead concentrated on building his own power, while Chiang Kai-Shek and his Nationalist Chinese forces did most of the heavy lifting against their mutual enemy. Envoys and advisers sent by the Roosevelt Administration, including General Stillwell, did what they could to help the Communists while sabotaging the Nationalist Chinese. They assisted the mainstream media in whitewashing the behavior and ambitions of Mao's followers—even denying they were communists, so the American people would remain ignorant.

At President Truman's invitation, the Red Army also moved into Manchuria, where they armed and equipped Mao's weak guerrilla force with captured Japanese weapons, as well as weapons paid for by American taxpayers and furnished to Stalin via "Lend/Lease." Meanwhile, George C. Marshall cut off supplies to the Chinese Nationalists. Despite betrayals of the Nationalists by communist apologists high up in the US Executive Branch, Chiang still could have won the civil war. On three separate occasions, Chiang Kai-Shek had the communists trapped and on the ropes. Each time, George C. Marshall imposed a truce (which only the Nationalists honored) rescuing the communist forces from annihilation.

We flew over Mao's encampment some time after the

Japanese surrender. Dad varied our altitude drastically so I could get the big picture. Chiang's Nationalist Chinese had inflicted numerous defeats against the communists and was now poised to wipe out what was left of Mao's PLA ("People's Liberation Army").

"This is Chiang's last opportunity," Dad explained. "He can secure victory with one final push. But as we speak, his 'great American ally' is gonna snatch defeat from the jaws of victory yet again. Marshall will coerce Chiang into not pulling the trigger."

The opportunity to save China slipped away forever.

Mao escaped, regrouped, reinforced, and was resupplied by the Soviets, who were now flush with weapons, supplies, and money given them by the Roosevelt and Truman Administrations. Of course, Chiang never got that kind of support from the US. He also never got another chance to wipe out Mao's PLA. It wasn't too long before the situation was reversed, and the Nationalists had to flee to the island of Formosa.

The communists took over mainland China—thanks mostly to the US State Department.

"Stillwell and Marshall have the supplies and munitions we promised Chiang dumped in the Bay of Bombay or left in India," Dad explained, "rather than deliver them to the Nationalists. Marshal leaves China in 1947, having fucked the Chinese people and, ultimately, the world. The *Koumintang* grows weaker and the communists get stronger until all mainland China is enslaved by 1949."

But the world map wasn't red enough yet. The communists would invade South Korea, too.

There was no Secretary of War, anymore—only a "Secretary of Defense." There would be no more declarations of war by Congress, either. Truman sent American forces to South Korea as (the most substantial) part of a United Nations "police action."

The problem for the globalists was, the Supreme Commander was General MacArthur, who assumed the objective was victory, like in previous wars. MacArthur kicked North Korea's ass quickly, and had liberated the entire peninsula, when the Red Chinese hordes flooded across the Yalu River to surprise attack the victorious Americans and their token UN allies.

"The Chi-Coms are the go-to guys when the Cabal suffers a setback," Dad said. "They'll send troops, a virus, whatever, to put the agenda back on track."

MacArthur prepared to deal with this new enemy, reasoning that, since we were now at war with China, it was an opportunity to undo the mistake of helping the Communists enslave China in the first place. He would liberate that country, too, and let the Nationalists govern it.

The joke was on him: the betrayal of the Chinese had not been a mistake, but the intent all along. Marshall, now the Secretary of Defense, forbid MacArthur from having the US Air Force bomb the bridges across the Yalu River to cut the Chinese supply lines.

MacArthur didn't know what the true objective of the shadow government in Washington was. He was fired, and replaced by Yes Men who obediently maintained a stalemate for the duration of the "police action."

"After the 'Forgotten War' and all this other stuff was memory-holed," Dad said, "We built Red China into a superpower, too. They went on to conquer Tibet, gain *de facto* control over the Panama Canal, bought Hollywood, most of our politicians, and with those politicians' help, usurped our manufacturing. You remember when we jumped that bad warp and wound up in 21st Century North America? It was under the administration of the Red Chinese. But golly-gee, it's a good thing we stopped those dangerous Japs from taking over the Pacific!"

Almost everything I had believed about the "Great Crusade" of WWII was a filthy lie.

ΔΔΔ

There were some communist agents in the Hoover Administration, but they greatly increased their foothold in the federal government during the New Deal. The infiltration spread like fast-moving cancer after that. A Senator from Wisconsin began trying to expose the communist takeover of the US Government in the postwar years. He was proven absolutely right decades later after the end of the Cold War, when declassified Soviet documents, FBI radio intercepts, and unsealed Congressional records confirmed his warnings. But the communists already controlling the government and press made sure that it was Joe McCarthy who was demonized—not the domestic enemies he blew the whistle on. The demonization began during the Army hearings. He was accused of having no specifics to back up his accusations by a smarmy Senator Welch trying to mock him. McCarthy named a specific communist agent working right at Welch's law firm.

"Have you no decency?" Welch protested. "Have you no decency at all?" Welch even managed to shed a crocodile tear on behalf of his communist assistant for the benefit of those present, and the TV cameras.

Welch's emotional ploy was the right call. With the help of the mainstream media, the country turned against McCarthy. The fact that a hostile foreign power, traitors in the highest levels of American government, and the Army were all working together against the USA was evidently not nearly as dangerous as Senator McCarthy being a big meanie to a grown man giving aid and comfort to the enemy. McCarthy was thereafter condemned as "Tailgunner Joe." His name became the root of a new word synonymous with "unreasonable persecution."

The communist subversion of the federal government continued, eventually seeping down into local and state governments, and every institution—especially Public Education—so that children could be taught to hate America (as

I had been in my native coordinates) and believe socialism was a superior system.

Dad mentioned how Castro came to power in Cuba, then what would later happen in Iran, Libya, Egypt, and other countries around the world. The globalist Shadow Government liked to topple existing regimes and replace them with anti-American dictators. Communist tyrants were their favorites. And if the state in question rejected a Rothschild-owned Central Bank, that made "regime change" even more urgent.

"That's the pattern you mentioned before," I said, with sudden epiphany. "The Washington Establishment stomps one country, so that another one will become the big kid on the block. Germany and Russia. Japan and China. Or the CIA knocks foreign leaders out of power, only to replace them with somebody even worse."

Dad nodded. "One pattern, for sure. There was a charade sold as 'halting the spread of communism.' Meanwhile, behind the scenes, America went into astronomical debt *promoting* the spread of communism...especially right in our own country. That brings us more-or-less to Kennedy."

△△△

Dad took us to a big, fancy north Dallas home in 1963. Since the area was a bit too populous to set up the telescope, and listening devices, without us being spotted, we remained in the VTOL while Dad sent in some insect drones.

"This is Clint Murchison's house," Dad explained. "He's one of the oil barons pissed off about Kennedy cutting the Oil Depletion Allowance."

The drone floated past a living room occupied by attractive young women smoking cigarettes, then flew under a closed door so that its camera captured a wide angle on a large drawing room with several middle-aged men in suits seated roughly in a circle, on chairs and couches.

Dad pointed to a pudgy man with glasses, prominent ears,

and a thick, sausage nose. "That's Murchison, there."

Dad pointed to a grandfatherly old fart. "That's his fellow Texas oil man H.L. Hunt."

I recognized Lyndon Johnson, and pointed to him. "That's LBJ."

Dad nodded. "And that's J. Edgar Hoover." He pointed to a rotund, jowly guy with a receding hairline. "Director of the FBI."

I had read about Hoover.

"That cocksucker right there," Dad said, indicating a refined-looking gentleman sitting by himself like a detached observer, "is a Rothschild agent. He represents the banking cartel."

Dad pointed at another guy with a ski-ramp nose, who looked familiar. "Richard Nixon. It's kind of ironic he's involved in this."

"Involved in what?" I asked.

"They're meeting to work out the assassination," Dad said.

"Oh. But Nixon is a crook, anyway," I said.

"No shit—he's a politician. We only know about what he did because he was in a political party that's been historically less enthusiastic about destroying America—and because he had an attack of conscience about what happened to Kennedy. The CIA set him up with the Watergate shit. As a crook, Nixon's a lightweight compared to Johnson, and most of the scumbags who came after Nixon. Tricky Dick had always admired JFK, and had a soft spot for him. Legally, he won in 1960. It was only the cheating that pushed Kennedy over the finish line. Nixon refused a recount, saying it would undermine confidence in our system, or some bullshit."

"But this assassination wouldn't?"

"Exactly," Dad said, shaking his head. "Anyway, Nixon, as sitting Vice President, had the power to determine which electors voted in the Electoral College—his, or Kennedy's—knowing he had won with legitimate voters, mind you. Well, he chose the Kennedy electors. Kennedy went to the White House because of Nixon's choice."

"You're right, then," I said. "This doesn't make much sense."

Dad sighed. "Murchison owns a hotel in California. It's a honey pot. He's got film on mob bosses, on Hoover, Nixon, and who-knows how many others. And this ain't the 1990s or later, when shitbags like Bill Clinton can get elected no matter who or what he has sex with—or how he gets it. Nixon took a woman there he wasn't married to. Hoover was blocking farts. That's called leverage. Neither of them wants to bump Kennedy off, but it's either play ball, or be humiliated, ruined, and probably get greased themselves. The CIA has all kinds of goodies. They can slip some stuff into your food or water, to give you a heart attack. They can make sure you get cancer and die within a few years. That's how they tied off the Jack Ruby loose end."

I shook my head and watched the scene.

"I talked to Clark, and Connally," LBJ told Hoover. "They've got key men in the State Police and the Dallas PD who'll do the right thing. You need to handle the federal stuff. And lean on the Secret Service."

Hoover nodded, frowning. "I'll have the right boys in the right places. But we need to control who does the autopsy, or this will all blow up in our faces."

"Then figure that out," Murchison said.

The youngest, healthiest man in the room spoke up. "I've got a few shooters who do this kind of work. But we need another couple teams for insurance. Ideally, we want triangulation. We need to trip it as he drives by the Book Depository." He glanced at Hoover, then Johnson. "It will make it a lot more of a sure thing if you can remove as many obstructions as you can—like motorcycle cops and the security detail that would normally ride with him in the limousine."

"Who's that?" I asked.

"CIA," Dad replied. "I haven't identified him by name, yet."

Hoover scribbled something in his notebook.

"Maybe I can get Yarborough to ride in the Presidential Limousine," Johnson mused, aloud. "We can score a tufer."

"Clark says you've got a trigger man for the Book Depository nest," the young agent told Johnson.

Johnson nodded. "He's done some good work before. But speaking of obstructions, those trees are gonna make that a tough shot."

"He's talking about Malcom Wallace," Dad said. "Wallace has rubbed out a few people for Johnson. Most recent one was Henry Marshall—agricultural official who was investigating how Billy Sol Estes had misappropriated the Federal Cotton Allotment."

I looked at Dad.

"Sol Estes was one of Johnson's henchmen," Dad explained. "Along with Wallace; Johnson's aide Cliff Carter, and Bobby Baker. Well, Baker was more like a partner in crime, in the Senate. He had connections to organized crime. Was into shady real estate deals; money laundering; a call-girl service. But anyway, Henry Marshall is all over Sol Estes, and just a hair away from figuring out Johnson had his hand in the cookie jar with Sol Estes. Marshall's fatal flaw was that he couldn't be bribed. Johnson had Carter plan the hit, and Wallace pull it off. Police found Marshall's body at the scene of a struggle, lungs full of carbon monoxide, shot five times with a bolt-action rifle. Suicide, of course."

"Obviously," I said, through gritted teeth.

"Yup," Dad said, chuckling. "Just like Vince Foster. Epstein killed himself, too. There never was a John Doe Number Two. Building Seven collapsed because of burning debris. Biden won. He got 81 million votes. And Oceana has always been at war with Eurasia."

"Huh?"

"Never mind," Dad said.

"Who is Clark? I asked.

" Edward Clark. He's the shadow 'boss' of Texas," Dad said.

"So Connally is the figurehead," I said. "But Clark owns him, and is really in charge."

"Something like that," Dad replied.

"Just like whoever is President is just a stooge," I continued. "Owned ultimately by the Rothschilds, who are really running the show."

Dad shrugged. "There have been some rogues, who they weren't able to control: Lincoln, Kennedy, Trump. There've been some foreign wild cards who pissed off the banks, too: Saddam Hussein; Muammar Gaddafi. The bankers got no problem with mass murderers—as long as they know their place. They got a big problem with leaders who won't knuckle under: the Shah of Iran, Tshombe, Noriega."

Dad took us back to B.H. Station.

"JFK's father, Joe Kennedy, was a gangster," Dad continued. "The gangster's war hero son had a problem keeping his pants zipped—and keeping his side pieces secret. He made it to the White House thanks to a whole lot of dead voters in Illinois. Of course, nobody did anything about the cheating, and it only got worse. Sixty years later, election fraud will be so brazen, and so ubiquitous, that half the population will finally realize the whole system is rigged against them."

Dad continued debriefing as we returned our costumes and props to the wardrobe.

"But anyway, Kennedy was crooked, like all of 'em. He totally fucked the Cubans, too. He may have been a good PT boat captain against the Japs; but he was a piss-poor Commander-in-Chief against the commies."

"That's a pattern too," I said. "Right? Against Germany, or Japan, or the Iraqi Army, we fight to win. But against communist countries...not so much."

"Not so much," Dad agreed. "So the Cubans got a grievance for the Bay of Pigs fiasco. CIA has a grievance, for that and other reasons. Jack Kennedy actually wants to shut down the Agency, 'cause they're already getting out of hand. Brother Bobby Kennedy has been leading a crusade against organized crime, going after Daddy Joe Kennedy's competition from the Bad Old Days. So the mob has a grievance. Texas oil barons have a grievance, because of JFK's intention to cut the Oil Depletion

Allowance. And LBJ has a grievance. His past is catching up to him. Not only won't he be Vice-President for Jack's second term; he might actually go to jail, if Bobby Kennedy comes any closer to getting the goods on him."

"So these guys are to JFK like the Confederate agents were to Lincoln," I said.

Dad gave me a thumbs-up. "Bingo."

He played the audio recording of Jack Kennedy warning about the dangers of secret societies. Even the first time I heard it, it was obvious JFK wasn't referring to the Elk Lodge, fraternities or harmless university hijinks; but something truly dangerous, with a malevolent and sinister purpose.

"That speech would be pooh-poohed as 'tinfoil hat' fodder if anybody but Kennedy gave it," Dad said. "It's ironic, on the surface, because a secret society had been controlling him for years—but through cut-outs. He thought the bribes and blackmail were just politics-as-usual. He could live with that. It was just garden variety corruption. As long as he could keep screwing hot side pieces like Marilyn Monroe, pushing his space program, and his New Frontier bullshit...no big deal. But then he discovered his strings were being pulled on behalf of something much, much bigger. He didn't like the Rothschilds and their proxies getting richer by screwing everyone else. I think he had an attack of conscience—like Nixon would, later."

Dad pulled the wallet out of his pocket, opened it, extracted a bill, and handed it to me.

"That's a Kennedy Dollar," he said.

It was a two dollar bill. It was not a Federal Reserve Note. It simply said "United States Note," "United States of America," and "Two Dollars."

He handed me another one. It looked a lot like the five dollar bills I had seen before, with Lincoln's portrait on one side and the Lincoln Memorial on the other. But it also said "United States Note" instead of "Federal Reserve Note."

"These are silver certificates," Dad said. "Interest-free currency, from the US Treasury—not the Fed. It's backed by silver—real money. He signed the Executive Order on June 4, and these were the first two denominations put in circulation. Tens and Twenties were being printed by November. Jack Kennedy was putting the central bank out of business in America—taking control of the country back from the bankers."

"They couldn't let him do it," I muttered.

"Damn straight. The tens and twenties never went into circulation. They were canceled right after the assassination. The twos and fives were taken out of circulation. Yet another crazy coincidence."

I stated the obvious: "The bankers had him killed."

"Yup."

"What's the connection between the banking cabal and the communists?" I asked.

"Not just communists," Dad said. "Socialists, of every kind. Whatever they call themselves: 'liberals,' 'progressives,' 'social justice warriors.' You haven't caught that pattern? It goes back to Friedrich Engels. Fat cat capitalist paying to support a smelly radical who wants to overthrow his system and lock people like him in a reeducation camp? It's a lie. It's a scam. Always was. Robber barons want to secure absolute power for themselves— make it impossible for anybody who comes along afterwards to equal their success—but meanwhile, dress it up so that it appeals to low-IQ sheep, lazy deadbeats, and Bohemian intellectuals who hate their fathers and feel guilty about being raised with privilege. Make it sound like it's a system to help the poor, and the poor will jump onboard to make themselves slaves forever, dragging everyone down with them who isn't an educated fool or an insider to the scheme. Because *those* shitbags are in on it already, with or without the poor. But if the poor aren't miserable enough to accept it yet, you establish a central bank to take over their economy...then you can make them as miserable as you need to, while increasing your own wealth and power."

He sighed deeply and shook his head. "When I started learning about all this, I had an attack of conscience, too. That led me to escape the whole shit show."

I decided that, once Dad dropped me off back at the Dallas hotel, I would drink myself into a stupor.

CHAPTER 6: LAST CHRISTMAS BREAK

Dad collected the electronic equipment from my hotel room. I helped him shuttle it out to the VTOL.

"It's been harder and harder to track you down," I said.

"I know, Sprout. It'll probably be that way for a while, too. So, anyway, how do you like that Goat?"

"The GTO? It's fun."

"How about everything else—you're about finished with school, right?"

I nodded. "I've got a little interest from the NFL, actually. If I'm lucky, I might get to warm a bench."

"Really? What team?"

"Minnesota."

He snorted and wiped his face, laughing sardonically. "Oh my god. The Choke Kings? You must love the game more than..." He blinked his eyes as if squeezing away an uncomfortable thought.

"The Choke Kings—why do you call them that?"

"Because their every single post-season appearance ends in an epic choke," Dad said. "There's never been a team in any sport that shoots itself in the foot more than those snakebit clowns. I guess you won't draw any undue attention sitting on *that* bench."

"Not if what you say is true," I agreed, my mood darkening even further.

"Trust me," he said. "You can take all the best players from every team in history, put them under the best coach who ever lived, and give them years to gel as a team. But put them in Minnesota uniforms and call them 'the Vikings,' and they won't be able to beat a junior high team from Buttwater, Maine, made up of epileptics and asthmatics. Not in a big game, I mean."

"So they're cursed?"

Dad shrugged. "Fate has a hard-on for them, whatever the reason. Something for you to think about, before you go wasting precious years of your life."

We said our goodbyes, and I jumped back to Poly.

△△△

I finished my classes in a sort of daze. Most of my time outside class was spent in the library, or at BH Station using the computers, researching history to fill in the blanks from Dad's quantum leap of a history lesson.

A whole lot of historians were left-wing revisionists, but I was able to identify their deception most of the time, by what they omitted, distorted, or embellished in their books or web pages. Plenty of more accurate books were still available in 1963.

I told Dozier about the visit from Mr. Jorgenson, and he thought I was crazy to now be unsure if I wanted to go pro. I couldn't very well tell him my lack of enthusiasm was because of the team's reputation...which hadn't even been earned, yet.

"If you don't wanna get paid to play football for a livin'," Dozier said, "then you must not love the game as much as I thought."

After Christmas, I made the trip to Bloomington. I met the coaches, and a couple suits. They showed me around, asked a lot of questions, and invited me to talk about myself. On the plus side, Norm Van Brocklin said he liked the way I stood in the pocket to pass; how I sold the fake on options, and could fire bullet passes down the field for a high completion percentage. But I also got the impression he didn't tolerate mistakes very well.

At the end of my visit, he advised me to join the Reserves to keep the Draft Board away. I let him know I was already in the Air National Guard.

I left the meeting not really knowing what to think. The prospect of playing professional football didn't exactly seem glamorous anymore. At least not in Minnesota, under Van Brocklin...for the "Choke Kings."

△△△

I made the rounds for Christmas, except for Bloomington and the Orange Grove. Then I returned to Sierra Leone.

Mona Lisa (real name Niki) was 18 now. She looked nothing like the subject of Leonardo Da Vincci's famous painting. I called her that because she had a smile that could light up a city block. I got the warm squishies for her from the first time I saw it.

She was as sweet as ever; and even more beautiful than I remembered. Being around her made me happy and confused.

She was like a nanny or babysitter for her extended family. Most days, when their parents were busy, six or seven kids flocked around Mona Lisa. Her patience with them was impressive, and she obviously enjoyed governing them. One day I literally spent hours just observing her in action. She knew exactly when to coddle them, exactly when to admonish, when to joke, when to play, and when to demand seriousness. She could invent games for them to play off-the-cuff that were educational and, apparently, fun for the children. I think her smile was just as enchanting to them as it was to me and they did their best to please her—to keep it shining on them.

It felt like a *coup* when she spent time alone with me. I was flattered she set aside time from what she was apparently born to do. It was hard not to place her on a pedestal, but I coached myself in private. Talked myself down from the ledge.

She didn't pressure me in any way regarding marriage, but she did inquire a lot about the places I had been, and people I'd met.

Since learning she believed it would happen, I sometimes tried to imagine a life with her married to me. But how would that work? I pictured her sitting in the stands at Metropolitan Stadium (where the Vikes played), to cheer me on as I rode the bench. She wouldn't understand the game, would be miserable in the cold, and when word got out that we were a couple, would I be subjecting her and any children we had to overbearing scrutiny? The popularity of movies like *South Pacific*, *Sayonara*, *West Side Story* and *Kings Go Forth*—and even songs like Ricky Nelson's "Travelin' Man" showed that most Americans weren't uncomfortable with the idea of multicultural or even mixed-race romances. But then, in 2012 Kansas City, there were people (not only white people, either) who gave Dad and Tonya dirty looks just for being attracted to each other.

The majority was rarely the loudest faction. It was the outspoken minority that often made everything contentious and uncomfortable.

It wouldn't be exactly the same if we stayed in her country, but I doubted it would be any better. Only some place like Planet Valhalla would openly accept us together. But then I'd have to kiss football goodbye—along with a lot of other stuff I had grown attached to.

I knew her and me together living a white picket fence life was a pipe dream, but I still wanted to spend time with her. I still loved football, and building stuff. Being with her was very different from those passions, but it was just as appealing.

△△△

When Dayvon got me into his office again, he told me, "I may have found the butterfly."

I let my curiosity show.

"Don't worry," he said, "I'm not gonna spoil any games for you, but I may have found where the split is." He leaned across his desk and handed me a photocopy taken from a newspaper archive on microfilm. It was an article from a local paper about two young football players who were killed in an automobile accident. The car was a '49 Mercury and the two young men were Gus Bartok and Sean Kiley.

"Oh my gosh," I said, aloud. "I did it. I caused the split you told me about."

"So I'm right," Dayvon said.

I nodded. "I must have saved their lives when I adjusted the Merc's suspension."

"You fixed their car?"

I nodded. "And without those two, Stauchel never could have built the Pumas into winners."

"It goes further than that," Dayvon said. "Your boy, Bartok, went on to play for Buffalo. They were gonna be champs for a few seasons, anyway. But apparently, with him there, they were better, for longer. As far as I could tell, the split had somethin' to do with the Bills, in the old AFL, so that's where I started lookin'. That's how I found the link between that discrepancy and you: you and Gus Bartok went to school together."

I whistled. "Geez. If you found that just by looking through old microfilm, then the TPF can find me, too."

"Don't freak," Dayvon said, holding his palm up. "First of all, you're assumin' everybody follows football. They don't —especially the way I do. Second: why would they be lookin' for you under your current name? Do they know you as Isaac Jaeger?"

"No. All I had was my original name, when they came to erase my biological family."

"Well, there you go," Dayvon said. "They don't even know who to look for; much less where or when."

"But they knew where and when to find me for that attempted erasure in 1988 St. Louis. How? Why?"

"Maybe they found some connection between you and

your uncle," Dayvon suggested.

"That's what he thinks," I said. "But so what? I didn't know anything about time travel, or the CPB. What's ironic is, I still probably wouldn't, if they hadn't tried to erase me."

"Why do you say 'probably'?" he asked.

I shrugged. "I guess my uncle might have let the cat out of the bag eventually. But his *doppelgänger* rescued me from the Erasers, and jumped a warp to evade pursuit from those coordinates. That forced the issue."

Dayvon chewed his lip for a moment. "Erasers are trained to be very thorough, Ike. They not only erase the target, but all potential witnesses to the erasure, and anybody who might have the intelligence and interest to look at the official explanation and start connectin' dots. It probably wasn't just gonna be you and your family, but any neighbors who could have witnessed it. Anybody out walkin' their dog. Any honest police detective who might know or learn somethin' and realize the official story don't add up."

"Does the CPB control the official narrative somehow?" I asked. "How?"

Dayvon leaned back in his chair, hesitating to speak for a moment. "I mean, interested parties ain't normally gonna come up with a hypothesis that involves time travel. People will just automatically reject it. It sounds too crazy. It sounds even crazier than pedophile networks operatin' in Hollywood and Washington DC, usin' 'pizza' and 'hot dog' for code words. It sounds even crazier than a centuries-old international conspiracy controllin' the official governments of countries."

"Public incredulity protects the big secrets," I remembered, out loud.

"What's that?"

"Nothing. Just summarizing what you said."

"So, anyhow," Dayvon said, "they pretty much just have to keep a lid on the little stuff. So, say the official story is that a whole family was on a sailboat out in the middle of the Pacific ocean when all fell overboard and drowned. What if somebody who knew the family remembers that they were scared of deep water and would never have gone out there in the first place? Or some bored bank employee looks through their credit card purchases and figures out they were visitin' Carlsbad Caverns at the same exact time they were supposedly 6,000 miles away in the middle of an ocean." He imitated the sound of a siren. "Assets planted at those coordinates get activated, and they handle it. Sometimes the potential whistleblower gets discredited. Sometimes they get bribed to shut up. Sometimes they commit suicide or die in an unfortunate accident."

"Assets planted at the coordinates?" I reacted. "You'd have to have plants all through space and time! Every police agency; every news organization..."

Dayvon shrugged. "You've probably bumped into one without knowin' it. They're sleepers, and nine out of ten never get activated, anyway. I met this one sleeper in Katanga once. He was in his 50s. He'd been planted in the Congo's Colonial Police when he was 20, and worked his way up to a position of influence. Of course, some of his promotions came about because of another plant in the Colonial bureaucracy who could influence promotions."

He put his magazines away.

"But I'm not sayin' they have 'em everywhere to cover all bases. They've got these specialists, with supercomputers, that can predict human behavior, with all kinds of variables. So they plant sleepers at coordinates where stuff is most likely to go sideways...from their perspective."

"Wait," I said. "First of all, why wouldn't Simon have told me about the sleepers?"

Dayvon shrugged. "Maybe he was never briefed on it. Erasers and normal TPF agents don't have a need-to-know. I only found out because I went on special assignment in Katanga and had to work with one of those sleepers. Somethin' tripped the predictive algorithms and they expected a big breach, so they needed a bunch of us in-theater."

I ran my hands through my hair and closed my eyes,

evaluating all this information. "When you say they expected a breach, what do you mean?"

"It means there were various possible outcomes—includin' negative ones—and there was a high probability that a rogue would show up and nudge the chain of events in the wrong direction."

"Are you aware of any other coordinates where breaches are expected?" I asked, remembering Dad's mention of such a breach in Oklahoma City.

"That's just the one I was involved in," Dayvon answered. "But I heard scuttlebutt from other TPF agents."

"Was Oklahoma City one of them?"

His brow knitted and he shook his head. "I never heard of that one. 'Course, that don't mean it didn't happen. I probably only heard about the big ones—Sarajevo 1914; St. Petersburg 1917; Havana 1959..."

"Big ones," I repeated. "What makes them big ones?"

"Well, from an Eraser's perspective, it means we may get special duty. For the desk jockeys at the CPB, it probably means the variables include a lot of potential negative outcomes, so they definitely got sleepers planted. Probably multiple sleepers."

This immediately brought Dealey Plaza in 1963 to mind. "You heard what happened to Kennedy last month?"

Dayvon snapped his fingers and pointed at me. "Oh, hell yeah. The whole world heard about that. And you just know that's a big one."

Surprisingly, I didn't have a headache from trying to sort and understand all this new information. But I still didn't understand why the Erasers came after me without erasing Dad first.

ΔΔΔ

I spent most of my time in Sierra Leone with Mona Lisa, of course. She still didn't want to go on any "modern" dates. I took her sightseeing, sometimes driving, sometimes walking.

We both loved music, and spent a lot of time just listening to it together. Sometimes she would lay down with her head in my lap. Sometimes she would hold my hand. Sometimes she would recline back against me and close her eyes.

We smiled at each other a lot during those lazy afternoons, but didn't say much. Our silences were comfortable. Despite the sexual tension now and then, I felt at peace around her. When I was with Niki, I didn't think about other women. Not even Madalena. Not even Juanita. I didn't feel any need to use "game" or enforce "frame" around her. She didn't get bored with me or lose affection. She didn't shit test me.

I couldn't hide anything from her if I wanted to—she could read my moods as well or better than Dad could read my thoughts. Yet she still proclaimed love for me. Not that I understood much about love, but I thought she was sincere.

I had known Niki for three years, now, and the other shoe had not dropped. It didn't take Susan that long to lose interest in me.

Susan.

The lessons learned back then stayed with me. The more I saw how sincere and giving Niki was, the more my mind speculated about that other shoe dropping. Her beauty was unquestionable, but was her kindness and honesty just a facade? Was it luring me into a trap the way Professor Beth-Tiva had used her body to spring one on me?

I figured, the more perfect she seemed to be, the more dangerous the trap.

While saying goodbye, Niki placed her hands on either side of my head and smiled at me lovingly. "Your mind is too busy, Isaac. You should relax and slow down more. You can't solve all of life's riddles in a single day. Probably not in this lifetime."

"I don't have spiritual perception like you," I replied. "My brain is all I have."

She showed me a strange expression for a moment, then said, "Return to me soon. The days are long between your visits, and I miss you."

CHAPTER 7: SENIOR YEAR EPILOGUE

As with many seniors, my official studies slacked off somewhat when I returned after Christmas break. Unlike other seniors, it wasn't because I was partying. It was because I was obsessively studying history. I wanted to put everything Dad showed and told me in context; to fully understand it; to confirm it, if possible; and to discover how historians documented the events I had seen with my own eyes.

Even leaving time travel and the CPB out of the equation, I was going through a slow-motion epiphany whereby I became convinced that much of the world I perceived was a charade, masking a sinister, but unseen, reality.

I began getting drunk on vodka. But not privately, like Dad. In one of the most reckless decisions of my life, I got drunk at a pub a few miles from campus, where blue collar workers tended to congregate. In my infinite wisdom, I also decided to reveal my ability to travel time, to whoever would listen.

The bartender, worried about me, called the school and somehow got hold of Dozier to come give me a ride home. Dozier found me entertaining a group of loggers and linemen at a table, slurring my words and gesturing grandly while alluding to Hegel and dark, ancient conspiracies.

"Where the hell is Beet-Nomm?" asked one of my burly companions, still wearing his steel hard hat.

"Never heard of it," another one said.

"It's the focal point for both sides," I insisted. "It brings commies out of the closet. Before Vietnam, they were all too afraid to admit they hate America. But the anti-war movement gives them cover, see? They could go public now, more and more...'cause starting in about 10 years they'll be teaching your kids in school that communism isn't so bad, but America is."

"Bullshit," said one of them. "Parents wouldn't put up with that. They'd have the school board fire 'em."

I shook my head and waved my hands. "Right now, yeah. But it's changing, fast. Parents won't rock the boat. They think public school is free babysitting, see? They may not like what the teachers will teach us, but they'll just complain—not try to change it. But...where was I? Oh yeah: the false choice. Give people the illusion of choice, and they won't realize they're being screwed. The politicians and Henry Kissinger and Walter Cronkite and all those guys are gonna come on TV and tell you guys, 'here are your choices: One—you keep sending your sons over to this country in Asia you never heard of, so they can keep getting wounded and killed for no apparent reason...or Two— you pull them out of Vietnam, after all the blood and money that's been spent over there, and just let the commies have the country.' And you guys will think, 'well, those are the choices— we have to pick one.' What you're not supposed to say is, ' to hell with that! I don't like either choice. If it's important enough to have our boys over there bleeding and dying, then let's play to win! Let's go to by-god war and bomb the bridges, and ammo dumps, and North Vietnamese infrastructure. When they go to hide across the border in Laos or Cambodia, we chase them in force and wipe them out. We march north and kick their asses and don't stop until we're in Hanoi and Ho Chi Minh signs off on unconditional surrender.' That choice isn't on the table, see?"

"Sounds like Korea, only worse," one of the working men said.

"Yup," I continued. "If we win, that will upset the Russians, see? The big bad Russians. Their people are starving because their idiotic centralized economy makes it impossible for normal people to prosper. The Soviets are only dangerous because you made them dangerous. You and your parents...all the money you gave them through their buddy, FDR."

More than half of them soured at that remark, as if I had just blasphemed.

"All the secrets of ours," I continued, "given them by spies and traitors. You think those dumbasses could have figured out atomic power on their own? They murder everybody who's smart enough to think for themselves! Spies and traitors...Joe McCarthy warned you about them."

Some of the men laughed.

"Oh, *that's* where he gets his information—from Tailgunner Joe. So tell us, Future Man: when does this Beet-Nomm country invade and take over America?" He looked to his comrades with a twinkle in his eye and they all shared a laugh over the young dumb jock's drunken imagination.

"Oh, your boys will win over there. On the ground. In the air. Everywhere they're told to fight. Then the commies will stage a huge offensive—violating the Tet cease fire to catch us unprepared. Well, guess what? They get damn near destroyed for their effort. They got almost nothing left to fight with. But the sympathizers on TV will turn the truth upside-down and say it was a great success—that *they* hurt *us* and now Ho Chi Minh is guaranteed to win. So we'll start pulling out. But Nixon will bomb Hanoi. He'll bomb the hell out of them; and they'll come to the peace table and sign a peace treaty."

"Nixon?" one of them asked.

"But then once all the American troops are gone," I went on, "the commies will break the treaty, invade the South again, and take over. Congress won't have the balls to send troops back there to enforce the treaty. So we break our promise to the Vietnamese. We have to evacuate our embassy. We leave American POWs there to rot and die. It'll go down in history as America's first defeat...even though our military wasn't defeated...because people are too stupid to handle complex information, and the details will get memory-holed. And guess what? Some sleazy little pussy dope-smoking coward who dodged the draft will grow up to be President, and outsource American jobs to the commies in Vietnam."

A member of my audience rolled his eyes and wiped beer off his lips. "Now he's sayin' a draft-dodger could become President."

"It's just the next step," I insisted. "The next synthesis in the Hegelian Dialectic. Your kids are being prepared for it in school right now. They're gonna believe he stands for 'change.' They'll get out there and 'rock the vote' to help him lie and cheat his way to the top. And then he'll make sure the kids in school by then get brainwashed even harder. He'll have the schools teaching kindergarten kids that homosexuality is cool. Any parents who try to stop it will be declared a 'domestic terrorist' by the FBI."

They all laughed at this.

"Whatever he's drinkin'...maybe I should take some home for a rainy day!" one remarked.

"Then those kids will grow up and vote for a closet homo," I said. "And before that fart-blocking fraud is done, the Supreme Court will endorse homosexual marriage. And he'll light up the White House in rainbow colors to celebrate."

They guffawed, drawing the attention of everybody else in the pub.

"But it's even better," I said. "He won't even be American. He'll have an African father. He'll be raised overseas as a Muslim. He'll come over here under an alias; go to college as a foreign student, use a bogus Social Security Number from a state he never lived in, and when he does finally show the country his birth certificate, it's an obvious forgery."

Their laughter turned hysterical, and I laughed with them.

This was about the time Dozier decided to drag me out of there. I hadn't even noticed him and wondered how long he'd been there.

"But wait—there's more!" I promised, trying to imitate the old Ronco commercials I had seen in St. Louis, as Dozier pulled me toward the door. "If you order this sexually deviant, cocaine-addicted Marxist Muslim Manchurian President right now, we'll also send you Indefinite Detention absolutely free! Who am I kidding? You're gonna pay for that, too. So let's count up this incredible value: you'll not only get a crushing national debt that can never be repaid; you'll also get a covert takeover by the Red Chinese, a rigged election process worse than what's in the third world, an IRS that persecutes non-communists..."

By this time, Dozier had me outside and was cramming me in his car.

ΔΔΔ

I had my head over the toilet most of the night, puking out the contents of my stomach. I lay in bed the next day, wishing I could die, in between running to the toilet to vomit some more. The day after that, I was able to drink water, walk around, and contemplate eating again.

Dr. Dozier's diagnosis was alcohol poisoning, on top of the hangover. He brought me some green gelatin from the cafeteria, which was one of the only food substances I could imagine consuming in the state I was in.

After eating the gelatin, and realizing I would be able to keep it down, he suggested we should have a talk.

"You trust me, don't ya Ike?"

"Of course. Why?"

"I didn't tell nobody nothin' about Dr. Beth-Tiva, until you asked me to testify. Remember?"

"That's right."

"So you can level with me," he said. "I know you're not crazy. I know you're not stupid. Maybe you can't handle your liquor very well, but I wouldn't try to get you sent to the looney bin, no matter what you told me. We're friends. In fact, I consider you my best friend."

"Thanks, Brock. That means a lot."

"Glad it does. So...that stuff you were sayin' down at the pub: where did you get all that?"

"What did I say down at the pub?" I asked, wondering how much he heard.

"You were talking about the future. I mean, some specific stuff. And it wasn't flying saucers, ray guns, or anti-gravity machines."

"Honestly, I've never been that drunk before. Everybody talks crazy when they're plastered."

"Yeah, okay...but you said some stuff about Vietnam. That's a place almost nobody has heard of. I've heard of it, and can find it on a map, because my big brother has been there. He's an advisor. The stuff you were sayin' doesn't sound like you made it up. You use some of the same terms he uses. And you told us about regular combat troops gettin' sent there to fight, even though Johnson is promisin' he'll never do that. But my brother says we're already sendin' gunboats and fighter-bombers there...which makes him think that combat troops will be next."

"Maybe they're just to support the ARVN," I suggested, dizzily.

"My brother says the ARVN is a joke. And how do you even know to call them ARVN, anyway?"

I rubbed my head. "Army of the Republic of Vietnam. I can read acronyms."

"But where did you even see that acronym? That's what I mean. And not just that. You've been actin' awfully odd ever since Kennedy was shot."

"Who hasn't?"

"Yeah, but it isn't like everybody else. Most people are sad and mixed-up. But you don't seem very confused. Just mad. In a really foul mood."

"Don't you think everybody handles something like this in their own way?" I asked.

"Sure, but... Look, even before Kennedy was killed, there was parts of you that didn't add up. There's stuff you know that nobody else knows. You live like you're on vacation, sometimes; or like you escaped over the Berlin Wall, other times. You talk like we do, most of the time, but sometimes you talk like my grampa talks. But you ain't no square."

He pointed to my photograph of Juanita, on the wall. "That ain't your mama. Or your aunt. Or an older sister. She don't look nothin' like you. So I gotta wonder: why do you have some 20-year old snapshot of some chick up on your wall? I mean, you're a bigger lady's man than anybody I ever seen, but aside from that ginchy professor and maybe some older broads at the beatnik bar, you have normal taste in girls. Good taste. Girls around our age. And that photograph ain't from a magazine."

Dozier was far from the dumb, slow country boy so many assumed him to be. His analytical curiosity was starting to get a little scary.

I regretted having put the photo on my wall. Madalina and I were talking about children of our own, which meant I should have abandoned my other spinning plates, anyway. I didn't want to have wives and separate families all over the continuum, like Dad. I wasn't sure I could handle that, or feel right about it. I had tight enough game to keep Madalina from straying, and honestly, she was enough woman all by herself. But I still couldn't help but think about Juanita sometimes, and Mona Lisa other times, and wonder what could be.

"You know what else, Ike?" my roommate added, "You know more about engines than the writers for *Popular Mechanics*. Okay, so you're an engineerin' student. You'll talk all day about my engine and what I can do to make it run better, but you won't even let me look at your Studebaker's. I can tell by the sound it's way different from any other hot rod. It's faster than anything on a race track. And that new GTO—I've window shopped them at the dealers a lot. But when I get down on the pavement and peek underneath yours...I see parts like I never seen before. You can tell me that it's all space age prototypes from your daddy's research & development lab, like them crazy fat tires and wheels, but that don't ring true. When you was talkin' about the future, in the pub, *that* rang true. I think I can tell the difference, with you."

"Sounds like you've given all this some thought," I said, desperately trying to imagine a new cover story that could explain it all away.

"I may run slow, but I don't think slow. Ya know what else? Your radio in the Stude—it always receives stations perfect, no matter where you are. No static. No whine. Heck, no commercials; no station identification; no disk jockeys. Just great music. And I swear, that time you took me down to the speed shop so I could buy that high performance distributor? After we got back in your car and you started her up...the same song picked up exactly where it left off when you shut down about a half hour before."

I stared into my lap, not meeting his gaze. I never should have let him ride in my car. I should do something about the stereo before it made somebody else suspicious. I should be satisfied with just using the radio to listen to local stations, rather than my mp3 player.

"You can tell me that's coincidence," he said. "I hope ya don't, 'cause that would mean ya think I'm stupid. You could just refuse to tell me, I guess. I mean, it's none a' my business, really. And no matter what, I won't blab anything you tell me, if you don't want. But it sure does bother me sometimes—all this stuff."

"You ever read science fiction, Brock?"

He shrugged. "Now and then. No more than the next guy."

I stood, steadied myself, and dug in my pants pocket to ensure my keys were there. "Let's go for a ride."

I took the Goat up to Don Diego Road, with Dozier in the passenger seat. I ran flat out—no sandbagging—so he would see what it could do. Then I pulled over on the wide dirt shoulder, unlocked and raised the hood. He looked over the Pontiac engine and I explained each part he didn't recognize.

Once back in the car, I jumped a warp to Los Angeles in 2012, where I humiliated several nitrous-equipped imports at the street races. We cruised around, and wound up at the beach.

Dozier was noticeably uncomfortable, on top of being astonished. He asked a lot of questions, and I answered honestly. His reaction was one of sadness, more than anything. I asked him what was wrong.

"I mean, the technology is sumpthin' else," he said. "There's no Mars rockets, or jet packs, but those smart phones are real impressive. It's just...I don't know. The music is ugly. The people are ugly, most of 'em. And fat. But the morals...is the whole country this bad?"

"Yeah. 'Fraid so."

"I seen some really disgustin' stuff just since you brought me here. And my skin's crawlin', Ike. It's like, there's evil so thick I can feel it. But the people here don't even bat their eyes at it."

I knew he was referring to the Big Spooky. By 2012 it had grown considerably since the Kennedy assassination.

"I'd like to go back, now. I don't think I can stand much more a' this," he said.

Back in the parking lot at our dorm, he said, "Thank-you, Ike. And I want you to know, my lips are sealed."

"It's not like anybody would believe you, anyway," I quipped.

"I dunno. There's folks got a lot wilder imagination than me." He chuckled. "You really are the Travelin' Man. That song fits you better than I ever would have guessed."

I told him a little bit about Juanita, since he had taken notice of her photograph.

"So where did you come from, for real? Where and when, I mean."

"A trailer park in St. Louis," I told him. "1988."

"Was it as bad there as what I just saw?"

"Not quite. On its way, I guess."

"Well, I sure don't blame ya for choosin' to be here now, instead."

We started back toward the dorm. He flashed me a look of despair. "Jeez, Ike. Is that the future we have to look forward to?"

"One possible future," I said, quoting from *The Terminator*.

Up in our room, I explained everything as best I could: dimensional warps; timestreams; mapping, the Continuum Protection Bureau (CPB); the Temporal Police Force (TPF); and the Erasers.

"You could have spent the last four biological years of your life anywhere," he said. "Any*when*. Why in the world did you pick Yosemite Polytechnic?"

I laughed and said, "I wanted to play football."

He shook his head, trying not to laugh. "That simple, huh?"

"Yup."

"Well, now that you're done where and when are you gonna go?"

"I don't exactly know," I replied.

CHAPTER 8: BUILDING MY OWN LOGISTICS

Mine and Dad's tradition of spending the summer together had evaporated in his absences over the last few vacations. We had seen each other for my impromptu history lesson, so I figured that would be the last I saw of him for a while.

Dozier still had another year of college, and his father needed him to come back and help on the farm for the summer, as usual.

I spent quite a bit of time on Valhalla, researching the 20th Century on a computer, mostly. I spent my mornings and evenings with Madalina. She had kept to our agreement; but now that I had finished college, she quit taking birth control, and had me jump back to Earth for at-home pregnancy tests.

She was evidently quite fertile. I would be a father soon.

I had to cut my time there short after a few months, because even though the aging process came almost to a standstill on that world, a person's muscles would atrophy, too —unless you ramped up your exercise to lifting vehicles and throwing boulders.

Between Valhalla and BH Station, I did some more work on the miniature warp generator. I also caught up on other projects. I had another hangar built in Texas. I jumped to the early 1970s and made a tour of car lots around North America.

Dodge Daytona Chargers and Plymouth Superbirds were selling dirt cheap—even the Hemi cars. I earmarked the ones with automatic transmissions and column shifters for cleanup and sale at various 21st Century auctions. The four-speed models, whether 440 or 426 Hemi-powered, I kept in my new hangar. I began collecting parts to give one of them a complete suspension and powertrain upgrade right away. A nearly-stock version of the Daytona went 243 miles-per-hour back when it was legal for NASCAR. I would see what that aerodynamic body was truly capable of.

I made some more real estate investments around the world; made quite a bit of money off some sports wagers, and invested in precious metals, which I stored in safes on Dad's various properties until I would have places of my own to secure them.

I began searching for some coordinates where I could take Madalina and we could raise our child, with normal gravity and atmospheric pressure. I found a little island in the central Pacific that might be ideal, and jumped far enough back to acquire it, with period-correct currency...or simply by being the first to claim it. Maybe the 1300s would be a safe enough time to live there. I left a message for Dad, explaining that Madalina and I had mated permanently, what my plans were to raise our baby, and asking him if I could borrow a construction crew to help me establish some modern facilities there, where we could live peacefully, undiscovered, for quite some time. My own little country no Rothschild bankers could subvert. Nobody would be assassinated; we couldn't be swindled into any counter-productive wars, and nobody could force me to sell out to a foreign power.

Of course, we could spend every night in Valhalla if we wanted to, slowing our aging process enough to live perhaps hundreds of years, role-playing *Tarzan and His Mate*. And I figured Madalina was a good choice to spend that time with. The rush of our initial attraction was gone, but I still enjoyed being with her. She liked being with me, too. After all the plate-spinning (and especially after the nightmare with Dr. Beth-Tiva), my attitude about sex was changing. Certainly, sex with a new woman was still exciting. But I could be content with getting sex from just one woman—so long as she gave me plenty of it.

For the sake of our children, we would eventually have to leave our island paradise (I began thinking of it as "Happy Ever After Island), or bring other people there. But in the meantime we could jump to different coordinates now and then to avoid cabin fever.

With that iron in the fire, I invested in a new aircraft—a cargo plane which could take off and land on a short runway.

I still had all the navigation history for the warp generator I repaired in the P-40. I was able to pinpoint the exact coordinates it sent me to instead of 1935 Ethiopia.

I jumped to that future conflict, this time in a P-47 Thunderbolt, and destroyed the remaining Chi-Com helicopters during my second, unsanctioned attack on the PacFor base. Now reasonably safe from Chi-Com air assets, I returned in the cargo plane (a civilian version of the C-130 Hercules), and landed it near Tyler's family farm, loaded with food, ammunition, medicine, boots, socks, and brand new Mossy Oak cammies.

Tyler's family (unbelieving, at first) sent the word out. I stuck around long enough for the Jayhawkers to reach me. They arrived with four captured PacFor trucks. Kaiden's squad were part of the detachment. They all recognized me, though two of them were dead since the last time our paths crossed. What surprised me most was that their weary commanding general, Rex Winfield, personally came with them. He still looked exhausted, but almost managed a warm greeting for me.

"You know who hit the PacFor base again?" he asked, shaking my hand.

"That was me, Boss," I said. "Wanted to buy myself some friendly skies to get this bird in and out."

"By yourself? No co-pilot?"

I shook my head. "What you see is what you get."

He waved at the open ramp of the C-130, where his men were offloading containers, to be loaded into the trucks. "What I see looks pretty damn welcome, Jaeger. Where'd you get all this?"

"I scrounged it. You wouldn't believe me if I told you."

He placed his hand between my shoulder blades and steered me off to the side where we could talk in private. "How's everything on the Texas Front?"

I shrugged and said, "Not quite as bad as y'all have it." I had jumped to Texas in 2028 and assessed the situation as best I could, to supplement my cover story in case it was necessary.

"I can't hardly believe this haul," he said. "Is this a one-time deal?"

"I know you guys are in bad shape," I said. "I'll do my best to get you more supplies, when I can. You got a specific request?"

"Well, we always need more food and ammo. If you can swing it, though, we could really use some mortars, M-203s, and shells for both. High explosive and incendiary. Third generation NODs—night optical devices. Six meter radius. Vitamins—especially B, C, D and E. Zinc, Ivermectin and Hydroxychloroquine. Trauma kits. And any kind of water filtration systems you can find."

Dad had collected a lot of his military-grade weaponry from Mexican drug cartels, plus paramilitary forces around the world who had received American weapons as military aid. I had obtained the machineguns for my aircraft similarly; but I would have to expand my business operation if I was going to be Winfield's supplier. "No promises," I said.

"I copy. But try to remember my wish list."

"If I'm able to get some of that for you…is this a good place for me to bring it?"

"Let's go look at some maps, and we'll figure out where's best."

ΔΔΔ

I wished I could do more for them, but judging by their

overwhelming gratitude, you would think I had single-handedly kicked half of the Pacification Force back into the ocean.

I didn't know what the Americans' chances were, but getting what supplies I could to them had become one of my hobbies.

CHAPTER 9: HAPPY EVER AFTER?

I returned to Bakersfield to catch up with Angelina, my sister, and my old friends. Angelina asked me about Dad. Apparently, she hadn't seen him in over a month. Last she heard, he was on a business trip overseas. When she did see him, he was tired and gaunt, and never stayed more than a day or two. I didn't know what to tell her. She had friends in the neighborhood, but was lonely. She did seem happy to see me, though.

She told me that my commanding officer from the Air National Guard had called the house a few times, asking for me. Wanting to cruise around a bit anyway, I drove out to see him.

He knew I had finished my college degree, and told me about an opportunity the Air Force was offering. President Johnson's deepening commitment in Southeast Asia was driving a demand for pilots. He knew I was already a licensed civilian pilot, that my academic performance was good, and that I had some athletic accolades on top of all that. Slots were opening left and right at the Academy of Military Science back in Tennessee. If I took one, and got commissioned as an officer in the Air National Guard, he said I could go on to pilot training. He was also willing to put in a good word for me to get assigned to a fighter squadron.

I knew enough now that I didn't want to go to be part of a

pointless clusterfuck in Vietnam. But I did like the idea of flying a jet fighter.

The C.O. gave me some time to think about it. I mulled it over for a few days, weighing the pros and cons. The officer school would only take six weeks; but the flight training would take up most of a year. I knew the physical aspect of it wouldn't be all that tough for me, but I would also go for long stretches wherein I wouldn't be able to get near a warp generator. Or a woman.

Because I was young and dumb, I agreed to go. But despite all the futility of learning to be a fighter pilot for a war with the USSR that would never come; or a war in Southeast Asia we wouldn't be allowed to win, I enjoyed myself. I liked learning, and there was a lot of learning to do. I also missed the comradery of football; so going through all the training with other guys compensated somewhat for that.

I missed Madalina more than ever when it was all over and I had my wings. I returned to Valhalla in time to be there for her during the birth of our daughter, Sylvia.

ΔΔΔ

When Madalina was released from the medical center (now a permanent facility underground, with electricity and modern equipment), I walked her and the baby home. She held Sylvia in one arm, and wound her other arm around mine, clasping hands. She alternated between staring down at our daughter and beaming up at me. She looked so joyous, I couldn't help grinning back at her like a sentimental sap. I felt warm energy radiating out of her, that reminded me of when Mami held me as a boy and let me cry my eyes dry. I guess what I felt was the essence of motherhood. A chemical reaction between mother and child that could not be duplicated any other way.

"I've never been so happy, Isaac," she told me, squeezing my hand. "I have the man I love, and our baby. You are perhaps, biologically, still younger than me. But we are a perfect match, anyway."

"I like it when you're happy," I said, grinning like a fool.

Technically, she should have been a little less attractive than normal, since she had recently gone through childbirth. But it seemed she was even lovelier than before.

I kissed Madalina's cheek while opening the door to our home for her. She leaned into me to receive the kiss, closing her eyes, then let go my hand and entered our pre-fab-but-bare-bones two bedroom hut.

I sat her in the rocking chair and brought her some tea and snacks. The weather was always perfect on Valhalla, but I knew she got chilly anyway when sitting still for any length of time. I tucked a blanket around her and she rocked with the baby contentedly. When Sylvia began to murmur, and twitch her tiny arms, Madalina breast fed her. I took pictures of mother and baby while they rocked.

I studied the woman who bore my child and thought what I felt might be what other people meant when they spoke about love.

After a long, comfortable silence, Madalina re-bundled our daughter, stood, crossed the room, and handed her to me. Sylvia slept. I stared at my daughter while Madalina went to the kitchen and began putting a meal together. Sylvia was still a newborn. Her face probably wouldn't start showing personality for a while. She was so small, and fragile, I experienced goofy fantasies of protecting her from wolves, bears, and man-eating tigers.

I continued to hold Sylvia while we ate. Afterwards, her little eyes came open and she began to grunt and squirm.

"Well hello there, sleepy girl," I said.

Madalina got up and came around the table to take her from me. "She needs her diaper changed, Daddy."

"Really? She didn't even cry."

"That's her Romanian half," she said, smugly. "Our babies don't fuss like American children."

I snorted. "Whatever, Miss Mega-Ego."

"It's true, spoiled Yankee," she said, laying Sylvia down on the sofa to begin the operation. She was trying to understand and adopt my American sense of humor.

While changing the diaper, she made exaggerated facial expressions and chatted as if every noise from our daughter was an intelligible comment that invited profound thought. Madalina's hamming encouraged Sylvia to smile and continue in the back-and-forth of the conversation.

I realized Madalina was born for this role—a first-time mother who glowed with instinctive competence. It seemed she had matured 20 years in wisdom during childbirth. She had already been more mature than me before. Now, with the gap so wide, I wondered if her feelings toward me would cool as she waited for me to catch up.

With the diaper changed, she rocked Sylvia to sleep, then laid her down in the nursery.

I remained on the sofa in our small living room, sipping fruit juice and perusing my copy of Dr. Torstenson's notes on his team's quantum discoveries.

Madalina tiptoed back from the nursery and sat in my lap, sighing as she embraced me. "Maybe she will sleep for more than an hour this time."

I tossed aside the stapled sheaf of photocopied notes and slipped my hands up inside Madalina's blouse to caress and massage her back.

"Maybe she will be pretty like you, and smart like me," she said, then giggled and mussed my hair.

I slid one hand down to pinch her hip, which made her giggle more.

"Everybody knows I am the smart one," she teased.

"You must be," I said. "You picked me."

She slapped the back of my head, playfully. "Maybe she will have humility also, unlike her father." She combed her soft fingers through my hair, and gazed down at me, expression transforming from playful to rapturous. Her eyes were luminous with a mixture of compassion, vulnerability, good humor, and desire.

"Thank-you for the gift you've given me," she whispered, and kissed me like she hadn't seen me for years.

△△△

Madalina and Sylvia were celebrities for a while on Valhalla, and we were so proud of our baby girl, you would think we were the first couple to ever make one. Sylvia's face began to develop. She had Madalina's chin, cheeks, and nose, but my eyes, hair and complexion. Everyone remarked upon how she was a perfect blend of both of us. She continued being a good baby—hardly ever crying, then easily pacified. She smiled and laughed more frequently, especially when Madalina engaged in silly conversation with her. I guess I could never experience or even fully understand the bond between mother and child on a spiritual level; but the way my heart melted when Sylvia grinned, I imagined I could almost relate.

Fatherhood was a pretty awesome gig, I thought. The pregnancy also put some padding on Madalina that, frankly, she could use. It went to all the right places on her pint-sized body.

Dad had left a message when I was in Tennessee, relative time, congratulating us on the pregnancy, and agreeing to let me task one of his construction crews with the island project. In between officer training and pilot training, I dispatched the crew with detailed plans, and funding for materials.

I had told Madalina about the plan, and our little tropic island paradise. She was keen on the idea, once she understood we could get away occasionally to civilization.

I checked on our new home on Happy-Ever-After Island, tested the generator, air conditioner, and other amenities, and went back for my family.

Madalina revealed to me a bright idea about visiting Romania in 1995, first, so all her old friends from the orphanage could meet me and Sylvia. I shot the idea down right away. It was too dangerous. As far as her old friends knew, she had ceased to exist. Bringing her back from nonexistence would draw exactly the kind of attention we didn't want. Besides, if her old friends were really so important to her, she wouldn't have agreed to go to Valhalla anyway.

Initially, I won. But Madalina was devastated. She was depressed all the time, and burst into tears on several occasions. I began to second-guess myself.

She had never been anything but good to me, and was easy to please. She had never asked for much, other than to be with me and bear my children.

Dad wasn't there to talk me out of it. I gave in.

ΔΔΔ

We jumped to Madalina's home coordinates in Densus, and spent a few days tracking down her friends. After meeting a few of them, I grew restless. Nobody Madalina knew seemed to speak English, so I couldn't understand anything they said to me, or to each other. I wished Dr. Manfredi had perfected a way to simply upload a language into the brain. But all there was for me to do was sit on my thumbs while an endless parade of strangers made the same kind of noises and expressions over my daughter. I decided to shop for groceries and other supplies to stock Happy-Ever-After.

When I returned from that errand, Madalina and our daughter were gone.

CHAPTER 10: TRAGEDY AND RUNNING FIGHT

I checked our hotel room first. All Madalina's luggage, clothes, and the extra diapers and such were still there. At first, I assumed she must have run into another friend, and was visiting with them somewhere.

I waited for her to return, but she didn't. I hired an interpreter, and began asking questions to anybody who might know where she was.

I couldn't remember her friends' names, or what their addresses were. We checked the orphanages first. They didn't have up-to-date records of alumni's current contact info. For days the interpreter and I wandered all over, hoping we would stumble across a face or an address I recognized. It was much like trying to locate that aluminum pull-tab mixed in with the asphalt back on the runway at BH Station.

Nobody knew anything about Madalina, but like some cruel cosmic joke, every so often, we ran into someone who thought I looked familiar.

It was usually a tourist, and always a man in his 30s or older. Some would stare at me curiously, and never go beyond that. Others might smile, point, and/or snap their fingers in assumed recognition. I found this more irritating than intriguing. They apparently thought I looked like somebody who was fairly well-known at these coordinates. Not wanting to waste time answering questions, I generally avoided such people by slipping into a crowd, or turning to hustle away in the opposite direction.

Finding Madalina began to look like an impossible task. I didn't believe she had intentionally run away from me—that made no sense at all. It had to be something else. I couldn't get the police involved. How and why I was there without a passport would be just the first question they had for me.

Finally, I did come to a place I remembered. From there, I was able to speak to one of Madalina's friends, through the interpreter. The friend gave us the names and addresses she knew of hers and Madalina's mutual friends from the orphanage she could remember. The search became more frantic after that.

Through friends' recollection, I was able to narrow down the general area and time where Madalina and the baby were seen last. Some people in that area thought they might have seen them, but didn't see what happened to them.

Based on what I knew about the continuum, if I jumped a warp back to, say, a day or an hour before my family's disappearance, to remove them from harm's way before the fact, I would simply be splitting the stream. I might be able to protect Madalina and Sylvia's *doppelgängers* (so my own *doppelgänger* wouldn't lose them), but in my stream they would still be gone. This wasn't exact science, but I hoped that if I intervened at the perfect instant, the split would circle back into the stream so immediately that it wouldn't be a split at all.

I didn't know for sure that the Erasers had taken my family. There was plenty of evil in the world that could have happened to them without the use of warp generators and cloaking devices. I cursed myself for not considering that before. I should not have left them alone.

I jumped back to the time Madalina was last reported seen, and waited for her to emerge from the house she was reportedly seen in. I set up my observation point on a roof overlooking the street where the house was, thinking from a high elevation I would better be able to spot her in the foot traffic, predict which way she would go, and identify threats.

I watched droves of people go back and forth below. For a brief instant, I glimpsed a face that looked familiar. I only noticed her in the human kaleidoscope because she glanced up at me. But as quickly as I spotted the woman, I lost her in the crowd.

She wasn't anybody I knew; so where did I remember her face from? And what would anybody I had ever encountered be doing at these coordinates?

Something caused me to turn around from my perch on the edge of the roof. Maybe it was a sound, a vibration, a change in the temperature or light. Coming up behind me on the roof was a Predator-cloaked figure.

The sudden fear and panic froze me in place at first. The distorted light convulsed as it grew closer, confusing my eyes as to what I was seeing. Then I realized a cloaked weapon muzzle was swinging to bear on me.

It was probably all the martial arts and situational awareness Dad had drilled into me that saved my life that day. I pitched to the side and rolled across the roof as a suppressed shot hit the spot where I had just been less than a second before. I rolled to my feet and came up drawing my silenced M1911 from the holster concealed under my loose button-down shirt. I spotted the visual anomaly and fired. It went backwards and flattened on the roof. A .45 wadcutter makes a huge exit wound; but unable to see much in the way of detail, I fired again and saw the shape jolted.

Scared and furious, I approached the Eraser and knelt beside it, feeling the body with my free hand. My hand closed on something that felt like a rifle. The predator camouflage failed where I touched it, so that I could see parts of it near my grip. I pulled on it, but it was tethered to the body somehow. I holstered my pistol and used both hands to feel the weapon from one end to the other. I felt a cord of some kind. My hand closed over a connector. After fumbling with it, then giving it a stout yank, the connector separated and the carbine became visible.

It looked like it might be an M4A1, under all that now-inactive predator camouflage.

The Eraser's jumpsuit camouflage was still active, but I could see the two entrance wounds, and the area around them as blood seeped out to neutralize the camouflage. I checked the body for spare magazines, for a way to remove the jumpsuit, or a switch to turn it off. I scooted around the body, still groping around.

The suppressed gunshot and the sudden pain in my calf were just about simultaneous.

I dove to my stomach, putting the carbine butt to my shoulder and searching in the direction the shot came from. Another shot snapped over my head. I spotted the anomaly and fired four rapid shots.

At least one shot must have got him. He went down, his jumpsuit fizzing, sparking, then failing. I glanced down at my own wound. I thought it probably missed the bone, judging by the location. And it wasn't bleeding heavily enough to have sliced a major artery. Still, it hurt.

I limped over to the now-visible Eraser's body. I found his spare magazines, jammed them into my cargo pockets and thought about checking to see if he had some kind of identification. Then I noticed the sound of the approaching helicopter right before a machinegun burst stitched across the roof toward me. I jumped and rolled out of the line of fire as the burst nearly shredded the booth that covered the top of the fire escape that led to the ground level. I rolled to the side of the roof and looked below. A few yards farther along the roof, there was some kind of outdoor display cabinet where an old man was hawking his wares. I scrambled over to where it was below me. I glanced in the direction where I could hear the chopper (it was cloaked).

I jumped.

My good leg, ass, and back hit the rickety hutch. Wood splintered and merchandise smashed as the whole structure collapsed under my weight. The noise made everyone nearby jump and gape. Jagged wood, broken glass and pottery tore at my flesh. But it broke my fall.

I was at that early stage of a minor wound where the pain existed, but was obscured by the fog of adrenaline. I still had the carbine in a death grip. I climbed to my feet and right then the cloaked chopper appeared over the narrow street some thirty yards away. Shocked pedestrians turned their attention from me to the almost-invisible aircraft they could hear overhead.

I ran as best I could with my variety of wounds, firing at the chopper as I went. I flicked the selector lever to full auto and emptied the magazine at where I thought the tail rotor should be. I slipped around a corner just as the machinegun cut loose and chewed up the wall I had just passed.

People screamed as I hobbled down the alley at a double-time, trying to change magazines on the move.

I turned a corner into an even narrower alley, and backed against a wall to check my new wounds. I pulled a glass fragment out of my hip and a large wood splinter out of my thigh. My blood dripped to the ground from a dozen little areas of broken skin.

Changing magazines, my brain now had time for some thinking. I wanted to get back to where Madalina was scheduled to emerge. But the Eraser team was so determined to get me, they didn't seem to care that hundreds of locals were aware of their presence. They would kill them all if necessary.

Why were they after me? How did they find me?

I was in a big deadly mess, and had to get out of those coordinates, stop the bleeding, and come back with some serious firepower, body armor, and some predator camouflage of my own. That meant I had to get to the plane. I checked the digital map on my handheld computer, got my bearings, and chose a route.

The chopper's turbine engine grew louder and it passed by, directly overhead. If it had not been directly overhead, those aboard might have spotted me in the narrow gap between buildings. The bottom of the fuselage was what shielded me from view.

Once it was out of sight, I got moving.

I emerged from the narrow alley onto a street. Pedestrians, who no doubt had heard all the nearby gunfire, saw me and freaked out. I ran diagonally across the street to another alley that should give me good cover and concealment for about a block.

Shots rang out at ground level. One snapped the air right behind me. I couldn't place the Erasers in all the crowd movement. I sprinted the remaining distance to the alley and entered it. Ten yards in I stopped, whirled, and dropped belly-down with the carbine ready.

The light at the mouth of the alley bent strangely, and I squeezed the trigger. The Eraser went down, but there was another one behind him, who appeared to trip over his buddy and fall. I squeezed again and nothing happened. The carbine was jammed.

Cursing, I rose, pulled my .45 and pumped four rounds into the mass of distorted light. I turned and resumed my escape, hoping my bullets had found their marks, or I would take one in the back any moment.

The alley continued straight across the street, but I wanted to put buildings between myself and pursuit. I darted to the right on the street, causing more panic among bystanders, then turned left again, zigzagging into another alley.

All this time, I could hear the chopper stalking me. I stopped and caught my breath again, clearing the jam in the carbine.

The chopper grew louder, and then the sky distorted behind and overhead. This time it rotated in place, hovering. They had spotted me.

I wished I either had a BAR, or an M203. I was sure I could hit the cloaked chopper from there. With the BAR firing bursts of .30 full metal jacket, I could do some serious damage. With the 40mm shell from the grenade launcher on the M203, I could blow that bird right out of the air.

Even while thinking these thoughts, I put my feet to work. I don't know how the gunner managed to miss me, but I turned the corner without getting smashed by one of those heavy rounds.

The chopper was relentless, and I assumed there were more Erasers at street level closing in on me. Thanks to the adrenaline rush and my refusal to stop running for more than a couple seconds at a time, the hopelessness of my situation didn't fully register.

I was less than a mile from the field where I had landed the small civilian twin engine plane I had jumped here in.

The chopper was still dogging me. I assumed the pilot was so good at tracking me because of the reaction of the natives every time I emerged from an alley limping, bleeding, cursing, with the carbine swinging to and fro as I scanned for targets.

It was quite a surprise when I galloped out into a street that was seemingly empty, I looked around, gulped for air, and headed for an alley before the chopper could get close enough to spot me out in the open.

A building up ahead had a garage door that opened. A woman stepped out the door, turned and faced me.

"Come! Quickly!" She spoke English with an accent I didn't place from just those two words. She beckoned me urgently and backed through the garage door.

I had to pass the building anyway, so I swung to the edge of the opening with the carbine leading the way, ready to shoot depending on what I saw. Only the woman was inside the cluttered warehouse.

"Don't shoot!" she cried, frantically waving me toward her. "You've got Direct Action agents, and now local police after you." She glanced at my bloodstained pants. "Are you wounded?"

I just stared at her, stepping inside so that if the helicopter got close, I wouldn't be easily seen.

"My word," she exclaimed, doing a double-take at my wounded leg. "Yes—you've got a dreadful wound, it seems. Follow me. I need to get you to where that can be treated, and you can't be found."

Who was she? She wasn't Roma. She spoke perfect English, with an upper-crust British accent. She wore flats, a loose-fitting print dress, and a head scarf—not unlike many local women did. But how did she know about the Erasers? And me? She addressed me as if she knew me, and my situation.

I stood in slack-jawed wonder. She approached me, hips swinging in a wonderful, mesmerizing, feminine gait. She was sexy, I noticed, with a Tier One face and figure. Music was playing from somewhere. Or was I imagining that?

She grabbed me by the wrist and tugged me along with her. With her free hand, she pushed a button which lowered the garage door behind us. I let her lead me toward an empty corner of the building.

Two jolting realizations occurred to me at the same time. One was that this was the same woman I glimpsed below me on the street just before the first Eraser attacked. The other was that she was rapidly disappearing into thin air right before my eyes.

I heard strange noises; felt ridiculous sensations; and my vision blurred.

It was like she was disappearing into a doorway...only there was no visible doorway. It reminded me of how the floating bodies of my biological family disappeared into the cloaked van in back in the trailer park where the Erasers first came for me. Only there was no visual anomaly here, to suggest a cloaked object. First her nose and breasts disappeared, then the rest of her face and torso, with one leg, then the other...

I yanked my wrist out of her grip just before her hand disappeared.

Now she was completely gone, and I was terrified. As I backed away, my vision cleared while the noises and weird sensations subsided. But I could hear the music again. A boom box hanging by the handle from nails on the wall was the source. Just as I noticed it, the music stopped. A second later, the "play" switch on the cassette player clicked up into the "off" position.

Under different circumstances, I might have stayed there

and looked around the building. Instead, I found a man-sized exit door and scurried out of there.

For some reason, the chopper seemed to break off pursuit. Its engine and air-beating noise grew faint, then completely stopped, as if jumping a warp. Maybe it was low on fuel.

I didn't stop until I reached where I had stashed the plane.

As soon as I had enough altitude to clear the tallest trees, I jumped a warp to Valhalla. My thinking at the time went no further than that I should be safe there, and the alien atmosphere would cause me to heal faster.

CHAPTER 11: FUTILITY

I didn't realize how much blood I was leaking until I looked down and saw the crimson pool on the floor of the plane under the rudder pedals. I warped in over the airfield, which was about 20 miles from Dad's colony. There were other aircraft near the field, and a tower, though the place was unmanned most of the time.

I had heard a lot about how difficult carrier landings were, and didn't doubt it. But landing a conventional (Earth) plane on Valhalla was no joke, either. With the light gravity and strange atmospherics, you had to almost dive down to the runway. Then, if you touched down too hard, your bird might bounce up and come down on its nose. The mass of the plane remained the same, so you could snap off the landing gear or crack the whole bird up. Feeling light-headed by then, I put in a call for an ambulance, just in case.

I cut the engine long before my approach, and was able to stick the landing.

Normally, I would have waited for my ride in the tower, which had a dart board, a stocked book case, and furniture much more comfortable than the seating in the plane. Instead, I used the plane's first aid kit to bind my wounds as best I could. There wasn't enough for all the wounds; but the compress at least stopped the bleeding from the exit side of the bullet wound. After securing that, I decided to rest my eyes for a while.

I awoke as a couple of the shooters from the colony's security force carried me to the ambulance.

During the hovercraft ride, Nurse Vickie stuck an IV into me. She was a lot friendlier with just one patient to worry about than with a whole room full of them. She made conversation with me on the way to the aid station.

Dad wasn't at the colony and nobody had seen him for a while. I didn't explain the bullet wound or the loss of my family until I was alone with Lee, Manfredi, and Kyle, after I was patched up.

Dr. Manfredi handed me a crutch and some medicine.

"I know you don't want to hear this," Kyle said, "but you can't go back there looking for Madalina and the baby. They're watching those coordinates, and know at least something about you."

"Watching why?" I asked. "Because Madalina had been gone a while, then came back? How many informants does the TPF have?"

"A lot," Dr. Manfredi said. "But it might not even be that."

"Then what could it be?" I asked.

Manfredi sighed and frowned. "Some of my assistants have jumped to Densus at different points in the timestream. That's how we found Madalina, in fact. Perhaps somebody on my team made a mistake, and drew attention to themselves. Perhaps my own disappearance is what tipped them off. They have virtually unlimited time to investigate. If they somehow connected her to me, it makes sense they would have a sort of All Points Bulletin on her. When she reappeared, they would certainly want to interrogate her...and lay a trap for anyone who might come looking for her afterwards."

"It was pretty stupid taking her back there," Kyle said. "I know Simon warned you about jumping with others who aren't cleared."

All the excuses that came to my mind would sound lame, even to my own ears. I had grown weak, and lost control of my frame. I let Madalina persuade me to do something I knew was foolish. I took the risk because I wanted to make her happy. For my mistake, I lost her and my daughter.

"You should have at least asked for an exception," Kyle added.

"He cleared me to take her to the island," I said.

"But to take her back to Densus?" Lee asked.

"He wasn't here," I said.

"Then you should have brought it to me," Kyle said.

"You're chief of security on Valhalla," I replied, shrugging. "You're not in charge of policing the continuum."

Kyle's face flushed red, but he said, "Oh, that's right: I'm just a dumb flunky who works for your dad. Why should a big, bad genius college boy like you have to check with me about anything?"

My comment just came out unfiltered. I hadn't meant it as an insult. "That's not what I'm saying, Kyle."

"You dumbass," he growled. "Your idiocy jeopardizes this operation, and everybody at all of your dad's stations. Think about somebody besides yourself. Other people's lives matter just as much as your little romantic fling."

It was not a good time to get personal, to bully me, or to refer to Madalina and our baby as a "romantic fling."

I shot to my feet to face off with him.

I had always thought of Kyle as a huge dude. I had never even considered throwing hands with a big badass like him. All that changed in a moment. Also, I realized he only had a couple inches on me in height, and perhaps 20 pounds in weight. I had longer reach, and might be faster. Of course, there was the wounded leg and the crutch, too. Frankly though, I was angry enough to fight him no matter what the "Tale of the Tape" might be.

My retort was the model of intellectual *repartee*: "Fuck you, you piece of shit."

Manfredi got between us, extending his arms in both directions as if he could keep us separated by pushing against our chests. "Hey, hey, hey! Settle down. A pissing contest isn't going to solve anything."

"Let him go if he thinks he's so bad," Kyle said, sneering at me. "Let's see how much his superstar football skills are worth."

My temper had boiled over so fast, my mind hadn't kept pace with it. I remembered that letting my emotions get out of control would be disastrous, and consciously worked on my breathing.

Dr. Lee glanced at both of us and said, in a clipped, brittle cadence, "That is quite enough, Kyle! You will leave us at once, and complete the debriefing when you can once again behave like a professional!"

Kyle looked at the doctor, at me, and back to the doctor. His cheek bulged out, then the bulge moved in a wave across his mouth with the unseen swipe of his tongue. Without another word, he whirled and stalked out of the room.

"Sit and calm yourself," Dr. Lee told me. His tone was gentler than a moment before. It was more of a helpful suggestion than a command.

I began pacing instead, hobbling back and forth on the crutch regulating my breathing as I tried to quench my temper.

"Obviously the TPF is watching those coordinates and will be ready for you if you go back," Dr. Lee said. "Aside from that, you know what will happen if you loop back before your jump."

"I'll split the stream," I said. "There'll be two of me and only one of Madalina and the baby."

Dr. Lee nodded.

"Then what can I do?" I asked.

The doctors glanced at each other, and Lee said, "We don't know that there's anything that can be done. They've got her now. They'll have you if you go after her again. You got shot in the leg this time. What if you get shot in the head next time? Or maybe they'll take you away to wherever they have her, and either torture you to death, or until they get you to rat us all out. Either way, none of it helps Madalina or the baby."

"In other words," I accused, "they can't be helped. That's what you're telling me."

Manfredi stood there stiffly, eyes downcast. "I'm so sorry, Ike."

Dr. Lee wouldn't meet my gaze, either.

I felt hot tears leaking out my eyelids. I would have stomped out of there, kicking the door open on my way out, but my dependence on the crutch took away any chance of a dramatic exit.

ΔΔΔ

Without any agenda, much less a plan, I returned to the hut Madalina and I had shared, and just sat there in the living room, trying to think of some way to get my family back. I didn't sleep that night, and spent the next day still trying to scheme my way out of the morass I had blindly plunged into. I didn't eat, and suffered through another sleepless night. I came up with a dozen ideas, but each one had a fatal flaw I ran into when thinking it through.

On the third day, I was stir crazy, and wanted to get out of that hut. But I didn't want to face or communicate with anyone. I waited until the following night, traveled by crutch the distance to the airfield (not caring if some deadly alien creature tried to kill me along the way) and found my plane. I jumped to Happy Ever After, where I could be alone, but at least walk around the island to expend some angry energy.

I finally slept on the third night. It was fitful, not restful. I still didn't eat right away, but resumed exercising. The construction crew had cut a path around the island so that I could keep up on my roadwork. I had a gym there, too. I couldn't run yet, but I could limp along pretty fast. Working the speed, heavy, and double-end bags burned up endorphins and drove the hunger away. It also allowed me to concentrate on combinations and breathing. Simple stuff to fill my mind so I wouldn't dwell on what might be happening to Madalina and Sylvia, or my helplessness.

I finally resumed eating on the fourth day; but then drunk myself stupid after that, and wound up puking it all out for the next few miserable days. I hadn't learned my lesson after the history field trip. At least I kept to myself this time, and didn't get loose-lipped at a bar, with people around.

The hangover lasted more than a day, for sure—I lost track of how many days, though.

I resumed eating again, once able to hold food down. Then I cried for hours on end, in between screaming and bellowing my rage into the atmosphere of a world that couldn't hear and didn't care.

Emotionally spent, I collapsed into bed and slept for 14 hours. When I awoke, I felt like I hadn't felt since leaving my native coordinates.

Life was rigged against me—the whole damn game. Evil, relentless control freaks held all the trump cards. They didn't have to follow any laws or rules. They could do whatever they wanted to whoever they wanted, wherever and whenever they wanted. And their victims had no way to strike back, without making it worse for themselves. They were like the damned central bankers, almost. Everything worked to their benefit but to normal people's detriment. And the only way you could carve out a decent existence for yourself was to escape their attention.

Life sucks; then you die. That was the most common expression me and my peers used back in St. Louis. I had cheated that reality for a time, but now had come full-circle.

Nobody was on my side. The vast majority of people would never believe there was such a tyranny in the first place. The people who knew couldn't, or wouldn't, do anything to strike back at the Erasers and the CPB. I couldn't strike back at them by myself, without being captured or killed while doing minimal damage to them. I certainly wasn't going to get Madalina or my daughter back from them. They weren't going to let me take them back, or even reveal where or when they were holding them, and what they were doing to them.

Even Dad probably wouldn't help me, because rescuing Madalina, or striking back at the CPB was a harebrained suicide mission at best. Not that Dad was around, anyway.

I was beaten. There was no coming back from this.

CHAPTER 12: HOMECOMING

"**N**o matter what happens, there's always another hill to be taken."

I remembered Dad saying that a lot over the years. I assumed it was a military axiom of some kind. I always took it to mean, "No matter how good or bad life gets; no matter how you feel, what you want, need, or would rather do, the show must go on."

Another saying he often repeated was, "Suck it up and drive on." It seemed to come as a package deal with the other saying. And, of course: "What do you want—sympathy?"

Those three nuggets of encouragement were the answers to the reality of my generation: "Life sucks; then you die."

Dad also had his own version of that saying, naturally: "Life's a bitch; then you marry one." Or: "Life's a virgin, 'cause bitches are easy."

Madalina wasn't a bitch. She was...

Aw, never mind. She was gone, with our child. I would never get them back, and that was that.

Suck it up and drive on. What do I want—sympathy?

But I didn't know what hill was to be taken next. What hill mattered?

I lost count of how many days I spent, alone and miserable, on the island, thinking that if there was no hill to take, maybe I should just say to hell with everything. Suicide didn't have the same appeal to me that it did as a boy back in St. Louis. But what if I returned to Densus with all the firepower

110

I could carry and just went out in a blaze of glory? Do so much damage they would have to kill me, and take as many of them with me as I could.

That could be my hill.

In my mind, I did make some preliminary plans for that, for a while. I ate, exercised, and thought about Densus.

But over time, my attitude changed. I wasn't ready to die.

I guess it was selfish and probably cowardly, but there was still stuff I wanted to do—stuff I could take pleasure in. I still wanted to live a life.

Some girls will break your heart. You either kill yourself or drive on. My heart was broken again (though it wasn't Madalina's fault). I wasn't going to kill myself, so I had to drive on.

Even more selfish than wanting to live, without my family, I found myself getting lonely.

I hadn't gone without female companionship for quite a while, and I missed it. When preparing to settle down with Madalina, I intended to let all my other spinning plates spin off to some other romantic pursuits. But that was when I had her. Now I didn't have her. And no matter what I did, I would not have her again.

I accepted this reality about a week after the casting change in the nightly dreams that left me feeling empty and broken every morning. The dreams starred Madalina for about a month, but the role was gradually taken over by Juanita.

I had given up on ever going back to Juanita, after Madalina's pregnancy. But why give up now?

So a see-saw battle waged inside me for a while—Guilt in one corner, and aching Loneliness in the other.

Before Madalina had won me over, I had learned to not even notice loneliness anymore. Maybe I lost a piece of myself when I lost her—that piece that allowed me to be content, even when I went through a drought and couldn't enjoy all the things a woman can do for a man. Or maybe it was just a temporary weakness.

I mulled all this over while staring at Juanita's photo and reminiscing on our short time together.

Guilt was still putting up a hell of a fight in my mind, so I told myself I was going to visit the Orange Grove to see Mamita and my siblings. I didn't have to visit Hollywood, just because I'd be so close.

Sure, I didn't.

Juanita or not, I should have thought of visiting the Orange Grove sooner. Just seeing the place again lifted my spirits. It all seemed smaller now, but felt more like home than anywhere and anywhen else. The smell of the orange trees and the sight of the adobe hacienda made me smile. My mood improved dramatically just from that moment. I had picked up a '39 Chevy for these coordinates, and arrived dressed in the khakis of an Army pilot. I had to stick with the cover story, even for family.

Before I even shut the door of the Chevy, the kids exploded out the front door, over the scalloped adobe wall, and mobbed me.

Wyatt came up to my stomach, now. He, Debbie and Lana surrounded me, hugging whatever they could reach, shouting for joy and all chattering excitedly at the same time. They had grown considerably since I last saw them. Then Mamita rushed out after them. She stopped in her tracks. She covered her mouth with her hand, looking me up-and-down as if sure I must be an imposter and this was a prank. Then she ran toward me, arms outstretched, with a high-pitched wail. She wrapped herself around my waist and buried the side of her face into my ribs. Just like the house and orchard, she seemed tiny compared to my memories.

"Oh, *Pedrito*, you're finally here!" she murmured, in Spanish. Then she began sobbing, making a wet spot on my shirt.

"What's wrong, Mami?" I asked, returning her embrace and kissing the top of her head,

"It...it's just so good to see you, *mijo*," she said, little body shaking with her sobs.

The warmth and love was just as powerful as I remembered it. Still, I felt like a heel for the deception that caused her this unnecessary anguish.

The five of us stood there for a long moment, huddled together like tacks on a magnet. Mami cried, as did Lana, while Debbie giggled and Wyatt tried to bear hug me through the tangle, before letting go, backing up, and staring at me.

"Hey Pete, I got a beebee gun for Christmas. You wanna see it?"

"Sure," I replied.

Mami released me and wiped at her eyes. "That can wait, Wyatt. Let's get your brother inside. You check the car and bring in his things."

I held Debbie in one arm while Lana led me by the hand. We followed Mami into the house.

Everything was just like I remembered it—except my brother and sisters. Mami herself had barely aged at all since last I saw her.

In the living room, I sat on the couch with Mami and the girls. The front door slammed. A few seconds later, Wyatt staggered in under the weight of my duffle bag, which was bigger and heavier than him. He drug my crutch behind him.

"You didn't have to carry that, Wyatt," I said, starting to get up.

Mami caught my arm and tugged downward, shooting me a meaningful glance. I put my weight back on the couch.

Red-faced from exertion, huffing and puffing, Wyatt dropped the duffel bag with a thud by the end of the couch, stood up straight, and, now unburdened, panted, "Aw, it wasn't heavy."

"Well, you sure have gotten strong while I was away," I remarked, winking at Mami, who smiled with a twinkle in her eye.

"What's this for?" Wyatt panted, holding the crutch up. "Were you wounded?"

"I don't even need that," I said.

"You were limping as you came in," Mami observed.

"How would you know?" I asked. "Your back was to me."

"A mother notices such things," she said.

Debbie and Lana whimpered sympathetically, touching my face and arms and asking if I was okay. Their concern was so heartwarming, I almost laughed. My emotions were kind of haywire.

They asked a thousand questions. I used my cover story, but I tried to steer the conversation away from the war.

"How much of the Army Air Corps is in the Pacific?" Wyatt asked.

"Well, it's the Army Air *Force*, now," I informed him. "And now that we've licked the Germans, the rest of us will be transferred from the European Theater, soon."

"Hot dog!" Wyatt cried. "Our troops will be in Tokyo in no time!"

"Shouldn't be long before it's over, now," I said, then turned to Mami. "Have you seen Dad?"

"He's still over there, somewhere," she replied, her smile fading a bit. "He's been gone almost as long as you have, but he doesn't write very often. I worry so."

"I know you do, Mami." I licked my lips, preparing to modify the truth again, for their benefit. "I ran into Dad not too long ago," I said. We both passed through the same place at the same time." Of course, I failed to mention it was Dallas in 1963.

"Where was it?" Wyatt asked.

"How was he?" Mami asked.

"He looked worn out," I said, honestly.

Her worried look intensified.

"But that's normal for officers," I said, quickly. "Especially once you get up to lieutenant colonel. He'll be fine. You know how tough he is."

Mami shook her head. "This war is so awful. I know we have to stop the bad people; but I'll be so glad when it's over."

"It shouldn't be long, now," I said. "US forces are on Okinawa. That's the last island to take before Japan itself."

Mami made us a quick meal of tacos, apologizing that it wasn't fancier. If she'd known I was coming, she could have prepared something worthy of my homecoming. I reminded her that I loved tacos. She promised to prepare a feast for the next day.

After supper, we sat around the radio and listened to Captain Midnight, the Green Hornet (The choice of me and Wyatt) plus Fibber McGee and Molly (loved by the girls). Mami sat knitting, occasionally asking us for a translation. Debbie sat on my lap while Lana sat against me, clutching my arm and tightening her grip during the parts she found scary. Wyatt, with his air rifle in hand, transitioned between acting out the audio dramas, and improvising his own adventures on-the-fly.

Home sweet home. This was exactly what I needed.

The next morning I helped Wyatt with the outdoor chores, then he, I, and Lana took a walk through the grove while Debbie helped Mami with breakfast. Lana held my hand the whole time like I might disappear into thin air if she let go. They caught me completely up-to-date on the happenings of the Home Front, from a kid's perspective.

After breakfast, we all gathered around the radio again to listen to the big bands while Mami relaxed with her knitting, Debbie played with her dolls, Lana looked at the pictures in the Sears Catalog, and Wyatt and I read from our favorite pulp magazines.

Mami looked up from her needles at one point to ask, "Is there anything you'd like to do today, *Pedrito*?"

"I'm doing it," I replied.

She smiled. All of us smiled. We were all happy. I felt a pang in my chest, realizing that I could have shared this kind of family experience with Madalina and our own kids if I hadn't been so foolish.

Mami got up during commercials to bustle about, tending to various household matters to keep the home ship-shape.

She returned to the room from one such commercial break with a stack of letters, and handed it to me.

"Here is your mail from *Senorita* Sanders."

I was excited to have mail from Juanita. At the same time, Mami's raised-eyebrow inquisitive gleam embarrassed me a little bit.

"What?" I asked, defensively.

"You never told me anything about this girl."

"I met her in Hollywood," I said.

"And?"

"And what?" I wiggled the envelopes. "We wrote to each other."

"Is she your sweetheart?"

I shrugged. "We haven't seen each other since 1942."

"Juanita," Mami pronounced the name playfully. "Is she *Chicana*?"

"Her mother is part Navajo," I said. "She could pass for Mexican, easy."

"Is she pretty?" Lana asked, looking up from the catalog.

All my siblings were watching me for my answer.

"Nobody will ever be as beautiful as Mami," I said. The girls grinned. Wyatt made a wolf whistle, but blushed and apologized when Mami glared at him in silent reprimand.

"Will you read her letters to us?" Lana asked.

"Not on your life," I said.

My sisters giggled.

I put aside the pulps and started on the letters.

The first few mentioned how much she enjoyed our dates, and that she hoped I could come back to the States soon. She shared generic news and anecdotes about casting calls. She also told me that she had searched high and low for the Louis Armstrong song, but couldn't find anyone who had heard it or heard *of* it. In one of my letters, I had written all the lyrics for her. She surmised that it was really me who had written it, but was just too shy to say so—perhaps embarrassed that being a budding lyricist might be "unmanly."

She was cast as a chorus girl in a few musicals, before getting another speaking role as a cigarette girl in a romantic comedy. Her line was, "Say, what's with him?" Then she did get the role as a half-breed Indian girl in the western that the producer Lew LaPierre had mentioned. She had a handful of lines, and she helped the hero escape from the bad Indian tribe before she herself tragically died from an angry brave's arrow. It was a "B" picture, but the role got her noticed by the casting director on another "B" movie, who gave her a role as an Italian night club entertainer who secretly spied for the Allies against the Germans and her own countrymen. By the time I got to her last letter, she had landed a supporting role in an "A" feature, *Passage From Algiers*. She played a Bulgarian refugee with a heart of gold. It was a small part, with only two scenes wherein she had dialog, but she was on the set with one big star, one new star, several respected character actors, and a top notch director. She loved working with all those talented people, apparently, and had made a few contacts which might pay off.

In relative time, it had been quite a while since she had written.

There was still a package, also from Juanita, that I saved for last. I opened it and found it contained a Christmas card (1943), a portrait of her, some homemade cookies that were now bad, a pair of thick wool socks, and a record.

I threw away the rotten cookies, read the card, and took everything to my room. I put the record on the phonograph, turned it on, and carefully placed the needle on the record.

Juanita's voice came out the speaker.

"Hello, my Sweet Pete, and Merry Christmas!" I heard a chord progression on a piano that sounded like it was from "Here We Come a-Caroling." Juanita laughed. "There's a place here in Hollywood offering holiday specials on renting a recording booth, and even furnishes a piano. This record only lasts a few minutes, so here goes: my present to my soldier."

The piano played, and she began singing.

> Give me a kiss to build a dream on
> And my imagination will thrive upon that kiss.
> Sweetheart, I ask no more than this:

A kiss to build a dream on.

Give me a kiss before you leave me
And my imagination will feed my hungry heart.
Leave me one thing before we part:
A kiss to build a dream on.

When I'm alone with my fancies
I'll be with you.
Weaving romances
Making believe they're true...

I closed my eyes, feeling shivers at the beauty of her voice as she finished the song.

"Thank-you for showing me your lyrics," she said. "I remembered the melody, and came up with an accompaniment for the piano. I hope you like it. I guess you had Satchmo in mind...and I did originally have him come to the studio here. But his trumpet was all out of tune. It was frightful. And then *he* accused *me* of having a scratchy, gurgling voice. The nerve! Can you believe it? Well, I just up and told Mr. Armstrong to get lost, that's all! I would do it myself!"

She laughed again. It was a sweet, clean sound.

"Well, I hope you like it, Pete. You stay safe. I miss you. How about you end this war so you can come back to me on the double? Goodbye. Hugs and kisses."

I listened to the record over and over again, thrilling to the perfection of the notes when she sang, and the lilt in her voice when she spoke. I closed my eyes and visualized her feminine fingers on the piano keys.

Who was I fooling? I had to see her.

CHAPTER 13: THE SNOB SOIREE

After Mami's fancy roast beef supper, I found the Los Angeles telephone directory Dad kept in his office and flipped to the "S" pages. I couldn't find any Juanita Sanders listed. After thinking for a moment, I looked up Viola Fontaine, and found a listing. I copied down the number and address.

I dressed in my Class A uniform and took the Chevy to town. I found a pay phone and called her number. A woman answered on the second ring.

"Hello?"

How much could you tell about a person from one word? It resembled Juanita's voice, but quite different from what I remembered. Sort of detached and numb.

"Hi. Juanita?"

"Who is this?" Her tone was flat. Maybe suspicious.

"It's Pete. I'm back."

"Pete Eimbach? I'm afraid I haven't had the pleasure."

"Would you prefer Satchmo?" I asked. I cleared my throat, and gave my best Louis Armstrong impression singing the first line of "A Kiss to Build a Dream On."

"Oh! Oh, Pete, with the funny last name!" Her tone was lighter now; more open...but still missing something.

"Yeah, that's me. I know you got at least some of my

letters, because you wrote back."

"Yes. Yes, I did. It's nice to hear from you. What's buzzin', cousin?"

"Hubba hubba hubba," I replied. "I got it from a guy who was in the know: it was mighty smoky over Tokyo."

She chuckled. "Mister, how you love to blubber with that knocked-out squawk."

I duplicated her cadence. "It's like my lips are made of rubber every time I talk."

"Just as corny as ever. You haven't changed. Well, where are you?"

"I'm in town," I said.

She was silent for a moment. That wasn't the reaction I was hoping for.

"I guess I called at a bad time," I said.

"Well... I am almost out the door, as a matter of fact. There's this mixer I need to go to."

"Ah. Okay." I considered asking her if there would be a better time to call. But I didn't like that she sounded like such a different person. She was polite, and upbeat now that she knew who I was. But she didn't have the joy and enthusiasm at a chance to see me again that I would have expected from the Juanita I remembered. Maybe she had moved on. Maybe I should, too.

"I tell you what, Pete: why don't you meet me where I'm going—do you have a ride?"

"Yeah," I said. "But it's no big deal, if you have business."

"No. No. I just have to hobnob on the regular. Keep my name out there. It might be a kick for you. You have something to write with?"

I pulled out my handheld and opened the digital map program. "Okay, let's have it."

She gave me an address in Malibu.

I found a liquor store and inquired of the proprietor what kind of gift I should show up with at a party thrown by showbiz types. He was very friendly, probably because of my uniform.

He said there was probably no telling what the partygoers might be drinking in this crazy part of the world, but that I probably shouldn't bring any really hard stuff as a gift—even if that's what they were drinking there. A high percentage of movie moguls were from New York, and still had snobby New York sensibilities. So he picked out a bottle of wine.

I did a little sightseeing around Hollywood and the other L.A. suburbs on my way, to make sure I didn't arrive before Juanita.

When I did get there, so many cars lined the street that I had to park a quarter mile from the house in question. All the houses out here were big and expensive. I weaved my way through the vehicles parked on the cobblestone circular driveway, and could hear festive sounds from the house. Silhouettes fluttered on the backlit window shades.

I rang the bell and an honest-to-goodness butler opened the door. I greeted him politely and handed him the wine bottle.

"That's for the host," I said.

He took the bottle. "Thank-you, sir. Um, do you happen to have your invitation?"

"Viola Fontaine invited me," I said.

He looked me up-and-down. To his credit, he didn't act snooty. "I see. If you will please wait a moment?"

I shrugged. "Okay."

He closed the door. I waited for a few minutes before the door opened again. The butler didn't have the bottle in hand, but he did have Juanita.

She had cut her hair into a short style, like Jean Harlow or Bette Davis—and died it red. She had too much makeup on, no hat or gloves, but some jewelry. She was pale, and thin. Her look was quite different.

Dad had once told me that women generally wore more jewelry when they were ovulating. Some wore it no matter what. And some might subconsciously consider makeup and jewelry to be a sort of armor that would protect them from...something.

She raised her hands in celebratory fashion and showed

me a polished smile as she stepped outside to hug me.

The butler opened the door wide in invitation. Juanita turned to him and winked. "He's alright, Jack."

I think the butler had already figured that out by our perfunctory embrace, but he nodded and said, "Very well, madame."

She steered me through the vestibule, a hall, and into a huge room with a bar, a piano, and very scarce furniture. Dozens of people—maybe even a hundred—stood around socializing. Juanita smiled, waved, or winked at people we passed, who glanced curiously at me. I didn't get the warm greetings I had received in '42...or from the liquor store clerk an hour ago. Some of them stared as if Juanita had dragged a wet skunk in the house.

She stopped in a small clearing near the center of the room where we had space to stand facing each other at arm's length. She briefly grabbed my arms, looking at my face, my uniform, and back at my face.

"Look at you," she said. "You finally came marchin' home."

"Yup."

"And in one piece," she added. "Most of the boys look like they've been starving for months when they get back home, but you're even bigger than you were last time. Even your muscles have muscles."

"I guess I'm luckier than most, " I said. "I haven't missed many meals."

"I should say not," she said, then turned to a tight cluster of men and women chatting with each other while holding drinks. She introduced me to them and said, "He brought a bottle of wine for Mr. Schoenberg. Isn't that just adorable?"

The group engaged me in small talk for a moment, asking generic questions that they probably forgot my answers to as soon as the words left my mouth. But that was fair, because I forgot all their names as soon as they told me.

They resumed their previous conversation. Some fat guy said something that wasn't funny, but Juanita laughed at it as if it was. She turned to me, still keeping the phony laugh going, perhaps expecting I would force some fake mirth of my own. When I didn't, she sobered and pointed to the bar, making a circling gesture with her other hand. "Why don't you get yourself a drink, Pete. Mix around; meet some people. I'm sure a lot of them will be excited to meet one of our real-life heroes."

It felt like a brush-off, which annoyed me. But I took it in stride and navigated through the crowd to the bar. I asked for a rum and Coke, got one, and sipped at it as I scanned around the room.

It was an ugly scene, to me. *What a bunch of pretentious phonies.*

In each little sub-group, there was either one life-of-the-party type surrounded by an entourage hanging on their every word, or two people with huge, fragile egos competing for that role, tying to assert their dominance by controlling the conversation. Every other member of the sub-group was either sucking up in one way or another, or scheming how to supplant the ones who were currently dominating. That was the impression I got, and I'm still pretty sure it was accurate.

I searched back in the direction I had come from, but didn't see Juanita. I continued scanning. There she was—she had moved into another group. She was chatting with animation to some actor I recognized from several movies, whose name I couldn't recall, and who was probably 20 years her senior. He said something and she laughed, touching his arm. She said something back. He wiggled his eyebrows but played it cool. She said something and touched his arm again. He made a crack and she nearly doubled over, laughing. She slapped at his suit jacket as if she were drowning, and just clutching at anything to keep her afloat. A regular comedian, that guy. For her next comment, she changed up and touched his other arm. At one point, she glanced toward the bar, spotted me, and met my gaze for an instant. I can't be sure what my expression was, but I assume it was blank. Hers wasn't, but I can't quite determine what it actually was, either. She refrained from touching the actor for a little while, and nodded with serious contemplation as he spoke. I finished my drink and asked for another.

While I waited for my refill, Viola Fontaine began touching the older actor again. I stopped counting after the tenth time she made physical contact.

My drink was ready. I took it and thanked the bartender. I wandered away from the bar and through the crowd. I gave myself a tour of the house, concentrating on the construction and furnishings; trying not to notice the pretense and fakery of the fat-cats or their wives and mistresses.

I wandered out onto the back yard. There was a big, fancy patio with a swimming pool, cluttered by the same kind of little social groups that littered the inside of the house. The fact that a house right on the beach had a swimming pool in the back yard told me a lot about this neighborhood and the sort of people who lived here.

A circle formed around some guy who appeared vaguely familiar (another actor, I assumed) dressed in a Marine Corps uniform. He was speaking boisterously and gesticulating with both hands. He was the only other guy I had seen in uniform, even though many of the men in attendance looked young enough to serve.

Somebody asked the marine a question and he beckoned them forward from his audience. He proceeded to demonstrate some slow-motion self-defense moves that looked like basic *judo* to me. His sycophants laughed and applauded his act.

Some skinny guy in a suit with glasses bumped into me, turned, then looked me over in a way that made me uncomfortable.

"Well, I beg your pardon," he said. "Another one of our brave boys back from the field of battle. You're no dog-faced soldier, but it certainly looks like they tore you down and built you over again."

He held a martini in one dainty hand and swished it around so that the olive orbited the glass. He inclined his head toward the marine. "I don't suppose *you* would like to demonstrate some of the hand-to-hand combat you used on the Japs?"

"I'm a pilot," I said. "I never went hand-to-hand with any Japs."

"But I'm sure they trained you," he insisted.

"Why don't you go get another drink?" I suggested. "Or better yet, sit down somewhere and clear your head for a while."

"Come on. I volunteer. Show me one of those moves. Just be gentle with me."

"Look, Mack," I said, getting irritated that this drunken twink wouldn't just take a hint and leave me alone, "if it gets to the point where I decide to use a move here tonight, I ain't gonna be gentle."

The queer recoiled a bit, but then smiled and licked his lips. "Mmm. That sounds intriguing."

"Would you like a cigarette, sir?"

I turned my back on the drunken faggot (definitely not a wise maneuver at certain coordinates, but in 1945 not too dangerous), to place the voice. The cigarette girl who had spoken was Tier Two, with a cute smile and the sort of shapely hips that usually framed a decent caboose. Tier Two women looked as good or better than most Hollywood actresses from any era, for my money. Juanita had been Top Tier in 1942, but no longer stood out from the pasty-faced, flat-chested, square-hipped broads the movie moguls evidently preferred for some reason which was lost on me.

"Hi there," I said.

"Welcome home, soldier boy," the cigarette girl replied, with a sweet sincerity. Then she noted the aviation wings. "Or should I say, fly-boy?"

"I like either one, coming from you," I said.

Her grin widened. She was probably used to being treated like a flunkie or a whore by the Hollywood set, and appreciated somebody who noticed her, and treated her like a person.

"Yoo-hoo! I'm talking to you!" intoned the little creep to my back.

I ignored him. To her I said, "Just how blatant is this individual gonna get, do you think?" I rolled my eyes back without moving my head, so she would know who I was referring to, but he wouldn't.

"Honestly, I don't know," she replied, in a hushed tone. "I haven't run into this one before tonight. But you probably don't want to rough him up. Word is, he's related to a real big shot in the pictures."

"Thanks," I said.

"Excuse me, cigarette girl!" the faggot called, in a demanding voice.

I feared he was going to insult or otherwise embarrass her, to throw his weight around and punish her for diverting my attention. I wasn't sure I would stand for that.

"Yes sir," she said, carrying her tray toward him.

I turned, so I could watch both of them.

"I would like a cigarette." He dropped a coin on her tray, making eye contact with me the whole time, and took a butt.

She turned to me with a flirty smile. "They're on the house for our men in uniform. Take as many as you like."

I shrugged and grinned. "Thanks. I don't smoke, though."

Her eyes opened a little wider. "Interesting."

"You know what," the faggot said, dropping more change on her tray. "I'll take a whole pack." And he did...her last one... while frowning at me in disapproval.

"Thank-you, sir," she told him. "I'm sorry I couldn't be of help to you," she told me.

"Here," I said, taking her tray. "I'll be of help to you, Dumpling. Let me carry this back to where you get reloaded. Lead the way."

"Oh," she said, wrinkling her nose and grinning. "A gentleman."

As we made our way back inside, I heard my would-be buttboy behind me tsk and say, "What a boor."

I followed the cigarette girl through the house, enjoying the way her rump wiggled. We entered the huge kitchen, where all sorts of employees of the caterers either bustled or loitered. The girl took her tray back from me, put away the change, and re-stocked from the stack of cigarette cartons on the counter. She opened a pack, extracted a cigarette for herself, and positioned it between the tips of her index and middle fingers.

"I'd ask you for a light," she said, "but..."

"Why, sure," I said, pulling the period correct Zippo from my pocket and flicking it alive. "A good scout is always prepared."

"I don't get it," she said.

"There's a lot that a lighter can be handy for," I said. "Not just smoking."

She helped me light her, then leaned back against the counter, took a puff and blew it out. "Thanks, fly-boy. I'm Irma, by-the-way."

"Pete," I said.

"It's nice to come across a normal person at one of these things," she said.

"That's just what I was thinking."

We flirted for a few minutes. She jotted down her name and phone number for me before leaving the kitchen to make her rounds again.

I pocketed her digits and wandered through the house toward the front door. I passed by Viola not too far from the kitchen, and didn't pause. She was still playing social butterfly, chatting with another older man.

I had had enough of this experience. I probably could have survived hours of it with the Juanita I remembered from 1942. This Viola, however, was a cool fish, who only warmed up when schmoozing with men who could help her career. An actress, in other words. I had wished her success in Hollywood. I guess this was what getting my wish looked like. I wondered how Tinsel Town had done this to her. How did it get to her—or had she done it to herself? She had been an island of decency and authenticity before, maintaining her integrity in shark-infested waters. Now she struck me as just another breed of shark.

I had spent too much time at the party, and felt icky all

over. Hanging out at the Orange Grove would be a much smarter investment of my time.

I bid the butler (another rare normal person, I thought) good-night, walked through the front door, and out into the warm California night.

CHAPTER 14: EXCAVATING JUANITA

I strolled leisurely toward the street, in no particular hurry. I breathed deep of the sea level air and gazed up at the stars and half-moon.

The front door slammed behind me and I heard clicking on pavement. "Pete? Pete!"

I stopped and turned. Viola hurried toward me, stumbling a bit on the cobblestones. "Pete! Where are you going?"

I shrugged. "Not sure. Might wander out to the beach before I head home."

"Why? What's wrong?"

I shrugged. "Don't worry about it. Go on back and enjoy yourself. Congratulations on all the film roles, by-the-way. Maybe some day I'll get to see 'em."

"I have you to thank, in a way," she said. Her voice was softer now than it had been.

"It's your talent that they see now, Miss Fontaine. It's got nothing to do with me."

"Why did you call me that?" she asked.

"That's who you are, now. Right?"

She shifted her weight onto one leg and heaved her shoulders. "Won't you come back inside?"

"Nah. Thanks, but I don't think so."

"Why not?"

"Not my cup of tea."

She chewed on her lip. "No. I suppose it isn't."

"See you in the funny papers," I said, waving as I turned to resume my stroll away from her and the party.

"Pete...wait."

I turned and sighed. "What?"

She showed me her palms. "Um, wait right here for a minute, alright? Don't go anywhere, please. I'll be right back."

I shook my head. "I told you: don't worry about it. Go do your thing. I'll do mine. No hard feelings."

She pleaded with her eyes. "Just stay right here. Humor me?"

I sighed again. "Okay."

She turned back toward the house, tripped on the cobblestones, removed her high heels, and trotted barefoot to the door. She disappeared inside. I gazed up at the night sky and felt silly for coming here. I thought of Madalina and felt sad and guilty for thinking I could rebound. This big steaming heap of disappointment was probably what I deserved.

The actress emerged from the front door again, wrapping something around her shoulders I assumed was a mink stole. She carried her shoes and a stylish purse. I turned and resumed my stroll, slow enough that she could easily catch me.

She caught up and paced herself abreast of me, her breathing a little heavy. "You're really going to go down to the beach? Why?"

"You've been in California all this time," I said. "And we're right next to a beach. Don't you ever take time to look at the moon and stars reflected off the ocean? And on such a warm, nice night like this?"

"You are such a romantic, aren't you? Right off the cobb."

I looked askance at her. She avoided my gaze, expression changing—almost like she was ashamed.

"I'm sorry, Pete. That sounded critical. But a romantic isn't a bad thing, at all. And you're right: I have seen it before and it really is impressive."

"Well, I want to look at it, since I'm here," I said.

"It is a nice evening for it," she said, still breathing a little hard.

"Did you take up smoking, too?" I asked.

"Now and then I have a cigarette," she said. "Why do you ask?"

I shook my head. "Just wondering why you get winded so easily."

We walked along the road silently for a bit, while she got her breathing under control.

Before reaching where the Chevy was parked, there was a clear area in between estates, which led down to the beach. I turned left toward the crashing breakers some 200 yards west.

She stopped. "Wait a minute, please."

I stopped. "What's cookin'?" I asked.

She grabbed my shoulder for balance. "I don't want to get sand in my nylons."

She bared one leg, then the other, and stuffed her nylons in her purse. "These are hard to come by, these days," she said. "I don't mean offense, but you seem kind of impulsive tonight."

I shrugged again. "I get that way, sometimes. Don't you?"

After a long hesitation, she mumbled, "Not really. Not anymore."

Under our feet, the grass gave way to sand.

"I thought you were enjoying the party," she said, with a catty tone.

"Why's that?"

"You seemed to be enjoying yourself with the cigarette girl."

"She was a nice girl. Not trying to impress or manipulate anybody."

"I'll say she was nice. She sure was quick to give you her number. You two must have impressed each other."

"Wow. You had time to keep track of *my* social progress in there. Now *that's* impressive."

"What is that supposed to mean?" she demanded.

"How many times did you pass out your own phone number?"

She didn't answer right away. "These get-togethers are ultimately about business."

"Yeah."

"They are," she insisted. "The movie business. When you've made it...when you're a star...you don't even have to go to them anymore. But when you're looking for your break, you've got to go out there and play the game. Mix. Make connections. Or you'll never get up the ladder."

"Ugly business," I said. "I wasn't even there for an hour, and I could tell it stinks on ice."

"Jealous?" she challenged.

I shrugged again. "Disappointed, I guess. But like I said: if it floats your boat, go right ahead. I'll go my way. No hard feelings."

"I should let you go on your way," she huffed, "if you're going to be like that."

"Why don'tcha?" I asked. "It was pretty obvious back there you've got no use for me."

We reached the surf. She took my arm.

"Oh, Pete...I'm sorry. Of course I'm very fond of you."

"Yeah, I know. Ain't I adorable?"

She scrunched her face up in confusion.

"Your comment to the butler," I reminded her.

"Oh," she said, looking away. "I didn't mean to offend you."

"Us peons have no right to feel offended when you sophisticated movie people put us in our place," I said, breezily. "In fact, we should feel flattered that you find some of us so 'adorable'."

Her gaze lowered. She appeared to be inspecting the manicure on her splayed fingers.

"All right. Fine, Pete. It was rotten of me to act like that. It's just that..."

I cut her off. "Save it. Excuses are just gonna make me sore. Do what you wanna do. Don't do what you don't wanna do. That's how you keep it on the level."

"If it's that easy for you, you must have it pretty good."

"Yeah," I agreed, sardonically. "I've got it just aces. Everything's comin' up roses."

She tightened her grip on my arm and leaned her head against it. "I need to just shut up. Every time I open my mouth, I make everything worse."

I watched the waves rolling in, reflecting the moon and stars. A warm land breeze moved the air around us.

"Were you wounded?" she asked. "You've been limping all night."

"It's better than it was just a few days ago," I said. "Bullet missed the shin bone, but nearly severed a tendon. Doc sewed it together, but warned me it's gonna be a while before I can move like I used to. Had some other junk in my lower body at first, but it's pretty much healed, now."

"I'm sorry, Pete. I've been a real shrew, not even considering what you must have seen over there."

"Don't pity me," I said. "I've been kicked around, but my brain still works, and my body, too. Soon it'll be good as new. A horse throws you off; you get right back in the saddle."

I was talking about Madalina and the Erasers, but she assumed I was talking about the war.

I did happen to be a combat veteran who had actually seen a little action on Valhalla and in America's future—just not against the Germans or Japanese. So I didn't feel guilty so much anymore about dressing like a soldier from these coordinates. Naturally she would come to the wrong conclusions about who, when, and where. Big deal. It was the "what" that counted for most, and allowed me to wear a WWII uniform without cringing.

"I'm not gonna spend the rest of my life crying in my beer about what I've seen and what happened to me," I said. "And I don't want anybody else to do the crying for me."

She let out a deep breath and softened up a little more. "All right, Pete. You want to sit down?"

"You'll get sand on your party rags," I said.

"If you'll give me a lift home, then no cabbies will see and I won't be embarrassed."

"Okay," I said, and we lowered ourselves to the ground.

"Will you be going back, once you're healed?" she asked.

I shook my head. "Naw. The Japs won't last much longer."

She brightened. "Really?"

I nodded. "We're pounding on their front door right now. They're licked, but just too proud to admit it."

She clung to my arm, still, now rubbing her cheek against my shoulder. "That's wonderful," she said. "Once they quit, there's nobody else to beat, right? The war will be over."

"The war will be over," I agreed.

"Won't that be great, Pete? Why so glum?"

I shrugged. "Nothing you'd understand. Nothing I could explain to you."

She stretched up to kiss my cheek. "We don't have to talk about it."

The tide, at its farthest advance, didn't quite reach our feet.

"You were right about the reflections off the ocean," she said. "It's a sight."

I nodded. "Last time you wrote me, you had landed a part in *Passage From Algiers*. I'm guessing you're higher up the ladder now than you were then."

"Still just playing supporting roles," she said, with a sigh. "But I've read for a couple leading roles. I did another musical and got to sing two different solos, so I'm moving up. And there's this chemical I found out about, that lightens the skin. My last treatment still hasn't worn off, so maybe…"

She trailed off. I stifled a groan. That's why she was so pale.

"What?" she asked. "The sawbones says it's safe."

I just shook my head.

"What?" she repeated.

"I miss Juanita," I said, shaking my head. "I would have liked to see her again."

"It's just part of my new look. That's all."

"I like the old look," I said.

She let go of me and leaned away, to stare at me in indignation. "You rude bastard. Damn you!"

"So you smoke *and* cuss, now. This Viola Fontaine is a class act."

She shot to her feet and brushed sand off her clothes in violent swiping motions. "I think I'll go home, now."

"Why?" I asked. "You could just go back to the party."

She whirled to storm away, but had only made it two steps before she stomped back. "Go ahead and have your fun insulting me, Pete. It so happens that this town likes exotic-sounding names, but hates exotic-looking women. They disapprove of me without a makeover; and you disapprove of me with it. That just leaves me with all kinds of choices, doesn't it?"

I stood to face her. "You should count disapproval a badge of honor from people who hate what is beautiful." I wiped some makeup off her face with my sleeve. I grabbed her wrist and shook it, so that her jewelry flashed in the moonlight. "What the hell is all this garbage—armor? You trying to protect your real self, or bury her?"

Her expression changed from angry to confused. "You're not making sense, Pete."

I let go of her wrist. "You know what I like about the cigarette girl? Out of everybody in that house, she's the one who most reminds me of Juanita."

"You keep using my name like I'm dead, or somebody else. "I'm still Juanita, Pete."

"No, you're Viola Fontaine. And I don't like Viola Fontaine very much."

Her eyes widened as she stared at me for a long, wordless moment. I didn't realize she was fighting a battle to control her face until she began to lose it. First her mouth contorted, which stretched her lips, pulled at her nose, and wrinkled her chin. This transformed into a full-faced grimace. She murmured and gasped; then the tears began to flow. She turned away to leave the beach, but I pulled her back into an embrace.

"Let go of me!" she cried out, struggling to break free of my arms.

I pulled her in tighter. She resisted, and pounded the side of her fists against me; but finally just collapsed against my torso, sobbing uncontrollably and clutching the back of my uniform as if she were terrified to let go.

I thought this might be a good sign. Maybe she still had a soul, after all Hollywood's attempts to suck it out of her and drag it to Hell.

Her tears made my jacket wet, but had little power over me. After several minutes, her sobbing subsided. As her breathing normalized, she let go and drew away from me, averting her gaze. "Would you call a cab for me?" she asked, wiping at the streaks of mascara down her face with a handkerchief and studying the wet, dark smear on the white cloth, afterwards.

I took the handkerchief from her, firmly but gently. "I'll give you a ride."

I wiped her face, from her eyelids down to her chin, removing all the makeup I could. She stood there unmoving, like a little girl recovering from a spanking, leery of further reprimand.

After my last wipe of her face, I examined her in the soft glow of the moon. Her natural beauty was still visible, with some of the armor now removed.

I held her arm and steered her up the beach, through the field, and to the Chevy. It seemed a good sign that she didn't start jabbering to cover her embarrassment in a big production of false bravado. If women had any conscious idea how much more attractive vulnerability made them, they probably wouldn't try such theatrics.

I opened the passenger door and held it for her. She took my offered hand and slid into the seat without protest or resistance. I closed the door once she was situated, walked around, and slid behind the wheel. I asked her how to get to her place and she gave me directions in a small, bare voice.

$\triangle\triangle\triangle$

I parked in the driveway of a modest one-story house in Pasadena. "You don't have a car of your own?" I asked.

She shook her head. "Not yet. Maybe I can afford one, after a few more A pictures. But the buses and trolly can take me just about anywhere I need to go."

I walked her to the door. She found her keys, then hesitated, turning to me. "Would you like to come in for a nightcap?"

"Don't feel obligated to do anything you don't want to do," I said.

She gave me a sad smile. "Sweet Pete. I know you're not a masher. And there's no roommate to worry about, here. I think I'd like some company for a few minutes."

"Okay," I said, and followed her in.

She gestured at a sofa. "Make yourself at home. What would you like?"

I shrugged. "You got rum and Coke?"

"Give me a minute," she said. "I'll fix you right up."

I sat on the sofa while she went to a bathroom. I heard water running for a moment. From there she went to a bedroom, then to the kitchen.

She sang to herself while fixing drinks.

Since the Yankee come to Trinidad
They got the young girls all goin' mad.
Young girls say they treat 'em nice,
Make Trinidad like paradise.
Drinkin' rum and Coca-Cola...

Her voice still rang just like a bell, hitting every note perfectly and effortlessly, with a *vibrato* so subtle you had to listen for it.

She brought out the drinks and sat on the sofa with me. She held out her glass and I clinked mine with it. "To an end to war," she said.

She was barefoot, had removed the jewelry and washed her face. She looked a lot better this way.

We both took a pull from our drinks.

"You're absolutely right," she said, staring into her glass.

"About what?" I asked.

"That party. Hollywood, in general. It's all a bunch of drips, creeps, and phonies. Not to mention the whores...of both sexes...literal and figurative."

"So, you *can* see it," I said.

She nodded. "I can see it. I guess...I don't know...I kind of lie to myself. I pretend 'it's all what you make of it.' I pretend I can lie down with dogs and not get up with fleas. You know how normal people have it all wrong? They think it's just the pictures that are make-believe. They don't understand that us show biz fakers are always acting—even when we're not on a sound stage. Those 'insider scoop' magazines, and the newsreels that show you footage of stars caught in natural moments away from the set? That's all fake, too."

"It rubbed off on you," I said.

"You don't have to smash my nose in it, Pete. I get it. Everything you've said to me—and probably all the stuff you didn't say—my conscience has said it already."

"So why are you still here?" I asked.

She took a sip from her glass. "You make everything sound so black & white."

"People like everything black & white right now," I said. "Tojo bad; Mao Tse-Tung good. Hitler bad; Stalin good. Nazis taking over Poland bad; commies taking over Poland good."

Her brow wrinkled momentarily and she swallowed half her remaining drink. "What am I supposed to do—go back to the farm?"

"Would that be so bad?" I asked.

She didn't answer.

"Are you happy here, Juanita?"

She smiled sadly as a tear leaked out one eye. "Thank-you

for calling me Juanita. I...well, it can be exciting, sometimes. When you get that call from a casting director. When you show up on the set, not knowing what to expect...then all the gaffers and gophers running around, while the director talks to the camera man and the sound guy. Then he talks to the actors. And he talks to you; says what he wants and needs from you in the scene. You're a part of something. You've got an important role to play. Then he yells, 'action,' and the magic starts. It's hard to explain how thrilling it can all be."

"I can understand some of it," I said, gulping down a big portion of my own glass. "I guess a better question would be: are those exciting moments worth everything else that comes with them?"

She wiped the tear away. "I don't know."

"Good singers can find jobs outside Hollywood," I said.

"As smart as you are, Pete, you're still a little naive. Show business is show business. It's just on a bigger scale, here."

I thought about this quietly for a while. "Can't you just be phony when you're in front of the camera? Then be yourself when you're not?"

"I thought I could do it that way," she said, quietly, like she was talking more to herself than to me.

I finished my drink and stood.

"You need to visit the latrine, soldier?" she asked, being facetious to lighten the mood, perhaps. Or to change the subject.

"Yeah. Then I better head out."

"One thing this town teaches a woman is that men only want one thing from us. It figures you would prove it wrong, Sweet Pete. Here you've got me alone, with some booze in me, and you're volunteering to leave." She pointed down the hall. "The bathroom's right there."

I went in, drained my bladder, washed my hands, and came out to find her waiting for me in the hall with a fresh drink.

I smiled at her gesture, but said, "Thanks just the same. But I'm still not a big drinker; and I have kind of a long drive."

"You don't have to drink and run," she said. "I won't kick

you out. I'm a big girl. And Uncle Sam certainly thinks you're responsible enough to handle a lot more than a little bit of rum."

I studied her, and understood what she was offering. To make the matter crystal clear, she said, "I appreciate your nobility, Pete; but I don't expect you to be a gentleman. Should I spell it out for you? Fine. I honestly don't *want* you to be a gentleman, either."

CHAPTER 15: VIOLA WINS

I took her in my arms, right there in the hallway. She gave me a smoky look, as our faces drew together. Her eyes didn't close until our lips touched.

I don't remember what happened to my second rum & Coke. We undressed each other down the length of the hallway and didn't even unfasten from each other long enough to gracefully mount the bed.

Juanita was more genuine that night than she had been since I got back. But she still wasn't the same woman I remembered. Aside from the physical changes, her performance in the sack was pretty experienced for a virgin. Which meant she was probably not a virgin when I got my first dose of her. Not that I prefer virgins anyway. It just disappointed me a bit. She probably gave it away on a casting couch to some fat slob who lasted five minutes and forgot her name just as quickly—all so she could be promoted up from Second Chorus Girl From the Left in a dancing scene.

Her lack of innocence did not interfere with our enjoyment at all. It was probably cathartic for both of us. I still hurt over the loss of Madalina and the baby. The intimate attention of a woman was a welcome distraction, and a much needed emotional release. For her, maybe sex that wasn't transactional was a big improvement and an emotional fulfillment to some degree or another.

She cried after the first time we made love, but clung to me with desperate strength. I just held her for a while after that, and eventually she began talking. She rambled on about her feelings, until she seemingly inspired herself to go for another round. We dozed for a while after that. Then she woke me in the best possible way.

We slept in late the next morning, then made it again. We showered, ate breakfast; then attacked each other, winding up back in bed one more time.

We were both in good spirits when we cleaned up again for lunch. She held onto my hand or my arm, played with my hair, and sat in my lap, just the way an infatuated woman will do. The way they all would, if they wanted to keep a man. We made silly jokes and laughed together.

At one point I asked if there was anything she needed to do for work. She said her latest gig had wrapped. Normally she would call her agent, or go "be seen" in the right places, to land her next job. But, she said, she was having more fun with me.

ΔΔΔ

When I did return to the Orange Grove, I jumped a warp back to the same night I left, so Mami wouldn't worry, and so I could spend more time with her and my siblings.

Mami asked me how the date went, and I told her it went pretty well. She said I looked happier than when I first arrived. She suggested I should have Juanita over some time.

I went back to Juanita and spent three weeks with her. It didn't make me forget about Madalina, but it helped. She smiled and laughed a lot, and so did I.

I took her dancing, and record shopping. Sometimes we just sat around listening to music. We both lamented the loss of Glenn Miller, but Juanita held out hope that he had been in a German POW camp and would show up any day now. We went to the beach together, on picnics, to an amusement park, and on drives as far as San Diego and the Redwood Forest. I was on leave, as far as she knew, and in no hurry to go anywhere or do anything in particular.

I lost track of time, and so it was that one day when I took her shopping, we heard a ruckus outside the department store we happened to be in. People were gathering on the street outside. They clapped, raised their arms, hooted and even danced. Cars stopped; drivers honked their horns like it was New Years (even though it was August), then stepped outside, leaving their doors open and engines running.

Juanita and I shared a perplexed look.

"People around here don't do that for movie stars," she said. "Maybe President Truman is in town?"

We stepped outside, along with everyone else still in the store.

In the 21st century there were "flash mobs." This impromptu celebration had the same kind of energy, but there was no attempt to synchronize dance moves.

Somebody waved a newspaper around, but I couldn't make out the headline. A radio blared from a hardware store, but with all the honking and cheering, I couldn't understand the announcer's words.

I grabbed the elbow of a passing sailor, who was howling at the sky like a wolf, clutching an open bottle of whiskey by the neck.

"Say, Mack: what goes on?" I asked.

He turned to me, looked me up and down, and said, "The Japs surrendered. we used some kind of secret weapon on 'em—blew 'em to smithereens. The war's over!"

Juanita's gaze turned from him to me. Her eyes widened.

"Say, doll," the sailor said to her, "you rationed?"

She wound her arm around mine and said, "Sorry—I'm afraid so."

He walked away toward another woman.

"Lucky for that anchor-clanker, there's plenty of girls to choose from," Juanita said.

I glanced around the spontaneous celebration. Even in a city swamped with young men from every service, the ratio was still about three-to-one in favor of the fairer sex. In my mind,

I pictured the famous photo of the sailor in Times Square who sucked the lips off some random, unsuspecting woman during V-J Day.

"There sure are," I agreed. "More than enough to go around. He's sure to get lucky. I might, too."

She backed away from me, cocked her hips, put one hand on her waist, and twisted her lips while glaring at me.

I pointed to a blonde across the street. "You think she'd resist if I just walked up, grabbed her and stole a kiss?"

Juanita's eyes narrowed. "You'd better save that for *your* girl, soldier. Now plant one on me, if you know what's good for you."

We made out right in the middle of the street. It was something unheard of at these coordinates, only acceptable at that moment because the euphoric *zeitgeist* had hit such a dramatic peak.

"You were right. It's finally over," she breathed, when we broke the kiss. "We met because of the war. I didn't see you for three years because of the war. Now it's over and you won't die in some god-forsaken jungle 8,000 miles away."

She peered at me, curiously.

"What's the matter, Pete? Aren't you glad it's over? You don't have to go back. I would think you'd be jumping for joy."

"Sure, I'm ecstatic," I said, wishing I could be as happy as people from these coordinates. But I knew too much. "The world is free. There are blue birds over the white cliffs of Dover."

"Say, I don't get it," she said. "What's eating you?"

I shook my head dismissively. "Don't worry about it. I guess it's time to celebrate."

"Now you're talking," she said. "How do we want to celebrate?"

Now I smiled, coming up with the answer to her question: "Why don't you come meet my family?"

ΔΔΔ

The timestream had caught up to the model of refrigerator in Mami's kitchen. And as long as nobody got a peek at the vehicles in Dad's garages or the temperature wheel and generator, I figured it was safe to have a guest over.

I spent some extra dimes at a pay phone calling the Orange Grove, and asked Mami to set an extra plate for supper. She hesitated to break Dad's rule about visitors; but I assured her it would be okay. Her eagerness to meet my girlfriend probably helped convince her to make an exception. After I hung up, Juanita remarked that she had no idea I could speak Spanish. I warned her that Mami could speak a little English, but not always fluently.

I drove Juanita out to the orange grove. Her hair was too short for my liking, but she hadn't dyed it again, and normal shampooing had washed the red out of it. Her skin was even starting to gain back its golden luster.

I introduced her to Mami and my siblings as we sat around the radio listening to a big band program and some news reports. Mami asked questions, and I translated between them. Wyatt and the girls could speak English fine. They had plenty of questions, too.

We ate supper together, listened to *The Lone Ranger*, and had "a grand time," as many people at these coordinates would say.

While driving Juanita home, she said, "You would never know you're adopted, the way your mother dotes on you. And Wyatt does sort of resemble you."

"Who says I'm adopted?"

"Well, your hair and complexion, for two. Remember: I figured this out three years ago."

I shrugged. She was right on all counts.

"Watching you with your family," she said, staring out the windshield at the stars, "it makes me want to have that, too."

"Have what?"

"A family."

"You've got a family, back in the Four Corners. Right?"

"Yes. But I mean I want one of my own. My own children. My own husband. There's no more war. Maybe this is the time to settle down."

I took my eyes off the road for a moment to study her. "Are you on the level?"

She nodded, smiling.

"You're ready to give up Hollywood?"

"I think I'd rather have what your mother has," she said. "At least what she'll have when her husband gets back."

"And do you have anybody in mind for a husband?"

"Maybe," she replied, grinning.

"And how soon would you like to do this?"

She continued gazing out the windshield with a dreamy expression. "Mmm...first we should find a house. Somewhere between your parents' place and Shiprock."

That narrows it down," I said.

"It's got to have pretty scenery," she said. "Out in the country, but with electricity and indoor plumbing."

"That's all the rage, now," I said.

"Probably up in the mountains. Then, an engagement of a month or two—time for our families to make arrangements. My parents will definitely want it in a church. Our church outside Shiprock, if you don't have something different in mind."

I shrugged.

"A honeymoon in Cairo, in a brand new autogiro," she sang, "then off to Rio for a drink. We'll settle down near Dallas, in a little plastic palace..."

"Your geography is a little off," I said.

She scooted over and leaned against me, her head on my shoulder. "Oh, it's not as crazy as you think."

"Now who's corny?" I asked.

"Next year we can stop being careful," she suggested, in a sexy tone. "If I conceive at the right time, we can have our first child in the spring."

"How many kids you wanna have?" I asked.

"Oh, I don't know. At least two, I think. We can decide if we want more after that."

"This seems pretty rushed," I said. "You sure you're ready for such a big step?"

"Not with anybody else. Just with you, Pete. Don't you want that with me?"

I liked the sound of everything she was saying. Just getting her away from the movie crowd for a while had restored a lot of her inner beauty. She looked more and more like a woman who should have my children. Once the Hollywood was completely out of her, she would be a woman I'd love to come home to. Maybe she could exorcise the ghosts of Madalina and Sylvia.

"I'll buy that dream," I said.

Yeah, I was rebounding. And that night was the zenith, for Juanita and me.

The next day, I set about finding a house for us that fit her requirements. I also began working on a romantic evening for me to formally pop the question. My biggest concern was whether or not I could trust her implicitly enough to tell her everything. If so, we could relocate to Happy Ever After. It wouldn't go to waste.

When I returned from my first scouting trip, I found out about the call she received from her agent. She was excited and even more celebratory than before: she had been offered the leading lady role in a swashbuckling pirate movie alongside one of the top leading men—perhaps a little past his prime, but still a box office draw, and athletic enough to pull it off.

This was her big break, finally.

"I thought you were done with Hollywood," I reminded her. "You wanted what my mother has."

Oh, she still felt the same about that, she informed me. But couldn't I understand? She had been working so hard for this break. Opportunities like this only happened once—but for most people, not ever. Now it was there to grasp and she dare not miss it. After the film wrapped, we could go on with our plans. She would have achieved what she set out to, and could leave the show business life on a high note.

I could understand. That's how I had been about football. I didn't savvy the appeal of show biz, once you knew how slimy it was under the surface. But then, plenty of people didn't understand the appeal of playing football, either.

I continued trying to set stuff up, and for a while it remained good between us. But once shooting started on the movie, she became increasingly distant, if not cold.

Reality finally dawned on me.

If I clung to our little fantasy of love and family, she would grow tired of my persistence and eventually resent me. I knew what happened after that. If I passed this shit test and she fought to avoid losing me, as she had outside the party, then I would be stepping onto a roller coaster ride that might never end. Maybe I could win out over Tinsel Town one day, but was the struggle worth it? How old and unhappy would I be by then?

I didn't want a roller coaster ride—even as just a spinning plate.

I abandoned my foolish plans for a house and honeymoon, and quit Juanita cold turkey. A clean break would ache for a while; but would be the most merciful way to end it in the long term.

ΔΔΔ

I returned to the Orange Grove to continue my visit, and think about my life.

We were all pleasantly surprised when Dad showed up. He arrived like a returning soldier—just as I had. Mami cried tears of joy, as did the girls. Wyatt and I were also quite happy to have him back.

Juanita called the house a couple times. Dad, instinctively understanding the situation, told her I wasn't there and he didn't know where I was.

I explained the situation to him later—from losing Madalina and the baby, to my whirlwind romance (Part II) with

Juanita. He was surprisingly understanding about it all.

"It's hard to resist the fantasy, Sprout. White picket fences. Country picnics. Unconditional love. The best women can make you believe in all that. It's not easy to give up on that dream."

I sighed and changed the subject. "You think Dr. Lee is right about how me and Madalina got on the CPB's radar?"

"It seems like the most sensible explanation right now," he said, shrugging.

"You can call me stupid for taking her to Densus," I said. "I deserve that, and worse."

"It's not like I haven't been stupid myself," Dad said. "And most of the stupid stuff I've ever done involved a woman. As much as I wish I could give you all the benefits of my experience...there's just some stuff you have to go through yourself, before you'll believe me. Even though you're...well, anyway, it doesn't matter now."

"What doesn't matter?" I asked.

He shrugged again. "Anything. There's no point to anything. Everything is meaningless. And evil always wins, in the end. We can cheat Fate for a while, but she'll find us eventually. The best we can do is have some fun before she does."

"Fate found me, I guess," I said. "Found Madalina. Took her from me. And our baby girl. Got in between me and Juanita, too."

I didn't fully appreciate how tired Dad was, I guess. He fell asleep right there on the chair before saying anything else.

It wasn't that way for me. I lay awake late into the night, thinking about what he said, and scrutinizing my own thoughts.

That was the last chance we had to talk. He took Mami out on the town the next day/night, while I watched the kids. The next morning, he was gone again.

CHAPTER 16: I FIRST
GO A-VIKING

I guess, if somebody had a reason to check, and mid-'60s technology and record keeping been up to the task, they could have discovered that Ike Jaeger was in two places at once that summer. But why would they?

While I was, technically, back East/down South completing Flight School, I also showed up in Bemidji State University to attend training camp with the Minnesota Vikings. They had drafted me in the 18th round.

Head Coach Norm Van Brocklin greeted me with a handshake and a, "You better not turn out to be a pussy, Jaeger."

The Minnesota franchise was young—having only started as an expansion team three years before...when I was a sophomore at Poly. They were an *ad-hoc* team of rookies and has-beens skimmed from around the league. The NFL had rejected previous attempts to start a franchise in the area...until the AFL came courting. Suddenly, the NFL had a change of heart and seduced Minnesota away from the upstart league in 1960. The hostile takeover shook up the draft for both leagues. The Vikings began play the next season with a hodge-podge collection of athletes.

Nearly every professional team represented a specific city; but the Vikings would represent an entire state. Nevertheless, their home games would be played in Minneapolis, at

Metropolitan Stadium.

While a member of the staff was showing me around the facilities, he informed me that the "Viking" mascot was inspired by the dominant Scandinavian demographic which had settled in Minnesota back in the frontier days.

When an assistant coach took me back to the equipment cage for pads, helmets, uniforms and practice jerseys, I now remembered having seen the team play a few Sundays in the lounge at the dorm. I had assumed the team uniform was black (since the lounge TV was black & white) but now realized it was purple. The artwork on the helmet was simple—white horns, like what Norsemen wore on their battle helmets in artists' depictions—if not in reality.

Though the team was young, and had relatively modern equipment, the head coach was in stark contrast. Van Brocklin came from the rough-and-tumble postwar school of professional football. When he was a rookie, helmets didn't have faceguards, and his team at that time (the Los Angeles Rams) was the very first to decorate their helmets with a logo, only the year before. Players were still wearing leather helmets when he played in high school.

Van Brocklin skipped his senior year to serve in the Navy during WWII. He was an All-American in college, played in the Cotton Bowl, and finished sixth in the Heisman rankings.

Players, sports reporters, and other coaches called him "the Dutchman"—but not to his face. He had a foul mouth, a foul temper, and a foul opinion about newfangled ideas in the game. He was a chain-smoker—actually smoking on the sidelines during games as he insulted players from both teams. Players smoked and drank in the dorms, too, sometimes showing up at practice hung over. Coach Van Brocklin was not a stickler for self-discipline.

I noticed pretty quick that many players feared him, but few respected him as a coach—especially the youngest players. Being a bench-warming rookie from an obscure school with a College Division team, nobody confided in me; but the general scenario at Minnesota was easy for me to read.

One player who didn't care for Van Brocklin much was the third round draft pick who was unveiled as a professional quarterback during exactly the same game that the Vikings were unveiled as a professional team. His name, which sounded vaguely familiar to me, was Fran Tarkenton.

Van Brocklin didn't care much for Tarkenton. He didn't appreciate many of his younger players. In fact, the younger they were, the more he seemed to despise them. His verbal abuse could be pretty intense—and went beyond Stauchel's occasional tirades meant to scare or motivate his players.

Nobody liked being dressed down and referred to as one of "the 36 stiffs,", but the rookies and second year players hated it the most.

The Dutchman wasn't big on physical conditioning, either. I had kept in good shape just through the discipline of training Dad had instilled in me, so the Dutchman's program didn't challenge me at all. But morale was still extremely low on the Viking practice field. The psychological factor made it at least as miserable as Stauchel's physically grueling program.

In the environment under Van Brocklin, there didn't seem to be any trace of the camaraderie which normally accompanied football.

In some circumstances, a group of men such as this might have bonded together, with resentment of the Dutchman's verbal abuse their common ground. That's how it was for the Pumas, that first training camp under Coach Stauchel. But for whatever reason, the team I found myself on wasn't united. Most of them seemed to just want to be somewhere else. Most of the Vikings didn't act like historic Vikings at all. More like French nobles who got their asses kicked, their villages burned, and their women raped by Vikings. A few players, however, did live and play very much like what one might expect from our namesake seafaring barbarians.

The Dutchman's organization resembled a street gang more than a football team. The coach ruled through intimidation. Players could drink, smoke, chew, stay out all night chasing broads, and nobody cared—so long as they showed up more-or-less on-time for game days, ready to bust heads and make the other guys bleed.

I was pretty much all alone; but that was okay for the time being. Still stinging from the loss of Madalina and the baby, disappointed about Juanita, and disillusioned by the Kennedy assassination and everything I learned afterwards, I wasn't exactly comrade material for a while.

△△△

I landed an assignment to the Minnesota Air National Guard, and my C.O. arranged that my schedule wouldn't conflict with any regular season games. He was an Ace from the European Campaign, and about the coolest commanding officer a young pilot could hope for.

Orders were cut to put me in the front seat of an F89H Scorpion, as part of a fighter squadron. The subsonic Northrop jet was an all-missile, two-seater, twin turbojet interceptor designed in the 1940s. I had never heard of it before because, frankly, it wasn't all that exceptional as a fighter jet. It was intended to defend against Soviet bombers; so nobody would ever really know how effective it would be in its primary mission. Obsolescence came fast in the world of military fixed-wing combat aircraft (as opposed to, say, tanks or battle rifles); so the other pilots were already talking about the Scorpion being replaced when I first got there.

I hadn't flown many jets, so it was kind of neat. I enjoyed wargames, formation flying, and some of the training sorties we flew. It was all pointless, of course; but what wasn't, during the Cold War against an enemy propped up by the same government that trained me and paid for my plane? Might as well have some fun.

△△△

Even though Minnesota was one of the weaker teams in the league, watching games from the bench was more exciting than watching them on TV. Of course, I would have rather been out there on the field myself.

Football was fun; but it looked like I wouldn't get much chance to play it. Tarkenton was the starting quarterback and probably a better leader than I could be. Still, watching Frantic Fran play was fascinating. He was cut out to be an AFL quarterback, and under-appreciated in the stodgy old league he found himself in. He accomplished a lot with very little; and never stopped scheming for a way to make plays on the field.

Minnesota's rag-tag offensive line didn't give Tarkenton much protection. Any other quarterback would have been hurried into throwing interceptions and incomplete passes when not getting sacked. But Tarkenton was determined to keep the ball moving downfield. He was a pioneer in the art of "scrambling." When the pocket collapsed (as it invariably did), he put his feet to work, leading defenders on a merry chase all over the backfield, until he either saw one of his mediocre receivers get open and launched the ball, or saw an avenue across the line of scrimmage, tucked the ball, and ran for positive yardage. He was something of a Houdini. Many times I thought for sure he had been tackled, only to see him escape and make a play. He was small, by pro football standards, and very agile. He was on his way to the Pro Bowl that year.

Van Brocklin was like Stauchel in at least one respect: he wanted his quarterback to stand in the pocket, no matter what. He berated Tarkenton on every offensive series for "running around like a chickenshit."

The defenses we played against didn't like Tarkenton much, either. Most defensive linemen were huge, plodding hogs who were easily exhausted if called on to pursue somebody more than a few yards. Scrambling Fran gave them fits.

On *our* defense, however, we had a lineman who did not fit that mold. Number 70, Jim Marshall, was quick for a defensive end. He was also durable. A second year player when the Vikings first took the field, he had played every game and attended every practice—and would for many, many years, setting an NFL record. He was fun to watch, as well.

One time he was not so fun to watch was at Kezar Stadium in San Francisco my first season with the Vikings.

For all Tarkenton's efforts during that road game in October, our offense just wasn't moving the ball. But lucky for us, the defense was showing some real promise my rookie year. They dominated the 49ers and forced eight turnovers. One of those turnovers resulted from Marshall sacking San Francisco quarterback John Brodie, who coughed up the ball. One of my fellow Viking rookies (defensive end and first-round draft pick Carl Eller) recovered the fumble and ran 45 yards for a touchdown. Eller was quick for a lineman, too.

On the very next 49er possession, our defense backed them up against their own goal line. Brodie connected with Billy Kilmer in the flat, but our defensive backs were on him immediately, and stripped the ball. Marshall had given up his pursuit of the quarterback when Brodie got the pass off, and charged up the field to follow the action. He arrived just as Kilmer was going down. Marshall came to a stop. Then the ball came loose, bounced up off the turf, and Marshall resumed forward motion. He scooped the ball up smoothly, perfectly, clamping his big right hand around it and running for open field. He ran 66 yards into the end zone with no pursuit, then hurled the ball into the stands to celebrate.

The only problem was, he had run to the wrong end zone, and scored a safety for the 49ers, not a touchdown for the Vikings.

He had reversed direction in the backfield to catch up with the ball carrier—traveling in the same direction that the opposing team was trying to go. He must have become disoriented or confused somewhere along the way. Without thinking beforehand, I jumped off the bench onto my feet, shouting, "No! No! They've got the short end of the field! We have the long end!"

Obviously, he didn't hear me, or any of his other teammates yelling at him. He didn't realize what he had done until, walking out of the end zone, a smarmy San Francisco player with a shit-eating grin thanked him for the two points. I saw his shoulders slump from across the field and could imagine the humiliation he must have felt.

I forced myself not to stare at him when he returned to the sidelines, not wanting to add to his embarrassment. Van Brocklin had some words for him—probably some kind of degrading insult, but I couldn't hear it over the nasty heckling of the crowd.

To Jim's credit, he trotted back out there on the next defensive series and played hard—as he would for the rest of the game. He sacked Brodie again before all was said and done. Despite the gimme points and free kick for our opponents, we still hung on to win, thanks to the masterful performance by Marshall and the defense.

The wags on TV and in the print media had cruel fun at Jim's expense for years to come. It seemed to me a crime that one of the greatest players of all time would evidently be remembered for one stupid mistake ("Wrong-Way Marshall" they called him). I made an effort to be friendly to him after that when we had occasion to interact.

I was impressed with how quickly he was able to shake off the stigma and shame from that blunder. He didn't need patronizing from some 18th round rookie, and made that clear by his increasingly taciturn responses to my greetings and praise for great plays.

△△△

I knew that Minnesota was cold in the winter. Those pick-up hockey games I played in Bloomington taught me how brutal it could be. The temperature was low, of course, in that northern state; and the humidity from all the lakes (I guess) made it worse. The bitter, wet cold made you feel like your bones were about to snap—especially in your fingers and toes. During home games I did a lot of jogging in place, and shaking of my arms to keep the blood flow going. We had heaters on the sidelines, which could let you feel a little warmth on your back; but it was still miserable.

The awful conditions at Metropolitan Stadium made it rough on other teams too, though. Nobody liked coming to play us in the late season games. The field could ice up, or become covered in snow in the space of one quarter. The turf was as hard as concrete when you got tackled into it. Even with cleats, it was sometimes hard to get traction. Coaches who brought their teams to play us in November and December could probably empathize with Napoleon retreating from Moscow. The Minnesota Hawk was like the Russian winter—our 12th man on the field.

When Cleveland came to play us at the Met, our defense had to deal with Jim Brown.

In "football weather" like we had in Minnesota, the ball was frozen. The quarterback's hands were frozen. The receiver's feet might be frozen if they'd been sitting on the bench for more than a few minutes. Even your ears were frozen, inside the helmet. The passing game was almost non-existent in extremely harsh cold. You had to be able to run the ball if you wanted to win a game out there with the Hawk in effect.

With Jim Brown, Cleveland could definitely run the ball. The man was a machine.

Brown could wear you down physically *and* psychologically. He always took his time climbing to his feet after a play, then trudging to the huddle. You hoped he was tired, or maybe even injured, because you didn't want him pounding the ball down your throat again on the next down. But his painfully slow movement in between plays inevitably led to an explosion out of the backfield once the ball was hiked.

I swear he went for an entire half without being tackled. But then the Hawk redoubled its efforts. The field became ice, covered with snow. A bitter arctic wind swept through the stadium, slicing right through our flesh as if we were naked, whistling in our ear holes as if to mock us. Some of the veteran players began growling a chant of "Odin, Odin, Odin..." as if the Norse gods were going to intervene in the game.

The next time Jim Brown got the ball, our linebackers converged on him in an epic collision. The pop of helmets was so loud I assumed one of them cracked. Brown didn't go down. His legs kept churning—reminding me of the way Dozier ran—but his cleats couldn't get traction. While spinning his wheels on the frozen turf as if trying to skate uphill, our defenders escorted him to the sidelines. His feet finally skidded out from under him as they shoved him out of bounds.

No thanks to me, the Vikings finished the 1964 season with its first-ever winning record.

Football up there wasn't as fun for me as it had been at Poly; but in some ways it was more interesting. Despite confinement to the bench, the harsh weather, the lack of team unity, and the despotic head coach, I decided to stick around for a while.

CHAPTER 17: OFF-SEASON

E ven with all the other stuff going on in the world, I still followed pro football. I was a fan as well as a player. After the 1963 season, the Chicago Bears edged out the New York Giants 14-10 at Wrigley Field for the NFL crown. I didn't care much for either team. But I liked both teams that played for the AFL title at Balboa Park. It turned out to be a bloodletting. The Chargers finally won a championship by annihilating the Boston Patriots 51-10.

After running roughshod over us that frozen day in the '64 season, Jim Brown romped for 114 yards and caught three passes during the NFL Championship in Cleveland to help the Browns blank the Colts 27-0.

The defending champion Chargers entered the next AFL Championship with a weak record and without their star receiver, Lance "Bambi" Alworth. Nevertheless, San Diego began play like a team that had finally discovered the secret sauce for winning championships, putting together a four play, 80 yard touchdown drive in the first quarter to put them on top 7-0 early. Then, on their next possession, Charger running back Keith Lincoln suffered a horrific, rib-breaking hit by linebacker Mike Stratton that not only took him out of the game; but wound up being known as "the hit heard round the world." The hit was one of those demoralizing setbacks that psychologically devastates a team. I felt bad for Lincoln, and for the hard-luck Chargers. But I cheered for the undefeated Buffalo Bills, with the toughest defense in the league and an offensive line anchored by Gus

Bartok. San Diego fell apart, and didn't score again.

I treated Dozier to a box seat ticket and we watched the game live, in War Memorial Stadium.

I hung out with Dozier for a few days over Christmas break. We shared war stories about our respective seasons.

The Pumas had put together another winning record, but with three losses failed to make a bowl game. It was Lancer's last year at Poly, too. He got picked up by the Denver Broncos, while Kiley had been drafted by the Atlanta Falcons in the 10th round the year before. He and Bartok were the only starters out of all the Pumas who went pro. The rest of us who went pro— including Sapper and Hussar—were picked up on-the-cheap for the second string.

It was Stauchel's last year at Poly, too. One of the big schools lured him away after noticing what he had done with his undersized *podunk* squad.

I asked Dozier what he hoped to do after college. At his size, weight, and speed, he didn't think he had any chance of playing professional ball. He was lucky to play in college. Sadly, he was probably right. He was a greater player than anybody could ever guess based on physical stats; but no coach besides Stauchel was ever likely to consider that. Dozier revealed that he was thinking of joining the Marines.

I did my best to talk him out of it, explaining how the Vietnam deployment would develop. But, he pointed out, if he didn't volunteer first, he would be drafted and likely used as cannon fodder anyway. He asked me what I had done and I told him about the Air National Guard.

Dozier's interest was piqued by my status as a pilot. He asked a lot of questions about flying.

We promised to stay in touch, and I left to make the rounds with Dad's families.

△△△

I had no mail from Juanita at the Orange Grove, and Mami

said she had stopped calling. That confirmed she had moved on.

I cruised Bakersfield in the GTO while visiting my family there. I put in some lab time at BH Station with Dr. Torstenson, and some gym time with Paulo, while visiting Carmen and the kids.

I delivered another cargo planeload to Winfield's rebel guerrillas. I was pleased to notice they looked less malnourished this time. The PacFor in that region had actually fallen back to a different base, because the Jayhawkers had been so successful at their interdiction missions of late. Tyler's sister and their parents were now able to operate their farm free of Chinese interference...whether or not Tyler was out on missions.

I delivered every item on Winfield's wish list, in bulk. They were astonished, and grateful—even Garth, who never trusted me.

△△△

I spent most of my nights, and a lot of my off-time in general, on Valhalla. Most of my Earth-time was spent at BH Station.

I completed the prototype of my miniature warp generator. In my first tests, I jumped some inanimate objects to nearby coordinates—like a football from inside a lab to about a quarter mile away and 10 minutes into the future. I was able to be there to see the football appear at the destination point of the warp jump. After a few successful tests, my first living test subject was an annoying Chihuahua.

The dog didn't make it. With more density than the football, I needed more energy to get it across the warp. It was then I realized I had to program a failsafe so that the generator wouldn't initiate a warp if the object or creature to be transported had too much mass for the power source.

After uploading the space-time mapping software to my miniature generator, the major obstacle I had to deal with was developing a battery powerful enough to open a warp for a man, his clothes, and any sort of weaponry on him.

Doctors Torstenson, Lee, and Manfredi, all intrigued by my project, put their heads together with me to come up with a solution. The first step was to thoroughly evaluate my blueprints.

My Mini Warp, as I called it, was already pretty efficient. But by replacing some microchips and other components, we reduced the amount of current required. Next, we developed the harness.

The harness strapped around the waist and over the shoulders, securing flexible panels against the body. The panels contained battery banks. By using a test dummy with the same mass and density as a man, we were able to successfully warp it to separate coordinates. We then tested the harness on a pig (destined for slaughter anyway), and successfully warped it, as well. We were able to warp it as far as from BH Station to Valhalla. (Actually, the amount of energy needed to warp an object seven millennia or light years distant wasn't that much more than what was needed to send it 10 minutes and a quarter mile away, because of the overlap of dimensions we bridged through. Everything was "close" when you had access to an additional seven dimensions. It was *accessing* those dimensions, to bypass the fourth, that was the primary power drain.)

So, fully charged, the harness could provide enough juice to the Mini Warp for a jump. But it couldn't handle two jumps on one charge. Obviously, this was a dilemma. I couldn't think of any circumstance in which I would want to take a one-way trip through the continuum.

The Mini Warp already had electrical contacts that interfaced (via the harness) with the body it had to transport. We added contacts that let energy flow in the opposite direction —energy in the form of body heat, that could be converted to electricity to charge the batteries. Dr. Lee also came up with a flexible solar panel that could be rolled up or folded to fit inside whatever the traveler was carrying with them.

But using solar power or body heat to fully recharge

the batteries could take quite a while. Dr. Torstenson replaced the inverter with an adjustable one, and added a variety of connectors (including glorified jumper cables) to the harness. For a faster charge, the traveler could now tie into different power sources—including foreign and American house current via wall socket.

We tested it multiple times before I finally used it myself. I chose to jump from B.H. Station, 2016, to Sierra Leone, 1964. If I couldn't get back, for whatever reason, I could simply take a ship or plane back to my adopted coordinates in the States.

The jump left me dizzy, with a headache. But I had made it. My clothes and body parts were all in the right place, and I was in Sierra Leone.

I found it unusually quiet around Dayvon's house and outbuildings. I knocked on doors, but nobody answered. The place was deserted.

Not knowing what else to do, I walked to the village.

Some villagers were out, attending to normal chores, but the village seemed mostly deserted, too. However, I heard a murmur of many voices from the church building. I approached the church door. Before I got there, it opened, and my Mona Lisa came out.

Once again, it thrilled me how radiant her smile was, just like the first time. She bounded down the steps and ran to me. I hardly had time to adjust to seeing her...how good she looked, and how happy her presence made me in a world where the Big Spooky was gradually building strength everywhere...before she embraced me. My thoughts and emotions went erratic, overwhelming me with sensory and psychological input. I know my reaction must have been exaggerated because of my present loneliness, but it felt so good to touch her I held her for longer than would normally be accepted.

While hugging her, the dizziness came back.

She let go and backed away to arm's length, but still holding my hands while she studied my face and eyes. I had a lot of questions, but before I could ask the first one, she said,

"I wasn't going anywhere, Isaac. I could feel you were here; and came out to see you. That is all."

"That's all?" I shook my head. "You could *feel* I was here?"

She nodded, still gazing deeply into my eyes. Then she frowned. "You wondered why I came outside. That is why." She smiled at me a moment longer, then sobered. "Grandfather, father, and most of the clan is in Freetown. My mother and I...nearly all the women, are here." She turned her head in a gesture to indicate the church behind her. "We're praying for Grandfather."

"Well, if you're praying for something, I'm sure you'll get it," I said. Then I thought about her look of concern and the implication of her words. "Why? What's going on?"

"Our Prime Minister, Sir Milton Margai, has passed away," she said. "His brother, Albert, took over the position, but..." She blinked and contorted her lips. She seemed fearful and uncertain.

I guided her toward the steps and sat down, pulling her down to sit facing me. "Hey, hey...what's the matter, Niki?"

She took in a deep breath and let it out, closing her eyes. "I don't understand it all, Isaac. Grandfather helped write a Constitution. He got Sir Milton and the government to accept it as the law. Now Albert is violating it. There is much conflict in the government. We are afraid there will be violence...that Grandfather might be attacked or..."

I could feel the anxiety sweeping through this normally happy-go-lucky woman. I squeezed her hand and caressed her knuckles.

"Do you feel he's in danger?"

She blinked several times, and nodded.

"What can I do to help?" I asked.

"I don't know," she said.

"Should I go to Freetown?" I asked. "I'll be one of his bodyguards, if necessary."

She bit her lower lip, glanced back at the church, then looked at me. "Will you come inside?"

"Huh?"

"Please come inside," she said, standing and tugging on my hands.

I stood, checking to make sure my M1911 was still in place, concealed under my loose, tropical shirt. I followed her into the church, brain still trying to catch up with all the new information.

Women were all over the inside of the church. Some were on their knees with clasped hands. Others paced back-and-forth between the wooden pews, gesticulating and mumbling quietly. Most of them had their eyes closed. I assumed the preacher was the only man present—standing toward the front, facing the sanctuary. He waved his hands and spoke loudly in a language I couldn't place, with his eyes closed.

"What is this?" I whispered.

"They are praying," she whispered back.

A woman whose eyes were open stared at me. One by one, everyone else opened their eyes. The room fell silent as they realized a stranger was among them. Niki's mother looked at me and approached us, curious gaze bouncing between me and Niki.

"Isaac is here," Niki said, hopefully. "He wants to know how he can help."

The woman's expression softened. She took her daughter's hand, touched my face tenderly, then settled her hand on my shoulder and bowed her head. Another woman bowed her head and rested her hand on my other shoulder. A third woman took my elbow and bowed her head. The women gathered around me until I was completely surrounded. They took my arms. I felt several hands on my back. They closed their eyes and mumbled.

One of Niki's aunts spoke clearly, her voice rising above the murmur. "Oh Lord, this man doesn't know you; but we understand you appointed him to come into Nikiruka's life. We ask You, if You sent him during this season of fear and trouble, to guide him into Your will. We know you can use the lost, just like you used that heathen, Nebuchadnezzar. Use Isaac to carry out your will, if that's why you brought him here."

Eyes closed, she kept talking and the other women kept muttering, for some time. At first, I was pretty uncomfortable, and I felt condescension against the women for their primitive faith. But a few minutes in, I also bowed my head and closed my eyes, out of respect for them and what they obviously believed, down deep inside. What could it hurt? I silently prayed too, just in case there was a God and He was listening.

I don't know how long it lasted; but when it was over, some of the women smiled at me. Some of them wiped tears from their eyes and hugged me. Some said, "God bless you."

In a stupefied daze, I let Niki escort me out of there.

"Are you okay?" she asked me, taking my hand as we took the trail into the foliage.

"Fine," I replied. "I just don't know what you all need me to do. And that scene back there was confusing...and a bit overwhelming."

"You felt the presence of the Spirit," she said. "That is what overwhelmed you."

"What spirit?" I asked.

"The Holy Spirit," she said, in a tone she might use with a child.

"Okay...was it supposed to tell me something?"

"I think He will guide you," she said.

"What makes you think so?"

She beamed at me. "While we prayed, I felt peace again. I have not felt peace since we first learned about Sir Albert and Grandfather."

"I guess that's nice for you," I said, "but it doesn't help me know what I should do."

"Don't worry, Isaac. You don't have to solve the entire problem by yourself, with full knowledge beforehand. Use what you know, and do what you can. The Spirit will meet you where you are, and either reveal to you what else to do, or add what you can do to His overall plan."

"You keep calling this spirit 'he.' Like it's a person."

"He is a person—part of the Trinity. You've heard of the Trinity?"

I shrugged. "Yeah." The America I had been living in was still a majority Christian country, so I couldn't help but overhear people refer to "the Godhead," "Holy Trinity," or "Father, Son, and Holy Ghost."

"What do you know about the Holy Spirit?" I asked.

Her lips compressed in a rare frown. "Very little. He is a mystery, and can't be explained."

"But you're sure it Exists?"

"Oh, absolutely. He leads me. He comforts me. He shows me truth."

She seemed every bit as confident, or more so, as Dad was that Fate was a living entity. Only Fate was a malevolent, sadistic killjoy; while the Spirit was a benevolent, generous philanthropist. At least as their observers saw them.

It was tempting to discount it all as silly superstition. But Dad was not silly, superstitious, or gullible by any metric, otherwise. And Niki had intuition which was uncanny. I couldn't prove it, but I had experienced the Big Spooky several times. Was it related somehow to an unseen spiritual force or entity?

All the scientists who wrote textbooks operated on the assumption that evolution was the source of intelligent life; but the theory itself had so many flaws that it required more faith to believe in than Christianity does. There were too many simple questions it couldn't answer without mental gymnastics and self-contradiction. Darwinism was so full of holes that the hypothesis had to be modified every couple years as new discoveries debunked previous assumptions. Yet it was much more comfortable to accept than a supreme being infinitely smarter than the most intelligent man; and a reality beyond what we could perceive, with facts we couldn't observe or test.

So were there intelligent beings who existed in the dimensions I could warp through but not perceive with my natural senses? Why couldn't there be? It was no more ridiculous than assuming there were little green men cruising the galaxy in flying saucers—which was probably a science fiction trope because some people actually believed in them.

"Until and unless this Spirit beams an idea into my brain," I said, "I have to go just on what I can conceive of logically."

"And what is that?"

"The way you seem to see it, Niki, your grandfather and his supporters are in a struggle with Albert Margai and his supporters, for control of Sierra Leone. Historically, the winner is usually whoever the army sides with. But to me, the greater danger is from the Erasers. This internal struggle is a landmark. If your grandfather prevails, it will definitely split the timestream. The TPF will dispatch a team to erase him, and probably his whole family tree."

She chewed on her lip, thoughtfully.

"Your home is the perfect place to do it," I went on. "If they do it in Freetown, there's too many witnesses. It will stink to everybody. They do it at your house out in the bush, no witnesses. They can make up a story about your grandfather dying of a heart attack; or getting eaten by a leopard, whatever. A few months and it's all down the memory hole. Albert Margai is the legitimate ruler. There never was a dispute. Sierra Leone has always been this way. Oceana has always been at war with Eurasia."

"People in the village know us," Niki said, shaking her head. Grandfather has many friends, all over the country. They will ask questions. They will demand an investigation."

I shrugged. "So what? If the media doesn't report on it, it didn't happen; and anybody who questions the official narrative is just a conspiracy theorist not to be taken seriously. Or a dangerous thought criminal, who needs to be locked up. That's what the police will do, instead of investigating."

"That is evil."

"It's happened over and over again," I replied. "It only gets worse. The artificially-induced mass delusion in 2020 is so ridiculous, you wouldn't believe it, even if I took you there and showed you."

"Why would these 'Erasers' conspire with media and government? How many officials even know they exist?"

"Almost nobody, I assume," I said. "Even leaving time travelers out of it, all these scumbags serve the same cause, ultimately. They do their part without even knowing who their real masters are. They don't need to know—they'll serve who they think their master is, and it works out just the same. A lot of them think their master is money. More money; more money; more money. Others serve their own lust for power. Others think they're working towards 'justice' for their own demographic. Some think they serve 'equality' or 'diversity' or whatever. They're all working toward the same bullshit in their own selfish ways, and are too willfully ignorant to know...or care...who and what they really serve. It's not like you can show them the truth and they'll change their ways."

Her eyes were fixed on me as we walked along, like she was waiting for me to finish.

"Scumbags don't need to know about the Erasers," I said. "They're gonna do what they do regardless. Erasers know about *them*. They want to keep the timestream intact. Which means the scumbags keep winning while decent people pay the price, are kept in the dark, and lose. I'm sure that's how the TPB wants to keep it anyway."

She took my arm. "You are right, Isaac. What you are saying is right."

I studied her face. "Do you even understand what I'm saying?"

"Not all of it," she said. "But I know you are right."

"About where they'll come for Dayvon?"

"Yes, that too. Yes, they will come like you said."

CHAPTER 18: EPIC AMBUSH

I banked on Niki being right about the attack, because I had no more reliable prediction to go by.

Knowing where an attack was coming was a huge advantage. It cut the enemy's surprise in half. All they could surprise me with was the time they would strike...and I could narrow that down.

I recharged my Mini-Warp, made a supply run to my hangar in Texas, and began preparing an ambush for the Erasers.

Part of my motivation was helping Dayvon. I also wanted to save Niki and all of her family I could. And hey, securing freedom and peace for the people of Sierra Leone was a worthy goal all by itself. But I also had scores to settle with the Erasers. They had murdered my brother, biological mother, father and sister, which was technically cause for revenge. Worst of all: they had taken Madalina and Sylvia from me. This was a chance to make them pay, and I was damn well going to do just that if I could.

That night I dreamed again of the warrior decapitating the multi-headed snake. I also dreamed again of the alien-looking creature. It gestured and struck down the warrior with some kind of evil magic. It spoke a word while doing so. But by the time I awoke, I couldn't remember the word.

ΔΔΔ

I worked from dawn to dusk every day, stopping only to eat or drink when Mona Lisa brought me something. She and her mother, aunts, and cousins helped in whatever way they could, but mostly kept out of my way.

With a bad taste in my mouth from recent developments, I tried not to notice how good it felt to see Mona Lisa so often. And we worked together well. She never questioned my judgment or tried to take over. But she did bring me water or tea without me asking. And she cooked for me, always concerned with my general well-being. She reminded me of how Mami just naturally thrived on serving others—and did so cheerfully.

Within a week, three of Niki's brothers and two of her uncles arrived. They reported that Albert Margai had suffered a no-confidence vote. Now, new national elections were being scheduled and Dayvon was trying to solidify support for himself as a candidate for Prime Minister.

I gave each of them a pair of polarized sunglasses. I also explained to them what I was trying to do. Not all of them believed in dimensional warps—evidently Dayvon kept those cards fairly close to his chest. So I was intentionally vague about what sort of assets the enemy would show up with. I also didn't explain the reasoning behind everything I wanted done.

Dayvon returned, fiery-eyed and resolute, with the rest of the clan surrounding him. We didn't get much chance to talk, because the Erasers came for him that day.

△△△

It was a well-planned strike. The helicopter gunship and armored vans all warped in within the same minute. They were cloaked, of course. The gunship would level the area with rockets and chainguns, then the Erasers would debark from the armored vans and mop up whatever was left.

Nearby monkeys screamed as the vehicles warped in. I heard the engines and rotor blades just a split second later. I was by then in the habit of carrying my remote trigger with me everywhere I went. I was outside, walking the perimeter, and did a visual search for the vehicles upon hearing them. It was broad daylight and my sunglasses allowed me to see them plainly.

My warp generator was stored inside a Faraday cage. I had placed electromagnetic pulsars (similar to what I had used on the Chinese PacFor) in the vicinity, and now saturated the area with pulses by using the remote trigger. The chopper was flying low toward the main house, about 600 yards away. The pulse knocked out all its electronics—including the cloak. The pilot had no chance to react at that altitude. His bird came down, hard.

The armored vans, apparently waiting for the chopper's gun run before they moved in, lost their camouflage as their electronically fuel-injected engines died. With or without polarized glasses, everybody could see them, now.

I had a clear view to where the chopper crashed. It hit the ground hard enough, the crew might be dead already. But I was taking no chances. I unslung Double Threat (the automatic rifle/grenade launcher combo I had designed and built in Dad's machine shop) from my back, loaded a high explosive grenade in the launcher, sighted in and fired. Direct hit on the cockpit. The wreck leapt off the ground one more time in a fearsome blast that shook the earth and trees. It hit the ground again, burning this time.

I turned and ran toward the trucks. Several of Dayvon's clansmen, armed with Sten guns, were trotting over to surround the troop carriers. I gesticulated as I sprinted toward them, barking orders.

"Clear the kill zone!"

"Stay uprange!"

"Get over there!"

"No—you stay right there!"

"You three: double-time to the chopper crash and check for survivors!"

Despite all the planning and drilling I had done with them, many were confused and didn't respond the way we had practiced. During that gaggle, the van doors opened and the Erasers began to spill out. Most were trying to shed their heavy now-useless camouflage as they stumbled along, but a few opened fire. I returned fire on the run and cut a few down before my first magazine ran dry.

"Return fire!" I shouted. "Kill the bastards! Just try to take one of the drivers alive!"

I reached the machinegun nest, locked-and-loaded the air cooled M2 Browning, and traversed while working the trigger. I swept fire through the vans and cut down all the Erasers I could see in the open.

I burned through an entire belt, and the vans looked like smoking, mangled Swiss cheese when I was done. The .50 caliber slugs tore men and trees to pieces, literally. They tore through everything. Armor would probably have to be inches thick to stop even one of those slugs.

I called Victor over (one of Dayvon's grandsons who picked up tactics and weapons training like a natural), and had him man the gun. I changed magazines in my rifle while walking to join the armed defenders, yelling, "Skirmish line!"

They formed a crooked rank, facing the demolished vans. I joined them and signaled for them to advance. Thus we began the hunt for surviving Erasers. I dispatched details to search the vans, and to secure wounded Erasers. The rest of us marched through the kill zone, looking for targets. When we reached the tree line, an Eraser who had got away shot one of Dayvon's sons. Sten guns erupted all along the skirmish line, riddling the man with 9mm bursts.

The remaining survivors wised up quickly, trying to avoid contact altogether.

I re-formed the skirmish line into a patrol, and led them on a search-and-destroy mission until night fell. We didn't find any more, but I knew some must be out there.

Releasing the clansmen to secure Dayvon's home and outbuildings, I unpacked some items from the Faraday cage I brought, including night vision goggles. I resumed the hunt alone, on foot.

I only caught up with one of them that night. I cut him down with a single round from Double Threat, got close enough to confirm the kill, and left him for the local predators.

When I returned to Dayvon's place late that night, I could hear women wailing. The wound to Dayvon's son was fatal. Two grandsons had also been wounded, but not seriously.

Their trigger-happy cousins almost opened fire on me, even though I announced myself before breaking cover. I chastised them for not pulling sentry duty correctly, and asked where I could find Dayvon.

He was interrogating one of the drivers, who was tied to a chair in an outbuilding.

When Dayvon recognized me, he took me outside, far out of earshot.

"That one give you anything? I asked, thumbing back toward the building where the prisoner was secured.

Dayvon thumped a small spiral notebook with a pencil. "I got his name, the name of his C.O., and everybody in his unit. Got his unit and all the intelligence on me they were briefed about for this mission."

"That sounds good," I said. "Anything else?"

"Like what?"

"Never mind. I'd like to ask him a few questions, if that's okay."

Dayvon grinned. "Least I could do, Ike, after how you came through for us, here."

When I was alone with the prisoner, I asked if he knew anything about the mission to kidnap Madalina and Sylvia. He pled ignorance, so I beat the hell out of him to make sure he wasn't holding out. I moved on to asking about the TPF's command-and-control, standard operating procedures, past missions, and what coordinates they had people watching. I planted my fist somewhere that would hurt any time he didn't answer quickly enough.

ΔΔΔ

The clan members who had been unfriendly to me

in previous years now stared at me curiously...but without hostility. Those who had been neutral or ambivalent were now friendly. Those who were friendly before now treated me like family.

Dayvon was busy taking phone calls and signing paperwork brought to him by messengers, but made time to chat with me the next afternoon.

"I owe you one, Ike," he said, while we were secluded in his inner office. "How did you knock out their cloaks?"

"Electromagnetic pulse," I said.

His upper lip curled into a grin that threatened to precede a laugh. "I'll be damned. Now that's some white boy shit, there. We was gonna use paint bombs, if the Erasers ever came for us."

"That's not a bad idea," I said. "And if you're stuck in 1960s technology, it's a great idea."

"None of my electrical stuff quit workin', by the way. Except my computers in this room."

"Sorry about that. What circuits you got outside this office are pretty robust. It's the microchips and microprocessors that are so delicate. EMPs fry those circuits. The old stuff is stout."

"I shoulda' known about those sunglasses," he said. "In the TPF, we had goggles that let us see each other when we was cloaked. I thought it was some high-speed shit."

I shrugged. "It works fine on the cloaking that uses LEDs. Not sure it will help if they develop active camouflage that uses something else."

He nodded and leaned back to stare at the ceiling. "I shoulda' been more prepared for this. This is exactly where and when I woulda' hit me, if I was plannin' the hit. My people barely got the damn Sten guns ready in time, and half of 'em couldn't hit the walls of a Costco, if they were standin' inside it. With a automatic weapon! And even after you spent time with 'em."

"I didn't do so good the first time I had to shoot at somebody, either," I said. "They'll probably do better next time."

"You think there'll be a next time?"

I shrugged. "You tell me. The TPF just lost an entire Eraser team and all their expensive gear. How many teams can they afford to lose?"

Dayvon finally burst out laughing. "Damn! I never thought I'd miss bein' around cocky white boys. But they grew on me, thanks to you."

"Depending on how the problem here is resolved, they might just leave you alone. Who knows? But if you succeed; and they decide it doesn't suck bad enough in Sierra Leone downstream from your split, they'll probably try again. But you have a better idea than I do how those people operate."

"Hell," he said, "I was just one of their hired killers. It's not like they invited me into their meetings and briefed me on their mission statement."

"Well, for whatever reason, they don't like it when the stream is split and there's an opportunity for people to live where it doesn't suck as bad. At least that's what I understood from what my uncle believes about it all."

"Sometimes I wonder," Dayvon said. "Maybe the universe can only handle so many alternate streams. If we split reality too many times, maybe there's a reaction like fission, and it all goes off like an atomic bomb."

I shrugged. "That sounds like something out of a science fiction novel. But who knows? Whatever their rationale is, they don't share it with the curious. They just have the curious killed."

ΔΔΔ

Dayvon didn't have much time to chat with me. I appreciated what time he did take.

The clan handled security, and the clean-up of the mess from the firefight. They also put out an APB for any of the surviving Erasers who might still be on the loose.

Dayvon had been vague, to his clan, about the enemies who might one day come for him. Some of them took the battle within stride, assuming it was some kind of demons who had attacked. Others suspected it was something else—and that I wasn't just some random guy, either. I don't know if Dayvon explained dimensional warps and the CPB; but he told them some kind of story that must have made sense to them.

I stuck around a few more days and spent most of my time with Niki. Her family was more trusting than before, and allowed us a lot of time alone together.

On one of my trips delivering weapons and equipment, I brought her gifts: a piano, a phonograph, and some records. We listened to music together; she played and sang while I listened; and we talked quite a bit.

I knew I was rebounding from Juanita. Still rebounding from Madalina, truth be told. But it was hard not to be smitten with this beautiful woman and her gentle spirit. She was so kind, vulnerable, and, in most ways, innocent, that I couldn't understand my own behavior toward her.

Why had I kept her at arm's length and not taken her seriously? Was it the racial difference? I didn't want to think I was that shallow. But there was a slightly nationalistic streak in me now and then. Sometimes when watching a fight—whether MMA or boxing—when all other factors were equal, I just naturally rooted for the white fighter. So there was some latent prejudice floating around inside me.

Maybe, deep down, at a subconscious level, it had to do with children. If we did get together, and she bore me children, they would be mixed. I had never had a problem with mixed-race people if they treated me with the same consideration I treated them; and most of my siblings (Dad's biological kids) were mixed. I did learn, in St. Louis, that it was risky to wander neighborhoods where most people looked a lot different than me. Maybe my hesitation was instinctive—some kind of primordial obsession with pure bloodlines or something. But my adopted mother (quite frankly the best mother a guy could have had) didn't look like me, either.

Maybe it was because Mona Lisa seemed so flawless. I didn't want get close enough to discover her flaws or, worse yet, be the cause of some. I knew better than to put any woman on a pedestal, but I guess I did with her, and was afraid of ruining her "perfection."

On a bright, hot day, Mona Lisa and I sat together under the shade of a tree by the river, sipping ice tea and chatting. She asked about the Erasers and their attack on her family. I did my best to explain it. When I got to the part about her grandfather's out-loud speculation regarding too many stream splits causing a nuclear reaction, she shook her head adamantly.

"What?" I asked.

"The potential is limitless," she said. "There can be infinite splits and infinite alternate realities."

"Why do you say that?"

"Because God is limitless, Isaac. His mind is infinite."

I shrugged. "Okay. Maybe. But how is that relevant?"

"Who do you think created the dimensions? Those, and all the creatures within them, are in his mind."

"What?"

"We are just figments in God's imagination," she said. "Did Mr. Einstein not say so?"

"Wait. Just wait. Are you saying that all the realities in the...*multiverse*...including this one you and I exist in right here and now, are just a simulation?"

Now she shrugged. "I suppose you could say it that way."

"But that would mean..." I scratched my head. "Okay. So what are we? Are we just part of the simulation?"

She nodded.

"But we can think, and reason, and create, and suffer emotions. You think we're just sophisticated AI—artificial intelligence?"

"Why not?"

"You're blowing my mind," I said, mulling over all the implications at a thousand miles-per-minute.

"Splitting the 'stream' doesn't hurt anything," she said. "God's imagination is limitless. He can track any number of variables. Multiply our alternate streams by a million, and they are still finite. There is no danger in that regard. There must be some other reason they don't want Grandfather to change history."

"If God is really imagining all this, why isn't it perfect? Why has he included all the injustice and all the evil dirtbags?"

She threw her hands up. "We have to accept that we may never understand why God does what He does. Why did He put that second tree in the Garden? Why did He create Lucifer, knowing what Lucifer would become, and do? These are questions I can't answer. Maybe He wanted us to love Him voluntarily; and the only way to know that was if there was an alternative to choose. I do not know."

We fell silent for a while. I tried to measure her theory against what my own logic could conceive. I guess she was deep in thought, too.

"What you're implying is that reality is not real," I said, finally. "That whatever is in the dimension where God is...is more real than anything we can see, hear, smell, touch...or think about."

"Yes," she said. "Precisely."

"It still makes no sense," I said. "Not only does He allow evil dirtbags to run the show...why would He let people like me slip through dimensions and live in a time period where He didn't put me?"

"Why would He allow people to communicate using radio waves?" she countered. "Why would He let men fly...or to build that dreadful bomb that can kill so many people?"

She leaned close and used one hand to pull her hair behind her ear on one side. "You remember our conversation about destiny?"

I nodded, suddenly, consciously, enjoying her proximity, her scent, her gestures, and her gaze.

"Maybe He allows such things so that people like you and I could find each other; and in the middle of all the world's tragedy, we could make something beautiful."

I stiffened and stared at her. "Were you...reading my

thoughts a minute ago?"

She set down her tea and showed me her signature smile.

"Oh, Isaac—it would be beautiful! I know it, even if you don't."

I took her hand, and let myself imagine a future with her. Would it, in fact, be beautiful?

"Isaac, I'm old enough. Won't you go see my father, and ask for my hand?"

Marriage, with a formal ceremony.

Dad thought all that was stupid bullshit, and I agreed. Not because I wanted to keep spinning plates. Because I didn't... not necessarily. It was the hype, the dog-and-pony show, and almost inevitable divorce-rape of the man that made me despise marriage, for starters. Both my parents had been married twice. My half-sister Allyson only had one divorce, but was working on getting remarried (poor guy) last I saw her. I had seen the same pattern with all the adults I knew back at my native coordinates. They went to such trouble to make weddings "perfect," then spent the majority of their time together making each other miserable.

Maybe none of that was the issue—perhaps because I still assumed there might be a way to find Madalina and finish the life I started with her. She could still be my happy ever after, if only I figured out a way to get her back without tipping off the Erasers again.

I reviewed all my serious romances—all of them ended badly. Madalina and I spent a short time making each other happy; but it ended in heartbreak anyway.

Niki pulled away and fixed me with a sad stare. "You don't feel the same. You're still not ready, yet."

I remained silent, not knowing what to say.

"It is so painful," she said, closing her eyes. "But I will wait for you. One day you will love me."

CHAPTER 19: 1965 SEASON

T hat conversation with Niki was the kind you don't easily forget. Surprisingly, I didn't simply dismiss any of her ideas. Although they were silly hocus-pocus by any conventional reasoning, I had to consider them. She couldn't prove them to be true; but I couldn't prove them to be false.

Fortunately, I had tested my portable warp generator, successfully. And my observations would help me improve the prototype.

I worked on a few more projects that summer, and also jumped back to watch a few Puma games. Poly had a slightly better defense than before; but not much of a passing game. The new coach stuck with Stauchel's Attrition Offense. They wore down defenses; but there was no big play makers like a power-running fullback, a fast halfback or a quarterback with a cannon to strike the knockout blow. They barely scratched out a winning season, but didn't make a bowl game.

I hung out with Dozier a little bit, and took him on some warps to witness Golden Age football. We watched Bronko Nagurski in action; Red Grange; Knute Rockne; and Jim Thorpe. I took him to watch the Dempsey-Jeffries fight and Dempsey-Firpo. We also went to a Beatles concert in our contemporary stream. It was one of those events where the Big Spooky transformed into a seemingly positive force. The euphoria was tangible. Dozier and I made time with two of the girls in attendance, whose defenses were down in the mass ecstasy of the moment, but not screaming and feinting like some of the younger female fans. We had a few double dates with them before returning to Poly.

We road-tripped to the dry lakes and made some high speed runs (my GTO wasn't as aerodynamic as the Stude, so didn't go as fast). We cruised Van Nuys Boulevard in LA, and raced anybody who was willing. We went back through Bakersfield, where I introduced him to my family there. We did more cruising, racing, and girl-chasing. My half-sister, Salvatora, was now 10 years old, and took a shine to Brock. It was obvious to everyone but him. He assumed she was just a friendly little kid, and exhibited the patience and gentleness that came naturally to him. It endeared him to her even more.

Dozier asked about my spinning plates and I brought him up-to-date. Unable to talk with Dad regularly, it was nice to have Dozier's sympathetic ear to bend on occasion.

He let me know what he was up to as well. Aeronautics had become so fascinating to him, he had changed majors. He talked frequently of becoming a pilot—and maybe even an astronaut. But not one of those astronauts who merely took a ride in a capsule. He wanted to pilot a craft that could take off from a runway, navigate the stars, and return to Earth, landing like an airplane. I told him it would be over a decade until the Space Shuttle came along—and even that wouldn't be able to do all he imagined.

△△△

I arrived at Vikings training camp in a little better mood than I had been the previous year. We got some new rookies in the draft; but some of them were traded to other teams before they ever donned our purple uniform. Of all the rookies who did join our roster, I assumed Mike Tilleman, a defensive tackle, would have the biggest impact. Another rookie, running back Dave Osborne, I thought wouldn't last long. He wasn't fast, compared to other pro backs. He didn't have great hands. He was tough; but not Brock Dozier tough. Returning in the backfield that year were Bill Brown and Tommy Mason. Brown was another tough ball carrier; and a reliable receiver as well. Mason was the stereotypical college superstar who fizzled as a pro. He had been the first pick in the first round of the 1961 NFL Draft, but wasn't as fantastic as you hoped a Round One, Pick One should be. I thought Minnesota's offensive line might have a lot to do with that. Despite having Mick Tingelhoff at center and Grady Alderman at tackle, it couldn't open up big holes for Mason to run through; whereas fullback Bill "Boom Boom" Brown could churn out a few yards per carry even without good blocking. Van Brocklin respected Brown. Brown could play old-school, smash-mouth football, and seemed to enjoy it that way.

Tingelhoff was nearly the opposite of Mason, in that his college career wasn't impressive (he didn't move to first-string until his senior year); but he really hit his stride as a pro. I had hit a major growth spurt my junior year in college, which supercharged my athletic abilities. Maybe Tingelhoff had a similar experience...just a bit later on in life.

I still hadn't made any close friends on the team; but some of the players lightened up with me—perhaps simply for the reason I was no longer a rookie. As in college, I was cool with the new rookies. It wouldn't hurt to cultivate a network of allies as soon as possible.

Most players still didn't like the head coach.

We lacked the cohesion of teams like the Packers...or some of the AFL teams; but I noticed little cliques existed within the Vikings. Players at least felt some loyalty to the other members of their clique.

Once he decided I wasn't trying to sabotage him to take his spot, Tarkenton warmed up to me a little, too. His arm wasn't as strong as mine, but he played at a higher level than I ever had. He was a first-class general on the field; and his teammates trusted him, even when he made mistakes. He had gone to the Pro Bowl last season, and engineered a victory for the Western Conference there. He passed for 2,000 yards every season, and had averaged 2,352 yards a season so far as QB at Minnesota.

I was just a second season bench-warmer. I studied Tarkenton because I knew I could learn from him. Not just about football—about leadership, too.

Van Brocklin and Tarkenton still didn't get along. I wondered if it was at least partly a conflict of Big Dogs for dominance of the pack. Maybe something short-circuited and the players' hierarchy had somehow merged with the coaches' hierarchy. They were both now playing king-of-the-hill on the same Ziggurat. Maybe Tarkenton would be content to play Lieutenant under a Big Dog he respected; but the Dutchman just was not that guy.

△△△

Despite all our problems, we went undefeated in the pre-season. And Van Brocklin had me play at least one quarter per game. Not only did I not embarrass myself, I actually made some good plays that helped win games. I didn't receive any compliments from Van Brocklin or Tarkenton; but some of the rookies gave me accolades.

Our regular season didn't go as well. We got stomped by the Colts at Baltimore, then lost a close one at home to the Lions. In Los Angeles, we managed to edge out the Rams. Then at home, we dominated the Giants to the point that Van Brocklin let me take the reins for the entire fourth quarter. I increased our overwhelming lead by two touchdowns. Then the Bears came to play us, with their new rookie running back, Gale Sayers.

Frantic Fran and his blood-and-guts backfield put up some big numbers again. But thanks to Sayers, it became a shootout.

Sayers wasn't a power runner like John Riggins or Brock Dozier; but he seemed no less a force of nature. He was swift; but what really set him apart was his fluidity. He was as graceful as a cat negotiating the obstacles on the field. He made talented defenders look incompetent. If he made the first would-be tackler miss, that was usually the last chance anybody would get to lay a hand on him. He danced and skated around defenders to find daylight. Sometimes he hit the brakes and let a defender slide past him. Once he found daylight, he simply outran everybody. He didn't just take the ball in the backfield, either. He fielded kickoffs and punts, too. We were leading 37-31 at one point. Our kicker, Fred Cox, booted the ball to the opposing four yard line. Sayers caught the ball and it was like he was Moses and our guys were the Red Sea. (Purple Sea?) He made one little move to avoid a tackle; and from there he just sailed all the way down the field for the score. Nobody touched him. He broke our spirit with that play. We didn't score again; and lost the game.

We bounced back in San Francisco, winning a shootout with the 49ers.

Amazingly, our defense came up with a way to contain the run and we beat the Browns by 10 points in Cleveland. We swept the Rams when they came to play us at home. The Colts trampled us again; the Packers swept us for the season; and the 49ers got their revenge.

We clobbered the Lions at Detroit; and managed to wrap up Sayers enough to beat the Bears by one touchdown in Chicago. That brought us to a 7-7 record.

Our pass rush was already good; but improved when we traded with the Rams for Gary Larsen. Now with him, Marshall, and Eller, the best quarterbacks in the league began to dread playing us.

Between Bill Brown; Tommy Mason; and Dave Osborne, we had the second best rushing offense in the league. Aside from that, and Tarkenton's second consecutive appearance in the Pro Bowl, we looked like a mediocre team—just as our record indicated. Our receiving corps and defensive backfield just hadn't come together; and our special teams were sub-par. We made too many stupid mistakes and incurred too many penalties.

The season was an improvement for me, personally, because I got to play in a few games. Getting to be on a professional football team was awesome all by itself. Actually getting to play (and even tossing a couple touchdown passes!)

was quite the bragging right, I thought. No matter what else happened in life, I had accomplished *something*.

CHAPTER 20: A SOLO MISSION IN SARAJEVO

While winter raged in Minnesota, I took off on an extended off-season vacation. I spent a lot of time on Valhalla, as usual; but spread myself around, too.

I visited Sierra Leone again. I was greeted like Charles Lindbergh in Niki's village. The election was underway and Dayvon had a commanding lead.

Niki and I were both wary and guarded with each other. I knew what she wanted. I think she knew I had too many reservations about giving it to her.

The Erasers had not returned; but another raid was expected.

That expected encounter occupied my thoughts frequently. Would they return with overwhelming force next time? An entire army of time-traveling assassins? No—Dayvon said they only had nine direct action teams. Casualties were usually zero. Turnover was negligible, and standards were extremely high. Not just anybody could be trusted with TPF secrets. And as Dad and Dayvon showed them: even the ones they thought could be trusted couldn't always. The TPF couldn't easily replace an entire Eraser team. So would they risk another team or two trying to take out Dayvon and his clan, after the loss? Was it *that* important that Sierra Leone become a dystopian hellhole? The stream had been split already, anyway, with

Dayvon internationally known now, in this one.

The TPF's roster was finite. What if they were carved down even more? Then they would have to be choosy about where and when they deployed assets.

I could do it, myself. I could pick off Erasers one at a time or by the handful—like I did in Densus. I could be a warp-jumping guerrilla, slashing them down to size piecemeal. And maybe, if I took some of them alive, I could find out what happened to Madalina.

It couldn't be simply an impassioned effort at revenge. It had to be a cold, calculating, strategic effort devoid of emotion, or I would certainly slip up somewhere and get caught or killed.

The more I pondered the idea, the more I liked it. And Dad wasn't around to talk me out of it.

Niki noticed how preoccupied I was. She knew I was contemplating something dangerous, but didn't try to make me divulge my scheme, or talk me out of it. She did plead with me to be careful.

The conception evolved into a plan. I would jump to coordinates where the TPF was likely to have assets in place, like they did at Dealey Plaza in 1963. But that one was off limits, since Dad was obviously up to something there.

I would lurk at another likely time and place, and try to identify the asset; snatch them away to coordinates they were unlikely to be searched for at; interrogate them, and then...

Well, the only logical course of action was to kill them. But I doubted I could bring myself to do that, if they weren't shooting at me or something. There was a line between killing and murder that I didn't want to cross.

That was the weak link in my plan. I almost gave up, because of it. But I could at least make preparations. I could scout some coordinates out, and try to find the TPF asset(s). I didn't have to initiate the chain of events that would lead to cold-blooded murder. In fact, maybe I could think of an alternative to killing them. But while I was coming up with an alternative, I could at least try to identify the TPF operatives.

ΔΔΔ

Whenever Dad or I jumped back farther than the 1950s, we ditched the polarized sunglasses. Dad's lab techs had ground some contact lenses for us that would defeat the visual cloaking technology used by the TPF. I wore my pair when I jumped back to Austria-Hungary.

I made several trips, as far back as 1912 Sarajevo, to "prep the battlefield." I stashed weapons and equipment at various locations, just in case. I mapped out the city so that I was familiar with its overall layout and many of its neighborhoods.

Dr. Manfredi had made progress on memory implants, to the degree that I was able to upload German, Hungarian, and Serbian into the region of my mind where language was stored.

I returned to Sarajevo in the spring of 1914. I was patient, and avoided drawing attention to myself. I didn't wander around asking strangers about secret societies, but I kept my ears open and frequented places where members of the Black Hand would likely visit.

I spent months in relative time performing my reconnaissance, before planting myself at a certain cafe in June, observing the comings and goings of Gavrillo Princip and his associates.

On my third visit to the cafe, I finally noticed the lady.

How I could have failed to notice the striking beauty of that woman the first or second time is a mystery. A gorgeous woman always stood out in a crowd...but not her. She blended in. I guess she should have set off alarm bells just for that uncanny oxymoron.

I had seen her before; and not just on my previous two visits to the Sarajevo cafe.

In the melting pot of this Balkan region—whether 1914 Sarajevo or 1995 Densus, her dark features meant she could pass for Bulgarian, Albanian, or someone of Mediterranean descent. In Dallas, she seemed as natural as any striking Tex-Mex beauty could be.

Here she was dressed in the bustle, petticoats, hat and gloves of an aristocratic lady just visiting the poorer neighborhoods to experience the exotic cultures on display. She sat alone at a table, occasionally sipping from a cup, reading a newspaper. She bore the same content, amused expression she'd worn in Dallas.

As usual, I had chosen a seat in the back corner of the cafe, so that nobody could sneak up behind me. That was a habit I picked up from Dad, which seemed especially wise after Densus. I wondered why the woman hadn't recognized me, as I had her.

She had to be a TPF asset. She frequented too many disparate coordinates—and two of them at major historical turning points.

I was tempted to march right up to her table and confront her; but that would be foolish.

I waited.

Another woman—not nearly as attractive—arrived and sat with her. They chatted for a while. I couldn't hear their discussion from where I sat. It looked like a typical conversation two women might have with each other at any coordinates.

The visitor left after about half an hour. Then my target drained her cup, dabbed her lips with a napkin, and rose from her table.

I waited until she moved through the door and turned right on the sidewalk before I moved from my spot. I hurried out and turned after her.

She was easy to tail, having a distinct feminine gait that would have set her apart as a unicorn in the US after 2000 or so. Even under all the fashion mumification, she had a great figure; and the motion of her hips when she walked could put an old man through a second puberty.

Occasional automobiles chugged by on the street, in between horse-drawn buggies and wagons. I worried that she would get in a taxi. Would I be able to find another one quickly enough to play the "follow that cab" game?

I remained from 50 to 100 yards behind her, depending on how many other pedestrians were between us. She strolled across a bridge. The run-down neighborhood gave way to an artsy sort of area with upscale theaters and store fronts.

She turned under an awning and nodded at a door man who let her into a six-story hotel.

Suddenly, the job became more difficult than I was prepared for. How was I going to find out what room she would go to without arousing suspicion? I broke into a run.

I slowed to a walk before reaching the awning. I tipped my hat to the door man. He nodded politely and opened the door for me. I stepped into the lobby—a classy room with plush carpet, a vaulted ceiling and expensive-looking chandeliers. I looked around for the woman, hoping she might have paused at the front desk; but didn't see her. It dawned on me I should just stake out the place, and tail her again next time she left.

I turned to exit.

There she was. She stood by herself not far from the door, facing my direction and looking right at me.

CHAPTER 21: INTIMATE YET NAMELESS

I've been made, I thought, heart pounding.

I didn't see any cloaked Erasers in the room, but she could scream for the cops and get me in a sticky predicament.

She fixed her amused smile on me and said, in English, "You might never find my room by inquiring at the front desk. What name would you ask for?"

I approached her warily. Her expression and body language were open—as if she were pleased to see me.

"You tell me," I said.

"I fear I've already made it rather too easy for you," she said, chuckling.

My face heated as I considered I might have just walked into a trap. But I still didn't see any Erasers—and I had tested the polarized contact lenses with the Predator camouflage and knew they worked.

She lowered her voice to a conspiratorial whisper as I came to a stop within arm's reach of her. "It would arouse the least suspicion if we were a married couple...don't you think?" In full voice, brimming with cheery enthusiasm, she said, "Darling! I was worried you wouldn't make it."

Her hand was soft and warm through her lacy glove as she took my arm with a familiarity one might expect only from a lover.

I played my part, holding my elbow out conveniently as if escorting a bridesmaid to the front of a church.

"You're in fantastic shape, aren't you?" she asked, at a discreet volume once again, clutching my bicep. "Not even breathing hard from that run to the front door." Her voice was just as attractive as she was. Her accent was aristocratic British, but sexy.

We walked so that it appeared I was steering her, when, in fact, she was steering me. We climbed the stairs and entered a room on the third floor, where she closed and locked the door behind us.

The room was spacious and elegant, with a wingback chair and sofa, across from a king-sized canopy bed. She pointed to a shaded lamp. "The hotel is wired for electricity. That can't be said for every building here and now, can it?"

I stared at her, with a dozen questions to ask but not knowing where to start.

"Let's not be boors and pull pistols on each other," she suggested, with a frown that tipped upward on one side of her mouth. She waved toward the sofa. "We can sit down and talk like civilized people. That would be much more productive, don't you think?"

We sat on the sofa, with a few feet between us but inclined toward each other. She removed her hat, then her shoes, and tucked her legs under her, in a comfortable, almost feline, position.

"I suppose your first question is how I knew you were following me. Well, you're certainly not my first stalker."

I considered her words. "Stalking is something a hunter does to game," I said. "Using it in a sexual context didn't become a common metaphor until the 1990s. Is that your native stream, or later?"

Her laugh sounded natural. Even the knee slap looked sincere. "Sexual? Now that's wishful thinking, isn't it?"

I thought about the way she used the word "arouse" a

few moments ago, because now she *was* arousing me; and I wondered if she had used the power of suggestion to turn my thoughts carnal.

"But you're a smart one, aren't you? Not just clever; but rather...intellectual, I say."

"If you intend to keep evading my questions," I said, "this is gonna take quite a while. Is that what you have in mind?"

"Why be hasty? We have all the time in the world," she said, watching me for a reaction. After a moment, she burst out laughing. While doing so, she leaned forward and touched my arm. "Oh come now—you have to admit: that was witty!"

I remembered how she took my wrist back in Densus. I liked her touch. Even through the gloves, it was intoxicating. Her laughter was pleasing to the ears. I found her voice both sultry and comforting.

"Yeah, you've got a sense of humor," I admitted. "Thats one in the positive column for you, anyway."

"Just one?" she replied, arching her perfectly sculpted eyebrows. "I could have caused a scene in the lobby; and made trouble for you. I could have shot or stabbed you, were I feeling particularly nasty."

"Why didn't you?"

She laughed again. "I suppose I wasn't feeling particularly nasty." She reached out and briefly squeezed my forearm this time. "Lucky for you, I'm not a nasty person in general. Not nasty in that way, at least."

Was there a note of innuendo in her statement? It felt like it. She turned me on in a ferocious, desperate way only a few women could. Partly because of her (perhaps) suggestive words, partly because she was sexy in general, and partly because of her accent and the way she pronounced the word "nasty" with such relish. It came out "nohstie," like how I imagined a proper-but-naughty English governess might say it.

Most Top Tier women simply rested on the laurels nature endowed them with; but here was a Top Tier woman whose every movement, expression, and syllable was designed to enthrall a man.

"Okay, granted," I said. "When did you spot me?"

Smirking, she said, "I assume you're referring to here in Sarajevo. April, 1913."

"Did you know I was in the cafe?"

"Of course. Why do you suppose I returned each day until you decided to act?"

"You tell me," I said.

She had never betrayed the slightest indication that she recognized me until greeting me in the lobby downstairs. But apparently she had. In effect, she had been toying with me— testing me, like I was a lab rat in her experiment.

"You're rather charming when you blush," she said, touching my shoulder and pronouncing "rather" as "raw-thuh." Her swiping motion might have been meant to be soothing. "You're obviously inexperienced at surveillance and such things. It's nothing to be embarrassed about."

I *was* embarrassed. I didn't like being second best at anything, including temporal espionage. She obviously outclassed me in her knowledge of spycraft...which might mean she was a professional of some kind. "You returned multiple times to the cafe just to see if I would make you?"

Her nose wrinkled. "Make me? Make me what?"

"Recognize you."

"I see. Right. That was one consideration. I also wondered if you were going to interfere with the Black Hand in some fashion."

"You thought I might stop the assassination?"

She shrugged. "Franz Ferdinand is due here in a few days. Why else would you be here, now?" She opened her handbag to retrieve a cigarette and holder. I watched in disbelief.

"A trifle anachronistic, isn't it?" she remarked, noticing my perplexity, using a 1970s vintage disposable lighter to apply a flame. "I'm careful about where I smoke, and who sees me. Dreadful habit, I admit."

"Women won't start smoking until the Roaring '20s," I

mused. "And by about the 2010s, the health concerns, taxes, and stigma put smokers...of both sexes...back in the minority. At least among people wealthy enough to afford an accent like yours."

She exhaled her first puff and laughed some more. "Oh, but you do have a sharp wit! You've complimented, insulted, and amused me all with one acidic remark."

"So, considering your colloquialisms too," I added, ignoring her comment, "your native coordinates are probably between 1990 and 2010. In some hoity-toity place like Soho, or in a castle with a butler, chauffer, and maids."

"Twenty years? Is that the most narrow estimate you can give? You need to work on your stereotyping skills, as well."

"How about we quit beating around the bush altogether," I suggested. "Just tell me who you are, why I keep running into you, and what your game is."

She took a luxurious drag from her cigarette and closed her eyes as she breathed it out. "I didn't want to scare you away before we had a chance to meet," she said. "If you remember our last encounter...during which I offered you an escape from mortal danger, I might add...your rejection of my help was rather cold. Any colder and I fear you may have shot me."

"That brings up more questions," I said. "Why were you trying to help me, if that's what you were, in fact, doing? What kind of warp generator do you use? Why were you in Densus? What made you turn against your pals in the TPF?"

She blinked rapidly while exhaling smoke, with an irritated frown. "Pals in the TPF? Why would you suppose I work for the Temporal Police?"

"I don't know. Maybe because we keep crossing paths every time I visit coordinates that are crawling with TPF informants."

"By that same logic, shouldn't I also assume *you* work for them?" she asked, leaning back.

"You know I don't. Erasers were chasing me all around Densus last time, trying to grease me in broad daylight."

The amused smile crept back onto her face. "Erasers.

Grease. Americans do like their morbid expressions, don't you?"

"Well, what do you call the invisible assassins who jump warps all over the continuum to murder people and their families?"

"I've always known them simply as Direct Action Teams."

Finally: a straight answer. Skeptically, I said, "But you don't work with them."

"I should say not."

"Then who should you say you *do* work for?"

She raised her eyebrows and asked, "Who do *you* work for?"

So she didn't know everything about me. That was a relief. And suddenly I was selfish about my new-found advantage. It might be foolish to divulge information that could give her any kind of edge.

She blinked once, meaningfully, and put the cigarette holder back to her lips. She wasn't showing much skin at all below the neck, but the air practically sizzled with sexual tension. The longer I sat with her, the more I wanted her.

"Not just anybody can afford a warp generator," I said. "Which means you're in the Continuum Protection Bureau, at the least. Were you defying orders by offering me an escape? Or maybe it's a mistake to believe you were working against them, just because you weren't shooting at me. Your 'escape' could have been nothing but an attractive invitation to a trap that would have killed me just as surely."

She shrugged to concede the point. "According to your theory, either that, the Temporal Police have gone rogue, or there's some sort of civil war underway at the Bureau."

"Am I wrong?" I asked.

"Yes. I don't work for the CBP, either."

"So whoever you do work for can also jump warps."

"Curious expression," she said. "'Jump warps.' I gather that's your term for time travel."

"What's your term for it?"

"There's no jumping whatsoever, when *I* travel. I merely

step through the portal. When I do, I'm in a different time and place."

"How does that work?"

"Oh, I couldn't begin to guess. It's all very technical, with spinning singularities and gravity calibration and that sort of thing. Do *you* understand the science behind it?"

I chewed on my lip. There were still aspects of warp generation and navigation that confused me, although I could build or repair the hardware needed to make it work. I could do the same for the software, without knowing exactly why everything worked together—though my engineering education had brought me much closer to an overall comprehension. But it might not be wise to volunteer my understanding of any of it. "Nope."

"But I think you do know," she said, touching my forehead with her index finger. "Cagey lad."

"Why were you in Densus?" I repeated.

She sighed. "I learned that there was a sudden escalation of radiological disturbances there. I went to investigate."

"Radiological disturbances?" I interrupted.

"Yes. The sort made when portals open. In this case, the disturbance was profound, due to the size of the Direct Action Team—the size and number of portals the individuals and vehicles came through."

"How did you know portals were opening? How do you monitor that, and from where? From when?"

"Terribly sorry. I can't say. And I wouldn't be capable of explaining the technology, even were I authorized to disclose that."

"So you're definitely not solo," I said. "You work for somebody—somebody who only provides you with limited information."

"*Touche*," she said, eyes twinkling. "You are a clever chap."

"Why are you watching me?"

She grinned. "I wasn't watching you. Not at first. I was assigned to patrol the Kennedy assassination. But I remembered your face. Also your hair; your walk; posture; body language. I just happened to have been on duty when the call came in for Densus, 1995. But I recognized you there. As you can imagine, that recognition was worthy of note. The lab technicians uploaded your image to the facial recognition data banks. Made more difficult by your ever-present sunglasses, of course. I must say, now that I can see your eyes, you're a bit dishy. I rather fancy them. I hope I get to see them without the contact lenses, eventually."

My heart rate accelerated. "What do you mean: 'uploaded my image'?"

She stared at me with a curious smile. "Don't play so gormless. You understand more of the technology than I do."

"You had a camera?"

Her eyes narrowed as she studied my face closely. This went on so long, the silence and intensity of her gaze made me feel awkward.

"What?" I finally asked.

She removed one glove, then reached out with her bare hand toward my head. I instinctively recoiled; but her hand was empty.

"There, there," she said, soothingly. "Just relax. There's a boy." She spread her fingers and combed them into my hair, feeling around the top and sides of my scalp. I let her do it—not recognizing any threat, and actually enjoying her touch and what it did to me.

After probing around extensively, she withdrew her hand and stared hard at me. "At least you can tell me what vintage your implants are."

"Implants?"

She inhaled sharply, hand covering her mouth, then resumed her exploration of my scalp. Again, she gave up after what must have been a fruitless search, scowling in confusion and disbelief.

"You don't have implants?" she asked, incredulous.

"In my head? No."

"Then how, pray tell, are you able to 'jump warps' as you say?"

I shrugged, at first considering what I should tell her about how the technology worked. Then some revelations hit me.

If she (and whoever she worked for) didn't have the same warp generation technology we did, then they were not Temporal Police from this stream. I witnessed her portal opening in Densus. That was not our tech. Evidently, her tech required cranial implants. Either she worked for some organization that devised a different way to travel through the continuum; or she worked for the TPF in an alternate reality, wherein they had achieved dimensional travel via a different technology. Or there could be any number of other explanations.

Then I recalled Dr. Manfredi's advances with the Multiple Sensory Interface. He could play back images from someone's memories—basically using the eyes as the camera and the brain as the film.

"I see," I said. "Through implants in the brain, a computer is able to access data stored in the mind—in this case, visual data that came through your eyes. Your people uploaded the 'picture' of me...taken by your eyes...into a facial recognition database or something. Then that image file was shared with other agents. When one of them here in Sarajevo saw me, there was a match. That alerted you."

She stared intently into my eyes for a while, not speaking, but seemingly searching for something. She appeared uncharacteristically serious.

Slowly, so as not to frighten her, I reached toward her head. Her eyebrows furrowed and her posture stiffened. I gently probed through her dark hair, along her scalp. When she realized what I was doing, she relaxed somewhat.

Along the top of her skull I felt four symmetrical indentations, slightly smaller than the diameter of my fingertips.

"There you have it," she said, breathily. "You feel mine, but

I can't feel yours. Not terribly fair, is it?"

Fairly confident I had found all the abnormalities on her skull, I nonetheless continued exploring as if not sure. My gentle probe was more of a caress, now.

She closed her eyes and tilted her head back as if enjoying it. "Is this what you Yanks call 'copping a feel'?"

"No, but I can demonstrate what that's like, if you want."

She opened her eyes and showed me the amused grin again. I moved my hands down until touching both sides of her face. Her eyelids drooped to half-mast and she leaned toward me, dazedly shifting her gaze between my eyes and mouth. By this point in my life, I recognized this as a sign that she was ready and willing to be kissed.

I bumped my lips into hers and was fairly zapped by the powerful sexual energy of the woman.

Our lips bumped twice more, and then she moaned as I slid my tongue into her mouth. The distance between us on the sofa closed to zero and we locked each other in a tight embrace.

Making out was fun with any attractive and enthusiastic woman; but was at an extreme level of intensity with this stranger.

I cupped, then squeezed, her breast. She gasped and shivered, moaning as if I'd just given her an orgasm.

"That was me copping a feel," I said, when our mouths separated.

She removed her remaining glove and began massaging the bulge in my period-correct trousers. "Does this qualify as well?" she panted, with a feral gleam in her eyes.

I helped her out of her elaborately-designed period-correct clothes. It took some time and effort; but her body was worth the wait.

Her libido was supercharged. The hotel bed frame was sturdy; otherwise we probably would have demolished it. By the time she was finally sated, it was late at night and I blacked out from exhaustion.

CHAPTER 22: RECRUITED

The heavy curtains were drawn, keeping most of the light out of the room the next morning. I awoke needing to piss. The sensuous spy who had rocked my world rolled over and stretched without opening her eyes, as I stumbled out of bed.

I washed my face and hands. My hair was sticking up in all the wrong places from how I'd slept. I tried to get that under control. When I returned, the curtains were slightly parted, she was sitting up in bed smoking a cigarette, with her glorious breasts exposed. Despite my worn-down, desensitized state, I felt a twitch in my loins.

Her gaze swept down-and-up my naked body.

"You look even more fit starkers than with your clothes on," she remarked. "Now come back to bed. I'm not quite finished with you."

The twitching intensified. I slid between the sheets.

"Is the plan to spend the whole day in bed?" I asked.

"Certainly not. You will take me to breakfast this morning. But I shan't leave this bed until you've properly serviced me."

"You're pretty demanding," I said.

She touched me in just the right way. "I dare you to complain."

Some time later, we sat in the bathtub together. I soaked, on the verge of falling asleep again, while she smoked some more, leaning back against me.

"Mmm," she purred, stretching again. "You've proven

yourself quite useful, for a Yank."

"I have to admit," I said, "if I'm going to be used, this is probably my favorite way."

She caressed my leg under the water. "And to think you were so bashful when I first made an overture."

I opened my eyes. "Were you offering sex in Densus?"

She chuckled. "One never can tell what turn things might have taken."

"I hope you don't think I'm too forward," I quipped, "but what's your name?"

She cut loose a raucous belly laugh that shook us both. When she caught her breath, she said, "We did rather put the cart before the horse, now didn't we?"

I waited for her to answer the question. When she didn't, I asked, "You're not gonna tell me?"

She sighed and took a drag of her cigarette. "I go by different names at different coordinates. To be quite honest: I've used so many different names that it's rather confusing, and sometimes I forget which name is real. What name do you think fits me?"

She was so coy, it should be maddening. But her playfulness enamored me all the more. "You haven't told me any of the names you use," I said, "so how can I pick one?"

"Oh, I want to know what name you would give me. Use your imagination. What do you know about me?"

I played along. "Well, like I speculated before: in your native stream, you probably entered young adulthood between 1990 and 2010. I'd lean toward the early '90s because you're intelligent. The kind of intelligence that comes from literacy. That all but disappears at the turn of the millennium. And you don't have any body piercings or tattoos."

She chuckled again.

"Your accent sounds authentic to me; so I'd say you were raised in Britain—either to a wealthy family, or you went to some snobby school where they taught you diction like in *My Fair Lady*."

"Oh, this is good," she said. "Please continue."

"But you're not Anglo-Saxon-Norman. At least not completely. Maybe your exotic looks come from a former British colony. You're 33 years old."

She stiffened. "What? How did you come to that rather specific conclusion? I don't look a day over 20!"

I shrugged. "True—you don't."

"Well thank-you."

"But you're in your early 30s."

"And why do you insist?"

"Your confidence. Maturity. Plus the texture of your skin. Your face and body are like a nubile young woman's, yes. But I can tell a woman's age by looking at her skin up close. There's a difference between the skin of a woman in her 20s, 30s, 40s... and so forth."

"Bollocks! You're clearly 'round the bend on that. But do continue."

"You're sexually experienced," I said. "Maybe you've even had training, for your job."

"You clearly take the biscuit," she said.

"But you see that part of the job as a bonus—not a burden. You're uninhibited and insatiable. Sometimes you go for long stretches without it. But you can have any man you want. So when you find one who's suitable, you let your passion run wild."

"It worked out well for you, didn't it?"

"Family," I said, "I'm not sure. Maybe you got along well with your father, but not your mother. I don't know—maybe the other way around. Probably an only child. But if you did have siblings, then you were likely the oldest."

"Quite entertaining," she said.

"You strike me as a 'Vivian'," I said. "If you don't tell me your real name, I think I'll call you Vivian."

"I rather fancy that name," she said. "And I think I'll call you Peter."

This time, I stiffened. She laughed.

"Why that?"

"Why not?" she countered.

Suddenly, the cooling water and the soft female flesh was no longer as relaxing. I nudged her forward to give myself room between her body and the back of the tub.

"No, don't get out," she pleaded, in a whining tone. "I'm comfortable. Isn't it pleasant to faff around like this? Don't ruin it."

I debated with myself whether I should cater to her comfort or my own. She reached behind her to place her palm against my face.

"We're having such a chuff. Let's not go getting narky with each other."

"What the hell are you talking about?"

She took my arms and pulled them around her waist. It did feel good. I sighed and relaxed.

"Just hold me a little longer," she said. "There's a boy."

"Tell me who you work for," I said. "How much do they know about me, and how do they know it?"

She sighed. "The Continuum Protection Bureau isn't the supreme authority. Perhaps they are, or were, when it comes to time travel. But they answer to a higher authority, which is international and rather...Machiavellian in nature. It tries to control or manipulate every nation, through government, media, and other institutions. It is usually successful."

This sounded a lot like what Dad believed.

"Ultimately, I suppose, this...cabal, if you will...did manipulate the entire world," she continued. "The results were catastrophic. There was famine, war, disease, death, on a scale like nothing ever in history. Out of the ruins of civilization, a new one began to form. Some technology had survived; some had to be reinvented. This new civilization developed a way to navigate the continuum."

"When did this happen?" I asked.

"This was...will be...oh, circa 2050, I think," she replied.

"Did America survive?" I asked.

"I'm afraid not. Not in the form you're familiar with. What was it, the 2020s, 2030s, when it collapsed? The economic implosion, the civil war, ethnic cleansing, nuclear strikes, invasion. Well, it was reborn, so to speak, later; but was rather weak and insignificant in the world I'm describing."

That fit with what I had learned about my relative future.

"My forebears went back and prevented the worst of the catastrophe. Well, the atomic bombings in Europe, at least. But in so doing, they split the world lines. Now the Cabal and their Continuum Protection Bureau ruled in one reality, while my organization policed a parallel line. Oh, it was all a bloody cock-up." She took another decadent drag on her cigarette. "In any case, time travel had to be regulated; so a new organization was activated. Safeguards were put in place, so it wouldn't behave like the CPB or TPF. Operatives were recruited from throughout the continuum. Terribly sorry to spoil your theory, but they found me in the UK in 1969. You assume that I'm incapable of learning and using the slang of future generations. Why? You yourself do it, don't you?"

"Okay. Point taken."

"Yes, my parents sent me to a boarding school where I was trained to behave as a proper lady. Your deductions are quite impressive, in many respects. I'm sorry I can't divulge the name of my true employer. I wasn't even allowed to know, at first. I was recruited by MI-7, and believed them to be my employer for a few years."

"MI-7? I thought it was disbanded after World War Two."

She patted my hand. "You're such a bright lad, Peter. It was, along with the other sections; except MI-5, for domestic intelligence, and MI-6—the foreign service. I'm sure you've heard of that one because of James Bond, 007, and all that. MI-7 was reactivated in 2051 as the *temporal* intelligence section. But as it turns out, MI-7 is subservient to an international agency which polices the continuum. This may strike you as mundane, but most of our efforts are focused on mapping the world lines. We do, however, hunt criminals, terrorists, and the like. We've crossed paths with the TPF many times. At first, we thought our relationship could be a cooperative one. But their atrocities just can't be overlooked any longer."

"So your outfit..." I said, "you're not in the assassination business?"

"I should say not. We are concerned with protecting—not destroying. We're also not obsessed with rogues such as yourself who escape their native coordinates and become millionaire time-tourists...at least, we're not overly concerned so long as you don't cock things up too much."

"Define 'cock things up too much.' What about rogues who split the stream?" I asked.

She leaned her head back against my shoulder. "But we all split the stream, don't we? We don't condone using knowledge of the future to make a personal fortune; but as long as you don't cause a major disruption, we won't have a strop about it."

"What would you call a 'major disruption'?"

"What the TPF Direct Action Team did in Densus," she replied, shaking her head. "That was a dreadful disruption."

I nodded. "Yeah. They caused a hell of a greater disruption than I would have, trying to 'protect' the locals from me."

Still shaking her head, she remarked, "Bloody barbarians. Protecting anyone is the last thing on their mind. If you're a hammer, everything looks like a nail. When in doubt, kill. Kill friends; kill family; kill witnesses. Kill, kill, kill."

"They killed my family," I blurted.

She stroked my forearm. "The TPF were given too long of a leash—much like the CIA was in your country. They've forgotten what the purpose was behind their original mission. Cowboys—the lot of them. *They* are the actual rogues, truth be told."

"Why?" I asked. "Why does it bother them so much that some people are able to escape their native coordinates?"

"There was a genuine concern over what might happen if the stream were split too many times." After a pause, she shook her head as if to clear that argument away, and said, "Think of it this way: humanity has emerged from chaos, and built order.

That order is seen as fragile, on many levels. With time travel, the danger of sliding back into chaos increases exponentially. They don't want that. *We* don't want that. All humanity is in agreement that order is better than chaos."

"In what context?" I asked.

"In any context. So—"

"Just what 'chaos' are we talking about, here?" I interrupted.

She sighed. "Suppose we allow rogues to run rampant all over the continuum. One of them helps the Axis powers prevail in World War Two. Another uses a weapon of mass destruction on South Africa. Another helps the Spanish armada defeat Nelson at Trafalgar. One ensures that Hannibal is victorious against Rome. Or weaponizes the Black Death, or Spanish Flu; or prevents the development of important medicine. Imagine what would happen if aliens were revealed before humanity is prepared to accept their existence. What if some change is made that prevents civilization from forming altogether? No alphabet. No wheel. No tools, or agriculture."

"If Fred Flintstone doesn't invent the wheel," I said, "Somebody else will, later. It's pretty much inevitable. If the Romans don't conquer Carthage, so what? They've still got Europe. But even if Hannibal takes Europe from them... so what? That's not chaos; it's just an alternative. If Hitler, Mussolini and Tojo win... maybe they murder almost as many people as Stalin and Mao did. So-what? Evil empires have always existed. And they're not examples of chaos. They're examples of order, taken to the extreme."

"I don't want to argue semantics with you, Peter, if you're going to be so... pedantic," she said.

"What's the big deal about having a bunch of alternate streams?" I asked.

"Untold numbers of radically different world lines would be extremely difficult to police."

"So why do you need to police them? Let the natives police themselves."

She shook her head in frustration. "That simply won't do."

"Why not?"

She made a flinging gesture with her hand, and sighed again. "As I said: I don't want to argue with you. My organization has its reasons. The CPB wants to preserve order, as do we. There is no good and evil, *per se*. That's novice, binary thinking. But you could say there are light and dark sides of everything. There's a light and dark side of you. A light and dark side of America. Of Britain. Of masculinity. Of femininity. Of money; of pride; of family; of music; of magic..."

"Are you talking about the *yin* and *yang*?" I asked.

"If you prefer, yes. Yes...yes, precisely!"

"And the TPF," I said, "they are the dark side of the effort to preserve order and keep chaos at bay."

"Well put, Peter. There's a boy."

"But your boss represents the light side."

"And we've rescued many a bloke targeted by the TPF," she said. "In Densus, it became obvious you were one targeted so."

"But *why* am I targeted?"

With much squeaking and splashing effort, she turned herself around in the tub, facing me. "I've been very accommodating in answering your questions, you must admit. Now I need you to reciprocate: Why are you here in Sarajevo?"

"I'm not here to rescue the Archduke, if that's what you're worried about."

She searched my eyes, soberly. "You're certain? Then what?"

"Yes, I'm certain. We were both there when Kennedy came to Dealey Plaza. Did I try to prevent that assassination?"

She stared at me a little while longer, then said, "Right. That's good, Peter. We can't allow a disruption of that magnitude. While it's true you could save one or two lives in either case...who knows how many thousands, or millions more lives might ultimately be ended if you go mucking about with history."

"Hard to imagine how either scenario could have turned

out much worse," I said. "But let's assume you're right: so what? It's just one reality in a network of streams. Everybody on the main river dies who's supposed to die. And everybody lives who's supposed to live. Just don't visit the stream where different people live and die, and it's irrelevant. Right?"

"Now you've got me worried again," she said. "I wish you wouldn't ask those questions."

"But how can you *not* ask them? And why be so certain it's right or wrong...light or dark...if you *can't* answer those questions?"

"I'll tell you how," she said, taking my face in both her hands, and kissing me tenderly. "Because we want to keep snogging and shagging for a jolly good while."

The sight and proximity of her fantastic body had already turned my thoughts carnal again. Now I was fully aroused.

"But we can't do that," she continued, "if I have reason to believe you're going to interfere with the Black Hand while you're here. And now."

"I won't," I said.

"But you were going to."

"I wasn't."

"Then what? Why else would you be here and now, of all the coordinates you could be faffing around at?"

"Same thing as at Dealey Plaza," I said. "Just satisfying my curiosity."

"I don't believe you," she said. "And I can't say emphatically enough that it's of primary importance that I believe your reason. And that the reason is not to prevent the assassination."

"I liked your idea about the faffing and shagging," I said, reaching for her. She intercepted my hand and deflected it to the side.

I could have easily overpowered her. My entire body throbbed with desire right then. But I had never forced myself on a woman and knew there would be no pleasure in it if I did. Those kinky games with Dr. Beth-Tiva were closer than I ever wanted to get to actual rape.

"Please, Peter," she said.

I puffed my cheeks and exhaled. "I was toying with an idea. Not sure I would actually do it. I probably would have chickened out. I thought maybe I could draw a team of Erasers here, then take them out."

"You mean kill them?"

I nodded.

"And that's it. Just kill the Direct Action Team, and leave, without trying to save Franz Ferdinand?"

"Yup."

"Turnabout is fair play, then?" She frowned and shook her head, but appeared relieved at the same time. "Oh you silly lad. So you want to murder the murderers. Then I suppose, should you live, you would go after another team. And another."

"The thought crossed my mind," I said, staring at her perfect breasts.

"What if I told you there's a plan to stop the TPF, the CPB... the whole corrupt hierarchy...without stooping to their bloody level? Prevent families like yours from being murdered ever again."

"I'm listening," I said, now wondering whether I wanted to suck her lips or her nipples first.

"I can't share details, but there is such a plan," she said. "But the timing is critical. It can't be put into action a moment too soon. And once it begins, there's nothing they can do to stop it."

"That sounds radical," I said. "I'd like to see that."

"Perhaps you can," she said. "What's better: perhaps you could even be involved—on a small level, truth be told; but involved."

"For real?"

She nodded. "I might be able to bring you in. As a mapping tech, that is. But if you prove yourself good at mapping...who knows? It's possible your classification could be raised to the point..." She blinked and smiled. "I don't want to get your hopes up, but this business often works like that: you prove yourself in one role, you get trusted with something bigger. I know someone that has risen up through the ranks in just that way."

"Why would you trust me now—with any job at any level?"

"Call it intuition. Also, we need self-sufficient individualists, who can think and act independently within parameters, with strong pattern recognition capabilities, self-discipline, and deductive reasoning skills—all of which I believe you have—or at least can be trained successfully for. What do you say—would you like to have a go at it?"

I grinned and began to show her just how much I wanted to "have a go." This time she was receptive.

"Mmmmm...Peter! You do like it, don't you?"

The bath water was by now tepid, but her multiple orgasms seemingly made it boil.

Finally, whimpering, she pushed my hands away and began to compose herself.

"What's the matter?" I asked, fearing I had been too rough toward the end.

"Absolutely nothing," she said, then opened her eyes and regulated her breath with a big gulp of air. She looked down at my lap and smirked. She wrapped her hands around me and asked, "But what shall we do with this eager fellow?"

We didn't make breakfast that morning. My stomach roared in protest by the time we made it to lunch.

$$\triangle\triangle\triangle$$

In all our hedonistic efforts, I almost missed what was most significant: there were good people out there, working together to accomplish good. Not all good men did nothing. Some were working together on a plan to oppose evil.

Maybe I could, too.

If you liked this fourth book in the *Paradox* Series, please rate it and consider leaving a comment or two as a review. Just as important: tell somebody you know about it!

Follow me on BookBub—a free site for readers that sends you a message when my newest books come out! You can also get book recommendations from me and other authors you like to read.